LAST YEAR

LAST YEAR

Robert Charles Wilson

A TOM DOHERTY ASSOCIATES BOOK
New York

LAST YEAR

Copyright © 2016 by Robert Charles Wilson

A Tor Book
Published by Tom Doherty Associates
175 Fifth Avenue
New York, NY 10010

www.tor-forge.com

Tor® is a registered trademark of Macmillan Publishing Group, LLC.

The Library of Congress Cataloging-in-Publication Data
is available upon request.

ISBN 978-0-7653-3263-9 (hardcover)
ISBN 978-1-4668-0078-6 (e-book)

Our books may be purchased in bulk for promotional, educational,
or business use. Please contact your local bookseller or the
Macmillan Corporate and Premium Sales Department
at 1-800-221-7945, extension 5442, or by e-mail at
MacmillanSpecialMarkets@macmillan.com.

First Edition: December 2016

Printed in the United States of America

0 9 8 7 6 5 4 3 2 1

Calm as that second summer which precedes
The first fall of the snow,
In the broad sunlight of heroic deeds,
The City bides the foe.

—Henry Timrod, "Charleston"

PART ONE

The City of Futurity

—1876—

1

Two events made the first of September a memorable day for Jesse Cullum. First, he lost a pair of Oakley sunglasses. Second, he saved the life of President Ulysses S. Grant.

The part about saving Grant's life was speculative. Even without Jesse's intervention, the pistol might have misfired or the bullet missed its mark. Jesse felt uneasy about taking credit for an act of purely theoretical heroism. But the loss of the Oakleys, that was a real tragedy. He had loved those Oakleys. The way they improved his vision on sunny days. The way they made him look.

Grant's visit had been carefully planned. That was how City people liked it: the fewer surprises, the better. Grant and his wife had arrived at Futurity Station in a special Pullman car, where they had endured a reception, complete with bands and a speech by the governor of Illinois, before a plush carriage carried them five miles down the paved road from the train depot to the steel gates of the City of Futurity. Jesse had ridden that absurdly smooth and perfect road many times—he had helped build it—and he knew exactly what Grant would have

seen: a first glimpse of the City's impossibly tall white towers
across the rolling Illinois plains, massifs of stone and glass;
then the enormous concrete wall with gaudy words and pictures
painted on it; the gleaming gates, opening to admit his carriage;
finally the crowd, both locals and visitors, jostling in the courtyard for a glimpse of him.

Policing the crowd was Jesse's job. He had been assigned to
the task by his boss, a man named Booking—the same Booking
who had issued him the Oakleys six months ago. Today Jesse
wore a freshly laundered City security uniform: white shirt,
blue necktie, blue blazer with the words CITY OF FUTURITY /
STAFF sewn in yellow thread across the pocket, a soft blue cap
with the same legend above the bill—and, at least outdoors,
the Oakley sunglasses, which Jesse believed lent him an air of
sinister authority. When he wore his Oakleys, his reflection in
the City's plate-glass windows looked like a prizefighter with
the eyes of a gigantic beetle. Newcomers invariably gave him
startled, deferential looks.

Jesse and three other security people had been assigned to
the viewing line. The way it was supposed to work: Grant's
carriage would enter through the gates; Grant and his wife
would disembark; they would be escorted across the courtyard
to the lobby of Tower Two in view of the guests already present.
Post-and-rope stanchions had been set up to maintain a distance between the crowd and the president, and Jesse was
assigned to patrol that boundary and make sure no one jumped
the line.

It should have been easy duty. The weather was sunny but
not unpleasantly warm, the current crop of guests seemed well
behaved. Jesse was eager to get his own look at Grant, not that
he had ever paid much attention to politics. So he watched
attentively as the carriage came in and the gate rolled closed
behind it. A valet took charge of the horses, and Grant and his

wife, Julia, stepped into the sunlight. Mrs. Grant stared without embarrassment at the fantastically broad and tall buildings
of the City, but General Grant himself appeared calm and
measured—not as fierce in this last year of his presidency as
the images of him that had been published in newspapers during the Rebellion, but just as sternly observant. He ignored the
marvels of the City and surveyed the crowd. Jesse imagined
the president's gaze caught and lingered on him a moment—
because of the Oakleys, perhaps.

Then Jesse had to give his whole attention to the job he
had been assigned to do. He began a slow walk along the rope
line, keeping a careful vigil. All the people on this side of the
courtyard were local guests of the City. That meant they were
well-heeled enough to afford the entrance fee, which implied a
certain standard of gentlemanly and ladylike behavior to which,
alas, they did not necessarily conform. Today, however, the
crowd was mindful, and there was very little pushing or crowding of the ropes. Jesse told one couple to keep their children
back of the stanchions, please, and he scolded another man for
shouting out mocking references to Grant's role in the Crédit
Mobilier scandal. Otherwise it was simply a matter of keeping
his eyes open as Grant progressed from the courtyard to the
Reception Center.

Had Jesse not been wearing the Oakleys he might have been
too sunstruck to catch sight of the man at the rope line who
reached into his overcoat with a purposeful motion. Long ago,
in circumstances far from the City and vastly less congenial,
Jesse had learned to recognize that gesture, and he broke into
a run without thinking. Some in the crowd stared at Jesse, but
no one had yet noticed the man in the overcoat, whose movements were deliberate and whose attention was entirely focused
on Grant. The man's hand emerged, bearing a pistol. The pistol
looked peculiar, but Jesse didn't think about that. He was racing

now, closing the gap between himself and the would-be assassin, thinking: a pistol was a bad choice at this range. Odds were, a hasty shot would miss Grant altogether. But Jesse hadn't been hired to play the odds. He had been hired to make the most effective use of his size and skills. He came at the gunman like a rolling caisson.

Jesse had been taught that the two overriding principles of City security were *protection* and *discretion*. The first and most important of these was protection—of the president, in this case—and it was Jesse's priority as he made contact with his opponent. He grabbed the assailant's gun arm at the wrist, isolating the weapon, and let his momentum carry his shoulder into the assailant's chest. The gunman was taken by surprise, and the air was forced from his lungs in a startled grunt as both men fell to the ground. Jesse let his weight immobilize the assailant's body as he dealt with the weapon. The assailant's finger was out of the trigger guard and his hand was at an angle to his arm that suggested Jesse had successfully broken or dislocated the wrist. Nearby guests, still more puzzled than alarmed, stepped back to form a kind of perimeter. Jesse took the pistol from the assailant's hand and quickly tucked it into the pocket of his now-soiled blue blazer. Then he twisted the assailant's arm behind him and wrestled him to his feet.

The daylight seemed suddenly brighter, which was how Jesse discovered that his Oakley sunglasses had flown off during the altercation. He spotted them on the ground just as a female guest took a step backward, crushing one lens under her heel and bending the arms out of shape. Jesse's sense of loss was immediate and aggravating.

But the second rule of City security was discretion, and he kept quiet. The gunman began to utter sharp obscenities. Jesse murmured apologies to the ladies present and hustled the miscreant through the crowd, away from Grant and toward the staff door of the Reception Center. The man was four or five inches shorter than Jesse and a few years older. Jesse was in an excellent position to observe his pomaded black hair, thin at the crown, and to register the tang of his body odor, salty and sour.

The staff door flew open as Jesse came within a couple of yards of it. Two City security men rushed out—security men from the future, Tower One men, which meant they outranked Jesse, who had been born in this century. They were staring hard at the assailant and spared almost no attention for Jesse himself.

Like most of the Tower One security people, they were as tall as Jesse and at least as muscular. One was a white man, one was brown-skinned. They braced the gunman and secured his arms behind him with flexible ties. "Thanks, chief," the white man said to Jesse. "We'll take it from here."

"My name's not chief."

"Okay, sorry, bro. And, uh, we'll need the weapon, too."

Abashed at having forgotten it, Jesse retrieved the pistol from his pocket and handed it over. It was sleek, complex, and finely machined. Definitely not a contemporary handgun. "I broke my Oakleys wrestling with this man."

"Sorry to hear that. Maybe you can pick up another pair from the supply room."

They frog-marched the subdued assailant away.

Jesse sighed and went back to the rope line. But Grant was in Guest Reception now, and the crowd was already beginning to disperse. There was no panic. A few people had seen Jesse tackle the gunman, but no one seemed to have noticed the pistol. From any distance, the encounter would have looked like an unexplained scuffle between a security guard and an unruly guest. Protection *and* discretion, Jesse thought. They ought to give him a damn medal.

He headed to staff quarters for his afternoon break.

Two colossal, nearly identical buildings comprised the City of Futurity. Both buildings could be described as hotels, if you stretched that word to the limits of its definition. Both buildings were designed to house, feed, and entertain large numbers of paying guests. But the two buildings were carefully segregated. The guests who resided in Tower Two had all been born in the world outside the gate: Jesse's world. The guests who occupied the other building had been born elsewhere, in a place that claimed to be the future. The second kind of guests didn't enter by the gate, as President Grant had. They came up from underground, through the Mirror.

Jesse worked in Tower Two and slept in a windowless room in one of Tower Two's sub-basements. He took his meals at the commissary on the same floor. Staff quarters were clean and acceptably private, but never entirely quiet. The sound of the machines that circulated the tower's air and generated its electrical power seeped up from an even lower level of the tower, a faint ceaseless murmur, like the breath of a sleeping giant.

Jesse took his break at the staff commissary. Employees were issued food chits with which they could buy meals from a choice of vendors in the commissary concourse: booths with gaudy signs proclaiming them as McDonald's, Burger King, Taco Bell, Starbucks. Locals had been hired to staff these kiosks, and most of them knew Jesse by name. He used a chit to buy coffee in a paper cup and a glutinous muffin on a paper plate from a woman wearing a hairnet: her name was Dorothy, and her husband had been killed at Second Manassas fourteen years ago. "Looks like you scuffed up your jacket," Dorothy said.

"You think I ought to change it? I'm off duty in a couple of hours and I figured on taking it to housekeeping after that."

She reached across the counter and brushed his sleeve. "You'll pass, if there's not a formal inspection."

"I busted my Oakleys today. The sunglasses."

"Oh, that's a shame. You want a second muffin, Jesse? Big fellow like you needs to eat."

"I'm saving my chits."

"On the house, then. Since you lost your eyeglasses and all."

He carried his two muffins and steaming coffee to a vacant table. There were twenty minutes left in his official break, but he had taken no more than a single bite when his pager went off. He unhooked the device from his belt and read the message on the tiny display:

jesse cullum to sec office asap

Summoned by his boss. He finished the first of his two muffins in a few hasty bites, wrapped the second in a napkin and put it in his jacket pocket. He had no choice but to abandon the coffee.

He used his pass card to summon an elevator. The City's elevators were astonishing to new visitors, but Jesse had long since grown accustomed to them. His pass card was a more enduring marvel. It was a kind of key: it opened certain doors, but not others. It let him into all the places where he might be expected to go in the course of his duties, and into none of the places where his presence was forbidden. He could not imag-. ine how this thin sliver of what was called plastic, or the slots into which he inserted it, knew or remembered which doors to allow him through. Everyone on staff carried a similar card, and each card was endowed with powers particular to its owner.

The elevator arrived with its customary pinging and sighing. Jesse stepped inside and pushed the button marked "21." The twenty-first floor of Tower Two was the administrative level. Jesse had been there before, but only on rare occasions. His boss, Mr. Paul Booking, usually came down to the staff room to issue the day's assignments. If someone was summoned to twenty-one, it was usually for a promotion, a dismissal, or a special assignment.

The elevator stopped and the door slid open on a wide, immaculate corridor. Jesse's shoes tapped cadences on the smooth and polished floor as he made for Booking's office. Secretarial persons gave him incurious glances from open doors as he passed. Some were men, some were women; some were white, many were not. And none of them was local. The City imported all its managers and paper-handlers from the far side of the Mirror.

Booking's secretary was a woman with features Jesse once would have called Oriental, though he knew the word was considered objectionable by people from the twenty-first century. She looked up from the illuminated screen in front of her and smiled. "Mr. Cullum?"

"Yes, ma'am."

"Thanks for being so prompt. You can go on into Mr. Booking's office—he's waiting for you."

Booking's office possessed a large window, and even four years in the City had not accustomed Jesse to the view from the twenty-first floor. Even calling it a window seemed to mock it. It was a wall of glass from floor to ceiling, so finely manufactured as to be almost indistinguishable from empty air. There were vertically hung blinds to ward off the sun, but it was late afternoon now and the blinds had been fully retracted. Jesse felt as if he were standing on the scarp of an artificial mountain. A flock of passenger pigeons wheeled over a distant creek, and isolated stands of slippery elms sparkled in the long light like scattered emeralds.

"Your jacket's a little scuffed," Booking said.

God damn it, Jesse thought. "Yes, sir, I'm sorry."

"Don't apologize." Booking sat behind his desk giving him a thoughtful look. Booking was bald and appeared to be forty years old or thereabouts, though it was hard to tell with people from the future. He wore a goatee so meticulously trimmed it seemed nervous about its own continued existence. He was generally kind to hired help, and he spoke to the security hands as casually as an old friend, though that was not a two-way street: Jesse knew Booking's first name only because it was printed on the badge clipped to his lapel. "You had an encounter on the reception grounds today."

"Encounter is one word for it. It didn't amount to much, in the end."

"Don't be modest, Jesse. I've seen the video."

Like his secretary, Booking kept an illuminated display on his desk. He swiveled it to show Jesse the screen. The pictures it displayed had been captured by a wall-mounted camera, so the view was distant and a little indistinct, but Jesse recognized himself in his uniform and his Oakleys, lumbering along the rope line. What followed was pretty much as he remembered it. He shrugged.

"President Grant is grateful to you," Booking said.

"He saw what happened?"

"You were quick and careful, but the president has a keen eye."

Jesse supposed Grant had seen enough gunplay in the war that he was still alert to it. "His gratitude isn't necessary."

"And we've got the bad guy in custody, which is what matters. Nevertheless, Jesse, the president wants to thank you, and he wants to do it in person."

"Sir?"

"And because President Grant is a special guest, we want to make that happen for him. So you'll be escorted to his quarters tonight at seven sharp. Which gives you time for a shower and a fresh set of clothes."

Jesse glanced back at the screen. The images were repeating in a thirty-second roundelay. He saw himself wrestling with the assailant. At that point, his Oakleys had already come off. "Is it absolutely necessary for me to meet him? Can't you just tell him I appreciate the thought?"

"It *is* necessary, and you can tell him yourself. But I want you to keep a couple of things in mind. First, Grant hasn't had the orientation yet. So he's going to be full of questions, and he might pose some of them to you. So you need to remember the rule. You know the rule I'm talking about?"

"If a guest questions me about anything I learned in my employment at the City, I should refer him or her to a designated host or hostess." Almost verbatim, from the handbook every local employee was required to read.

"Good. But in this case you'll need to find a diplomatic way to do it. We think it would be best if you present yourself to President Grant as a hard-working employee whose duties keep him in Tower Two and who doesn't know anything substantial about the future. Which is pretty much the truth—am I right?"

The question—*Am I right?*—was one of Booking's verbal habits. Jesse found it irritating, in part because it wasn't rhetorical. It required actual assent. "Yes, sir."

"In any case, I doubt Grant wants a lengthy conversation. They say he's a pretty tight-lipped kind of guy."

"I wouldn't know."

"Don't offend him, don't volunteer information, and if he asks questions let him know his assigned host or hostess can answer them better than you can."

"Sir," Jesse said.

"And if he asks about the assailant, tell him our people are handling all that."

"All right."

"Okay, good," Booking said. "One more thing, Jesse. If you carry this off the way we hope you will, the City will find a way to show its appreciation."

Jesse sensed an opening. "I broke my Oakleys," he said, "in that scuffle."

"Oh? I'm sorry to hear that. Do this right, and we'll get you a whole crate of Oakleys."

Jesse showered and changed into his reserve uniform and took himself to the commissary for a meal. There was a line-up at every booth, but Jesse was patient. He spent his chits on fried chicken and French-fried potatoes and a cup of coffee.

He sat at a table by himself. He could have joined friends, but he had been told not to say anything about his scheduled meeting with Grant, and under the circumstances it would have been hard to make small talk. In any case, the table where the security and housekeeping folks had gathered wasn't as attractive a destination as it might have been. Doris Vanderkamp was there, paying obvious attention to a lanky, freckled security man named Mick Finagle. Jesse had lately extracted himself from a romantic entanglement with Doris, and he thought she might be trying to make him jealous by fawning over Mick. Jesse had a low opinion of Mick Finagle. And Doris, for all her posturing and covert glances in Jesse's direction, clearly wasn't at her best. She was sniffling as if her perennial head cold had come back, and her forehead was beaded with perspiration despite the machine-cooled air. He felt a little sorry for her, a sentiment that would have enraged her had he dared to express it.

He made quick work of the fried chicken. The commissary's portions were lamentably small, and he often went back for seconds, but it was getting near the end of the month, and if he spent all his food chits he would have to resort to cash, which he didn't want to do. What he could afford was a second cup of coffee. He bought one and sipped it slowly, watching the clock above the elevator bank, until a City woman in trousers showed up to escort him to President Grant's quarters.

It was a well-known fact that women from the future often wore trousers. It had been remarked on in all the papers, especially since tour groups had begun visiting Manhattan and San Francisco. Visitors didn't mingle with locals even there, but they were visible as they moved through the streets, and the presence of women in trousers was impossible to ignore. A few unctuous churchmen had condemned the practice. Victoria Woodhull, the notorious female-rights campaigner, had expressed her approval. Most commentators took the generous view that customs vary not just from place to place but from age to age, and that these novel forms of dress said more about changing customs than they did about morality or propriety. Jesse agreed, he supposed, though he had met enough City people to convince him that their morals might be almost as fluid as their fashion.

What surprised him about this woman was not her trousers as such but the fact that she was wearing them in Tower Two. Tower Two employees were issued uniforms designed not to shock sensitive guests, including skirts for females. So this was someone from the other tower, dressed according to its rules. The woman's name, her badge said, was Elizabeth DePaul.

Whatever her assignment—and Jesse guessed it was more than just escorting him to Grant's quarters—she seemed slightly bored by it. Her face was well formed but plain. Her dark hair was cut to a masculine length. She was nearly as tall as Jesse, thickset but not in any way ungainly. Nor was she demure. Her gaze was frank and unflinching. Her badge said CITY SECURITY.

"Good work on the rope line this afternoon," she said.

Her accent was flat as well water and Jesse couldn't gauge her sincerity. "Thank you," he said.

"Seriously. I saw the video. You had the weapon out of the bad guy's hand before anyone noticed."

"Well, not quite. President Grant noticed."

"There's that. Are you looking forward to meeting him?"

"I expect we'll exchange a few words, that's all." *And then I can go back downstairs,* Jesse thought, *and have a beer.* The commissary allowed the sale of beer to employees between the hours of six and ten. He wasn't ordinarily a drinker, and the price of City beer had almost made a temperance man of him, but the occasion seemed to justify the expense. He asked Elizabeth DePaul whether she would be joining him for his conversation with Grant.

"Me? No. Though I wouldn't mind getting a look at him. See what he's like when he's not decorating a fifty-dollar bill."

Jesse failed to understand the reference but let it pass. "Have you talked to the gunman?"

"Not my department."

"He's just a lunatic with a grievance," Jesse said, "I imagine."

"I wouldn't care to speculate."

The elevator opened on the highest of the guest floors, where Grant had been assigned the biggest suite with the grandest view. Four City people waited in the corridor. Jesse recognized his boss, Mr. Booking. The others were unfamiliar to him. Prominent among them was a gray-haired man of maybe fifty years, wearing civilian clothes rather than a City uniform. The others seemed to defer to him. But no one bothered to make

introductions. Elizabeth DePaul pointed in the opposite direction: "That way," she said. There was only one door at the
end of the corridor. "Go ahead and knock. He's expecting
you. We'll be here when you come out."

Grant's second term as president would be ending soon,
and Jesse wondered whether he might secretly be happy to
leave office. It had been a rough seven years—rough years for
everyone, especially since the crash of '73; therefore politically difficult for Grant. The railroad scandals had reached
all the way into the White House, and his tenure in office had
not achieved all he had hoped or promised. He had promised
a reconstructed South—what he got were serial lynchings and
the Ku Klux Klan. He had promised peace with the Indians—
what he got were Crazy Horse, trouble with the Nez Percé,
and the Little Bighorn.

But he was still the hero of Appomattox, the man who saved
the Union, and Jesse could not imagine what to say to him or
even how to address him. He knocked, and Grant opened the
door. The two men stared at each other. Grant seemed speechless. Finally Jesse murmured, "Your Excellency, I was told you
wanted to see me?"

"Jesse Cullum." Grant put out his hand, and Jesse shook it.
"Please come in." Jesse stepped into the room and Grant closed
the door behind him. "Sit down. No need for formal address,
Mr. Cullum. I've noticed strangers often prefer to call me 'General,' and it doesn't displease me."

"Thank you, General."

The room was plush. Jesse's duties had occasionally taken
him into Tower Two guest rooms, so he knew how this one
compared. The furniture was of the future: finely made but
almost aggressively plain. The window was almost as large as

the one in Booking's office. Beyond the flawless glass, dusk had turned the western sky blood-red. Jesse imagined he could see as far as Montana by the fading light. Maybe the State of Oregon, if he stood on his tiptoes.

"Mrs. Grant is out taking supper with one of our hosts. She knows nothing of the events in the courtyard, by the way. And given that no shot was fired, I prefer to keep it that way. You'll forgive me for not introducing you to her. But I wanted to thank you personally for what you did on my behalf."

"I took away a man's gun, that's all."

"Your modesty is commendable. In any case, I think Mrs. Grant feels easier away from the window."

"The view makes some guests dizzy at first, but they usually grow accustomed to it."

"Yes, and I expect she will, and I will, too, but just now I feel like a swallow nesting on a cliff."

"May I draw the drapes for you?"

"Please, if you can—it's not obvious to me how they operate. How long have you worked here, Mr. Cullum?"

Jesse tugged the rod that rotated the vertical blinds. "Going on four years."

"From the earliest days, then. May I ask how you came to be employed at the City of Futurity?"

"It was an accident, more or less. I was traveling east from San Francisco and I had to leave the train unexpectedly." Because he had foregone the formality of buying a ticket, but he left that part out. "Futurity Station didn't even have a name in those days. It was just another coaling depot out in the middle of nowhere. I meant to head toward Chicago on foot, but my directions were bad. The next day I saw a plume of dust from the construction site and showed up looking for food and water. The people here fed me and offered me work."

"Just like that?"

"The City people weren't looking for publicity until the major construction was finished. They figured I'd be more use to them as a hired hand than I would be spreading stories about what I'd seen. The road you came by from the station? I was part of the crew that laid it down."

"And a fine road it is, though it pales by comparison with what lies at the end of it. Of course I've read a great deal in the papers about the City of Futurity. The testimony is unimpeachable, but the reality of it is so much more . . ." Grant groped for a word and gave up: "*Real.* You must have seen many marvels in your time here."

Jesse tried to imagine how this room must seem to Grant. The electric lights and the switches that controlled them, the cool air flowing from ceiling vents, the thermostat to adjust the temperature. The explanatory notes printed on paper and affixed to the walls: how to lock and unlock the door, how to summon an elevator, the finer points of indoor plumbing. A button for summoning a City host or hostess, if the instructions proved inadequate. "What seems to impress visitors most," Jesse said, "is the airship."

Grant winced. "I've seen photographs. And I've been invited to ride it. And not just me, but Julia as well, if she can be convinced. Is the thing as safe as they claim?"

"I've seen it go up and down hundreds of times without any problem."

"Though I suppose the greatest marvel is that these things have come among us at all, from a place that is and isn't the future. Do you understand it, Mr. Cullum, the story of where these people come from?"

"I would never claim to *understand* it, General. They say there is a whole sheaf of worlds, and that the City people have learned to travel from one to another. They live on one stalk in the sheaf and journey to nearby stalks. But for the traveler,

all those stalks look like the past." Jesse felt himself blushing at his own incoherence. No, he did not understand it. "I
imagine they'll explain it to you better in the orientation
session."

"We are their past, but they do not necessarily represent our
future. That's what the brochure says."

"I guess the brochure's right."

"I value your opinion precisely because it's *not* printed in
a brochure. All these mechanical marvels are impressive, but
I wonder about the nature of the people themselves. You must
know many of them."

"They prefer to keep us separate. But some mixing does
go on."

"As employers, have they treated you well?"

"Yes, sir. They cured me." He spoke without thinking, then
realized with dismay that Grant was waiting for him to continue. "When they hired me on, you see, the first thing they
did was send me to the City clinic—sort of a miniature hospital with a half dozen doctors on duty. At the time I was suffering from . . . well, it's not easy to discuss. Being a military
man, I guess you've had experience of camp sicknesses among
your troops."

What Jesse could not bring himself to say was that he had
arrived at the clinic barely able to pass urine without shrieking
like a cat with its tail on fire. Grant cleared his throat and said,
"I take your meaning."

"Sir, they cured that. And not with a syringe full of nitrate
of silver. They gave me pills. They said I had other conditions
that weren't so obvious, and they cured those, too. They gave
me injections to the arm that made me impervious to rubeola
and smallpox and other diseases whose names I can't recall. So,
yes, I can testify that they treated me well. For all I know they
may have saved my life."

Jesse wondered if he had said too much. For a few moments Grant seemed plunged in thought. "That *is* a marvel," he said at last. "I hope they can be convinced to share the secret of these cures."

"They plan to do so. I've heard it discussed."

"Perhaps they should have shared it when they first arrived. Many lives might have been saved already."

"Yes, sir, but who would have believed them? Who believed the City was anything more than a trumped-up Barnum show, those first few months? Now that the skeptics are routed, it begins to become possible. You know 1877 is the last year of the City, before they close the Mirror and go home. They say, in the last year, they'll be even more frank and forthcoming."

"Now that they've prepared the ground."

"Yes, sir."

Grant tugged at the sleeve of his woolen suit. Even now, with all the weight he'd gained since Appomattox, he looked as if he'd be more comfortable in a Union uniform. Or maybe his restlessness meant Jesse had overstayed his welcome. But he couldn't politely leave until he was dismissed.

Grant said, "And have they made moral progress, too? Are they better than us, or just cleverer?"

It was a dangerous question. "Hard to say, General. The ones I've met, they seem . . . I don't know how to describe it. There's a kind of bonelessness about them. The women in particular seem insolent, almost louche—I've heard them swear like infantrymen. But they're capable of great tenderness and intelligence. The men aren't dishonorable, but they don't seem to think much of honor in general, as an abstraction I mean. When I first came here many of them struck me as effeminate or unserious."

"They struck you that way at first, but not any longer?"

"Well, they have a saying: *The past is a different country;*

they do things differently there. Which I figure cuts both ways. You don't expect an Irishman to comport himself like a Chinaman, so why should we expect City people to behave just as we do?"

"In matters of custom, surely, but in matters of moral duty . . ."

"I'm not sure I'm qualified to render judgment in that department. They don't seem especially better or worse than the rest of us."

"Not more generous?"

"They've been generous to me, certainly. But visitors don't get into the City for free, do they? The price is paid in gold and silver, and all that gold and silver goes straight to the so-called future, where it lines somebody's pocket. How they came here is difficult to understand; what they want of us is not."

"Well." Grant stood up. "Once again I thank you, Mr. Cullum. Not just for your conduct this afternoon but for your forthright conversation."

"You have a keen eye, sir, to have spotted the pistol."

"I saw it briefly and from a distance—more the reach than the gun itself, though I had the impression it was unusual."

"I only handled it a moment myself. But yes, it was one of theirs."

"Not a Colt?"

"No, sir—whatever it was, it was not a Colt."

"That surprises me. Because your employers told me it was a Colt."

Jesse very carefully said nothing.

"I suppose they were mistaken," Grant said.

"I suppose they were."

Jesse shook the president's hand again and made his exit.

The next morning Jesse was scheduled to ride the perimeter fence. Fence-riding was lonely duty but he enjoyed it, at least when the weather was decent.

The City of Futurity possessed many walls and fences, many boundaries. The most significant and least visible of these boundaries was the Mirror itself, deep underground: a wall (and at times a doorway) between present and future. Then there were the walls that separated Tower One from Tower Two. And surrounding these, the massive concrete wall that enclosed the City itself.

But the City was situated in a much vaster track of land, purchased by proxy and demarked by a fence of steel wire mesh. The fence served multiple purposes. It prevented curiosity-seekers from mobbing the City walls. It kept hucksters and frauds from setting up booths or buildings within sight of guests. It allowed the City to make the land available to visitors from the future as a specimen of "the untrammeled tallgrass prairie"—apparently all such landscapes would be "trammeled" in the years to come. And it enclosed a herd of American buffalo for the same reason: The buffalo were due for a trammeling, too.

The attractions of the City were so great, and the price of admission so high, that it was not surprising that unscrupulous people occasionally attempted to climb or cut the fence. Which meant it had to be regularly inspected and repaired; which meant Jesse was up before dawn, signing out a mechanical cart from the horseless-vehicle barn. By the time the sun breached the horizon he was mounted on a three-wheeled self-propelled vehicle and passing through one of the gates in the City wall and out into the grassland.

The chill of the morning was a reminder that autumn was approaching, but the lingering wisps of ground fog vanished at the first touch of sunlight. The sky was as blue as a robin's egg, and when he reached the fence the air had grown warm, and grasshoppers flew from the wheels of the cart in brown flurries. From there Jesse followed a pressed-earth trail that followed the fence, humming a tune to himself, stopping occasionally to inspect a dubious weld or a suspicious gopher hole. He was orbiting the City at a radius of roughly a mile, and by noon he had not detected any irregularities worth reporting. He stopped the cart, stood to stretch his legs, pulled off his jacket and hung it on the handlebar of the three-wheeled vehicle. He took a bagged lunch from the carry-box at the back of the cart (a sandwich from the commissary, coffee in a thermos bottle) and ate sitting sidesaddle on the padded seat. It felt good to be out of the labyrinth of the City for a day, away from its tuneless hums and whispers. Out here, only the bugs were humming. His own breath sounded loud in his ears.

He unscrewed the lid of the thermos bottle. The lid did double-duty as a cup. It was made of plastic, the City people's material of choice for trivial things. The lid was small in Jesse's large hands, as if he were drinking from a thimble. But the coffee was pleasant and hot.

At this distance the City dominated the horizon. Its towers sparkled like twin escarpments of mica-flecked granite, the wall a varicolored reef at the foot of them. He watched an omnibus full of tourists exit the City on a paved road, headed for the eastern pastures where the buffalo were corralled and Wild West shows were sometimes staged. The paved road paralleled Jesse's trail at a distance of a few hundred yards, and as the bus passed he saw the passengers peering out. Wealthy people from the future. Men and women with complexions of all hues, sitting companionably with one another as the amplified voice of the driver droned out facts about the prairie. If the tourists noticed Jesse they would have registered only his uniform. Just another City employee, to be ignored—although had they

known a little more about him, they might have considered
him an artifact almost as interesting as the buffalo. Step up, all
you ladies in short pants, you beardless men. Bring your squab-
bling, spoiled children, too. See the Man from the Past. See
the untrammeled syphilitic drifter of the Golden West.

The bus rolled on and out of sight. Jesse savored the silence
once more, until the pager on his belt chimed, a sound that
never failed to startle him.

The message on the screen was another summons to
Mr. Booking's office.

Jesse sighed and called his shift supervisor to report his
position so another man could come out and finish riding the
fence. Then he poured out his coffee on the untrammeled prairie, brushed a ladybug off the seat of the motor cart, and drove
back to the City.

Booking's office hadn't changed, except that the woman who
had escorted Jesse to Grant's room last night, Elizabeth De-
Paul, occupied one of the spare chairs. She gave Jesse a long,
indecipherable stare.

"Have a seat," Booking said. "President Grant spoke to us
about his meeting with you last night."

Jesse searched his memory for any gaffe or revelation that
might have provoked this summons or even cost him his job.
He could think of a few likely candidates.

"The president was pleased," Booking said. "He called you
amiable and intelligent. He said he was glad to have had an
opportunity to thank you for what you had done for him."

"That was good of him."

"Well, we happen to agree. You have a fine record, Jesse.
This incident has made us wonder whether you aren't being

underutilized in Tower Two. We think it's time for you to take a step up."

"Kind of you to say so. What sort of step up?"

"Specifically, we're going to need experienced security personnel for next year's tours. Hard work but major rewards. Are you interested?"

Tour security was a coveted job. It might nearly double his income. He nodded.

"There's a learning curve, of course, but we'll have you up to speed by the new year. In the meantime I have a temporary duty assignment for you."

"Sir?"

Booking reached into a desk drawer, took out a small wedge of plastic, and handed it to Jesse.

Jesse stared at it. It was a pass card, visually identical to the one he already possessed.

"We'll need your old card back. You'll find this one opens a lot more doors. Tower Two *and* Tower One—the job involves some crossover. Ms. DePaul can explain it to you."

"Can she?"

"She'll be your supervisor from now on."

Everything comes at a price, Jesse thought.

"Oh, and I put in a call to the supply room. You can pick up a new pair of Oakleys next time you stop by."

2

"I'll contact you when I need you," Elizabeth DePaul had told him. "In the meantime, keep your pager handy."

Jesse waited the rest of the day. No page. He went to his dormitory room and slept. The bedside clock woke him at six the next morning. No page. He lingered over breakfast in the commissary. Nothing. By ten o'clock he had breezed through a second breakfast and enough coffee to call forth Lazarus. Boredom set in.

He went to the bank of elevators that serviced the guest floors and slid his new pass card into the slot. His old card would have been instantly rejected. His new one caused the small red light on the card reader to turn green. The elevator door slid open. Jesse stepped inside and touched the button marked MEZZANINE. A recorded female voice said, "*You have selected mezzanine.*"

Technically speaking, with the new card, he was permitted to do this. But he had been systematically excluded from the guest zones for years, and it felt like he was committing a trespass. Which made it even more interesting.

The mezzanine level of Tower Two was a vast rotunda. Its ceiling was three stories tall, a pale blue dome that glowed with

the light of hidden electric lamps. In the center of the rotunda
was a sort of desk or counter under an illuminated sign that
said VISITOR INFORMATION. Other City employees were posi-
tioned throughout the rotunda. The employee nearest the
elevator banks was a young woman with an immaculately crisp
uniform and a fixed smile. She glanced at Jesse as he stepped
out, registered his security badge, and lost all interest in him.
She was here for guests, not staff.

The rotunda wasn't crowded, but it was busier than Jesse
had ever seen it. He had visited the mezzanine before—once
just before the City opened for business, on a walk-through
arranged for employees so they might know what the guests
were paying to see, and a few other times on after-hours guard
duty. The security personnel who worked the rotunda by daylight were from the future and bunked in Tower One; the same
was true of the night shift, but when they were shorthanded
they sometimes called up local hires like him. Jesse had taken
night duty three times in four years. But the rotunda and the
guest galleries were different after business hours, when the
lights were dimmed and the gallery displays switched off. By
night, this echoing chamber had seemed to Jesse as dark and
ominous as a pharaoh's tomb; by day, it buzzed with life and
color.

The rotunda was the hub of a wheel. Four galleries projected
from it like fat spokes: the Gallery of Science and Industry, the
Gallery of Twenty-first Century Life, a Gallery of the Arts,
and a Guests' Gallery, which housed food vendors and souvenir shops.

It hadn't taken Jesse long to figure out that the mezzanine
was really just a sort of inside-out museum. A museum, in that
it collected and displayed artifacts of another time; inside out,
because its collections depicted the future rather than the past.
He had been told the Galleries, with their soft lighting and

genial atmosphere, were a way of acclimating guests. Anyone wealthy enough to buy a ticket for a week's stay at the City would have known at least roughly what he was getting for his money—a glimpse of the future—but the details could be dismayingly strange. It had been a full year after the City's founding before respectable publications began to admit that people from the twenty-first century had actually contrived to build a kind of vertical resort city on the plains of Illinois—a notion so expansive it barely fit within the compass of a human skull. Skepticism was natural. Derision would have followed, had the City not provided evidence of its claims.

The City itself was evidence. The Galleries were evidence, a way to ease the passage between the clashing rocks of awe and incredulity. An even more convincing demonstration waited at the far end of the Gallery of Science and Industry. Jesse headed in that direction.

Grasping the concept of travel in time wasn't the last hurdle a visitor had to surmount, merely the first. The future represented here was so strange as to be intimidating, and guests were introduced to it one marvel at a time. Once you were comfortable with the mezzanine you could proceed to other levels of the City, where theaters presented moving pictures, where a heated swimming pool made its own waves, where acrobats and musicians imported from the twenty-first century performed on a nightly schedule. It was a lot to absorb, but the guests shuffling through the mezzanine seemed eager enough to absorb it. Jesse moved among them, insulated by his uniform. They were wealthy, and he was not. The women in the crowd wore fine silk bodices with bustles (and Jesse had once lived among women who would have killed, perhaps not just in the figurative sense, to own such things); the men wore waistcoats, frock coats, plain or checkered trousers, wing collars, elegantly knotted ties. Most of the guests appeared to be from

the east, but the wealthy of Chicago were prominently represented, and Jesse saw a few less carefully dressed gentlemen
who might have made their fortunes out west. There was a
sprinkling of likely Englishmen and Frenchmen, too, and one
conspicuous southerner in a white cutaway sack coat. City
hosts guided visitors in groups through the various galleries,
and Jesse followed one of these groups as it entered the Gallery
of Science and Industry, hanging back so as not to make himself conspicuous.

The displays, dioramas, and mounted exhibits were eye-
widening but vague on details. That was by design, Jesse knew.
The rationale had been explained to him in one of the seminars
local employees were required to attend. Too much explicit information about the future would be disorienting; it might also
be unfair. In the world today men were laboring to invent a
practical electric light, for instance, and the existence of the
City of Futurity suggested that their labors weren't futile; but
if the City handed out engineering details, the native inventor
of such a light would be made instantly irrelevant; geniuses
would die unhallowed and impoverished simply because the
City had revealed too much too soon.

So the Gallery of Science and Industry spoke in generalizations, and the history it portrayed was a shadow in a shadow.
Here were horseless carriages, depicted in photographs and
displayed behind glass, and claims that these devices would one
day dominate the roadways of America, but no hint of whose
fortunes might be made or broken by the use of them. Similarly
the flying machine: soon to fill the heavens with commerce;
soon to transform the art of war. A huge diorama depicted
"Aircraft in the Great Wars of the Twentieth Century." Winged
airships hung in motionless combat against a painted sky full
of smoke and fire. Guests were free to infer that there would
be world-consuming wars in the coming century—but when,

or with whom, or with what result, the gallery was careful not to say.

Static in their displays, the airships looked wonderfully strange but not quite plausible. Jesse walked a circle around something called a jet engine, a full-scale model with sections cut away to display its internal works. Wires, ducts, tubules, rotors; steel, rubber, copper, aluminum. It looked as complex as a Swiss watch, heavy enough to crush a millstone, and about as likely to fly through the air as a blacksmith's anvil.

"Might as well be a carnival show," Jesse heard a guest whisper to his wife. *Patience, friend,* he thought.

The group approached the end of the Gallery of Science. One of the final dioramas depicted what looked like a sheet-metal hut on a desert landscape under a black sky, men in white diving suits posed next to it. Men on the moon, supposedly. Next to it was a panoramic photograph of the plains of the planet Mars. The skeptics in the crowd became increasingly vocal, and Jesse understood the sentiment. But he knew what was coming next. These tours were carefully timed.

"Step this way," the guide said. The guide wore a City uniform; she was from the future, and judging by the sly smile on her face she enjoyed her work. She used her pass card to open the door at the end of the gallery. A flock of guests followed her onto the outdoor deck of the mezzanine level of Tower Two. Jesse joined them, trying to look as if he had some official business here. The deck—a sort of wide balcony, like the porch of a plantation house—overlooked what City people called the *helipad*.

Four stories below and some few hundred yards away, the City helicopter rested on a concrete platform, poised to take flight. The airship flew on a strict schedule, every morning at eleven forty-five, weather permitting. Jesse had seen it fly many times before, but never from this vantage point.

"Unlike the gallery displays," the tour guide said, "this is the real thing. Ladies and gentlemen, the marvel of manned flight. Please don't be frightened by the noise, and please don't crowd the railing. You'll be perfectly safe here."

She wasn't joking about the noise. It began almost at once. It was two noises in one, Jesse thought, a bass note that beat in the chest and a metallic whine that rose to a scream. The air around the machine quivered with the heat of its engines. Ponderously, slowly, the airship's enormous rotary blades began to turn.

Jesse had learned a few things about the City helicopter from the descriptive plaques in the gallery and from the conversation of Tower One repairmen who occasionally bought meals at the commissary. The airship was called a Sikorsky S-92. The crystalline bubble at the front of it was called the cockpit, and that was where the pilot sat. Behind it was a passenger compartment, which seated twenty. The helicopter was painted blue and white, with the words CITY OF FUTURITY emblazoned in gaudy red letters on the hull. On the near side of the machine was a row of small windows from which the faces of anxious guests peered out.

Every guest who bought admission to the City was eager to see the famous flying machine, but only a minority ever volunteered to climb inside it.

"Surely," a woman said, "it must be too *heavy* . . ."

If she said anything further it was lost in the roar. Heavy the machine undoubtedly was. More than ten tons, loaded. Fifty-six feet stem to stern. The top rotors spanned the same diameter. A team of horses couldn't pull it. It was frankly absurd to imagine such a thing rising into the air.

But that was exactly what it did. The rotors grew invisible with the speed of their rotation, raising hurricanes of dust. Even at this distance the wind caused men to put their hands to their hats and women to flatten their skirts. The guests stepped back from the rails, momentarily terrified. Then, engines roaring at maximum pitch, the machine at last parted company with the earth—awkwardly at first; then decisively, ferociously, beating its way into the sky by brute force.

Jesse guessed this was what the tourists found so dismaying: the unexpected violence of it. The helicopter was a cousin to weapons of war, not birds or kites. It was no more delicate than an artillery emplacement. It leaped on legs of fire and iron. It was a factory for manufacturing elevation, and if its furnaces were banked for even a moment it would plummet from the sky like a monstrous aerolite.

Jesse felt a hand on his shoulder and turned. The hand belonged to Elizabeth DePaul, who must have come over from Tower One. She was wearing a security uniform with trousers. Her expression was solemn.

Now that the flying machine was airborne it moved with startling speed. It was already crossing the western properties of the City, and it would fly for forty-five minutes more, darting across the low hills like a steel damselfly before it returned to its base. "We need to talk," Ms. DePaul said.

Her face was long and just missed being handsome, but her eyes were unnerving, brown as sand and just as implacable. "You could have paged me."

"A little private conversation before we head over to the other tower, all right?"

"Yes, ma'am."

"And you don't need to call me 'ma'am.' "

"I don't know what else to call you."

"It's not the fucking army. Since we're working together, Elizabeth is fine."

A guest overheard the curse and turned to stare at her with slack-jawed astonishment.

"Maybe we ought to step inside," Jesse said. "Where we

won't offend the paying customers." He added, "You can call me Jesse."

She nodded at the now-distant helicopter: "You must have seen it fly before."

"Often. Never from this angle."

"Think you'd like to ride it?"

"I'd be a whole lot happier not to. I suppose, Elizabeth, where you come from, you rode helicopters like they were horses."

"I've ridden a few," she said.

Jesse had first seen the City of Futurity when the towers were still under construction. At the time he had been less impressed by the buildings themselves—as impressive as they undoubtedly were—than by the tower cranes that roosted on their steel frames like skeletal birds, lofting buckets of Portland cement with their beaks. The scale of the work was dreamlike, a mechanical ballet across the vault of the sky, but the work itself, he soon learned, was brutally physical. The City men had trained him to help with the simpler tasks, and for months he had hauled lumber and boiled tar, his face burned brown by the Illinois sun, as the towers rose to completion.

But the most impressive miracle had been in place before he arrived. It was underground, located at the midpoint beneath both towers, and it was called the Mirror. The Mirror was the boundary between present and future. As a local hire he had never been allowed to see it, had never been close to it, had never expected he *would* see it; but he wondered, with his new pass card, if that had changed.

"Here's the deal," Elizabeth said. "We have to work together, and that's fine. Booking says you're a smart guy, and you did a good job with Grant. But once we cross into Tower One, you're on my turf. So we need to lay down some rules."

They rode a service elevator from the mezzanine to a floor below the dormitory level, another part of the City Jesse's original pass card would never have allowed him to enter. The elevator opened onto a corridor, crude by comparison with the guest floors—pipes and ducts had been plumbed in plain sight along the ceiling—but wide enough for vehicular traffic. A cart adorned with a flashing red light passed by as Elizabeth spoke.

"Rule one, don't be a tourist. Don't rubberneck. You don't want to be staring at everything like a newb. Whatever you see, pretend to be unimpressed."

He wasn't entirely ignorant of what went on in Tower One. It was common knowledge among local hires that when workers from Tower One took meals at the commissary in Tower Two, a person at an adjoining table might overhear a few words of their conversation. By that method Jesse had discerned some interesting truths about the forbidden parts of the City, including the Mirror. The Mirror, people said, was as tall as a five-story building, and it had been given its name because its surface reflected light, except when objects or people were passing through, at which time it became transparent. It opened a passage between filaments of time—but what engine could power such a machine, what furnaces were stoked to drive it? It was never discussed.

He saw a sign that said ACCESS TO ALL MIRROR LEVELS, but Elizabeth passed it without turning.

"Rule two," Elizabeth said, "don't ask for explanations and don't speak unless you're spoken to."

They reached a concrete bulkhead in which a steel door had been set. A sign said, OBSERVE ALL TOWER ONE PROTOCOLS BEYOND THIS POINT. Elizabeth dipped her pass card in a slot and the door sighed open.

"And stay with me," she said. "Don't wander off. We have a meeting in exactly one hour with August Kemp."

August Kemp: a man whose name was familiar to everyone
at the City, even low-status locals like Jesse. Kemp was the
twenty-first-century financier who controlled the company that
had built the City of Futurity. Kemp crossed the Mirror at will,
and he had made himself familiar to the powerful and the
wealthy of this world—just this summer he had dined in Manhattan with Jay Gould and John D. Rockefeller, and in San
Francisco with Leland Stanford and Mark Hopkins. The idea of
a personal meeting with August Kemp seemed as implausible to
Jesse as the prospect of shaking hands with the king of the moon.

"Okay?" she said. "Is that copacetic?"

He had no idea what she was talking about. "Yes," he said.

He followed Elizabeth to another bank of elevators and up
a couple of levels to the staff commissary of Tower One. At
first glance it could have been mistaken for the commissary
of Tower Two. Same windowless enclosed space, many tables,
plastic chairs. Similar booths housing similar food vendors,
though there seemed to be a greater variety of them. "I'm due
for lunch," she said. "Are you hungry?"

He was. But the booths appeared to be set up for cash, not
chits. And the cash changing hands was a specie not familiar
to him. "I guess I'll do without."

"Are you sure? It's on my dime."

"Well, that's generous. Thank you—I'll have whatever
you're having."

"Bento box and a Coke?"

He nodded, though he wasn't sure she was actually speaking
English. She ordered from a booth called California Sushi, and
the box she gave him contained contrivances of rice and fish,
mainly. He carried his tray to an empty table, and Elizabeth sat
opposite him.

He unwrapped his utensils. "Chopsticks," he said, surprised.
"You can get a fork if you want."

"No need." He sampled a ball of rice.

"Where'd you learn to handle chopsticks?"

"I'm from San Francisco. We don't lack for Chinamen or
chopsticks. Is this supposed to be Chinese food?"

"Japanese. Sort of. Fast-food sushi. And 'Chinamen' is
offensive, FYI." She mixed soy sauce with a green paste and
dipped a rice roll in it. Jesse did the same. The paste was a kind
of mustard, apparently. He managed to chew and swallow
without breaking into tears.

He apologized for "Chinamen"—he knew better; it had been
covered in his orientation course. The word was commonplace,
but it risked offending visitors from the future.

"So," Elizabeth said, "maybe you can guess why we're going
to see August Kemp."

He was distracted by an overhead video screen. Several such
screens were suspended from the ceiling of the commissary,
and all of them were showing a baseball game. At least, Jesse
guessed it was baseball. The diamond looked right, though the
catcher wore a mask and the game was played in a stadium that
dwarfed the Roman Colosseum.

Elizabeth sighed theatrically. "What did I tell you about
staring?"

"Sorry." He was tempted to call her *ma'am*, just to antago-
nize her.

"I was saying, maybe you can guess what this is all about."

"It's about the attempt on Grant."

"Right. You handled the incident really well. If the guy had
pulled the trigger, we would have had a major shitstorm on
our hands. Worst case, a dead president, federal investigators
knocking at the gate, a major hit to the revenue stream, maybe
even an early shutdown. As it stands, no shots were fired and

we have the shooter in custody. He's a local, by the way. Some douchebag who's still angry at Grant for taking Richmond. The important thing is, you saved Kemp a boatload of money and rescued him from a potential scandal. Which makes you a very shiny object in his eyes. You know about Kemp, right? Majority shareholder and CEO, the big boss, you came to his attention, he's favorably disposed toward you, and that's why you're moving up in the world. All good, except for one detail."

"The pistol," Jesse said. "They told Grant it was a Colt. But it wasn't."

"The weapon was a Glock 19 with a full clip, most definitely not local."

"And why is that a problem?"

"Because the shooter came into the City with the most recent batch of local guests, only a few hours before Grant himself. We have him on camera for pretty much every second after he passed through the gate. He didn't interact with anybody, didn't go anywhere unusual. So the question is, where did he get the gun? As far as we can tell, it was already in his possession. But they don't sell Glocks in Shitstain, Missouri, or wherever he hails from. So we need to know how he obtained it."

"You're saying the pistol was smuggled out of the City somehow, delivered to the gunman, and the gunman carried it back in."

"That's one possibility."

"So he must have had collaborators."

"Most likely, yes. I've been asked to find out. The investigation will have to look both ways, inside the City and outside of it. And in the conduct of the investigation, it could be useful to have help from someone who's both reliable and native to 1876. Specifically, you."

"I see. Well, I appreciate your confidence."

"I'm kind of agnostic on the subject, to be honest. In other words, yeah, if we set foot outside the gate you might be help-ful to me. But until then—and especially here in Tower One—I need to be the one calling the shots. That's the arrangement, and I hope you're okay with it."

"I'm okay with it."

Jesse guessed she had said everything she had meant to say at that point, because the conversation lapsed into an awkward silence. He went to work on the remaining contents of his bento box. After a while Elizabeth looked at her watch. And Jesse looked at his. Their appointment with Kemp was still a half hour away. She said, "So, uh, you're from San Francisco?"

"Yes." Because she seemed to expect more from him, he said, "I was born in New Orleans, but my father took me west at a young age." She nodded and said nothing. If this was sup-posed to be polite conversation, she was no better at it than he was. "So where do you hail from, if you don't mind me asking?"

"Born in Minneapolis, but my folks moved to North Carolina. I joined the army when I turned nineteen. After I left active duty I settled in Charlotte and started working private security."

"You were a soldier?"

"Yeah."

"A soldier in a war?"

"I'm not sure how much I ought to say about that. The rules are kind of relaxed between us, but . . . well, okay, yeah. In a war. What about you?"

"I was eight years old at the time of First Manassas. My father was eligible but didn't like to pick sides. That's why he headed for San Francisco, where he couldn't be called up."

"How did you end up working for the City?"

"I was thrown off a train," he said.

Up on the television screen, a batter wearing a Red Sox jer-sey hit a ball into a fielder's enormous glove. Third out. The teams traded places. The game, Jesse discerned from fleeting captions, was being played in Boston. It was a cloudy day in the Boston of the future. Elsewhere in that world, perhaps, female soldiers were riding helicopters and firing Glock 19s. But Boston seemed peaceable enough.

"Oh, shit," Elizabeth said (and it was certainly true, Jesse reflected, that she had a soldier's vocabulary). He looked away from the baseball game and saw two men in security uniforms approaching from the direction of the elevator banks. "Castro and Dekker," she said, scowling.

"Enemies of yours?"

"Not enemies so much as just assholes."

The man in front, Elizabeth said, was Castro—he was big and well-fed, and he filled his uniform to capacity. Dekker was even bigger. His head was shaved to stubble, and his grin suggested he was the ringleader of the two. "Liz!" Dekker called out. "Is this your new partner?"

Elizabeth showed him the middle finger of her right hand.

"So your partner's a local," Dekker said, undaunted. He turned to Jesse. "Is this your first time in Tower One?"

Jesse met the man's eyes. "It is."

"I saw you looking at the game. You like baseball?"

"I've never played it."

"They got fiber-optic cables strung through the Mirror so we can watch in real time. Red Sox versus the Orioles. Hey, Castro, you're a baseball geek. Do they have baseball here in 1876?"

"Sure," Castro said. "But different leagues and shit. Teams like, you know, the White Stockings or the Red Caps. Knicker-bocker rules. No night games."

"No instant replays," Dekker said. "Right, chief?"

Jesse shrugged.

"So how do you like Tower One?"

"I haven't seen much more of it than this table."

"I bet you wish you could see the real thing, though. Step through the Mirror into the glorious future, am I right?"

No, you are not right, Jesse thought. For one thing, it never happened. A wealthy local could buy a ticket to Tower Two for a peek at things to come, but that was as far as he'd get. A few local hires found their way into Tower One, usually as entertainers or servants. But cross the Mirror into *their* world? No one had ever managed such a feat—as far as Jesse knew, no one had ever tried. "I don't give it much thought."

"Bullshit," Dekker said.

"Excuse me?"

"Bullshit you don't give it much thought. I never met a local who didn't lie awake wondering about it."

"Like wetbacks," Castro said. "Sneak into the twenty-first century, get a job at Swift or Tyson."

"Mirrorbacks," Dekker said, laughing. "Except we have a perfect fence. Sorry, bro, but this is as close as you'll ever get to the World of the Future."

"My name's not bro."

"I don't really give a shit about your name."

Jesse stood up.

"Whoa," Dekker said. "You're pretty big for a local, but you don't want to be getting in my face here."

Jesse put out his open right hand. "My name's Jesse Cullum."

Dekker was clearly startled. It took him a moment to comprehend that he was being offered a handshake. Then his grin came back. He accepted the offer. Enthusiastically. More than enthusiastically. Jesse felt as if he'd put his hand into a laundry mangle, but he managed not to show it. He squeezed Dekker's hand in return. "Elizabeth," Jesse said, "do you think I'd lose my job if I knocked Mr. Dekker down?"

"Unfortunately, yes."

"In that case, Mr. Dekker, I'll just ask you to excuse us. Ms. DePaul and I have business to conduct elsewhere."

Dekker's grin had become an outright sneer. His friend Castro was trying not to laugh.

Elizabeth stood up. "He's right, Dekker. We have to go. You can compare dicks some other time."

Dekker released Jesse's nearly lifeless hand and leaned toward Jesse's ear. "We'll see who gets knocked down."

"At your pleasure," Jesse said. "Chief."

"And by the way, your partner? It's not 'Ms. DePaul.' It's *Mrs.* DePaul. She's married, didn't she tell you that?"

"Dekker, you're such an asswipe," Mrs. DePaul said.

They took a staff elevator from the commissary level. As soon as the doors closed, Elizabeth said, "Dekker never fails to mention my husband."

"It's none of my business."

"Because my husband's in prison. Five years on a trafficking charge."

"I'm sorry to hear that. But it's still none of my business."

"Dekker likes to use it against me, like it's some big secret or something."

"Your husband's crimes, whatever they may have been, surely don't reflect on you."

"Why did you offer to shake his hand, by the way? Dekker's completely steroidal. He could have broken bones."

"It seemed like the gentlemanly thing."

"You might want to save that behavior for actual gentlemen."

The elevator stopped at one of the guest levels. A half dozen women in identical cuirass bodices and ruffled skirts stepped inside, probably waitresses or barmaids. Locals, by the sound of their voices. Jesse knew that such employees were well paid, often hired away from places like Thompson's Restaurant in Chicago or Delmonico's in New York City. "Afternoon, ladies," he said.

Some of them giggled, not especially politely. They scorned his western vowels, he guessed, or the way he carried himself. "You're a long way from Tower Two," a redheaded one said.

About a thousand yards. But she was right. It was a long thousand yards.

"Is it true," the woman asked, "General Grant's visiting?"

"Yes, ma'am, he is. I saw him myself."

"Enjoying a taste of the future. Where women and niggers can vote and gal-boys can marry each other." She winked at Jesse. "You may be an old hand in Tower Two, but you're just a pie-eater over here. Be careful till you get your bearings."

The waitresses left the elevator at another level.

"Is that true?" Jesse asked.

"Which part?"

"Who can vote and all. Where you come from."

"Women vote. African-Americans vote. And you don't have to be straight to get married."

"Straight?"

"Heterosexual. Boy-girl."

Jesse was still pondering that when they reached the administration floor.

Something about Elizabeth DePaul made Jesse think of horses.

Not in an insulting way. She wasn't big or ugly, though she wasn't small, nor was she pretty in the polished manner of the waitresses he had encountered in the elevator. But she had the dignity of a well-bred horse. A certain horsey implacability. Brown eyes that seemed to express a cynicism born of bitter experience. And beneath that, a pride that was neither false nor self-flattering. He had seen that combination of traits before, in some of the Tenderloin women among whom he had grown up, and he had learned to recognize it even in the faces of strangers, especially the strangers who eked out a living in the streets south of Broadway and north of Market. It was a survivor's look. Such people were useful and dangerous, often in equal parts.

And she was a soldier. According to the dioramas of Tower Two, the twenty-first century was a land of marvels. But, by inference, it was also a world that contained wars. And prisons, if Elizabeth was to be believed; and prisoners; and prisoners' wives.

Like the commissary, the administration level of Tower One was a replica of the same level in Tower Two: the same tiled floors and subdivided offices, the same gentle sound of tapped keyboards and cool air hissing from concealed ducts. Clerical workers looked up as Jesse and Elizabeth passed, and a few of them were startled enough to look twice, though they were too well trained to stare. What exactly was it, Jesse wondered, that made him so conspicuously a local? He felt like a belled cat.

He followed Elizabeth to the office where August Kemp and the Tower One security administrator were waiting. It was a big office, and it housed a big desk, and several plush chairs and a sofa. The window was like the window in Tower Two, except that it looked east. Outside, ominous clouds tumbled across the sky. Far below, in a sward of mottled green, the City's captive buffalo huddled in anticipation of rain.

Both men stood up as Elizabeth and Jesse entered. The man behind the desk was the Tower One security chief, Elizabeth's boss. He was a dark-skinned man of middle age with a hawkish face and fiercely observant eyes, and his name was Barton. "Please sit," he said crisply.

Jesse and Elizabeth stationed themselves on the sofa. August Kemp remained standing.

Kemp was not what Jesse had expected. In Jesse's experience wealthy men tended to wear their authority in plain sight, an expectation of obedience as conspicuous as a Sunday hat. August Kemp was the right age for such a man: hard to tell with future people, but Jesse pegged him at fifty years or more by the grain of his skin. But he was lean as a whippet hound and tan as a cowherd, and his clothes seemed not only informal but unserious: denim trousers and a shirt on which pictures of tropical fruit were printed. His white hair was abundant, and he wore it loosely. His teeth were conspicuously perfect. He displayed them in a broad smile.

"Mr. Cullum, I don't want to embarrass you with praise for your handling of the apparent attempt on President Grant's life. I understand the president has already thanked you, and you know you have the gratitude of the City of Futurity."

"Yes, sir, I appreciate that," Jesse said.

"The gunman is in custody, and we've had time to interrogate him. Mr. Barton can fill you in on the details."

Barton cleared his throat and said, "The suspect is one Obie Stedmann of Calhoun's Landing, Louisiana. A few months ago there was an encounter between what Stedmann calls his 'rifle club' and federal troops, a shoot-out that left fifteen dead, two of them soldiers and the rest of them Stedmann's buddies. The army claims it prevented a lynching. Stedmann calls it murder and blames Reconstruction in general and Grant in particular. When he read in the papers that Grant would be visiting the City, he started to make plans. He traveled to Chicago, spent a night there, then came to Futurity Station, where he spent a week prior to Grant's arrival. We don't know what he did during that time, but we know what he *didn't* do. He didn't make an attempt on Grant when Grant's Pullman car arrived at Futurity Station. Probably because it wasn't possible. Guests bound for the City are escorted from their train to the coaches by a security detail, and Grant's security was tight as a drumhead. We believe that's why Stedmann decided to take Grant from *inside* the City."

"Which would have been a problem for him," Kemp interjected, "because it's not easy to buy a ticket on short notice. We're generally booked up at least six months in advance."

"It's not easy," Barton said, "but it's not impossible. Tickets come up for resale if guests cancel. We have a generous rebooking program, but not everyone takes advantage of it. Tickets can be resold. And while we discourage scalping, despite our best efforts, it happens. Stedmann managed to buy himself a ticket, though it must have cost him a small fortune."

"He bought something else, too," Jesse said. "A pistol, if I'm not mistaken."

Kemp nodded as if Jesse had said something wise. Barton said, "You saw it yourself. A clip-loading handgun, not of contemporary design."

A Glock 19, specifically, Jesse thought.

"We've gone to great lengths," August Kemp said, "to keep a careful boundary between the City and this world. It was part of the design of the City from the beginning. Our concerns are both pragmatic and ethical. We want to protect locals from ideas and technology that might be destabilizing or dangerous out of their context. And we want to protect the City from misunderstanding and needless litigation. Obviously, the boundary is going to be a little porous no matter what we do. We permit a limited trade in authorized souvenirs, and if one of our Tower One visitors is out on tour and misplaces a smartphone or a wristwatch, so be it. No great harm done. But a weapon? Every handgun we allow through the Mirror is itemized and assigned to a member of the security detail. No unauthorized carries are permitted. Zero tolerance. Finding such a weapon inside the City would have been bad enough. The possibility that Stedmann bought it at the railway depot is shocking, absolutely unacceptable."

Elizabeth said, "Have you got anything out of Stedmann about the gun?"

Barton said, "He gave us his backstory, but he won't say anything about buying the weapon. So here's what we want you and Jesse to do for us. First, you head out to Futurity Station and see if you can reconstruct Stedmann's movements. Your focus should be on the purchase of the weapon—who was the vendor? Are there more weapons being sold? Contraband other than weapons?"

Kemp addressed Elizabeth directly: "The details are in your inbox. This is your first trip into the field, isn't it?"

"I worked transit a few time between here and the railroad," Elizabeth said. "So I've been out of the gates. But basically, yes."

"We'll get you suitable clothing, but you'll need to take cues from Jesse when it comes to deportment. Are you good with that?"

"I had the orientation sessions—"

"And that's great," Kemp said. "But a little brushup is always helpful. And Jesse's a native. Remember that. It's *his* world out there, not yours."

"I understand," she said.

"Jesse, are we on the same wavelength here?" Kemp registered Jesse's blank expression and said, "Are we in agreement?"

"I think so."

"That's wonderful. Elizabeth, again, we texted you details. Jesse, I probably don't need to tell you this duty comes with a pay raise."

"That's very kind," Jesse said.

"You're one of our most loyal local employees and one of

the least troublesome. And that's the attitude you need to take into the field. Do you have any other questions before we break this up?"

Jesse thought about it. "We're working as a team. Elizabeth and me, I mean. And I need to help her pass as local. Correct?"

"Right."

"But if the gun was smuggled out of the City, the trail might lead right back to Tower One. And I'm happy to follow it. The trouble is, I'm conspicuous here. Twice today I got pegged as a local, and your clerks all peer at me like I'm Lazarus come forth. What am I doing wrong? Can you tell me that?"

August Kemp looked at Barton, who looked back at Kemp. Neither spoke. Finally Elizabeth said, "It's your beard."

"There are men with beards here."

"Not like yours. You look like a refugee from ZZ Top. You look like Zack Galifianakis auditioning for a Civil War comedy. Don't guys in 1876 ever shave?"

"Some do," Jesse said stiffly. "And not all your men are beardless."

"Right. With a little trim you could pass in *both* worlds."

Kemp said, "We've got a styling salon in Tower One. Off hours, it's available for staff. I'll book you an appointment. You'll need to learn to find your way around Tower One in any case, since we're moving you here for the duration of this assignment."

"I thank you," Jesse said uncertainly.

"Any other questions?"

Plenty, Jesse thought. But none he could bring himself to ask right now.

"And, oh," Kemp said, "I understand you need a new pair of Oakleys. Did you stop by the supply room?"

"I did," Jesse said. "They're all out of Oakleys."

"I'll look into it," August Kemp said.

3

The clothes Jesse was issued for his trip to the railroad depot were strangely made.

He had to wear them even so. The last "authentic" items of clothing he had owned were the trousers, shirt, and flannel underwear he had been wearing when he arrived at the City, and the first thing the City had done was to send them for delousing. Today—given that he was supposed to pass as a modestly successful businessman—a drifter's shabby pants wouldn't do. So he had been instructed to report to the supply room to be fitted for passable substitutes.

Which they had given him, and which he had put on this very morning. And judging by the reflection in the mirror in his dormitory room, he did look more or less like the sort of modestly successful shopkeeper he had often passed in the streets of San Francisco. Except that the shirt was too perfectly clean. And the collar was too white. And the waistcoat felt slick, as if the cotton had been woven too closely. Add to that his recent shave and haircut, and he felt both newly minted and altogether ridiculous.

"You'll do," Elizabeth said as he climbed into the coach and settled on the bench opposite her. He was grateful for the comment, but she was hardly in a position to judge. Her own clothes were imitations and, to Jesse's eye, looked it.

The carriage was also a replica, assembled in the twenty-first century and imported through the Mirror. From a distance it would be indistinguishable from an ordinary hackney coach, but it rode differently: the City people had installed a complex suspension. But the coach didn't have to fool anyone. It was part of the fleet of coaches and horse-drawn omnibuses that conveyed guests from the City to the train station on a weekly schedule.

The coach jolted as the driver urged his team through the gate and away from the City. Rain streaked the windows, rendering the Illinois prairie in a molten palate of greens and yellows, and Jesse's mood wasn't much sunnier. *Trouble ahead,* he thought. Or, to be fair, maybe not. Maybe he could winkle out enough facts to satisfy Elizabeth and her bosses, and his life would resume its prior course uninterrupted. But there were other possibilities.

Last night he had dreamed of his sister Phoebe. Again. The same dream, as familiar as it was terrible. He had been back at Madame Chao's, and there had been a room in flames, and Phoebe in a box, and his father spilling blood from his cupped hands.

He had awakened in a cold sweat. He showered and dressed, then made his way to the commissary for breakfast. He told Dorothy, the war widow who worked the counter at Starbucks, that she might not be seeing him so often now that he was being moved to Tower One.

"New job," she said, "that's nice! Making a name for yourself. You *look* like it, too."

"This is special. They dressed me for a trip out to the depot."

"As a fashion plate?"

"I'm not at liberty to speak of it," Jesse said, meaning he didn't want to.

"You'll have the ladies all agog, that's certain."

One lady who was not all agog was Doris Vanderkamp, taking a break from her work cleaning guest rooms. Doris's on-again, off-again case of the grippe seemed to be in abeyance today, and her face was more pretty than haggard, dark curls framing mischievous eyes. She joined Jesse at his table without waiting for an invitation. "Well, well, well! Jesse Cullum, spiff as a new dime. Almost enough to make a girl *miss* him."

"You're looking fine as well, Doris."

"All this time I figured your only aim in life was to collect your wages and smile at the boss. But it turns out you're *ambitious.*"

"Pretty soon you'll have fewer opportunities to insult me, so you might as well get the job done while I'm here."

"I don't mean to insult you—at least not at the moment. But you're an inconstant lover, Jesse, you have to admit it."

He wasn't much of a lover at all. His entanglement with Doris had been born of his desire, her availability, and a certain spirit of recklessness that had arisen between them like a summer storm. There had never been a future in it. He suspected Doris had known that long before their intimate friendship ran on the rocks. Her consequent resentment of him was a form of social theater, for which she possessed a remarkable talent.

"I hear they partnered you with a big old girl from the twenty-first century," she said. "Some female ogre with pants on."

"Ogre's not an apt word. Though she's not as small and pert as you."

"That's a pretty thing to say." Doris reached out and covered his hand with hers. "I forgive you nothing, you idiot."

Then she took a handkerchief from the folds of her dress and blew her nose into it. Her cold was coming back, Jesse thought.

"I had a word with Dekker this morning," Elizabeth said.

Jesse turned his gaze from the window. The rain came down hard and heavy, as if children were pelting the coach with gravel. The City's helicopter would remain in its hangar today. Outdoor events would be postponed and rescheduled, and both of the indoor pools in Tower Two—one for women, one for men—would be crowded with guests, who seemed to take a particular pleasure in bathing in heated water while a storm beat at the high glass walls.

But all that was behind him. Ahead, the streets of Futurity Station would be awash in mud and worse.

Dekker, Jesse thought: the man who had insulted him and then attempted to crush his hand. "Was he in a better mood today?"

"Pretty much the opposite of a better mood. After you talked to him in the food court? His pass card went missing. He had to call the security office to get a new one. The old one turned up this morning, stuck in a flowerpot on the commissary floor."

"I'm sorry to hear of his troubles."

"Dekker blames you."

"On what grounds?"

"There's a security cam video of him hassling you, but it's from the wrong angle, so it didn't prove anything—assuming that's when you lifted the card."

"Are you suggesting I stole it?"

"I think, if you *did* steal it and dump it in a flowerpot, it would have served that asshole right. But I didn't *see* you do it, and I was sitting less than a yard away. Are you a pick-pocket?"

Jesse considered the question. He didn't want Elizabeth to think of him as someone who had gone around skinning wallets in his earlier life. Nor did he want to lie. "What you're talking about sounds more like sleight of hand."

"What, like stage magic? So you're a magician?"

"No. Nor was my father . . . but he learned a few card tricks in his youth."

"And that's how you lifted Dekker's pass without anyone noticing, including Dekker?"

"I imagine, if I had done such a thing, I might be reluctant to admit it." In fact he was angry at himself for having done it at all. It had been an intolerable risk for a trivial act of revenge.

"Your secret's safe with me. Dekker can't prove anything, and everyone in Tower One security except Dekker thinks it's pretty funny." She thought for a moment. "It's important to you to keep your job."

"Yes, ma'am. I mean, yes."

"Any particular reason?"

"None that I care to discuss."

"Okay. That's interesting, though, about your father being a magician."

"He wasn't a magician. He earned his keep by opening doors. Do you come from a family of soldiers, Elizabeth?"

She laughed. "No. My father was an electrical engineer until he smoked himself into a premature coronary. My mother worked as a beautician, but these days she mostly watches Fox News and goes to church."

"I'm sure they're fine people."

"I'm glad *somebody's* sure." Moisture in the air had made the windows opaque, and Elizabeth scrubbed the glass with the heel of her hand. "But you know the saying? 'All happy families are alike, but every unhappy family is unhappy in its own way.'"

"Who said that? Some wise man from your century?"

She shrugged. "I think I heard it on *Oprah*."

Futurity Station was a smudge on the northern horizon now, as if someone had run a sooty finger across the wet Illinois plains. If Jesse craned his head he could see the rest of this convoy of coaches and horse buses bending toward the rail town like ants to a cabbage. And when the veils of rain parted he could see a skyline of wooden structures, the largest and tallest of which was the three-story Excelsior Hotel, where they would be spending the night.

The depot's smell preceded it. Jesse saw Elizabeth wrinkle her nose. Two years ago the City had installed waste disposal amenities for Futurity Station, but the town had rapidly outgrown those niceties. The weather could only have made it worse, Jesse imagined; the streets would be flooded and wet air would enclose the stench like a dome. "Sometimes I wonder why you're here at all."

"I'm here to make sure you don't screw up."

He smiled at what she probably intended as a witticism. "Not you personally. You twenty-first-century people. The guests in Tower One. What do you come here for? I don't see the attraction. I understand well enough how it works for *my* people: the wonders of the future, a better draw than anything Barnum ever dreamed up. We pay to see your moving pictures and swim in your heated pools and ride in your helicopter, and if we can't afford a week in the City we can come to Futurity Station to buy trinkets and catch a glimpse of the airship. But *your* people, the people who leave the twenty-first century to come here—what's the draw? I don't see it. People are still out of work from the Panic of '73. We're little more than a decade gone from a war that filled the streets with widows and legless veterans. The Indians are in rebellion, and the South is proving as difficult to reconstruct as a broken egg. It's a little surprising to me that so many guests should care to drop in and visit just now."

He was obscurely pleased that Elizabeth didn't have an easy answer for him. She sat in thoughtful silence for a moment. Then she said, "The Mirror is a machine. It has limitations. It won't take you to last month, because it can't do that kind of precision—a short jump is like threading a needle. And it won't take you back much farther than a century or two, because a longer jump would require a ridiculous amount of energy. So we have a window of opportunity, and you're in it."

"But that's not the only reason."

"Well, no. And in a way you're right—not everybody *wants* to visit. You notice we don't get a lot of black tourists? Because a place with a recent history of slavery doesn't seem like an ideal vacation spot to most African-Americans."

"I've seen black people in the tour groups."

"Sure, if they have an academic interest or a family history that matters to them. But think about what the City has to do to keep them safe. Armed escorts, gated hotels in San Francisco and New York."

All that was true. Just last winter the *New York Tribune* had managed to place a reporter in a tour group, and the result had been such sensational headlines as NEGRO PRESIDENT ELECTED IN THE FUTURE and IN FUTURE AMERICA VICE RUNS RAMPANT. But City authorities refused to confirm or deny the stories, and since there was an apparently endless supply of lies and rumors—no fewer than fifteen books had been published this year alone, all claiming to reveal "secrets the City won't

tell," all mutually contradictory—the controversy had amounted
to nothing substantial.

"And yet you come," Jesse said.

"Because you're what we used to be. Or we like to think
so. If I say '1876' to somebody back home they're going to
picture, I don't know, cowboys and Indians, or maybe a shady
New England town with an ice cream parlor and fat politicians
in waistcoats and celluloid collars, some kind of Disneyland-
Main Street-Frontierland deal . . ."

"Dear God," Jesse said.

"Of course it's bullshit, and we kind of know that, but—
look at it this way: If somebody in 1876 invents a time machine
and offers you a trip to see the Crusades, say, or the building
of the pyramids, wouldn't you accept?"

"I suppose I might. As long as I was guaranteed protection
from the Saracens or the pharaohs."

"Well, yeah," Elizabeth said. "Exactly."

The convoy from the City of Futurity pulled into a long coach
barn next to the rail depot at Futurity Station.

It wasn't the depot Jesse remembered from his arrival here
four years ago, when he had been unceremoniously evicted
from the baggage car of a westbound express. Back then, it
hadn't even had a name. It had been a coaling station and a
water tank then, not a locus of human habitation, but four
summers of proximity to the City of Futurity had turned it
into a boomtown with hundreds of permanent inhabitants.

The new train station had been constructed in partnership
with the Central Pacific Railroad, and one of its purposes was
to protect paying guests from the idly curious. Today's paying guests were returning from the City to meet either the

westbound train at six o'clock or the eastbound at seven; later, the same convoy of vehicles would carry fresh guests back to the City. Jesse and Elizabeth waited until the other conveyances were empty before leaving their coach. Their coachman, a local hire, handed down their luggage: a cloth valise apiece for Elizabeth and Jesse, each containing fresh clothes and sundry supplies, including a pistol and ammunition. Jesse exchanged a wave with the coachman before heading to the south end of the cavernous enclosed carriageway.

The rain had subsided to a drizzle. "Let me carry your bag," Jesse said.

"I can carry it."

"It's better if I do. For the sake of appearances."

Elizabeth gave him a hard look but handed over the valise.

The Excelsior Hotel across the street was fully occupied. Just one room had been reserved for them, and Jesse nodded at the desk clerk and signed the register as *Jesse Cullum & wife*. The Tower One security boss had warned Jesse of the necessity of the subterfuge. If he had a problem about sharing quarters, Barton had warned him, he needed to get over it. But Jesse didn't anticipate any problem. Apart from a certain inevitable awkwardness.

A bellman escorted them to their room, three stories up. As soon as they were alone Elizabeth opened the window. A rising wind billowed the cloth curtains and seemed to mitigate the stench of the town. *Unless*, Jesse thought, *we're just growing accustomed to it.*

In any case the daylight would be gone within hours. He cleared his throat and said, "You should know . . . I'm not a sound sleeper. Sometimes in the night . . ."

Elizabeth turned away from the window and gave him her full attention. "Sometimes in the night *what*?"

"I suffer from nightmares. Sometimes I wake up. In an agitated state. Possibly shouting."

"This happens often?"

"I'm hoping it won't happen at all. But I thought you should know. If it does happen, don't be frightened. As soon as I'm fully awake, it stops."

He was gratified that Elizabeth nodded as if he had said nothing surprising. "I'll bear that in mind," she said.

They shared an evening meal in the hotel's dining room, then returned to their room and made a plan for the following day. Elizabeth used a device like a fancy pager to report back to Barton at the City. Then they went to bed.

There were two beds in the room. Jesse turned down the gaslights as Elizabeth undressed. She was unselfconscious about it. Her dress looked conventional, but the stays and buttons were false. It was held together with something called Velcro, which made a sound like a dog's fart as she unfastened it. Underneath she wore briefs and a cotton halter.

Jesse's clothes were more simply made. City-issue underwear for men came in two varieties, briefs and shorts. Jesse preferred the briefs. They kept everything in place without getting in the way. As he put his hand to the mantle of the lamp Elizabeth said, "You sure you've never been in a war?"

She was looking at the various scars on his body. "Not a war that was formally declared."

The gaslight flickered down to nothing.

"Must have hurt like hell," Elizabeth said.

He didn't answer.

He put himself to sleep as he often did, by thinking about the complexities of time travel. It was a more reliable soporific than counting sheep.

The concept had been explained to him early in his tenure at the City. The City people had been careful to communicate the idea that time travel was not (as they said) *linear*—that there was not just one history but many histories, side by side. They talked about a philosophical problem called the Grandfather Paradox: if a time traveler killed his grandfather in the cradle, would the time traveler himself then cease to exist? But it didn't apply, they said, because in this case past and future were different worlds. City people could kill all the grand-fathers they liked—all it meant was that this world's future would not perfectly replicate the future from which the City people came.

Jesse thought about all those threads of time laid side-by-side like fibers in a rope, each thread a world with an identical history. The Mirror was a device that braided histories to-gether, so that human beings and physical objects could pass back and forth. It amounted to time travel because every ac-cessible world was identical to the source, but *less ancient*. A nearby history might be only a few seconds or minutes less old, so that traveling to it would seem like traveling a few seconds or minutes into the past. More distant histories were separated by years, centuries, eons. But as Elizabeth had said, there were practical limits to what a Mirror could do. Traveling to a nearby history required relatively little energy but an impossible de-gree of precision. Traveling to a very distant history required little precision but an absurd amount of energy.

What *kind* of energy it required Jesse could not begin to guess. But he knew, intuitively, that the Mirror was the most remarkable thing the City people had produced—more remark-able than a helicopter, more remarkable even than a photograph of the icy plains of Mars. It was more than a machine—it was a *metaphysical* machine. It was a steamship that plied the winding rivers of heaven itself.

Phoebe was crying.

That was unusual. Phoebe was twelve years old, and she took pride in her maturity. She had taught herself not to cry when she was unhappy. But she was crying now, and Jesse was frustrated because he couldn't locate the source of the sound.

The walls were on fire.

The walls were on fire, and his father stood in the center of the room, cupping blood in his hands. His father's expression was sorrowful. He bowed at the waist like a man at prayer.

"I tried to stop it," Jesse said, or tried to say.

Phoebe was inside a steamer trunk, he realized. He went to the trunk to open it. But it was locked, the key was nowhere to be found, and the brass fittings were too hot to touch.

"I'm sorry," Jesse's father said.

He opened his hands. Blood and unspeakable things dropped to the floor.

In the trunk, Phoebe screamed.

"You're safe," someone said.

Jesse became aware of the room, the stink of his own sweat, the rawness of his throat, the cotton sheet coiled around him like a rope.

"You're safe."

It was Elizabeth who spoke. And she was holding his hand. Or at least compressing his hands against his body in a kind of wrestling grip, so that he couldn't lash out at her. "Thank you,

I'm awake now," he managed to say, and she released him and took a wary step back.

He was profoundly embarrassed. "Elizabeth, I'm sorry . . ."

"Nothing to be sorry for." She was a dark presence in a room lit only by moonlight. "You okay now?" Her voice was soft and had no anger in it.

"Yes."

"All right then."

She went back to her own bed.

No further words were spoken. Outside, the rain had stopped. A cooling wind came through the window. Elizabeth's bed creaked as she turned on her side. Jesse pulled his blanket around his shoulders and stared into the darkness and waited for morning.

4

He woke at dawn. He dressed and washed and waited while Elizabeth did the same, then escorted her to the hotel's dining room. She insisted on taking all her meals here, where City officials periodically inspected both the food and the kitchen. Jesse objected that this would anchor them to the Excelsior, but Elizabeth wouldn't be moved: "You people don't have practical refrigeration. You put lead oxide in your milk and God knows what in your sausages. You call dysentery 'the summer complaint.' So this is where we eat, period, full stop."

He didn't argue. He was still ashamed that he had troubled her with his nightmare, but he couldn't bring himself to speak about it, and she didn't raise the subject. Which was just as well, since they had the day's work ahead of them.

Futurity Station was more circus than town, Jesse thought. Like a circus, it had an air of impermanence and expedience. And like a circus, its main sources of revenue were dreams, deception, sex, and theft.

Their plan was to pose as a married couple, not quite well-heeled enough to afford admission to the City, who had come to Futurity Station for a glimpse of the flying machine and to buy any futuristic contraband they could lay their hands on. This morning they would get the lay of the land by way of a leisurely stroll, and the weather was ideal for it: vivid sunlight and a pleasant warmth, the town's gaudy signs and wooden sidewalks all washed clean by last night's rain.

The town had two main streets, one parallel to the train tracks and one perpendicular to them. The first street was called Depot, the second was called Lookout. Most of the respectable establishments—hotels, a barber, an apothecary shop, a Methodist church—were situated on Depot, west of the train station. Lookout Street was home to saloons, pawn shops, penny theaters, music halls dedicated to burlesque shows and minstrelsy, and, at its southernmost extremity, rows of bleachers where customers could buy a "guaranteed best" view of the regularly scheduled fly past of the City airship.

Jesse and Elizabeth began by dawdling along Depot Street. Any hour before noon was early for a town like Futurity Station, but the sidewalks were far from empty, and daylight hours were especially suited for the respectable tourists they were pretending to be. It was the element of pretense that worried Jesse. He had reminded Elizabeth as tactfully as possible that she must not swear or swagger or express her opinions too freely or do any of the ten thousand other things City women did without thinking and which might, in the year 1876, raise eyebrows or start riots. Her response had been to roll her eyes and say, "So they tell me," which had not entirely reassured him.

But she carried herself convincingly enough as they strolled, taking his arm and keeping to his side. Her skirt and bodice must have made her uncomfortable in the warm weather, but the City outfitters had also provided her with a straw hat with a flat brim and blue ribbons, which disguised her short hair and gave her some protection from the sun. They stopped briefly at an apothecary shop with a soda fountain, and she put on a plausible show of interest in the patent medicines on the shelves and the array of red and blue bottles of all sizes, but when the druggist asked whether he could serve them she smiled and said, "No, thank you, maybe we'll stop by on our way back to the hotel."

At the western end of Depot Street they passed a shop offering novelty items and curios—it looked too respectable to be a source of contraband weapons, but something in the window caused Elizabeth to pause and tug him toward the door. A table inside was stocked with books claiming to be guides to the City or fictional accounts of future history, most with stamped covers featuring lurid or fantastical illustrations. Elizabeth picked up a novel that gloried under the title *America's War with Mars*. "I guess H. G. Wells is screwed," she murmured.

He didn't know what that meant, but he smiled in response to her smile.

The proprietor of the shop, a skinny man with a mustache and a striped shirt, bustled out from behind his counter. "Is there anything I can help you with?"

Elizabeth said, "There's a book in your window . . . at least, I *think* it's a book." She pointed. "May I see it?"

The shopkeeper made a tragic face. "I'm not sure you would like to, frankly."

The book in question was made of paper without boards, like a pamphlet. But it was thick. The title of the book was *The Shining*. "It sounds as if it might be religious," Elizabeth said.

"Quite the contrary, I'm sorry to say. It's an authentic book of the future, left behind by a visitor, but the contents aren't suitable for a female reader. If it weren't such a significant artifact I should be ashamed to sell it."

"Are such books typical reading material for the people of the future?"

"I wouldn't care to speculate, ma'am. But if you're interested in the future, we have many other publications that discuss it. Our hand-colored lithographs are popular with the ladies, and we also offer engraved spoons, decorative mugs—"

"Thank you, I'll look," Elizabeth said.

Which gave Jesse an opportunity to take the shopkeeper aside and ask about the price of the book, which was predictably astronomical. He said, "Don't you have any less expensive editions?"

The shopkeeper glanced at Elizabeth, who feigned interest in a display of commemorative ribbons, and leaned toward Jesse's ear. "That's an astute question. You're right, the book has been copied to a contemporary edition." He tipped open a drawer to show Jesse a crudely bound volume on which the words *The Shining* were stamped in flaking gilded letters. "Completely unexpurgated—you understand the need for discretion. If you're interested—" He quoted a number, less than half the price of the original but still startling.

"I *am* interested," Jesse said. "If I can come back for it later."

"The edition is nearly sold out, and it's not available at other vendors."

"Well, in that case." Jesse took out his wallet. "Will you hold a copy for me?"

The proprietor nodded knowingly and scribbled a receipt. Jesse accepted it and said, "Can you tell me whether there are other items like this for sale in town? I don't mean books exclusively. Any artifact or object. But authentic ones."

"City people don't approve of such transactions, so that's a ticklish question. Such items do come up for sale from time to time. Mainly on the south side of town. More than that I'm reluctant to say."

Did he want to be bribed? Jesse had been supplied with enough cash to appear convincingly prosperous, and more was available if they needed it. But if the shopkeeper had any sense he would have negotiated an arrangement with the other clandestine sellers in town. "Any recommendation would be welcome," Jesse said flatly.

"Well . . . there's a certain vendor on Lookout Street. The shop is called Onslow's. Onslow might be willing to show you his private stock. But his goods aren't cheap, and he only deals with genuinely interested buyers."

"This whole town," Elizabeth said, "is August Kemp's nightmare."

They followed Depot Street until the sidewalk ended in a clutter of squatters' shacks, then crossed the street and turned back toward Lookout, dodging a flock of female tourists with sun umbrellas and bright calico day dresses. "What does Kemp have against Futurity Station? It hardly seems to threaten him."

"Kemp tries to keep a strict wall of separation between our guys and your guys. Guests from the twenty-first century get a guided tour of 1876, and guests from 1876 get a sanitized glimpse of the twenty-first century. But they're not supposed to mix, except when Kemp arranges it. Policing the wall between them is how he makes his money."

"Looks like there's plenty of money being made here."

"But it's not Kemp who's making it. It's diluting his product. Authenticity is everything when it comes to the revenue stream. People who pay to see the Old West don't want some kind of theme park where ersatz cowboys kick back in the ranch house with Netflix and a bag of Doritos. They want the real thing."

"Or so they think." Jesse had met a few cattlemen. He did

not despise them, as a class, but he couldn't imagine spending money for the privilege of looking at one of them.

"That's why Tower One guests coming from the City go directly to the tour trains, no dallying at Futurity Station. Kemp won't give them more than a glimpse of this town, because it reeks of—well, *lots* of things, but from Kemp's point of view it reeks of *inauthenticity*. And authenticity is what he sells."

"I suppose I see what you mean. But Kemp gave up true authenticity as soon as he built the City, didn't he? It changes everything just by being there."

"That's why the City has a limited life span. Five years as a tourist resort in what still plausibly resembles the past, then he hands over the buildings and the land to Union Pacific and turns off the Mirror for good and all."

"Because beyond that point it becomes too obvious that our histories differ."

"Right."

"But there's money to be made mingling past and future." He was thinking of the price tag on that *Shining* book.

"Well, yeah, and Kemp knows that. That's why, come January, we stop being so coy about where we come from, we start handing over our medical and scientific knowledge—we turn the country into one big Futurity Station, and Kemp milks it for twelve months before he switches off the lights and hands over the keys. But not *until* then."

"You make Kemp sound mendacious."

"I don't know what that word means. But it's not such a bad bargain if you think about it. You guys get a jump on things like electricity and the combustion engine, plus all the lessons we learned by doing that stuff crudely and badly. You also get a better look at the way we really live up there in the twenty-first century, which might make your pastors blush and your matrons clutch their pearls, but are you going to turn it down?"

They reached the intersection of Lookout and Depot. Turning south onto Lookout was like stepping onto the midway of a traveling carnival, Jesse thought. Here, every commercial establishment had been hung with yard-lengths of bunting—to celebrate both the centennial year and Grant's visit—and painted with fanciful illustrations of flying machines and ringed planets. What was offered inside these buildings appeared to be random collations of pamphlets, mounted tintypes of the City, toy helicopters carved in wood, festive whirligigs, fried sausages, steamed corn, pickled eggs, and doughnuts. Jesse cast a wistful glance at the sausage sellers. He was a big man. He liked to eat plentifully and regularly. He wasn't sure Elizabeth understood that about him.

At the southern reach of Lookout was the Stadium of Tomorrow, a high wall of pineboard that blocked any view of the prairie. Here the gimcrack vendors gave way to restaurants and saloons. Where there were saloons there would of course be whorehouses, and some of the crude shacks on the side streets, sleepy in the sunlight, looked as if they might conduct that business after dark.

Onslow's Unusual Items was a small storefront situated between a tavern and a magic-lantern theater. Jesse and Elizabeth slowed as they passed it, but they needed to agree on a strategy before they went in. "Let's take in the show," Elizabeth suggested.

"The magic lanterns?"

"The Stadium of Tomorrow. It seems to be where everybody's headed."

"It's a cheat," Jesse said. "I've heard all about it. It's just stacked bleachers facing south. All you get for your nickel is some patter and a look at the airship when it flies over."

"A place to sit and talk," she said.

He shrugged. It was the City's dime, not his.

"Money back if the flying machine don't show," the ticket seller told them. An easy promise to make: It was a rare day the City helicopter didn't fly, weather permitting, and the weather today was fine. "Entertainment starts in a few minutes."

They headed for the less desirable seats, where the crowd was thinner and they could speak without fear of being overheard. A peanut vendor wandered past, and Jesse bought a bag for himself and one for Elizabeth. If she didn't want her portion he would eat it himself. But she accepted the bag with only a brief dubious look. He guessed roasted peanuts were unlikely to be dusted with poison or infected with deadly diseases, even in 1876. She ate from her portion unselfconsciously—like a man, Jesse thought—brushing shell fragments from her billowing dress with the back of her hand.

"So here's what we know," she said. "The would-be assassin bought a Glock here in town. He was working solo, without partners or connections, so the weapon probably came from a novelty vendor like Onslow. The question is, how does the vendor lay his hands on an automatic pistol?"

Jesse thought about it. "Most of the goods in these shops are lost items or copies of lost items, like that *Shining* book. Supposedly, the merchandise comes from tour groups. You put a hundred or two hundred City people on a train to New York or San Francisco, lodge them for a week, carry them back—they're bound to leave a few things in the Pullman car or the hotel room. At least that's the story I've heard." City management was aware of the trade and for the most part had ignored it.

"So someone like Onslow," Elizabeth said, "must get his goods from a City employee, or someone with access to a City employee."

"That's a whole lot of people, though, and lots of them are local hires. Railroad porters, hotel staff, coachmen—"

"What if Onslow decides he's tired of fencing two-bit cast-offs? He knows he can sell anything that's authentically City, way more than he can get his hands on. He might figure he'd be better off with a steady supply—someone on the inside feeding him a little of this and a little of that, in quantity and on a predictable schedule."

Horses and riders marched out onto the parade grounds of the Stadium of Tomorrow for the warm-up show. The riders wore spangly red-white-and-blue uniforms and put their mounts through some synchronized rearing and prancing. A brass band played "The Girl I Left Behind Me," and the audience gave back a tepid round of applause.

"It would affect the nature of his stock," Jesse said. "It wouldn't be random, and it wouldn't necessarily be the kind of thing that people tend to leave behind."

"So we need to see his stock."

"Onslow might be reluctant to show us. If he has a source inside the City, he'll know all about the attempt on Grant. If we're too obvious, he'll play dumb. But he's a businessman," Jesse said, "and if he scents cash, he's bound to show us *something*."

It was almost noon. The horse show came to a desultory conclusion. The parade grounds cleared. There was a wooden tower to the left of the bleachers, and a man in nautical garb climbed to its highest point, a sort of crow's nest, where he trained a theatrically huge brass telescope on the southern horizon. Down on the ground, in what would have been the

center ring if this had been an actual circus, a master of cere-
monies in a claw-hammer coat addressed the crowd through
a megaphone. Something about how the people in the bleachers were about to witness an "indisputable miracle of the
future," meanwhile consulting a pocket watch on a chain and
glancing at the tower, where the man with the telescope eventually rang a bell and shouted, *"Airship ho!"*

The crowd grew hushed with anticipation. Elizabeth leaned
toward Jesse's ear and said, "That was pretty fucked up last
night. The way you were yelling. Maybe we should talk about it."

"No," Jesse said, horrified.

The helicopter appeared first as a mote on the southern
horizon, small as a blown leaf but remarkable for the precision
of the curve it etched against the blue September sky. It seemed
to increase in size as it approached, and the noise of it increased
in step until it rattled the bleachers, thunder with a clockwork
rhythm in it. At its closest approach the airship hovered in
midair for all to admire. Then it darted at the audience, deft
as a steel dragonfly.

"That's Vijay," Elizabeth said. "The pilot. Showing off. He
can't resist a crowd."

Jesse guessed the people in the bleachers believed they had
got their money's worth. Some of the women covered their
eyes or clutched their husbands' arms, pleased and terrified
in equal parts; some of the men cringed into their seats. For an
interminable moment, tons of screaming steel hung suspended
above their heads. Then the airship veered away.

Elizabeth was still talking into Jesse's ear, shouting to make
herself heard: "We call it PTSD. Post-traumatic stress disorder. I mean, I'm not diagnosing you, and you can tell me it's
none of my business. But it's nothing I haven't seen before, and
it's nothing to be ashamed of."

"You think I have some kind of disease?"

"I'm a veteran—I know lots of people who are dealing with PTSD."

"Is your husband one of them?"

It was an ugly remark and he regretted it immediately. But she only blinked and said, "Actually, yeah."

The helicopter flew to the south. Before a minute had passed it was almost invisible, a dark comet carving the blue meridian.

"I'm sorry," Jesse said. "I shouldn't have asked."

"Let's go see Onslow," Elizabeth said.

He had almost let himself forget that Elizabeth was a married woman—whatever that meant to women of her time.

It wasn't that Jesse cherished any illusions about the sanctity of marriage. He had learned about the hypocrisy of married men at an early age. And it wasn't that he was attracted to Elizabeth, in the romantic sense. Of course he'd noticed that she was *attractive*, for a woman of her unusual height and strength. But she was out of bounds. She was Tower One. Her marriage was none of his business . . . any more than his night terrors were any business of hers.

Still, now that she had reminded him of it, he couldn't help wondering about her life in the twenty-first century. As hard as it was to picture her as a soldier, it was harder still to picture her as a soldier's wife, the wife of a soldier who woke at dawn with the echo of a scream in his ears. The way she had clasped Jesse's hands, he realized, had been a sort of medical intervention, kindly but impersonal, like a nurse binding a wound.

There was much he didn't know about her.

They walked into Onslow's Unusual Items like a pair of tourists, giddy from the helicopter show. Jesse looked around as the shopkeeper—presumably Onslow—waited on another customer. The large front room of the shop was walled with shelves and stocked with the same kind of merchandise every other such store in Futurity Station sold. If Onslow had something better to offer, he didn't keep it in plain view. All that distinguished Onslow from any other vendor on Lookout Street was his girth (generous) and the plain straw boater he tipped to his female customers. His chin was clean shaven, but his sideburns were making a determined march on it. His eyes were narrow and calculating.

The bell over the door tinkled as Onslow's previous customer left. Onslow turned to Jesse and said, "How can I help you?"

Elizabeth, as they had arranged, remained at the far end of the store so Jesse could speak freely. He mentioned the name of the store they had visited on Depot.

"I know the place," Onslow said. "Did you buy the book in the window?"

"A copy of it," Jesse said. "But don't tell my wife."

Onslow grinned and touched a finger to the side of his nose. "If that's the sort of thing you want, you've come to the right place. Genuine editions or copies as you prefer and can afford. *Harry Potter. Fifty Shades of Grey.* The works of Lee Child—"

"Thank you, but I already have a book. I'm interested in something more substantial."

"A display piece? A watch, say? Something electrical? Such things don't come cheap, as I'm sure you know."

"Well, I haven't thought it through. What can you offer me?"

"Do you have a price in mind?"

Jesse gave a number that seemed excessive even for the successful businessman he was pretending to be. He hoped it wouldn't make Onslow suspicious. In fact it had the opposite effect. Onslow said, "That rules out the more spectacular items."

"I might be convinced to go *slightly* higher—what do you call spectacular?"

Onslow unlocked a drawer, took out a rectangular object of glass and plastic and placed it on the counter. Jesse recognized it as what Elizabeth would call a smartphone. Tower One guests carried them. He feigned ignorance. "It's not very large. What does it do?"

"It does more than you can imagine." Onslow touched a button. Instantly, images welled up on the screen of the device. "It makes pictures that move and speak. It plays music. It can even add and subtract."

Elizabeth stopped pretending not to overhear and joined them. Onslow repeated his description of the device. She turned to Jesse and said, "Why, that's marvelous! Can it possibly do what the man says?"

Here was another interesting fact about Elizabeth, her ability to lie without blushing. "I don't know. I suppose it can."

"It almost seems alive. *Is* it alive? I mean to say, will it work this way forever? Or does it need some kind of fuel?"

"That's a fine question, Mrs.—"

"Cullum," Elizabeth said promptly.

"A fine question, Mrs. Cullum. On its own, no, it would not work indefinitely. But its functions can be restored with this." He took another device from a different drawer, a glassy wafer with a wire dangling from it. "You attach the wire like so, and put this under sunlight for an hour or two."

"Sunlight?"

"Nothing more, nothing less."

"It fuels itself with *sunlight*? How is that possible?"

"I don't pretend to understand it, Mrs. Cullum. I can tell you *what* it does, and I can tell you how to *make* it do what it does, but I'm as ignorant as an infant regarding its works."

"Have you sold many of these?"

"Just a few. They're scarce, as you can imagine."

Jesse said, "It's a costly item."

"I'm sure it must be! Has Mr. Onslow mentioned a price?"

"Yes, but—"

"In that case, Mr. Onslow, would you excuse us while I talk this over with my husband?"

"Of course."

Out of earshot, Elizabeth said, "This pretty much nails him."

"Does it? How so? The device is something a tourist might have lost, isn't it? There's nothing to say he got it directly from the City."

"The device, sure, but not the charger. The City makes sure its guests have access to electrical power everywhere they go. The City hotels in New York and San Francisco run generators around the clock—even the City's Pullman cars are electrified. Nobody needs to bring a solar charger through the Mirror, and nobody does."

"So we shouldn't buy it?"

"Waste of money."

"We ought to buy *something*," Jesse said, "if only to keep up the charade."

He went back to the counter and looked wistfully at the phone. Onslow said, "Have you come to a decision?"

"Is the price negotiable?"

"I'm sorry, no."

"In that case, can we see something a little less costly?"

Onslow was visibly disappointed. "There's an assortment of simple goods in the drawers at the side. All individually priced. You're welcome to look."

It was a chilly invitation, but Jesse dutifully open one of the drawers Onslow had pointed out.

His eyes widened.

The drawer was full of Oakley sunglasses in plastic wrappers.

"I'll take one of these," he said.

They went back to the dining room of the Excelsior for their evening meal. The room was crowded tonight. A dozen or more press men, in town for Grant's visit, filled the air with cigar smoke and forced levity, but Jesse managed to secure a reasonably private table in a darkened corner. He ordered mutton stew with a side of boiled onions; Elizabeth ordered roast beef. A waiter drew the curtains and lit lamps as sunset colored the sky.

"We don't know for sure if it was Onslow who supplied the pistol," Elizabeth said, "but we can be fairly sure he has connections inside the City. So we need to look at the supply side, any City employees Onslow might have had contact with. I'll call Barton tonight and let him know what we found out."

"It's a different town after dark," Jesse said, "when the shops close and the saloons open up. It would be easy enough to follow Onslow, see who crosses his path."

"I guess we could do that."

"Not *we*," Jesse corrected her. "A respectable woman would be out of place in the kind of establishment Onslow is likely to frequent."

"I'm respectable now?"

He smiled and said, "In a dim light you'd pass."

"So what are you suggesting?"

"I can scout the south end of town while you talk to the City."

"Uh-huh. Or you could just go out and get drunk."

"I could get drunk and hire a loose woman and come back

with my pants on sideways, but is that really what you imagine I mean to do?"

She laughed. "I guess not."

At least she gives me the benefit of the doubt, Jesse thought. "I'm sorry I raised the subject of your husband, back at the helicopter show. It's none of my business and I shouldn't have presumed."

"Are you curious about my husband?"

He didn't know how to answer that.

She said, "His name's Javiar. I met him in high school. He dreamed about doing something big, like becoming a doctor, but he was a west Charlotte kid with all the baggage. We enlisted about the same time. Nineteen years old, both of us, we got married at city hall and signed up a month later, how crazy is that? I ended up in signals intelligence, but Javiar was infantry. Multiple tours. After we mustered out it seemed like we had a chance. I got a job with Riptide, that's a security company that hires a lot of vets. Javiar hired on, too, and that was okay for a while, but he didn't last. They eventually fired him for not showing up, or for showing up drunk, some combination of the two. So I was the breadwinner, and we had Gabby by then."

"Gabby?"

"Our daughter. Gabriella. When Javiar got bored with looking for work he took up with some of his old friends. Who were mostly petty criminals. Breaking and entering, low-end drug dealing. He was happy to spend my paychecks but he resented having to ask me for them. He got angry. Often. He finally saw somebody at the VA hospital, got diagnosed with PTSD. Okay, you don't know what that means—it's something that happens to people who've had some kind of shocking or terrifying experience. Humiliating for these guys who come back from the front and suddenly they can't sleep through the night, can't think straight, get in fights, drink, do drugs, maybe end up on the street or in jail. So I tried to nurse Javiar through it. Talk him down when he woke up screaming. Tolerate his fits of anger. I drove him to the hospital and I made sure he kept his appointments. All that. But."

Jesse waited as she took a sip of water.

"But he was out of control. It wasn't just the PTSD. I think PTSD just opened the door to something that was inside him long before he enlisted. It got to where he was obviously danger- ous, not just to me but to Gabby. He fired a gun in the house."

"Is that why he went to prison?"

"They took him on multiple charges, including a botched drug deal where he pushed a guy into a wall and broke his hip. But I testified against him in court. Because by then it was clear to me that Javiar wanted to hurt us, and that he *would* hurt us, or try to, sooner or later. I wanted him behind bars long enough to get Gabby and me to a safe place. Which is why I'm at the City, actually. The City's security service offered me a pretty generous contract. It means I'm away from Gabby for months at a time, which is bad, and it means my mother is caring for Gabby while I'm in 1876, which I'm not real happy about. But at the end of my tour I get a paycheck big enough to take us out of North Carolina altogether. Divorce, name change, new job. That's my plan."

Jesse was too startled to say more than, "I see."

"The moral of the story is, I'm not shocked by the fact that you wake up in a cold sweat in the small hours of the morning. I don't think it's some kind of weakness you have."

"Do you think I'm dangerous? Like Javiar?"

"I don't know you well enough to say. But on slim evidence, no, I don't think you're dangerous." She added, "In that way."

Clearly, she knew she was treading on troubled ground. But Jesse guessed she wanted to clear the air. She valued honesty.

After a moment's thought he said, "You twenty-first-century women remind me of whores."

Elizabeth stiffened in her chair. Her eyes went narrow and hard.

He said, "That's not an insult. I don't mean you have loose morals or that you're venal or contemptible. I was raised around whores, and for the most part they treated me well. What I mean is, whores tend to speak frankly. They see much, and they take a cynical view of things. Listening to their talk spared me a host of polite delusions. It made me harder to fool, and it forced me to think honestly about myself. Do you understand?"

She was a long time answering, but she said, "I guess so."

"I think you're an honorable woman, Elizabeth. And I hope things go well for you and Gabby."

"Okay. So what would you say to a whore who asked you about your bad dreams?"

"I would thank her for her concern," he said, "and I would tell her it's a subject I don't care to discuss."

Futurity Station was a different town after dark. It was still a circus, Jesse thought, but it was a night circus now: fewer lion tamers, more cooch shows. Storefronts closed and saloon doors opened. Lookout Street was crowded with men, many of them spitting tobacco with carefree abandon, and on the side streets gaslights gave way to torches.

Onslow's store was shuttered now, but there was a saloon around the corner. Jesse went inside and was assaulted by the smell of adulterated liquor and cigar smoke and the bodies of unbathed men—four years of sanitized City life had made him as sensitive as a woman.

The saloon served beer at tables, like a German establishment, but featured frontier attractions: faro, poker, California pedro. Jesse spotted Onslow standing at the bar. He turned away and took a table at the far end of the room and paid for pickled eggs and a pitcher of beer.

He thought about what Elizabeth had said about PTSD. The letters, she had explained, stood for post-traumatic stress disorder. *Post*, a Latin word meaning *after*. *Traumatic stress*, self-explanatory. *Disorder*, because the people of the future liked opaque words; since the condition was treated in hospitals, Jesse guessed the word was a euphemism for *disease*.

Did that mean he was suffering from a disease? Maybe so, by Elizabeth's standards. But it didn't feel exceptional enough to qualify as diseased: His condition wasn't exactly uncommon. *The whole nation has PTSD*, Jesse thought. It was a plague that had started at Fort Sumter and grown virulent at Manassas. Its nightmares were lynchings, Indian wars, and the pick-handle brigades that hunted Chinamen on the docks of San Francisco. *And if we ever wake up from such dreams*, he thought, *then yes, we'll likely wake up screaming*.

Onslow drank continuously and methodically for most of an hour, his back to Jesse. He didn't stir from his barstool until three men entered the saloon and approached him. One slapped him on the back as the other two laughed amicably. Onslow accompanied them to a table. Jesse tried to memorize the features of these men, insofar as the flickering light of the kerosene lanterns permitted. Two of the men were strangers to him, but one looked tantalizingly familiar. He couldn't be sure . . . but he thought it might be the coach driver, the one who had handed down his and Elizabeth's bags after the trip from the City of Futurity.

He left the saloon before he could be recognized in return. He needed time to think.

He thought about the man who looked like the coachman.

If he was a City hire he would probably be staying at the
Excelsior. Maybe the desk clerk could identify him, or maybe
Elizabeth could talk to Barton about it. Jesse stood in the dimness beyond the torchlight, in the shade of a wooden building
he took to be a brothel by the sounds emanating from it, and
watched the saloon for most of another hour, but the coachman didn't emerge. He was about to give it up when the door
of the building behind him flew open and a woman stepped
out to empty a slop jar into the alley. He turned and exchanged
a look with her, and before he could walk away she said, "My
God, is that Jesse Cullum?"

He stared, speechless.

"It *is*!" she said.

He knew her, of course. Her name was Heddie Finch. She
used to work at a white bordello on Pike Street, back in the
Tenderloin. "Well, Heddie," he said. "You're a long way from
home."

She stepped away from the light that shone through the
half-open door. It seemed to dawn on her that Jesse Cullum
might not want to be recognized. "How are you, Jesse?"

"I'm all right. You?"

She shrugged. "I left San Francisco after the trouble. A lot
of us did. Some went to Sacramento, or back east. I ended up
here. But not permanently, if I can help it—Illinois winters are
colder than a nun's cunt. I swear, Jesse, I thought I'd never see
you again, not after—"

She registered his expression and stopped speaking.

"I'd appreciate it," he said, "if you didn't mention my name
to anyone."

Whispering now: "They still talk about you in the Tenderloin. The man who shot Roscoe Candy. We all thought you
was dead."

"I left right after I killed him."

Her eyes went wide. "Is that what you think? Oh, Jesse! You *shot* him all right. Dead center. But you didn't *kill* him, worse luck."

5

Jesse braced himself for bad dreams. Running into Heddie Finch had provoked all kinds of troublesome memories. But from the moment he put his head on his pillow, he slept as soundly as if he had dosed himself with laudanum. When he next opened his eyes Elizabeth was standing by the bed, fully dressed, and sunlight streamed through the window curtains.

Another bright, cloudless day, cooler than the one before. Over breakfast Elizabeth described her wireless conversation with the security chief Barton back at the City. Barton had thanked her for what they had learned, but his only advice was to "keep Onslow under surveillance." Spy on him, in plainer words. But Jesse had a better idea. "Do you carry your phone when you go out?"

She nodded. Jesse supposed it was tucked into some hidden compartment of her day dress, probably secured with Velcro.

"Will it work from anywhere in Futurity Station?"

"As long as it's within range of the repeater on the roof of the hotel, yeah. Why?"

"Keep it with you. We may need it. The first thing I want to do is talk to the owner."

"The owner of what?"

"Of this hotel. Or at least the manager."

"What do you think the manager of the Excelsior can tell us?"

"He can tell us who runs this town."

The hotel manager, a cadaverously thin man whose name Jesse promptly forgot, was reluctant to speak to them until Elizabeth reminded him that they were from the City.

The manager escorted them to his office, a room furnished with a few chairs and a pedestal desk with a chased silver inkwell on it. "We have excellent relations with the City of Futurity. We allow you to install your machines, we let you inspect the kitchen, we let you poison the bedbugs—I don't know what more you could possibly want."

Jesse said, "There's no problem with the hotel. Everything's very satisfactory. You're doing a fine job."

"Well, we try."

"When you say 'we'—?"

"Speaking for my staff and myself. The hotel is owned by a partnership in Chicago, as I'm sure you know."

"The Excelsior is the town's preeminent business, isn't it?"

"I like to think so. We've been here since the beginning, when the agents of the City and the railroad first put these lots up for sale."

"I'd guess a gentleman like you knows everyone worth knowing in this town."

"You give me too much credit. But I keep my eyes open."

"The town's high rollers, could you name them?"

The manager's face clouded. "I'm not sure what you're asking."

"Well, say we wanted to throw a party for the men who

matter in Futurity Station. Who would be the first five names on the list?"

"Is this—are you actually planning such a party?"

"Remains to be seen," Jesse said.

"Well. Five names? I would have to say . . . Karl Knudsen, who holds leases on half the properties on Lookout. Billy Mingus, the restaurateur. A shop owner, Elbert Onslow. Casper Brigham, if I have to name another hotelier. Oh, and of course Marcus Frane. Mr. Frane would be at the top of the list."

"Marcus Frane?"

"He owns the Stadium of Tomorrow."

"Does Mr. Frane live in town?"

"He winters in Chicago but he's usually here until the end of September. He stays at the Dunston House when he's not supervising the show."

"Can we find him at the stadium, if we want to talk to him?"

"This time of day, almost certainly."

"Thank you," Jesse said, standing. "That's all very helpful."

"You're welcome. About this party—"

"We'll let you know if we need to make arrangements."

The manager was wrong. Marcus Frane wasn't at the Stadium of Tomorrow. The ticket-taker directed them to the Deluxe Barber Shop on Depot Street, where Frane was holding court with a half dozen cronies.

Or thugs, Jesse thought. More thugs than cronies by the look of them. Their presence suggested that Frane was the right person to talk to, though possibly dangerous.

Elizabeth came into the barber shop with Jesse, which made everyone sit up and stare. Frane's men occupied all the chairs, but only Frane was getting service. After a long moment the barber whipped away a cotton bib as if he were unveiling a statue, and Frane wiped his face and gave Jesse and Elizabeth a long, thoughtful look.

"We'd like to have a word with you," Jesse said.

Frane was a big man, neither very young nor very old, strong and confident in his body. He stood up. "I'm afraid we haven't been introduced."

"We're from the City."

"Is that so?"

Elizabeth spoke up: "Yes. That's so."

In this case, her frankness was as good as a calling card. Frane asked the barber to take a break. He told his boys to wait outside. The doors creaked closed. The shop seemed suddenly larger. Sunlight striking bottles of pomade made rainbows on the ceiling. "I don't have any beef with the City," Frane said. "Does the City have a beef with me?"

"I'd say the City does pretty well by you," Jesse said. "It flies the airship that puts paying customers on those bleachers of yours every day."

"What of it?"

"Given how much you benefit from the City, we hoped you'd be willing to do the City a favor in return."

Frane paused long enough to take a cigar from his pocket and trim it and light it. "What kind of favor?"

"We both know this town runs on contraband. Men like Elbert Onslow make their entire living from it."

"Is this about Onslow?"

"In a way."

"So go talk to him. I don't deal in contraband, and I don't have much to do with Elbert Onslow."

Though you drink with him, Jesse thought. Jesse was fairly sure Frane had been one of Onslow's companions in the saloon last night. "Mr. Onslow might be reluctant to tell us what we want to know."

"I don't see how that concerns me."

"Mr. Frane, has the City ever interfered in your business?"

"No—"

"No, nor has it interfered in Onslow's business. What goes on in this town doesn't always please us, but our attitude is live and let live. Everybody gets along and everybody makes money. As long as everything stays within certain limits. The trouble is, Onslow overstepped those bounds. He's been buying from someone who shouldn't be selling, and we want to know the name of the person he's dealing with."

"Ask Onslow."

"He has every reason not to tell us. The City isn't the law here. What Onslow's doing is underhanded, but it isn't illegal. We can't easily dispossess him and we're too civilized to burn his shop down. All we want to know is who he buys his guns from."

Elizabeth gave Jesse a sharp look. He probably shouldn't have mentioned guns. But it had the desired effect on Frane, who grew more serious. "If Onslow's selling guns, I don't know anything about it."

"But you can find out. And when you do find out, you can tell us."

"Are you drunk? Onslow's not stupid—if he won't talk to you, he won't talk to me."

"We think you're wrong. We think he'd be willing to share the information on a friendly basis, if you ask him politely. Or you can be impolite and unfriendly, if the first approach fails."

"You want me to intimidate a fellow businessman, for no better reason than that you're unwilling to intimidate him yourself?"

"You seem like just the man who could do it."

Frane drew himself up to his full height. He had the thick hands and scarred knuckles of a brawler, and his nose had been broken at least once. Jesse had seen plenty of men like Frane in San Francisco, men who had prised gold out of mountains and imagined themselves transformed into imperial powers. Men who wore silk hats and pissed in the street. "I'm not your servant," Frane said. "Do your own dirty work."

Jesse could see Elizabeth's impatience in her face. She was itching to speak. But she had agreed to let him handle this. "I remind you again," Jesse said, "we represent the City of Futurity."

"Maybe so, but you don't own my land, you don't own my bleachers, and you don't own the bright blue sky. I'm not about to strong-arm Onslow just because some hired bull strutted in here with the word 'City' on his lips."

"I'm sorry you feel that way."

"And I'm sorry you're blocking my sunlight."

"What the fuck!" Elizabeth exclaimed as the door swung shut behind her. One of Frane's henchmen overheard her and laughed derisively. Jesse steered her farther down the sidewalk.

"You're attracting attention."

"Does it matter? Before midnight, everyone in town will know we're City operatives."

An operative, Jesse thought—*is that what I am?* "Before midnight we'll probably have what we came for."

"And what leads you to that conclusion?"

"Yesterday at the bleachers you mentioned Vijay."

"Sandeep Vijay, the helicopter pilot—what about him?"

"He's a friend of yours, you said."

"We're not best buds, but I know him."

"You have your phone. Can you call him?"

"Sure, but why would I— *Oh.*" She paused. Jesse was

gratified to see the smile that evolved on her lips. "Yeah, I can talk to Vijay."

They took a midday meal at the Excelsior. Because there was nothing to do but wait, the conversation grew halting and awkward. Jesse was silent much of the time, casting glances through the window. President Grant had left the City this morning, and a little before noon a crowd of gawkers and newsmen had descended on the train station to look at him. Grant had waved at the crowd but said nothing—it had taken a gunshot to silence the eloquent Lincoln, but Grant was mute as a crawfish.

Then the depot had reverted to its customary business. Later today a convoy of twenty-first-century visitors would be escorted onto a City train bound for a week-long tour of Manhattan. Of Futurity Station they would experience nothing but its pervasive odor—like an outhouse on a summer afternoon, Jesse thought, a mingled perfume of shit and slaked lime, which even Jesse found galling, though he wouldn't give Elizabeth the satisfaction of hearing him say so.

He had taken delivery of his copy of *The Shining* from the store on Depot Street. It sat on the table now, and Elizabeth pointed at it with her spoon: "Are you actually going to read that?"

"I don't see why not. I'm braced for the obscenities. I'm not expecting *Pilgrim's Progress*."

"Whose progress? No, never mind. You seem pretty well-read for a guy who claims to have been educated by prostitutes."

"My father loved books."

"I thought you said he was a doorman. Or a magician."

"He could read, and not just the Bible. He kept three volumes of Gibbon in a sea chest by his bed. I didn't go to school—his books were my school."

"But he opened doors for a living?"

Jesse saw by Elizabeth's frankly curious expression that she wasn't going to let the matter drop. "He was a large man, like me. I inherited his size. He wasn't a doorman as I imagine you understand the word. He earned his income as a bouncer. Do you know what I mean?"

"A big dude who kicks out troublemakers?"

"Essentially."

"Kicks them out of the whorehouse?"

"To be blunt, yes."

"So your father was a bouncer at a whorehouse in San Francisco?"

"Originally in New Orleans. When war broke out he bought us passage to California by way of Cape Horn." On a decaying freighter that wallowed in heavy seas like a damp cork. Jesse had been eight years old, and he had vomited himself senseless in the storms off Tierra del Fuego. Coming on deck after the weather cleared, dazed and drained, he had mistaken the petrels wheeling over the ship for angels. "He found similar work in the Tenderloin." Similar but even more dangerous, in a city where women were scarce and the troublemakers tended to be hardened veterans of the gold fields.

"Sounds like a rough life."

"Because of my size, he made me his apprentice. By the age of thirteen I was working the door at Madame Chao's on weeknights. I took some knocks." Some of which had nearly killed him. "I saw my father bloodied more than once and sometimes badly hurt. But coming to California kept him away from Manassas and Shiloh, which was the whole purpose of it."

Not that it had saved him, in the end.

"Do you think less of him for that?"

Jesse was puzzled by the question. "Think less of him for what?"

"Dodging the war. Not doing his bit for the Union. Or the Confederacy or whatever."

"His sentiments were Union, but he lived in New Orleans. He was smart to get away."

"As opposed to cowardly."

"What would you have had him do, Elizabeth? Abandon me and Phoebe in a New Orleans parlor house and head north to enlist?"

"Who's Phoebe?"

He had spoken without thinking. "My sister," he admitted.

"Younger, older?"

"Younger."

Phoebe had been just two years old when they began the journey to California. She had slept through the storms as blissfully as if the swells were God's way of rocking her cradle. Briefly, Jesse had hated her for it.

"What about your mother?"

"She died delivering me, just as Phoebe's mother died delivering Phoebe."

Elizabeth blanched.

Jesse said, "I suppose women never die in childbirth, where you come from."

"Not the way yours do."

"And you'll hand it over to us next year, I suppose, the medical knowledge that protects your mothers and infants."

"I guess so."

"And I guess we thank you. Though I can't help wondering how many women and children must have died while you waited."

That sounded harsher than he meant it to. Jesse regretted the words, but Elizabeth didn't answer, and he saw by the tilt of her head that she was listening to the sounds coming through the open window: passing carriages, the chiming of the railway station's big clock. Top of the hour. A stilling of voices. High noon. Right about now, down at the bottom of Lookout Street in the Stadium of Tomorrow, the barker would be finishing his spiel about the wonders of the future, the sailor in the lookout tower would be aiming his theatrical telescope at the southern horizon.

Elizabeth caught Jesse's eye, acknowledging a shared secret. She had talked to Vijay, the helicopter pilot. Vijay had agreed to fly a different route today, west and south of Futurity Station. The customers on Marcus Frane's sun-beaten bleachers might catch a glimpse of a dark speck moving against the horizon, but that was all they would see.

"Now we wait," Jesse said.

Frane's response came in the form of an anonymous note delivered after sunset to the front desk of the Excelsior:

> *The man you want is Isaac Connaught he drives*
> *a coach from the city he is Onslows man.*

"Awesome," Elizabeth said. "Nice work. With any luck we can head back to the City tomorrow. I'll call Barton and let him know."

"Do that," Jesse said. "I'm going out."

"Going out for what?"

"Some business of my own."

"What business?"

"Do you trust me?"

"I don't know. Should I?"

"I'll be back by midnight," Jesse said.

He made his way to the brothel where he had met Heddie Finch the night before, dodging the drunks who loitered outside the saloons. He knocked at the door and made it a point to smile when the doorman opened up.

My old job, Jesse thought. He knew it was important to state his business as succinctly as possible. "I'm not a customer," he said. "I've come to see Heddie Finch."

The doorman was untypically short for his calling, but he made up for it with his enormous width. He looked like a boulder balanced on a pair of bowling pins. "She ain't here."

"That's all right. I just want to talk, but I'll pay the going rate if I have to. I'm an old acquaintance of hers."

"Good for you. But she still ain't here. Plenty of other girls, though. Come in and take your pick, or move along—one or the other."

Jesse was inclined to believe the man. "Will she be back tomorrow night?"

"She won't be back at all. She left town. What's one buggy old whore to you, anyway?"

"Left town?"

"That's what I said."

"For where?"

"I ain't her keeper. She took what little she owns and headed for the train station in a hurry. It ain't unusual for these gals to pick up and leave, if they think they can get away with it."

Heddie had always been flighty and easily scared. But never without good reason.

Jesse thought: *Am I the reason?*

"Now move along, lummox, you're blocking the door."

Jesse moved along. He needed to think about Heddie's hasty departure, but he didn't want to let the question distract him. He had another task to attend to.

He found the alley that ran parallel to Lookout on the west side. The alley was unlit and fouled with trash and the occasional dead animal, but there was moonlight enough for Jesse to pick his way north, counting buildings, until he reached the back door of Onslow's shop. No light came from inside. The door itself was heavy and was secured with a rusty padlock. Jesse had no key, but he had the boot at the end of his left leg. It took three vigorous kicks to lift the hasp from the doorframe.

He waited to see whether anyone would respond to the noise, but no one did. The building was dark and seemed to be empty. He took two steps inside and counted to ten, waiting for his eyes to adjust, and even then he could see little more than a few ghostly outlines. He was in a room walled with shelves. A bulky presence in front of him was probably a table. He put his hands out before him and took another step. The shape of the table became more distinct. Cautiously, he swept his arm across the surface of it and found what he hoped had been left there: a finger-loop oil lamp. He pulled off the shade and took a book of City matches from his pocket, little paper lucifers attached to a sandpaper striking board. The lamp was nearly empty of oil, but there was enough in the font to support a small flame.

In the fresh light Jesse scanned the room, which seemed to be where Onslow kept his stock. The shelves were bounteously full. Jesse admired the novelty and variety of what he saw. Then he found a burlap bag abandoned in a corner, and began methodically to fill it.

Coming through the lobby of the Excelsior with the bag draped over his shoulder made him feel like some kind of criminal St. Nicholas. The night clerk gave him a hard stare but said nothing. Upstairs, Elizabeth was waiting for him. "Where'd you go?"

He came inside and closed the door. "Onslow's back room."

"You broke in?"

He nodded.

"Uh-huh," Elizabeth said. She stared at the bag. "So what's that? I hope to hell it's not full of Oakleys."

"I wish it was. It wouldn't be so cursed heavy." He emptied the bag on the bed. He didn't know what a Glock automatic pistol weighed, but he guessed about two pounds. And here were twenty of them.

6

The woman's name was Zaina Baumgartner, her title was "events manager," and her job was to arrange stage and screen presentations in both towers of the City—show business, in other words.

Jesse had not known many show people, certainly none from the twenty-first century. He wondered if Baumgartner was a representative example. She was tall and almost unnaturally thin, her gestures were nervous, and she seemed to regard Elizabeth and Jesse as lesser creatures bent on distracting her from the more important things in life. Elizabeth's first words on stepping into Baumgartner's Tower One office were, "We need to ask you a few questions." Baumgartner said, "But I have a screening."

Four days had passed since Jesse and Elizabeth had arrived back at the City. They had delivered their bag of automatic pistols to the security chief, Barton, whose reaction was a wide-eyed "Holy shit!" Since then Barton had been holding daily conferences with Elizabeth in his office. Jesse had not been invited to these sessions, but Elizabeth had apparently agreed to retain him as her partner: She had called him to

accompany her to this meeting with Baumgartner, the purpose of which she declined to explain.

"This is urgent," Elizabeth said.

Which didn't stop Baumgartner from walking out of her
own office. "The screening is scheduled for *five minutes ago.*
It's the new version of *Manned Flight.* All the department heads
are waiting! Follow me."

So they hustled to keep up with Ms. Baumgartner as she
made for the elevators. "Gearing up for the final year," she said.
"It's going to be just *ridiculously* busy. The film we're screening now is an improved version of the one we've been showing
to local guests since the City opened for business. But that's
only the tip of the iceberg. Starting in January we're booking
major talent, local and home. Mr. Kemp wants a Cirque du
Soleil show that will perform for *both* towers. You cannot
imagine the complexity! And we're trying to book local celeb-
rities as well. Maybe a lecture by Mark Twain—"

Jesse said, "Twain? The 'Jumping Frog' writer?"

Baumgartner seemed to notice him for the first time. "You're
local yourself, are you not?" She asked Elizabeth, "Should I be
discussing this with him?"

"He's been vetted."

"Well, then, yes, Twain. Why, do you *know* him?"

"Not personally." Twain, aka Sam Clemens, had acquired
a certain reputation in Virginia City and San Francisco, not exclusively literary. Clemens had vanished from San Francisco for
a few months after a friend of his killed a bartender by breaking a bottle over his head. Nor had Jesse been much impressed
by the frog piece when it appeared in *The Californian.* It was
just another mining-camp story, as far as he could tell. But it had
been well received, and if City people wanted to see him, then
Twain must be destined for a sterling literary career. Unless
the City destroyed that career by the very act of announcing it.

"Well, it's difficult," Baumgartner declared, bounding off the elevator as the doors opened on the theatrical level. "I'm sure you can imagine!"

Elizabeth said without much real hope in her voice, "We have just a few questions—"

"They'll wait, won't they? You can sit at the back of the theater and we'll talk after the presentation, how about that? Then you'll have all my attention—I promise."

Elizabeth shrugged. They filed into the cinema behind Baumgartner, who abandoned them in the back row and headed for the stage. There were only a few people in the seats down front, some of whom Jesse recognized as bosses from the City's entertainment division. Baumgartner took up a hand-held microphone and addressed them from in front of the enormous screen. She told them how difficult it had been to design an introduction to cinema for audiences of the 1870s: "Motion pictures were first shown to the public in the 1890s, and when those people saw a moving train on the screen some of them actually *ran away from it*. So it's always been a question of introducing locals to movies in a way they can easily assimilate. That's why we have a five-night sequence, where the first night is a lecture and some brief examples—it conditions them, so what comes after isn't so alarming. And that's only the first hurdle! Think of all the cinematic conventions these people have never absorbed, things like continuity, cross-cutting, close-ups. The version of *Manned Flight* you're about to see builds on everything we've learned about presenting movies to an unsophisticated audience. It's simple, it's relatively short, and by modern standards it's fairly static. But it's also viewer-friendly and gauged to impress naïve viewers without frightening them."

Jesse could only guess what all this meant. Not long after he was hired by the City, he and the other local employees had

been given a special screening of the various films offered to
paying guests. The shows had impressed him mightily, but she
was right about how difficult they had been to understand.

"And *Manned Flight* is only the first of our enhancements
to the film program. Next month we'll be introducing revised
versions of *Cities of Tomorrow* and *Wonders of Science*."

All guaranteed not to provoke undue terror in their audiences. Baumgartner stopped talking and took a seat; the lights
dimmed; the movie began. Jesse watched with interest. The
scenes of gleaming airships darting among the clouds were as
astonishing as they were unsettling, but he liked the animated
sequences best: cartoon illustrations of the early years of aviation, featuring mustachioed men of the relatively near future
and their comical adventures with flying machines. The sons
of our generation, he thought. Sons and daughters: apparently
there would be women among the pioneers of aviation.

Elizabeth sat close to him in the darkness, the blue cotton
cloth of her City trousers pressed against his thigh. It was a
pleasant feeling, which he tried to ignore. City women had a
free-and-easy demeanor that did not mean they were either
free or easy. That was one of the mistakes local men too often
made when they were hired for City work, and it was a fatal
one: A single unwelcome advance could put you out the door.
Likewise uttering racial or national insults, even if you didn't
recognize them as such. Jesse was fortunate in that regard: His
time at Madame Chao's had taught him how to speak placat-
ingly to people of all extractions, from Samoan sailors to
Dupont Gai hatchetmen. *Watch your mouth and keep your
hands to yourself* was the first and firmest rule. And the last
thing he wanted to do was insult Elizabeth DePaul, who was,
after all, a married woman, even if her husband was currently in
prison. But still, sitting thigh-to-thigh with her in the flickering

shadows of *Manned Flight*, he couldn't avoid the truth that he liked her. He liked her very much, in complicated ways.

Jesse had slept well for five consecutive nights since his return from Futurity Station. He felt freer and less worried, which might be a danger in itself: He couldn't afford to let down his guard, especially in light of what Heddie Finch had said about the monster Roscoe Candy. Impossible as it seemed, Candy still lived. That was very bad news. Worse, Heddie knew where Jesse could be found, and Heddie had left town the day after she spotted him. Was it possible the news of Jesse's whereabouts might reach the ears of Roscoe Candy? If so, might Candy come looking for him—or worse, for Jesse's sister, Phoebe?

The movie ended with a last giddy aerial view of a flying machine dipping its wings toward some vast, impossible city. Then the theater lights came up and Baumgartner spent a maddening quarter-hour glad-handing the assembled managers before she made her way up the aisle to where Jesse and Elizabeth sat. "We can talk in the green room," she said cheerily. "Thanks for your patience!"

The room to which Baumgartner led them was furnished with a conference table and some folding chairs, a coffee urn, and the clutter of used paper cups. Baumgartner settled into one of the chairs and said, "Well, I think that was successful!"

"No doubt," Elizabeth said. Elizabeth had asked Jesse to keep quiet during the interview, for the same reason he had taken the lead in Futurity Station. This was her investigation now, on her turf. "It's amazing how much thought has gone into the film program," she said.

Baumgartner beamed. "Isn't it? August Kemp has been

personally involved, so we've all been doing our very best to get it right. He has a way of motivating people—his enthusiasm is contagious!"

Everyone professed to love Kemp. And most of that love seemed reasonably genuine. August Kemp was apparently one of those wealthy men who inspire devotion in their employees. Most of them. "What about you, Ms. Baumgartner? Are you a hands-off manager, or do you like to get up close and dirty?"

Something in Elizabeth's voice made Baumgartner frown. "Before we go on, can I ask what this is all about? Mr. Barton arranged the interview, but he wasn't clear about its purpose."

"We're looking at how supplies get distributed once they come through the Mirror. There have been problems with bottlenecks—shipments of nonessential goods clogging up inventory while more important items wait to get tagged."

"I see. Well, I'm deeply involved in the work, but not so much that end of it. I haven't noticed any problems if that's what you're asking."

"Specifically, in August your department received new digital projectors?"

"We upgraded all five cinemas. Four-K two-D Barcos. New switchers, new interfaces, everything running off Android tablets—plus more lamps and lenses than we're ever likely to need."

"All arrived in a timely fashion, undamaged?"

"Yes! No problem at all."

"Anything included that wasn't on the bill of lading?"

"Not to my knowledge. Like what?"

"You unpacked these items yourself?"

Baumgartner hesitated and stroked her nose with the thumb of her right hand—it seemed to be a nervous habit. "Well, some of them. Mostly I leave that to the technicians."

"Any technician in particular?"

"We have a team."

"Do unauthorized personnel have access to your store-room?"

"If so, I'm not aware of it. You'd need the right card to get in. Security, isn't that your department?"

"And are you on friendly terms with any Tower Two employees outside of the entertainment division?"

"Because of the work I do, I have informal contacts with a lot of people in both towers."

"Do you have contacts with any *local* people in Tower Two?"

"Like this one?" She waved her hand at Jesse, as if Elizabeth had brought him in on a leash. "As a rule, no."

"All right. Let me read you a list of five names, and you tell me if you recognize any of them." Elizabeth took a notepad from her hip pocket and flipped through pages while Baumgartner fidgeted. Elizabeth read the names slowly, and Jesse watched Baumgartner for any visible reaction.

There was none he could detect, but he was distracted by the last name Elizabeth read: Mick Finagle. Finagle was a Tower Two security guard, the one toward whom Jesse's old girlfriend Doris Vanderkamp was currently directing her affections.

"No," Baumgartner said curtly.

"Are you sure?"

"Not *absolutely* sure. I'm introduced to people on a daily basis, for all kinds of reasons, and I don't always remember names. But nothing rings a bell. Honestly, this is starting to feel like an interrogation."

"Are you aware of any contraband circulating among the staff in your department?"

"Contraband?"

"Drugs," Elizabeth said.

She had chosen a moment when Baumgartner was once more

reflexively rubbing her nose. Now her hand fluttered under the table like a startled bird. "What are you suggesting?"

"Are illicit drugs, such as cocaine, circulating in the entertainment division in Tower One?"

"Certainly not! I mean, as far as I know."

Elizabeth penciled something into her notebook. "Okay. Thank you, Ms. Baumgartner. We may need to speak to you again, but that's all for now. In the meantime, if you think of anything that might be pertinent, please contact me. Anything you choose to say will be held in the strictest confidence." She lowered her voice and added, "We're not interested in punishing anyone. Management is aware of how hard you work on behalf of the City. We just need to be aware of what's coming through the Mirror, and we'd be grateful for any help you can give us."

A threat and a promise in one package, Jesse thought. Neatly done. He followed Elizabeth out of the room, leaving Baumgartner dumbfounded and twitching. In the privacy of the staff elevator he said, "So what does Baumgartner have to do with guns?"

"Barton thinks the weapons came through the Mirror along with a shipment of theatrical gear. It's reasonable to assume illegal drugs might be coming in by the same route. Baumgartner's coke habit isn't the secret she thinks it is, and it gives us leverage."

"Coke?"

"Coke, yeah, you know: cocaine. When she powders her nose, she literally powders her nose. You understand?"

"Why would anyone bring cocaine from the twenty-first century?"

"What do you mean?"

"When she could just send someone to the druggist in

Futurity Station. Coca wine, coca tooth drops, powdered cocaine—"

"Holy fuck," Elizabeth said.

Wednesday night was Netflix Night in the Tower One Staff Common Room. Elizabeth might be there, and that was a temptation, but Jesse had attended the event last week and hadn't felt especially welcome, so he took advantage of the free time to cross over to Tower Two and visit the commissary. He was hoping to run across Doris Vanderkamp, preferably not in the presence of her new beau.

Doris was unpredictable, but on slow weeknights she typically lingered in the commissary waiting for company to drift by. And true to form, here she was, working her way through a bucket of fried chicken and dropping crumbs onto the pages of *Frank Leslie's Illustrated Newspaper*. "Interesting story?"

Doris glanced up, her dark hair bouncing like a nest of coiled springs. "*You*." She sniffed and returned her attention to the paper. "Seems like the Spaniards caught up with Boss Tweed."

"May I sit?"

"Don't know why you'd want to. Everyone says you go around with that big-shouldered Tower One woman nowadays."

He settled into a chair. "And you go around with Mick Finagle."

"Are you jealous, Jesse Cullum?"

"Of course I'm jealous. Any man would be."

"Liar." But she gave him a grudging half smile.

"Have you seen him lately?"

"Who, Boss Tweed?"

"Mick."

"How would that be any business of yours?"

"None, except that I need to talk to him."

Doris closed the newspaper and pushed it aside. "What do you need to talk to Mick about?"

"About that head cold you can't seem to get rid of."

"Are you drunk?"

"You know me, Doris. I'm the original teetotaler. I don't drink hard spirits. I also avoid Vin Mariani and Mrs. Winslow's Soothing Syrup. But back in San Francisco—"

"In your earlier life. Which you're always so careful not to talk about."

"Back in San Francisco I knew folks who went to Chinatown from time to time. What they learn there is that a pipe can be a good deal easier to pick up than it is to put down. And I've seen what happens when such people don't get what they need. Sweats, shakes, the runny nose. They try to make it up with laudanum or patent medicines, or they boil poppy heads for tea."

"Nice friends you have. No wonder you don't mention them more often."

"Now, I'm not suggesting you're one of those sorry souls. The Doris I know would never fall to that level. But your symptoms tell a story. What would I find, I wonder, if I searched your dormitory room? A bottle of laudanum, maybe, lurking at the back of a cupboard?"

"What you would find would be my *shoe*, planted in your *fundament*." But her belligerence was forced. "Jesse, what's this all about? Speak plainly; I'm not good at puzzles."

"We both know things come into the City from time to time. Things the City people don't approve of. Some of the restaurant girls and show people have habits worse than yours, Doris, and if some nervous dancer needs a dose of paregoric I don't see any earthly reason why she shouldn't have it—though the City people are prudish that way. But when it gets too obvious to overlook, when it leaks from Tower Two to Tower One? Bad things start to happen. Rooms get searched. People get fired."

"What's all this got to do with me?"

"It has to do with Mick. I don't suppose Mick's the only one doing business with the druggist in Futurity Station. But he's one of them. Don't deny it—his name is already on a list. And knowing Mick, he's not doing anyone any favors. Mick's not much more than a glorified teamster, but he has the mind of a businessman. An eye for profit and the *quid pro quo.* You scratch my back, I'll scratch yours. Which tends to make other people—innocent people—people like *you*, Doris—a party to his affairs. And those same people risk getting drowned, if Mick's boat sinks."

"His boat's sinking, is it?"

"He doesn't make you pay for those little bottles of Bateman's Pectoral Drops, does he?"

"You bastard—you *have* been in my cupboard!"

"You and I were intimate friends, Doris. An intimate friend notices things."

"Like I noticed you crying like a baby in your sleep?"

"I think Mick brings you your paregoric, and in exchange you do him some kind of favor. Maybe something as trivial as carrying a package from one place to another. His pass card won't let him into the guest floors, but yours will. Suppose someone gave you a little something upstairs, and Mick told you to hand it off to Isaac Connaught, the coach driver. Has anything like that ever happened?"

Doris had utterly forgotten *Frank Leslie's Illustrated Newspaper.* She bared her teeth in an expression that would not have looked out of place on a Bengal tiger. "I will have your guts for garters if you get me fired from the City!"

The part about carrying packages had been little more than a guess, though it was rumored that Doris had had a brief dalliance with Connaught before she started her affair with Jesse. "I want to *prevent* you from being fired, if it's at all possible. That's why I'm here. Yes, Mick's boat is sinking, and you need to get clear of it as quick as possible. I can help you."

"Maybe his boat is sinking because some great huge lummox *torpedoed* it."

"I work for the City like everyone else. I'm doing my job. If you want to keep on doing yours, you ought to cooperate."

"You can't fire me!"

"*I* can't, but the people who *can* fire you will be looking at you very closely, very soon. Let me tell them you're being cooperative."

"Whatever that means!"

"It means we should have a frank conversation. For instance, about those packages you delivered to Connaught. What was in them, Doris?"

For a long moment he was sure she was going to slap him. Then she rolled her eyes and sighed. "I don't know. They're always wrapped. Pasteboard boxes in brown paper, to look like something I might carry in or out of a guest's room."

"All right. These packages, are they heavy?"

"Some heavier than others."

"How often do you pick them up?"

"Once a week, the same day the guests leave."

"Always from the same room?"

"No. Mick tells me which room. Always one that's just been vacated. When I make up the bed I look underneath. If there's a package I carry it down to the stables and hand it off to Connaught. Honestly, that's all." Her anger had drained away. "I guess it's enough to get me fired."

"Not if you're willing to tell the story twice."

"Tell it to who?"

"A security boss called Barton in Tower One."

Her eyes widened. "I can't cross over to Tower One!"

"I'll escort you."

"What do you mean—*now*?"

"The sooner the better."

She cast a long glance at the newspaper, as if she wanted to hide under it, then pushed away from the table. "If we're being so damned honest with each other . . . what'll happen to Mick? Because I don't want anyone to think I gave him up just to save my skin."

"No one will think that." He took her arm before she could call him a liar yet again. "Come on, Doris. Don't be afraid. You always said you wanted to see the other tower."

He left Doris with Barton, who promised she wouldn't be fired if what she told him was honest and helpful—a promise Jesse hoped he would keep.

He was in bed by eleven o'clock, and he dreamed of Madame Chao's house in San Francisco.

Jesse is seventeen years old. His father is drunk, but not bad drunk.

"Working drunk" is how Jesse thinks of it. The smell of whiskey hovers over his father like a sullen angel. It's the end of a long night—within grasping distance of dawn—and Jesse's father has been on the door of Madame Chao's for many hours. Jesse has been serving drinks in the parlor: His aversion to alcohol makes him a reliable employee, which Madame Chao appreciates.

The parlor is empty of clients. Most of Madame Chao's girls are upstairs, though Ming and Li are on the sofa, conducting an earnest conversation in Dupont Street patois. Jesse, collecting empty glasses, listens with half an ear as his father speaks. It is one of his father's mumbling monologues, a tutelary speech directed at no one: The only evidence of his drunkenness is that he doesn't care who's listening. Tonight it's something about whalers. "Whaleboat men are the worst." From the point of view of a whorehouse bouncer. "Stinking of carcasses and train oil, strong as bulls from lofting their irons . . . coarse and ugly from months confined among men no better than themselves, arms thick as hawsers, hard on the women and harder still in a fight . . ."

Jesse and his father and his sister, Phoebe, share an attic room, stiflingly hot on summer nights like these. Jesse is ready to sleep but he dreads the walk upstairs, passing through layers of increasingly hotter air to lie and sweat through the restless hours until a distant noon bell wakes him. He prays for morning fog, the benediction of an ocean breeze.

The last glass has been returned to its cupboard and Ming and Li are dozing in each other's arms when there is a knock at the door: three loud, insistent pounds. Jesse's father rouses from his introversion and takes his station. He slides the wooden cover from the peephole and puts his eye to it. He mutters something inaudible, probably a curse. He says to Jesse, "Go fetch Madame Chao."

Then he opens the door, and Roscoe Candy enters the whorehouse.

Jesse doesn't hesitate. He's up the stairs in an instant, rattling the door of Madame Chao's room. A smell of burning flowers seeps around the jamb, acridly sweet and almost rancid, like a fire in a funeral parlor. Madame Chao (who encourages Jesse to call her Big Sister) has smoked her evening opium. Madame Chao has a healthy respect for the poppy and is meticulous in her habit. She won't touch the pipe before midnight or after dawn. And even now, Jesse knows, she won't be incapacitated.

But she might be dangerously slow. He calls out, "Big Sister!" into the darkened room. The creak of bedsprings. A lazy pendulum of footsteps.

Madame Chao's face is an obscure history, written in parchment. She's been running this house for more than two decades, but no one knows much about her. The squat brick house called Madame Chao's has been here since before the rebels took Fort Sumter. It was here when the '49ers arrived. It's older than the Catholic church on Mission Street, Jesse's father likes to say, and Madame Chao—well, Madame Chao is older than God. She blinks at him from the darkness: "Yes?"

He whispers Roscoe Candy's name. Big Sister frowns and narrows her eyes. "Evil man. All right, I'm coming."

She dresses quickly. Descending the stairs, she leans on Jesse's arm. At the age of fifteen he towers over her, but she still makes him feel like a child. No one in the house questions Madame Chao's authority. Visitors occasionally do, but they generally come to regret it.

Roscoe Candy might be an exception. Roscoe is making himself a big man in the Tenderloin. He has all the necessary traits: a high opinion of himself, contempt for his enemies, a small army of enforcers. And—of course—money. Money from the gold fields, Jesse has heard, acquired mainly through claim-jumping and intimidation. Not enough money to impress respectable San Francisco, but enough to make a big noise in the Tenderloin. Candy is buying saloons and whorehouses from Broadway to Market.

In the parlor, Jesse's father stands unhappily at his post by the door. Roscoe Candy is on the sofa now, casually groping Ming. He has a hand up her silk chemise and a nasty grin on his face. He looks like a fat clown, with a striped schoolboy cap on his head and his red checked vest straining at its buttons. But he's not a clown. He's as tall as Jesse's father, agile and strong despite his fat. Under his frock coat he carries a flensing knife of steel and bone ivory. He has made himself a legend with it, using it to disembowel more than one of his enemies. Men from the gold fields still call him Roscoe Gut-Cutter.

Jesse senses that his father both despises and fears Roscoe Candy. This makes Jesse ashamed and curious. Jesse wonders how he would take down Roscoe Candy, if he ever had to do such a thing. A hand with a knife in it is dangerous, his father has taught him. The hand as much as the knife. Watch the hand. Jesse would watch Roscoe's hand. He notes that Roscoe is right-handed: That's the hand he's using to squeeze Ming's breasts.

"Ming," Madame Chao says, "stop bothering this man and go upstairs. Now!"

Ming escapes, careful not to show her relief. Roscoe Candy fixes his eyes on Madame Chao. "Shoot, she weren't bothering me." His voice is incongruously high-pitched, like the yelp of a small dog. "I like a little yellow girl now and then. Diddeys that would fit in a teacup, that one. Sweet little thing."

"Not open for business," Madame Chao says.

"Well, that ain't the kind of business I want to conduct just now anyway."

Candy and Madame Chao begin an earnest, low-pitched conversation. Jesse wants to know what it's about, but he can't make out the words. Madame Chao speaks soothingly but fingers the jade bracelet she wears around her left wrist: She's nervous. Candy's meanness simmers under his words like a kettle coming to boil.

Jesse sneaks another glance at his father, who seems relieved that Roscoe just wants to talk. His eyelids have crept back to half-mast. His mouth moves as if he is whispering to himself. It's this last habit that worries Jesse most. Jesse knows his father is a working drunk and that liquor has been a part of his daily life since before Jesse was born. But it seems as if liquor affects him differently these days. It takes him deeper into himself. Maybe because of his age, Jesse thinks. His father is no longer young. Nor as fast as he once was. In body or mind.

But his father snaps to attention when there is a noise on the stairs.

Jesse follows his glance: Phoebe has come down from the attic room.

Jesse's father has been careful to insulate Phoebe from the work of the house, though she is in no way ignorant of it. Madame Chao has been cooperative, maybe because she's fond of Jesse's father. Phoebe knows better than to come downstairs after dark or before the first light of morning. But maybe it's first light now. The night has certainly seemed long enough.

Madam Chao looks up. Roscoe Candy looks up. Phoebe freezes on the stairs.

She's eleven years old, dressed in her plain cotton nightgown, which is torn in places. Phoebe's mother was a pretty mulatto woman whom Jesse barely remembers, and Phoebe's skin is the color of wheat ready for the harvest. Her hair is dark and lustrous, and her eyes are brown. She has been having her female bleeding for three months now.

Phoebe seems startled to find a stranger in the parlor at this hour, and she turns away hastily. Jesse is horrified to see that her nightgown, long overdue for replacement, is torn from hem to thigh. Nothing Madame Chao's girls would blink at. But Roscoe Candy lets out a long appreciative whistle. "I didn't know you kept such girls here—I thought it was all yellow-for-the-white trade. Are you doing business I don't know about?"

"No business," Madame Chao says curtly. Madame Chao speaks eloquent English but puts on the patois for customers and people she doesn't like. "Not business girl."

"Everything's business," Roscoe says, smiling in a way that bares his teeth. His face is round, his features small. The devil's face, *Jesse thinks, as it might look if you painted it on an egg.*

"Not for sale," Madame Chao insists.

"Grooming her for some other customer?"

Madame Chao has no response.

"She's just ripe," Roscoe says plaintively.

Phoebe isn't stupid. She turns and flees upstairs. Jesse looks at his father. His father gives him a warning look.

"Does she come with the house?"

"Not for sale. Not the girl, not the house. You have plenty of saloons, plenty of fuckhouses. This one is mine."

Cornered, Madame Chao has thrown down the gauntlet. But she's not defenseless. She pays protection to one of the Six Companies. Roscoe Candy ought to know that.

"Well, maybe I'm negotiating with the wrong person, in that case."

Roscoe stands up. He heads for the door. Jesse's father steps aside to let him pass. But Roscoe pauses and walks to Jesse, stands in front of him. Roscoe is nearly as tall as Jesse and twice his weight. Roscoe puts his chin up and pouts out his lower lip. "I don't appreciate the way you've been staring at me."

Jesse knows better than to argue. He says, "I'm sorry."

And then he is on the floor, his ears ringing and his vision uncertain. Roscoe has clubbed him with one of his big fists, and Jesse didn't even see it coming.

"Remember me," Roscoe says.

Jesse will. But what he will remember even more acutely is the casual way Roscoe Candy strides to the door, and the way Jesse's father bows his head and opens it for him.

———

Jesse woke from the dream sweating.

It wasn't a dream so much as a memory—a memory enacted in the theater of his mind as if it were one of those moving pictures Ms. Baumgartner was so proud of. All of it had happened almost exactly as he had dreamed it. It was a memory refusing to be forgotten.

Just like the other dream. The one that always made him scream.

He glanced around the darkened room, still groggy. This wasn't his old dormitory room in Tower Two, it was his new room in Tower One—only slightly different, the bathroom door *here* instead of *there*, the closet to the left rather than the right. Disorienting. For a split second he thought Elizabeth might be standing over his bed, as she had stood over him in their hotel room in Futurity Station. But of course she wasn't. It was a silly thought.

He put his head into the pillow and slept dreamlessly until morning. There was no sunlight in this windowless room to mark the dawn, only the insect buzz of the electrical alarm, followed by another buzz from his paging device: Barton, telling Jesse to come to his office ASAP.

Jesse arrived just behind Elizabeth. Barton was waiting inside, and so was August Kemp himself.

Kemp was smiling, so the news would likely not be bad. Jesse reminded himself again that Kemp was a powerful businessman, though he lacked what Jesse thought of as a tycoon's demeanor. He wore blue jeans and a shirt without a tie, and he addressed his employees as if they were his social equals. But the future people often behaved that way. To Jesse they seemed like children who had grown up without ever learning how to comport themselves as adults. But appearances were deceptive. Power was power, whether or not it wore a tie.

Barton said, "There have been some developments in the investigation and we'd like to bring you up to speed."

Kemp seemed to find this declaration too abrupt. "Actually," he said, leaning against the plate-glass window with his hands in his pockets and a God's-eye view of the Illinois prairie at his back, "we want to thank you for your hard work. You were absolutely essential to our success here. Great job, both of you."

Barton said, "Here's where we stand. Jesse, you sent us Doris Vanderkamp, who was hugely helpful. Doris admits she acted as a go-between for Isaac Connaught and Mick Finagle. She gave us Finagle, and when we called in Finagle he broke down and basically told us everything. The contraband has been coming through the Mirror concealed in shipments to the theatrical division. Baumgartner turned a blind eye in exchange for regular deliveries of cocaine from the pharmacy at Futurity Station, supplied by Connaught. The contraband itself was mostly personal electronics and solar chargers, but it included some weapons. That's how a lunatic came to make an attempt on Grant's life with an automatic pistol. As for the shooter, Grant's people don't want the event publicized— we turned Stedmann over to a U.S. marshal and a couple of Pinkerton men, to dispose of as they see fit. All that's left is making sure none of this ever happens again. Questions about any of that?"

"About Doris," Jesse said. "I told her she wouldn't be fired."

"We sent her to the City clinic for detox. There'll be follow-up testing, of course, but if she can stay clean, she can keep her job."

"Thank you," Jesse said.

"Anything else?"

"What about the rest of the contraband weapons?" Jesse couldn't help thinking of the bag of Glocks he had lugged out of Onslow's back room. "Apart from would-be assassins, who's buying them?"

"We're looking into that," Kemp said. "But now, today, this morning, we're taking one of the ringleaders into custody, and we thought you and Elizabeth ought to be present."

Jesse said, "Where do we find this miscreant?"

"He works at the Mirror," Kemp said

In the corridor connecting Tower One and Tower Two there was an elevator operated by a red-and-yellow-striped card reader: for employees of Jesse's status that meant NO ADMIT-TANCE. August Kemp, on the other hand, owned an all-pass card: The doors slid open for him as if operated by invisible servants. Jesse followed Elizabeth inside, where there were only three choices on the elevator's push-button array: MIR-ROR LEVEL ONE, MIRROR LEVEL TWO, MIRROR LEVEL THREE.

Kemp pushed ONE. "I assume," he said, "you two have had the standard employee briefing about how the Mirror works."

"For what it's worth," Elizabeth said.

Kemp smiled. "I don't understand it, either. Maybe no one does. No one but the physicists, and they seem to have trouble explaining it in English. But if you have any questions, I'll try to answer them."

After a long descent, the elevator slowed. The door opened on a vast space.

Jesse's father had once taught him a trick: if something confuses you, imagine describing it to a five-year-old. Jesse pictured Phoebe as a child, the quizzical expression she had so often worn. *What's the Mirror chamber look like?*

Well, he imagined telling her, *it's deep under the ground, for one thing. Like a cave or a coal mine. So it has no windows. But it's not cramped or close or crude like a coal mine. Picture a room as big as two or three cathedrals and square as a box, bathed in artificial light. And clean—cleaner than a rich woman's kitchen, despite the constant work that obviously goes on here. The floor is crowded with machines made for lifting and carrying and for less comprehensible functions. The men tending the machines wear white cotton pants and shirts, as if they're about to whitewash a barn, and badges to identify them. The room has four walls, but one of them consists almost entirely of what they call the Mirror. Because it really does look just like a mirror. A mirror in the shape of a half circle, ten stories tall.*

"It reflects the light," Jesse said, an observation that sounded simple-minded, but he was startled by the effect, as if the already enormous chamber of the Mirror were twice its actual volume.

"It doesn't always," Kemp said. "It's transparent when anything's passing through, reflective when we maintain it at minimal power. There's a scientific explanation—something to do with the energy gradient between conjoined universes—photons bounce right off the interface, apparently."

"Thank you," Jesse said, not that Kemp's words meant anything to him. "And the future's on the other side?"

"In a manner of speaking. The Mirror bridges a distance of approximately one hundred and forty-five eigenstate-years through ontological Hilbert space. What's on the other side eventuated from a world identical to yours, but it's not *your* future."

Whatever else it might be, Jesse thought, the land beyond the Mirror was Elizabeth's home. The place she would go when she returned to her jailed husband and her daughter. A mere one hundred and forty-five eigenstate-years from here, as the crow flies.

The room is so huge it does peculiar things to sound, he imagined telling Phoebe. *Voices and machine noises seem small and far away. But there's a hum under all those other sounds, soft but powerful, like the drone of a gigantic bumblebee. The air smells of metal, the way a copper kettle smells if it's been left out in the sun.*

"What's important," Kemp said, "isn't what makes the Mirror work but what it does. The use we put it to. That's what I'm proud of. I was on the other side when we opened it for the first time. And it didn't open onto this room, I can tell you that. It opened onto pure black Illinois earth. Ancient silt and glacial till. Groundwater came pouring out. So the first thing we did was dig. We tunneled out a foundation for the entire resort, pumped it dry, stabilized it, began to build on it. Jesse, you were among the first local people to show up on our doorstep. But by then most of the work had already been done. Our people had already gone out to establish our claim to the land, to buy the property we needed to buy—to bribe the people we needed to bribe, where there was no other choice. How the Mirror works is a mystery to me. But what we built around it, that's what I understand. That's what I'm proud of. And that's why it pisses me off when some asshole decides he can walk all over me just because he wants to sell iPhones to the locals."

There was real anger behind the words. Kemp wasn't entirely the amiable mannequin he appeared to be. "Which greedy asshole are we taking into custody?"

"Well, I'm not going to point at him. You see the forklift parked by the cargo elevators? He's the guy tying down a palette of boxes."

Jesse identified the slablike white doors of the cargo elevators. It was hard to make any reliable judgment from this distance, but the smuggler was obviously a large man.

"We have a security detail standing by on the second tier if anything goes wrong. But I thought you two might like to do the honors."

"Thank you," Elizabeth said, sounding genuinely pleased.

"We just need to escort him upstairs for interrogation. No big deal. But you might want to keep your flex cuffs handy. All right? Let's do it."

Kemp strode across the floor with Barton beside him and Jesse and Elizabeth hurrying after. Jesse was careful to keep his eye on the smuggler, who went on loading cartons onto an aluminum skid until Kemp was within thirty feet of him. Then he looked up and froze in place.

"He's made us," Elizabeth said.

So he'll stand or he'll run, Jesse thought. Not that there was anywhere to run to.

The gap closed to twenty feet. The smuggler stood upright, watching them approach. Then his eyes narrowed. Jesse saw it coming. The smuggler broke and ran. But he didn't run *away*— he came at August Kemp, and he came at him head-on.

Jesse and Elizabeth sprinted forward, trying to put themselves between Kemp and the smuggler. There wasn't time for anything subtle. Jesse threw his body into the smuggler's path, and the smuggler's own momentum did the rest of the work— he tumbled headlong over Jesse, though not before planting a knee in Jesse's ribs. Jesse rolled and managed to pin the man under him long enough for Elizabeth to lean in with her plastic cuffs and secure his hands behind his back.

The smuggler's attention remained focused entirely on Kemp. "Fuck you," he said. Jesse stood and hauled the man to his feet as Kemp's standby security detail came hustling down the stairs from the second tier, a belated thunder of booted feet on metal treads.

Jesse brushed himself off and took stock. No harm done.

He might have bruised a rib, but nothing was broken. "Good work," Elizabeth said.

"All I did was get in the way."

"No, you were great," Kemp said, only slightly shaken. "Thank you, Jesse. One of the best hires we ever made. You too, Elizabeth."

Which was fine, but it left Jesse with an unanswered question. The smuggler had come at Kemp as if he hated him and no longer needed to conceal it—more like a partisan with a grievance than a guilty grifter. What had Kemp done to make an enemy of a man whose name he barely knew?

He took a last look at the Mirror as they moved toward the elevators. All of the chamber was duplicated in that vast mirage, and his own reflection was part of the minutiae of it, a tiny figure in a cavernous space. Then a Klaxon sounded, and the workers in white suits began to clear the floor—preparing for a fresh shipment to come through, Kemp said. Jesse hoped to see the Mirror open onto the world beyond it: the fabled future. But the elevator door slid shut before that happened.

The investigation was over, Barton had said, nothing left but the tidying up. But some of that tidying had to be done at Futurity Station, and he wanted Jesse and Elizabeth to do it.

So they traveled to the rail town with a convoy of departing guests late on a Wednesday afternoon. The crowds that had been drawn by Grant's visit were gone now, which meant they could book adjoining rooms at the Excelsior. *Elizabeth will have her privacy*, Jesse thought as they checked in, *and I'll have mine.* Come morning they would talk to the town's druggist about reporting any future spike in the sale of coca or opiate compounds, and then they would attempt to recover any contraband that remained in Onslow's back room.

They arrived in time for a meal. The light of sunset through the curtained windows of the hotel's dining room added a roseate glow to the gaslight, but Elizabeth seemed broody and distant over supper. Jesse guessed she was thinking about her home, and he tried to distract her. "August Kemp seems pleased with us."

"Good for August Kemp."

"So you don't worship at his altar? Everyone else seems to."

"It's not Kemp they worship, Jesse. It's his bank account."

"I'm sure he's a wealthy man."

"Multibillionaire, according to *Forbes*."

Jesse tried to imagine what that could possibly mean. What did a billionaire buy with his money, up there in the twenty-first century? Airplanes? Spaceships? Entire planets? "How did he make his fortune? Not exclusively from the City, I imagine."

"By inheriting a family business, first of all. Big holdings in the hospitality industry, high-end resorts and cruise ships mainly. But Kemp wasn't some kind of trust-fund baby. His father groomed him to take control of the business, and he turned out to have a talent for it. He expanded into some really difficult markets, shouldered out some high-powered competition. There's Kemp money in that orbital hotel they're building, for instance. But the City is his personal obsession."

"Men such as that tend to make enemies."

"What he went through to build the City, of course he made enemies."

"What do you mean? What did he go through?"

"There were all kinds of legal and regulatory obstacles he had to deal with. The safety of the Mirror. The whole question of people carrying things through and bringing things back.

What Kemp brings back is mainly gold, so how is that regulated? From the legal point of view, is Kemp *importing* gold? Not from any recognized foreign country, no. So is Kemp pulling gold out of a hole in the ground—is the Mirror a kind of *gold mine*? None of the written regulations apply, and Kemp had to lobby hard for laws that would work to his advantage. And you can't imagine the number of interest groups who want to piss in the pot, even over trivialities. Antique dealers, for instance—they didn't want a flood of Duncan Phyfe sideboards and Currier and Ives prints driving down the market. That's why anything a tourist brings back from 1876 gets an indelible stamp and a registry number. There are layers and layers of this bureaucratic stuff. Labor laws—Kemp hires a certain number of locals, like you, but does he pay them minimum wage? And is that calculated in our currency or yours? What's the exchange rate? A fair wage by 1876 standards looks like a slave's wage in twenty-first-century dollars."

"I guess all that kept him busy," Jesse said.

"That isn't the half of it. Medical considerations. No offense, but you can't visit 1876 without a shitload of vaccinations. The CDC argued for an enforced quarantine on anyone coming back through the Mirror. Kemp dodged that one, but we still have to be careful—even a single case of smallpox or yellow fever would be enough to shut us down. One of the first things Kemp's people did, even before the foundation of the City was laid down, was to send over an epidemiological team to sequence influenza viruses and prepare vaccines."

"I apologize for our diseases. We'd do without them if we could."

"Plus all the ethical considerations. The whole question of treating you guys as a tourist destination. And thereby fucking with your history, which might be morally objectionable. Or *not* fucking with it, which *also* raises moral questions. So yeah, Kemp ran into lots of opposition, including an entire political movement aimed at stopping him. Which he crushed, or marginalized, or simply ignored."

"The man we took into custody," Jesse said. "The smuggler. Do you suppose he's one of Kemp's enemies?"

Elizabeth hesitated. "Why do you ask?"

"He came for Kemp as if he bore a grudge against him."

The hotel's dining room was nearly empty now. A waiter trod softly between the tables, floorboards creaking under his feet. Beyond the window, a carriage passed in a gentle music of hoofbeats and harness reins. "Probably just some slacker," Elizabeth said, "looking to make a little easy money."

But that wasn't the whole story, Jesse thought. She knew more than she was saying.

Autumn was beginning to show its muscle. Jesse's room in the Excelsior was chilly even with the windows shut and the curtains drawn, and he had piled the bed with blankets. Elizabeth, in the adjoining room, had left the connecting door ajar—*in case of trouble,* Jesse thought with some embarrassment: *in case his demons visited during the night.*

He fell asleep quickly and woke an uncertain time later. He hadn't been dreaming, or at least he didn't think so. But here was Elizabeth, standing at his bedside. She had lit a lamp in her room, and its soft and uncertain light came through the open door, just enough to see that she was hardly dressed and that the expression on her face was solemn. He summoned his wits and said, "Did I wake you?"

"No. Couldn't sleep. Can I sit?"

On the bed, she meant. He nodded and shifted his legs to make room for her. The bed frame creaked as she settled onto the mattress. He waited for her to speak. After a long moment she said, "Tell me what you think of me."

"I'm sorry—I don't know what you mean."

"What do you think of me? Simple question."

No, it was not. It was far from a simple question. He said, "I think you're a brave and competent woman. Why do you ask?"

"You said City women reminded you of prostitutes."

"Only in their frankness."

"Only that?"

She must consider the question important or she wouldn't have come to him in this state of undress. He tried to answer honestly. "There was a time when I thought your men had no conception of honor and your women had no conception of decency. But that's not true. It's that you hold these ideas differently. You're not afraid to say what you think. And you don't hold out chastity as a virtue." He hesitated, feeling foolish. "Is that correct?"

"As far as it goes."

She shivered and drew up her shoulders until the tremor passed. "You're cold," he said.

"Uh-huh. Can I come in?"

He opened the blanket for her. She couldn't have missed seeing the aroused state of his masculinity, even in this subtle light. But the sight seemed not to shock or offend her. She pulled the blanket over herself and pressed herself against him.

After a few silent moments she said, "Do you have a condom?"

One of those French letters they sold by the box at the City pharmacy. "No."

"Then it's a good thing I brought one."

Once again she astonished him. And she went on to astonish him some more.

———

By the long light of morning the town seemed transformed. *Or maybe I'm the one transformed,* Jesse thought. The season's last tourists moved through the streets in chattering clusters, men in straw hats and women in bustles with sun umbrellas ("Like an impressionist painting," Elizabeth said, whatever that meant), the summer making its last faint show, a fragile warmth fretted with wood smoke. He could have walked all day with Elizabeth on his arm. But they had work to do, even though the events of last night, of which they were careful not to speak, made the duty seem trivial by comparison.

Futurity Station's pharmacist was a small, round man, easily cowed: The merest hint that they represented the City's interests was enough to reduce him to fawning cooperation. Yes, he had sold coca powder in significant quantities to Mr. Isaac Connaught, but only because Connaught had told him the City dentists were suffering a shortage. Yes, he had found the claim plausible. Yes, he had taken a profit on these exchanges; why would he not? Yes, he would report any such future transactions to an agent of the City. And no, he was not aware of any arrangement Connaught may have made with Onslow. The pharmacist's obvious nervousness tended to belie the last statement. But the rest was all more or less in accord with what City security had deduced, so Jesse simply shook the breathless man's moist hand and left.

They walked toward Onslow's, making no particular haste. "I know so little about where you come from," Jesse said.

"You've seen the movies."

"I wonder if the movies don't hide more than they reveal. Before the City ever came, some people thought the future might be a place where everyone was wealthy and happy. And when I first came to the City, I thought that might be true. The

nations at peace, the poorest men richer than our own captains
of industry."

"Kind of true," Elizabeth said. "Kind of not. Mostly not."

"What about you? Are you wealthy, where you come from?"

"I wish I could say yes."

"Are you poor, then?"

"I wouldn't say so. But a lot of my neighbors are what's
called working poor. Single moms holding down two McJobs
and maxing out their credit to pay for day care. My neck of
the woods, a lot of us are one paycheck away from the trailer
park. I'm a little better off than that—I get paid pretty well for
the time I spend on this side of the Mirror, which helps. Why
do you ask?"

"So many things I don't know about you."

"I'm pretty average." She glanced at him from under her sun
bonnet, which she had neglected to tie: the strings dangled
fetchingly over her shoulders. "There's a lot I don't know about
you, either."

"Such as?"

"Like what you do with your money. City wages are pretty
good by contemporary standards, right? But you don't seem
to spend much."

"Most of it goes to support my sister."

"You mentioned her before. Phoebe, right?"

"Yes."

"You support her?"

He hesitated. He said, "It's a long story. Maybe best not told
by daylight—not on a pleasant day like this."

Lookout Street had the aspect of a midway at the end of the
season, underpopulated and sad despite its declarations of
gaiety. A board had been nailed across the door to Onslow's
shop. The words OUT OF BUSINESS were chalked on it. Onslow himself had probably left town. He'd been tight with

the local business leaders, but attracting the wrath of the City would have made him *persona non grata.* "Keep walking," Jesse said. They could get into the building more easily from the rear.

It was his second time in the alley behind Lookout: It was uglier but less threatening by daylight. Elizabeth muttered a few curses as they stepped past trash barrels overflowing with encyclopedic examples of everything that met the definition of "waste." Most noxious was the carcass of a horse, picked to bone and sinew by dogs, from which a thrumming cloud of flies arose when Jesse kicked a stone at it. "Oh, God," Elizabeth said, covering her mouth.

"Do animals never die where you come from?"

"Of course they do. We try not to let them decay in public places."

"That must make city life more pleasant," Jesse said.

The back door of Onslow's had also been boarded over, but it wasn't much work to pry off the barrier. The broken hasp still dangled free. Jesse pulled the door open and propped it with a loose plank. He stood on the threshold a moment, listening for any sound that might indicate that the building was occupied. There was only silence.

He stepped inside, Elizabeth behind him. "It's been cleaned out," she said.

As expected. All the shelves were empty, nothing on the crude table but the dusty oil lamp Jesse had lit on his last visit. *Nothing to see,* he thought. At least until Elizabeth spotted the hinged door under the table.

The little door was two feet square and equipped with a simple rope handle, and he had missed it in the darkness during his last visit. Jesse shifted the table and yanked the rope. The door clattered open. There was darkness underneath.

"Should have brought a flashlight," Elizabeth said.

"Light the lamp and hand it to me."

He crouched on the floor. When Elizabeth handed him the lamp he hovered it over the hole. A sour-smelling plume of air rose from the dimness. "It's not a cellar," he said. "Just a space somebody dug out of the clay."

"Is there anything *in* it?"

"Boxes."

"Boxes of what?"

"Empty boxes. Lots of empty pasteboard boxes." He grabbed a few samples and hauled himself to his feet.

He put the boxes on the table. Elizabeth picked one up and inspected it. It was a twenty-first-century box, as colorful as a lithograph and about the size of a brick. GOLD DOT, it said in bold lettering. PERSONAL PROTECTION. It also said 9MM LUGER and 147 GR.

"Hollow points," Elizabeth said appreciatively. "Twenty rounds to a box. How many empty boxes down there?"

"Well, I don't know how deep the hole goes."

"Jesus! And you think it was just gun collectors buying this stuff?"

"Collectors, souvenir hunters, wealthy curiosity-seekers— anybody with money, I imagine, up to and including our would-be assassin. A Glock is the perfect item of contraband, in some ways. Much of what you people bring with you is incomprehensible to us, but everybody knows how a pistol works. And the Glock takes these specialty rounds, so Onslow's customers would have had to come back to him from time to time, if they were using their pistols in earnest."

Jesse might have discussed it further, but he was distracted by a noise from the alley. Someone stumbling over something metallic, followed by a low and urgent *"Hush."*

He exchanged a look with Elizabeth. No need for words: She was good that way. She stepped into a corner of the room where she wouldn't be immediately visible to anyone coming through the door. Jesse looked around for anything he might use as a weapon. He took up the oil lamp and held it behind his back. There was time for nothing more.

Two men came into the room from the alley, one after the other. Both were big men, cheaply dressed. Jesse recognized neither of them. The one in the lead—barrel-chested, almost six feet tall—carried a handgun. Not the futuristic kind. It looked like an ordinary Colt. *Lethal enough,* Jesse thought. The man behind him was armed with a leather cosh.

Jesse held out his empty right hand in a warding gesture. One advantage to being left-handed was that his opponents tended to watch the wrong hand. Misdirection: a useful skill his father had taught him. The gunman gave him a scornful smirk. Jesse kept his eyes focused on that grin as he took a half step forward and swung the lamp out from behind his back.

He caught the gunman's pistol hand in a square blow, shattering the lamp's glass mantle and carving bloody gashes in the gunman's forearm, but the man kept his grip on the weapon. So Jesse stepped inside the gunman's reach and clutched his damaged wrist and twisted until the Colt clattered to the floor. He was vaguely conscious of a ripping sound as he did this—that was Elizabeth, separating the Velcro folds of her skirt to gain access to the pistol she kept tucked inside it. And he was aware of the second man, right arm raised to bring the cosh down on him—he was in no position to do anything about it—and he was aware of the thunderous discharge of Elizabeth's gun, the sudden reek of hot powder, a ringing in his ears as loud as a fire siren. And then nothing at all.

7

Much later, he woke up.

It wasn't as bad as waking from one of his nightmares, but it wasn't a pleasant process. There was a feeling of foreboding attached to it, a sense of emerging from a comfortable darkness to some unpleasant and onerous duty, even if it was only the duty of opening his eyes.

"Much later" was a mere intuition, but he felt as if some substantial amount of time had passed. He was in a clean white room populated with sleek, chiming machines—a City room. He was in bed. His right arm was connected by a flexible tube to a transparent bag of liquid, and there was a throbbing pressure in the general neighborhood of his face.

He closed his eyes for another moment or hour. When he opened them again there was a stranger hovering over him, a woman in white. Jesse parted his gummed lips and said, "Are you a nurse?"

"I'm your doctor, Mr. Cullum."

"Am I back in the City?"

"Yes. Lie still, please. We've been keeping you under sedation. Are you in pain?"

He was, now that she mentioned it. He nodded, which made it worse. "What happened to me?"

"Linear fracture of the skull. But you're doing fine." The female doctor tapped the keyboard of an electronic device she held in her hands. "If the discomfort becomes difficult to tolerate, don't be shy about letting us know—we can adjust your meds. We want to keep you here for a couple more days to monitor your recovery."

Jesse felt recalled to sleep before he could ask any questions of his own. *The meds*, he thought: medications. Some twenty-first-century anodyne. Sleep, distilled and bottled. Sleep delivered directly into his veins, as soft and pure as winter snow.

He woke again, and this time his first question to the female doctor was about Elizabeth: Was she all right?

"Elizabeth DePaul? We had a look at her when you both came in, but she wasn't injured."

"Does she know I'm here?"

"I can't answer that question. A Mr. Barton in security said he'd come down and explain everything once you're awake. Do you think you're ready to see him?"

"I surely am."

"I'll let him know."

But it wasn't Barton who showed up at Jesse's bedside that afternoon. It was August Kemp himself, August Kemp the billionaire, teeth as perfect as ivory dominoes and a smile like a squire conferring a knighthood. "Jesse! Good to see you awake. Are they keeping you well fed?"

The lunch cart had just been by. "They gave me tuna salad.

And something called Jell-O." Which was neither solid nor liquid but came in interesting colors.

"Well, fuck that. You can get yourself a steak if you like, as soon as the doctor signs your release form. You put your life on the line for us, and that earned you a big bonus."

"I thank you," Jesse said. "What about Elizabeth?"

"She wasn't hurt. She shot and killed one of your assailants. Elizabeth made an emergency call from Onslow's store, and we had people on site pretty quick—we keep a response team and a couple of vehicles at the railway depot. It was a huge deal for the locals, seeing you carried away in an armored vehicle. We could have charged admission."

"Who were the gunmen?"

"According to the survivor, they were hired by a curio dealer in Chicago who had been fencing Onslow's surplus inventory. The storefront at Futurity Station was just a fraction of Onslow's business. The Chicago middleman had wealthy customers all across the country—not just for guns but all kinds of contraband: electronics, books and magazines, even clothing. Onslow had been paid for a shipment he failed to deliver—he skipped town as soon as you started to pressure him—and the Chicago dealer sent a couple of men to enforce the agreement. You and Elizabeth just happened to get in the way."

"The dealer is out of business now?"

"Our people shut him down. You would not believe the kind of stock he was holding. Shoes alone—he could have opened a fucking New Balance store. I had to fire half the inspection staff down at the Mirror and more than a few senior managers in a bunch of divisions. Complete housecleaning."

"Sorry to have caused such a fuss."

"You have nothing to apologize for, my friend."

"Did you give Elizabeth a bonus, too?"

"Better than that. We gave her three months' paid leave."

"Paid leave from the City?"

"She's in North Carolina now."

North Carolina of the twenty-first century, he meant. "Did she say anything about me before she left?"

"She was down here a few times when you were unconscious and sedated. That was quite a blow to the head you sustained. She was worried about you, but she was also anxious to get back to her family."

"Naturally so."

"As for you, you're not just getting a bonus, you're getting a permanent pay raise. You'll be housed in Tower Two again, now that the investigation is over, but you'll have a lot to show for it."

"And will Elizabeth be coming back, when her leave is finished?"

"That's up to her," Kemp said.

He moved back into his old dormitory room in Tower Two. The room was unchanged since he had left it. What had changed was his social standing.

More than a few Tower Two employees had lost their jobs or been reprimanded for their role in the smuggling operation, even if all they had done was turn a blind eye to a dubious transaction. Many of them blamed Jesse for that. He was treated to cold stares along with his breakfast coffee; former friends were suddenly reluctant to exchange words with him. So he volunteered for night duty and fence-riding, both solitary jobs.

Riding the fence was thankless work, but he liked the open air and the company of his own thoughts. As the seasons changed and the mornings grew cold, the supply room equipped him with a plastic overcoat stuffed with goose down and a balaclava hat like the knitted hats British soldiers had worn to keep their heads from freezing during the Crimean War. In early December a storm blanketed the prairie with snow, deep enough that Jesse exchanged his three-wheeled cart for a vehicle with tracks and skis. Riding the fence took longer under such circumstances and seemed even more pointless: Any would-be trespasser who managed to trek all the way from the Union Pacific depot to the City's borders in the heart of winter ought to be given a medal for perseverance, in Jesse's opinion. Often during his work he saw the tracks of wolves. Once, a palsied old cougar met his eyes through the steel mesh of the fence.

During these expeditions Jesse had ample time for thought. He thought about Phoebe, and in his mind he composed the letters he would later scribble on paper (his handwriting was a schoolboy's scrawl; he had never had much opportunity to practice it) and mail to her along with his bonus money. He thought about the guns and ammunition that had passed through Futurity Depot, and he wondered where they had gone, and who had paid for them, and whether the weapons had ever been fired. And he thought about Elizabeth. And tried not to think about her.

Most days, the sun was at the horizon by the time he headed back to the City, the last light obscured by clouds or diffused into bleak, brilliant prairie sunsets. He worked hard enough to exhaust himself, which ought to have helped him sleep but often did not. On those nights when his terrors woke him, he switched on his electric lamp and sat up—roused to an involuntary vigilance by his traitorous imagination—and waited for the deliverance of dawn.

After Christmas some of the animosity toward Jesse began to wane, and he joined the rest of the Tower Two staff for a New Year's Eve party in the commissary. All the local employees not on holiday duty were there, every security person, every cook and housekeeper, every waiter and waitress and towel-holder and coat-check clerk, and there was much drinking and a great deal of singing. The hilarity and talkativeness of some of the partiers hinted that the influx of coca powder from Futurity Station might not have entirely ceased. But Jesse didn't care about that. Some irregularities were to be expected, because everyone knew the new year, 1877, wasn't just new. For the City of Futurity, it would be the last year. Twelve months from now there would no bunting, no confetti, no party hats or lewd songs. By the time 1878 rolled around, this circus would have pulled up stakes and moved on.

Doris Vanderkamp approached him when the electric clock on the commissary wall marked ten minutes to midnight. Doris had become something of a pariah, too, for her role in exposing the smuggling ring. They had been avoiding each other for that reason. "Dance with me," she said, a little drunkenly.

She was pretty in her disarray, ringlet curls unraveling at her shoulders. "Are you sure you want that, Doris?"

"I would rather dance with you than not dance at all. I don't want to be lonely when the year turns. Dance with me, Jesse, just for tonight. You owe me that much."

The clock turned minutes into seconds, today into yesterday. The boundary between past and future was called the present, Jesse thought. It was where he lived. It was where everyone lived. He took her in his arms and danced.

PART TWO

Runners

—1877—

8

The town was called Stony Creek, but the name didn't matter. Jesse guessed he'd forget it sooner or later, as he would forget the town itself. Stony Creek was a New England town like every other New England town he had ridden through by rail or buckboard in the last six months, not that he knew much about New England towns except by reputation: dour Yankees, whitewashed houses, teetotaling Congregationalist churches. And maybe that was the case; but the towns, as towns went, seemed pleasant enough from the perspective of an outsider. This one surely did, by the light of a late spring morning.

He stepped off the Pullman car into a chorus of birdsong. The trees on the north side of the tracks were full of birds, all vocalizing. It made Jesse wish he knew something about birds or their calls. He guessed some of the birds might be sparrows. He asked the uniformed stationmaster about it. "Sparrows," the stationmaster said, looking him up and down, "bluebirds, goldfinches, ovenbirds, uh-huh—the whole choir."

Stony Creek was a one-street town surrounded by small-hold farms, with a brickworks and a pottery factory on its outskirts, cut through by a river that turned all the requisite mill wheels. The train depot smelled of sun-warmed lumber, creosote, coal smoke, wildflowers. The stationmaster was a squat box of a man maybe ten years older than Jesse. His uniform was dusty black wool trimmed with gold braid, and he looked at Jesse's canvas bag with an undisguised, almost avaricious curiosity. Jesse asked him about a residential hotel in town.

"Staying long?"

"Probably not more than a day or two."

"For that, the Morgan House. For a longer stay, Coretta Langstaff rents rooms by the week. Depends on your business, I suppose."

Yankee manners ruled out a direct question, and the stationmaster was clearly chafing under that constraint. Jesse said, "As a matter of fact, I'm looking for someone. Maybe you can help me."

"I guess that depends on who it is you're looking for. Do you represent the law?"

"No, sir, I don't. But I don't mean anyone any harm. There's a family trying to find their daughter." This much was almost true. "Not a child but a grown woman. They think she might have arrived here around this time last year. Unaccompanied."

"This woman have a name?"

"She probably isn't using her family name."

"Is she in some kind of trouble?"

"I'm not at liberty to say what drove her from her family. I'm to tell her they hold nothing against her and want to see her again, if she's agreeable. I have a letter to deliver. That's all."

"Are you some kind of Pinkerton man they hired?"

"Not Pinkerton, but hired by the family, yes."

"Well, it's none of my business," the stationmaster said.

"And I shouldn't have asked. I thank you for your time." Jesse tipped his hat and made as if to walk away.

"It's an unusual situation," the trainman called after him, "a woman traveling unescorted."

Jesse turned back. "Maybe the kind of thing folks remember?"

"I don't know anything about it. But a woman from out of town has been staying at Widow Langstaff's for most of a year now."

"And which way is Widow Langstaff's?"

"East. Just this side of the millpond. There's a sign in the window."

New Englanders weren't such bad people, Jesse thought. More generous than they were given credit for. Back in San Francisco he would have had to pay for information like that.

He thanked the stationmaster and set out to walk. Stony Creek's main street was pressed earth, white with dust. The birds kept up their chorus, the breeze was soft as cotton. Passing strangers glanced at Jesse; curious faces peered at him from the sun-silvered window of a barber shop, the shaded porch of a dry-goods store. Jesse ignored them all. His bag was heavy in his hand. The bag contained a change of clothes and a pistol, and in his pocket was money enough for two fares to New York City. Of these, he expected he would require all but the pistol.

After a walk long enough to draw out a light sweat on his forehead, he came within sight of Widow Langstaff's house. The house resembled its neighbors: heavy cornices, gabled roof, a long porch furnished with wicker chairs. Bookending the chairs, two tall ceramic vases with dried cattails sticking out of them. A sign in the window offered ROOMS TO LET. Jesse stepped onto the creaking porch and knocked at the door.

The door opened, wafting out a scent of dusty carpets and wood polish. A gray-haired woman gave him a long up-and-down look, just as the stationmaster had. Maybe it was a New England custom. "Yes?"

"Mrs. Langstaff? My name is Jesse Cullum."

"You want to rent a room?"

"No, ma'am, I'm sorry but I don't. I want to speak to one of your guests."

"Anyone in particular?"

The true name of the woman he was looking for was Mrs. Standridge, Claire Standridge. She wouldn't be using Standridge, in all likelihood. But she might have stuck by her given name. Runners often did. "Her name is Claire."

"Are you a relative?"

"No. I have business to discuss with her."

"Well, she's upstairs. I'll see if she's available. You said your name was Cullum?"

"Tell her I represent her people from the City."

"Which city?"

"She'll understand."

"Well—you can wait in the parlor if you like."

"Thank you, but it's such a nice day I'd rather sit out here, if it's all the same to you." For the kind of conversation he hoped to conduct with Mrs. Standridge, the porch was likely to be more private.

"Suit yourself," the widow Langstaff said.

Jesse wedged himself into a wicker chair and watched the street. The life of the town rolled by, what there was of it. A cargo truck drawn by two scrawny dray horses. A man on horseback. Another young man in creased trousers and a straw hat came quick-striding along, in a hurry to get somewhere—love or money was involved, Jesse guessed.

Then the door creaked open and a dark-haired woman

stepped out onto the veranda. She looked at Jesse closely, more sadness than curiosity in her eyes. She was tall, of an indeterminate age somewhere north of thirty, and she wore a white day dress and a small, ridiculous hat. "Don't get up." She settled into the chair beside Jesse. "I thought someone like you might show up sooner or later. Mrs. Langstaff said your name is Cullum?"

"Jesse Cullum."

"And you're from the City." A deliberately ambiguous statement, on the off chance she had misunderstood.

"I work for the City, yes."

"A local hire?"

"Yes, ma'am. I've been in the City's employ almost four years now."

"And you've come to take me back?"

"It's not in my power to compel you to do anything at all, Mrs. Standridge. I'm just a messenger."

She flinched when he said her name. "And the message is?"

"Eighteen seventy-seven is the last year the City will operate, as I'm sure you know. August Kemp means to shut down the Mirror as soon as winter sets in. And once that door is closed, no power on Earth can open it up again. The City discourages runners, obviously, but there's no penalty for changing your mind, and we'd be happy to pay your way and protect your anonymity, should you make that choice. But the time has come. It's a choice you have to make."

"So this is Kemp doing due diligence? Covering his ass in case my family tries to bring a lawsuit against him for losing me?"

Mrs. Standridge had lived in New England for a while now, according to what Jesse had been told, but apparently she hadn't lost her futuristic habits of speech. (At least not for the purposes of this conversation—Jesse hoped she was more careful when she spoke to her Yankee neighbors.) "I don't know any-thing about Mr. Kemp's motives, but the offer is genuine."

And now she'll send me away, Jesse thought, *and that'll be the end of it. Or she'll begin to talk.* If she began to talk, chances were good that she would leave with him.

She looked across the rooftops of the houses across the street, to the peak of a wooded hill and the small clouds that drifted lazily beyond it.

"Last summer," she said softly, "a lightning-rod salesman came through town."

Jesse knew better than to prompt her with a question. He let her silent thoughts play out against the homely sound of birdcalls, a barking dog, children playing somewhere out of sight. Wind chimes were suspended from the ceiling of the porch, but the breeze was so gentle that they gave out only the occasional bright *ting.*

"I don't know if you can understand how it seemed to me, Mr. Cullum. How it was for me before I came here. I was raised in a relatively wealthy family. My father owns a chain of automotive-supply stores. And I married a man who is even more successful. So my life has been good, by conventional standards. Home in Manhattan, a vacation house in Malibu. My husband was a decent man, *is* a decent man—often out of town, maybe something of a philanderer, sometimes photo-graphed with women he refuses to talk about, but we liked each other well enough. It's just that he didn't understand my . . . nostalgia."

"Nostalgia?"

"That's the word I use. Can you be nostalgic for a place you've never really been? Well, I was. Strange as it sounds. It started after we were married. I began to read history com-pulsively—I guess you could say obsessively—long before August Kemp started selling tickets to it. American history, I

mean; America before the Internet, before television, before
cars, before electric lights. I read history books and old nov-
els, books out of print for a century and half." She smiled, not
happily. "I collected stereoscopes and daguerreotypes. Scenic
views of New York and Boston. My husband called it un-
healthy—I made the mistake of wondering out loud whether I
was actually channeling a past life. I thought about seeing a
psychic; he wanted me to see a shrink."

"And did you?"

"I looked up my family genealogy instead. What I found
was the usual assortment of European immigrants, most too
recent to be interesting. But my maternal grandfather's line went
way back. Like a golden thread. Old New England stock. The
names of people, the places they lived—it all seemed familiar
to me, like something I had once known and forgotten. Sometimes, when I closed my eyes, I could see it perfectly clearly.
Another world. Church steeples and wooden sidewalks and
women in bustle skirts, all clean and simple and bright and *new*.
Do you have even the faintest idea what I mean?"

Jesse's father had once given him a children's book—
probably left behind by one of Madame Chao's inebriated
clients—in which there was a fanciful drawing of a pirate's cave
strewn with jewels. On more than a few nights Jesse had
imagined himself into that cave, a private kingdom where rubies
rubbed shoulders with emeralds and no one was ever startled
awake by the simulated ecstasies of hardworking whores.
The cave had seemed real enough in his mind, occasionally
more real than the world around him. "I think I understand."

"Of course I was fascinated by the idea of August Kemp's
resort when I heard of it. The idea seemed so compelling and
at the same time so implausible. I still don't understand how it
works. Leaves of the past pressed together like the pages of a
book. Absurd. But true."

Jesse nodded. The nation's newspapers had reacted to the advent of the City with the same incredulity. The claims made on the City's behalf could not possibly be genuine, but reporters sent to debunk the fraud had come back converted, bearing photographs of the flying machine in which they had been permitted to ride.

"I tried to put it out of my mind. The cost of a week at Kemp's resort wasn't trivial, even for us. Almost like flying into orbit for a vacation. Which was what my husband said when I raised the question. It would be a titanic waste of money. I was disappointed, but I could hardly contradict him. So we flew to Switzerland that winter. An awkward trip. There were arguments. Skiing bores me. The time passed slowly, as it does in marriages that have decayed into friendships. I think Terrence sensed that."

"Terrence is your husband?" *Is* or *was* or *will be*, Jesse thought: time travel caused those ordinary words to tangle up like shoestrings.

"Yes. And he genuinely wanted to make me happy, and he knew he wasn't succeeding at it. So for my thirty-sixth birthday he conceded the point and booked us the full tour. It was a wonderful surprise . . . though I knew, even then, that I wanted to leave him. And not just him but the world we lived in. I knew I'd take the chance if the opportunity presented itself. I knew it without ever really admitting it to myself, if that makes any sense."

"It makes perfect sense."

"We signed on to the 'Springtime in New York' package. Very exciting, going through the Mirror, and especially when we left Futurity Station on the special train, watching the old America slide by the window, all those sleepy depots and smoky little towns, cities without skyscrapers. New York, of course. They took us to see Adelina Patti at the Academy of

Music. Dinner at Delmonico's. That was the night I made my run. Delmonico's invented Lobster Newburg, did you know that? But as it happens, I hate lobster. So I excused myself and found my way out of the building. It was the Delmonico's on Broad Street, a fine June evening, and there I stood on the street corner, all by myself, dressed in my period clothes, the kind they give us so we don't shock the locals, Velcro instead of buttons and stays—do you know what I'm talking about?"

"Yes, ma'am."

"And money in my purse, because I had made preparations. And a whole world in front of me. It felt . . . *wonderful*. For a short time. I learned better very quickly. An unchaperoned woman in New York is liable to be mistaken for a prostitute. Renting a room, buying a train ticket, even shopping for clothes, all much more difficult than I had anticipated. I learned to pass myself off as a widow. Because, God knows, the Civil War left no shortage of widows. But it's a difficult lie to maintain. So I refined the story. I told people I had been engaged when my betrothed was killed at Waynesboro. Or I said I'd been traveling with my brother when he was taken ill. I told all sorts of lies, a lie for every occasion. Eventually I arrived here. I had convinced myself that this town would be different. I chose it because I have relatives—I suppose you could say *ancestors*—here. Not that I would dare introduce myself to them. I planned to make my own home here, on my own merits. I would join the church, I would be absorbed into the community. I had no better plan that that. It seemed sufficient." She gave Jesse another smile with no discernible trace of happiness in it. "Do you know the story of the painted bird?"

"No, ma'am."

"I read about it in a book. A man catches a bird and paints it different colors and releases it. The painted bird tries to go back to its flock, but the flock doesn't recognize it anymore—the other birds turn on it, kill it. Well, I haven't been killed. But otherwise, Mr. Cullum, I am that bird. I dress incorrectly, no matter how hard I try. I've been told I have a peculiar accent, that I talk like a sodbuster or a Negro. I don't defer to men exactly as I should. I stare when I ought to cast my eyes down. I say the wrong words at the wrong time. In a thousand subtle ways, I am that painted bird. Which is why I live alone in a rented room. Which is why I've nearly run out of money and can't find decent work. Which is why I have no friends to speak of."

Jesse waited for her to go on. Three women strolled past the house, twirling sun umbrellas. Their conversation was a tangle of tenor voices fading in the warm spring air.

"One of the tenants here has a tumor on his face. It covers most of his right eye. Where I come from, it would have been treated and removed. So I find myself thinking, what if I get sick? Something as simple as appendicitis could kill me. A fever could kill me. I've had all the shots, but what happens when the vaccines wear off? As for the charm and innocence I hoped to find—it exists, it really does, but consider what it's buried in. Racism. Misogyny and homophobia so absolute as to be nearly universal. Hatred of the Irish, the Italians, the Chinese— not that many of them are seen in these parts. Europe is as far away as the moon, Asia might as well be Mars. And—did I mention the lightning-rod salesman?"

"Just briefly."

"Late last summer I was standing at my window when a lightning-rod salesman came down the road. A *lightning-rod* salesman! You won't understand this, but it was exciting to me—it was like something out of those old stories I loved so much. He was pulling a cart with his name painted on the side in bright red circus writing: PROFESSOR ELECTRO. A crowd of children following after him. A perfect day for it, too, sullen and hot, storm clouds swelling on the horizon. So I ran down to see him—I couldn't help myself. But you know what Professor Electro was? Professor Electro was an old Jew with yellow eyes and a smelly blue Union jacket, hardly more than a beggar—so drunk or demented he could barely mumble his pitch, and the children were mocking him obscenely, and he looked as if he had endured so much serial humiliation that he would have been grateful if a bolt of lightning had struck him dead on the spot."

"Disappointing," Jesse said, though he couldn't imagine what else she had expected from an itinerant peddler.

Mrs. Standridge turned in her chair and looked at Jesse as if he were the one who had disappointed her. "The point is, I accept your offer. Yes, you can escort me back to the City. The sooner the better."

Jesse had been hunting runners for the first few months of 1877.

His bosses at the City had given him the assignment, ostensibly as a reward for his work with Elizabeth, also as a way to make profitable use of his skills and to get him away from Tower Two, where he was still viewed with suspicion. As it turned out, he liked the work. In those few months he had seen more of the country than he had ever expected to, and the constant travel was usefully distracting. It tired him out and helped him sleep.

"Runners" were people from the future who booked passage on one of the City's excursions and jumped ship, generally with the aim of staying permanently in this century. Such people couldn't be compelled to return—the City had no such legal authority in the America of 1877—but they could be offered a last chance at a ticket home without sanction, if they could be found. Most runners were like Mrs. Standridge, imaginative individuals acting out of romantic illusions; most, like Mrs. Standridge, were happy to accept a reprieve from the reality they had been forced to confront. That was true even of the less idealistic runners, the ones who planned to make a fortune by "inventing" some device they had read about in a history book or investing in a commercial stock they knew would improve. As a rule, the practical aspects of the question confounded them. Or they came to understand that the money they had hoped to earn wouldn't buy them, in this century, anything they really wanted.

There were rare exceptions. In the weeks before he set off to retrieve Mrs. Standridge, Jesse had been sent after a runner named Weismann who had been frequenting saloons in the Germantown district of New York City. Weismann was a man in his fifties, older than most runners, grim-faced and morbidly serious, and according to the City's hired detectives he had been haunting these dives for the purpose of suborning a murder.

Jesse tracked him to a barroom near the Stadt Theater, where he went to Weismann's table and introduced himself as a City agent. Weismann merely nodded. "All right," he said. "Sit down, Mr. Cullum. I won't go back to the City with you, but I can buy you a beer."

"Thank you," Jesse said, sitting. The saloon was a basement establishment, lit with old nautical lanterns that did little more than insult the darkness, and the sawdust scattered on the floor reeked of hops and urine. "But you might want to change your mind about what you've been doing lately."

Weismann had been drinking, not enough to make him properly drunk but enough to put a hitch in his motions. He turned his head to Jesse as if the hinges of his neck needing oiling. "And what is it you think I've been doing?"

"Endangering yourself, for one thing."

"Endangering myself how?"

"By approaching immigrants who have criminal connections and attempting to arrange the killing of a man in Austria-Hungary, cash on delivery of evidence that the man in question is dead."

To his credit, Weismann didn't try to deny it. "It's not a risk-free enterprise, true."

"Such men are more likely to steal your money than trust you as an employer. You ought to have figured that out by now."

"I know what I'm doing. I don't threaten easily, and I don't carry cash."

"Maybe so. But you've been discovered, and you have to stop, so you might as well go home. Free ticket to the City, Mr. Weismann, and no questions asked. It's a generous offer."

"What makes you think I have to stop?"

"Suborning a murder is against the law even in the Bowery. We have witnesses who will go to the police if you don't give it up."

Weismann nodded, still neither surprised nor intimidated. "I guess Kemp can afford to buy himself some Tammany justice, if that's what he really wants. But I don't see any police here—do you?"

"There's the door," Jesse said. "You can walk out and go into hiding, and I have no power to stop you. But there won't be any murder. We've seen to that."

For a moment it seemed as if Weismann might actually call Jesse's bluff, stand up and leave the saloon without looking back. Then his eyes took on a harder focus. "You're a local hire, obviously. How much did they tell you about the man I want killed?"

"He's a customs agent in a town called Braunau am Inn. An innocent man. Whose offspring will commit monstrous crimes, if history unfolds in our world as it did in yours."

"A man who'll be the father of a monster. I'd rather kill the monster himself, but he won't be born for twelve more years. Given that, it doesn't seem like such a bad deal. One innocent life against the death of many millions. If killing him is a sin, no one has to go to hell for it but me. So I cordially invite you to fuck off and leave me to my business."

"But it won't work," Jesse said patiently. "Kemp wrote to the Austrian officials to warn them. And even in Austria, August Kemp's name rings bells." An Austrian envoy had been among a delegation of European dignitaries who had toured the City of Futurity last year, with only a little less fanfare than President Grant himself. A more querulous, contrarian group of people Jesse had never encountered. But they had been as impressed by the City as all the other visitors. An English lord had fainted aboard the helicopter. "They'll intercept your man, if you succeed in hiring one, before he can get close to his target."

"Maybe," Weismann said. "Maybe not."

"And Kemp did something else. Something you might approve of."

"I doubt it."

"When he warned the Austrians about your hired killer, he warned them about the target at the same time—including enough detail about this man's philandering that the customs service will likely fire him to head off a scandal. They were also warned that he was a potential danger to his household servant, one Klara Pölzl."

"So?"

"Well, think about it. You're trying to prevent an act of conception by killing this"—Jesse recalled the name from his briefing—"Alois Hitler. But the conception can't happen if Alois never marries Klara. And even if he does marry her, the circumstances of their marriage will be altered. Bluntly speaking, the fucking will happen differently, producing a different result."

"It's possible," Weismann admitted. "I've thought of that myself. And maybe Kemp's right. But he could be wrong. Alois Hitler is a genetic gun, cocked and loaded and aimed at six million human beings. It's not enough to just hope the gun misfires."

It was becoming clear to Jesse that Weismann wouldn't be talked out of his project, perhaps for good reasons. Many millions dead, up there in the unimaginable future. Something the educational dioramas at the City neglected to mention. "All right," Jesse said.

"What?"

"All right. I'm not going to pull a pistol on you and drag you back to Illinois by main force. Do what you think is best. Will you answer a question, though, before I leave you to it?"

Weismann shrugged suspiciously.

"According to the City, there are more worlds and histories than can ever be counted. A world next door to this one and a world next door to that, and so on, like grains of sand on a beach. And there's an Alois Hitler in each of them. At best, you can only kill one. What's the point?"

"That sounds like something August Kemp would say. But it's a bullshit argument. This world has a twin, one Planck second away in Hilbert space. And that world has a twin. And so on. Hall of mirrors. But each one is as real as any other, and they're interconnected. If I stick a pistol in your mouth and blow your brains out, that act is reflected in every domain of Hilbert space that follows from it."

"But there's the 1877 in your history books, where you *didn't* blow my brains out."

"And that's also real and unchangeable. So there are Hilbert vectors where you live, Hilbert vectors where you die. Does that make it okay if I kill you now?"

"No. That does not make it okay."

"Because right now, right here, for moral and ethical purposes, there's only one of you. You're not a shadow or a reflection or a possibility. You're as real as I am. And this world is real. Back home, back in what you call the future, some of us understand that. We think Kemp is doing something immoral by turning this version of 1877 into a tourist attraction, as if it were some colonial backwater where you can lie in the sun and drink mai tais while the natives die of cholera. Some of us refuse to look the other way while Kemp monetizes an *entire fucking universe*." Weismann drained the stein that had been sitting in front of him. "Maybe I'm more radical than some, but I'm not the only one. I'm just willing to make a bigger sacrifice."

"Shall I say that to Kemp?"

Weismann stood up, his chair teetering behind him. "Tell August Kemp to bend over and fuck himself," he said. "Or, better yet, ask him who invented the Mirror."

A week later, the City's Pinkerton men reported that Weismann had bought passage to Hamburg on the steamship *Frisia*. If you want a thing done right, Jesse supposed, better to do it yourself. He wasn't sure whether he should hope for the success of Weismann's project. One relatively innocent life in exchange for millions sounded reasonable, but it was a hard bargain for poor old Alois. Maybe, if Weismann got close enough, he could effect a compromise by shooting off the man's balls instead of killing him.

Mrs. Standridge was quiet, almost melancholic, on the train back to New York, which gave Jesse ample time to contemplate the unanswered questions her story had raised. "You said you left New York with enough cash to buy clothes and transportation and to rent a room for a year?"

She nodded abstractedly. The Hudson River valley rolled past the window, dimming into sunset. The passenger car was foggy with cigar smoke. "It seemed like enough, at any rate."

"Banknotes or specie?"

"Banknotes."

"May I ask where you got them?"

"I told you, my family back home is more or less wealthy."

"Yes, ma'am, I understand that. And I figured the money must be paper, because your husband would have noticed if you were carrying bags of coins through the Mirror."

"Not just my husband. Going through the Mirror is like getting on a plane: You have to pass through security screening, including metal detectors. A bag of gold would have set off all the alarms, literally and figuratively."

"Paper is more portable."

"It would have been. But I didn't carry paper, either."

"Then where did your money come from?"

She hesitated. "I'd rather not say."

"Then I apologize for asking. It's just that I'm curious."

"If it were up to me I'd tell you all about it. But I don't want to get anyone else in trouble." She hesitated. "I will say that a greenback isn't hard to duplicate with twenty-first-century technology."

"Your money was counterfeit?"

"My money was in every practical way indistinguishable from money issued by your banks, let's put it that way."

"You're inflating the national currency."

"The country's in a recession, if you haven't noticed. The goldbugs might disagree, but a little inflation isn't a bad thing under the circumstances."

Which left the question of who had slipped her the fake paper. But she refused to talk about that.

He watched from the window as the river came into sight: the Hudson, grown dark and turbulent as daylight drained from the sky. Not far to go now. "One other thing if you don't mind. From when you first heard about August Kemp's resort to when you crossed the Mirror, how much time passed?"

"Terrence barely paid attention when Kemp's first resort opened. It took years for him to come around."

"You said, Kemp's *first* resort."

"*Ah.*" She nodded. "They warned us not to talk about that with locals. But the rules are different between us, aren't they?"

"I expect so," Jesse said. "Really, it's an open secret. Rumors get around." Which was almost true. Back at the City, some claimed Kemp had opened other Mirrors into other times, other places. Those who knew the truth of the matter would neither confirm nor deny it.

"The problem is historical drift," Mrs. Standridge said. "Kemp is selling tickets to history as we know it, but as soon as the City is constructed, that history begins to mutate. So he closes after five years, before the drift becomes too obvious. Then he opens the Mirror on a *new* 1872—or 1873, or 1874—all fresh and unsuspecting and completely virginal. The City in Illinois is the second one he's built. Next year he'll open a third."

So—if this was true—there had already been another City, in one of those next-door worlds Kemp talked about . . . and had some other version of Jesse been hired to work at it? He guessed not; the Mirror was said to be imprecise; that other City might have arrived months after Jesse passed the spot, or might have been fully staffed months before he reached it. Still, it was an eerie thought. "I suppose he learns from experience."

"I'm sure he does. And so do his enemies."

"And who might they be?"

"I don't really know a lot about it." Ms. Standridge turned her head and closed her eyes as if she wanted to sleep, or wanted Jesse to think she wanted to sleep. "Will you be traveling with me all the way to the City?"

"Maybe, maybe not," Jesse said. "I go where they send me."

Once they had passed through the bustle of the Grand Central Depot at 42nd Street and Vanderbilt, Jesse hired a coach to carry them to the Broadway Central Hotel.

The hotel had been considered one of the finest in the city when August Kemp's men took it over and refurbished it. Kemp had reportedly offered the building's owners a deal they could hardly refuse: He would install elaborate new amenities— electric lights powered by a dedicated generator, improved heating and fire protection, a twenty-first-century kitchen— in exchange for exclusive use of the facilities by City tourists for a four-year period. At the end of that time the hotel would revert to its owners, who would be supplied with enough spare parts and diesel gasoline to keep the amenities running for another decade. Newspapers had since taken to calling the hotel the "Electric Grand" for the way its electric lights shone through the many windows of the eight-story building; gawkers came from miles around to see it, and on pleasant summer evenings the crowds were thick enough to block traffic on Broadway.

Tonight the crowd seemed unusually dense despite the cool spring weather, and Jesse directed the coach driver to a gated side entrance to avoid the press of bodies. He showed his City identification to the gate guard, who examined it methodically before waving him through. In the lobby of the hotel Jesse handed off Mrs. Standridge to the night clerk, a man named

Amos Creagh. Creagh was a local hire, a beefy veteran of the Army of the Potomac who owed his stiff right leg to an injury he'd suffered at Chancellorsville. Creagh had not yet forgiven General Lee for the insult. Jesse sometimes took meals with him. He stood by now as Creagh welcomed Mrs. Standridge—there was no mention of her being anything other than a valued guest arriving at an odd hour—and summoned a bellboy to escort her to the elevator.

"Strange night," Jesse said once Mrs. Standridge had gone to her room. "Big crowd on Broadway."

"That ain't the half of it," Creagh said.

"Why, what's up?"

"I guess you haven't seen the papers? Big trouble. Oh, and that City woman you're always asking about? The big-shouldered gal?"

Elizabeth DePaul. "What about her?"

"Arrived by train this morning, along with a whole raft of City bosses, including August Kemp himself."

9

ALARMING TRUTHS ABOUT "FUTURITY" EXPOSED

The advent of the City of Futurity on the Illinois plains south-west of the city of Chicago four years ago has inspired intense curiosity among all those who have heard of it. It is a curiosity about the years to come, a curiosity the operators of the City have exploited, but have been reluctant to entirely satisfy. The City's spokesmen, including its founder Mr. August Kemp, eagerly boast of scientific and mechanical wonders, but they have reserved comment on political and social subjects until a comprehensive written account can be prepared and formally presented to the president of the United States. That document was handed to President Hayes last week, on the condition that its contents remain private until a general publication to take place at the end of 1877. Two other documents, said to contain useful advice for medical practitioners and mechanical engineers, are already being brought to press.

Absent these disclosures from Mr. Kemp, rumors have proliferated. Citizens of Manhattan have had ample opportunities to observe the behavior of individuals visiting from Mr. Kemp's "future," and many peculiarities have been noted. It is not a secret that Negroes, Orientals, and women in masculine dress mingle freely with white men in these crowds. Some have understood that observation as evidence that the world of the future is blind to distinctions of race or sex, as in a radical dream-vision of universal egalitarianism. Others take it as a token of the sort of haphazard morality too often associated with great wealth and aristocratic excess.

Until now it has been impossible to know the truth of these matters, but certain letters sent to Mrs. Lucy Stone Blackwell of the American Woman Suffrage Association and lately published in the *Woman's Journal* appear to be genuine, and, if authentic, constitute a shocking indictment of "the world of futurity." According to Mrs. Blackwell, she began receiving these anonymous letters on a monthly basis beginning in September of 1876 and continuing until March of this year. The author of the letters claims to be an unnamed visitor from the future, and his communications contained predictions of both near and distant events. Mrs. Blackwell naturally dismissed these missives as fabrications, but as the nearer prophecies seemed to come true, including detailed statements about the controversy between Mr. Tilden and Mr. Hayes, and the compromise that eventually resolved it, she gradually became convinced of the letters' authenticity.

It is no doubt flattering to Mrs. Blackwell that the author of the letters, who signs himself only as "an American citizen who wants to speak honestly," thinks of her and other radicals as harbingers of the future condition of humanity. This is no doubt what has moved Mrs. Blackwell to expose these communications to the public. We cannot view their contents with equanimity, however, for the letters are incendiary. Our nation has survived a great conflict, and we have no wish to see old wounds reopened, yet the anonymous "American citizen" would do exactly that. By denouncing home rule for Southern states as a "Jim Crow" regime that exchanges slavery for serfdom, the letters threaten to reignite racial tensions and stoke the embers of sectional discord. By holding up female suffrage as a moral ideal that ought to be enacted into law, they threaten to pit husbands against wives and daughters against fathers. By their endorsement of the broadest possible conception of the territorial rights of Indians, they repudiate our army and would push the former president's ill-advised "peace policy" beyond the point of absurdity. And even these horrifying assertions pale next to the claim that our nation will one day become one in which men may enter into marriage with men, and women with women. It is, we are inclined to say, so grotesque a proposition that it simply cannot be true, though observation of the behavior of visitors from the future does little to dispel our fears.

Similar letters are rumored to have been mailed to other prominent or notorious persons, including Mr. Frederick Douglass and Mrs. Woodhull, but only Mrs. Blackwell has admitted to receiving them, and perhaps we should thank her for doing so. If the claims are not true, we hope Mr. Kemp or his representatives will say so. In the event the claims are verified, we may take solace in Mr. Kemp's oft-repeated declaration that the future he represents need not be our own. Indeed, that knowledge would serve a tutelary purpose, in that we would then labor mightily to avoid such an outcome.

Jesse took a sip of orange juice, spilling a drop on the folded page of the newspaper. The word "outcome" became an illegible blot.

He was still not entirely accustomed to taking breakfast in the restaurant of the Electric Grand, where the morning meal

was presented twenty-first-century style: a buffet table offering eggs, miniature sausages, thinly sliced bacon, and various
breads, along with juice and coffee dispensed by luminous machines. He had chosen juice because the dispenser was simple to
operate, but he kept an eye on the coffee machine as the tourists used it, planning to make an approach as soon as the crowd
thinned. He dabbed the spot of juice from the newspaper with
a napkin, which caused an entire paragraph to disappear. When
he looked up, Elizabeth DePaul was standing at his table.

"We meet again," she said.

Jesse stood, banging a knee on the table edge. "Elizabeth!"

"Don't freak out. Do you mind if I sit?"

"No! Please. I mean, of course." He added, "I looked for
you last night."

She was dressed twentieth-century-civilian style, denim
trousers and a white shirt, no Velcro bustle, no City jacket.
Apart from that, she hadn't changed much since she had pulled
her gun on Jesse's would-be assailant in the back room of
Onslow's curiosity shop. Her hair had grown out a little. *Six
months,* he thought. Three months back in her own time, three
more here, doing City work far from Jesse's runner hunts. He
had almost despaired of seeing her again.

She was carrying a plate, which she set down in front of herself. Pineapple wedges and a crescent roll. "Yeah," she said, set-
tling into the chair opposite him, "the desk guy mentioned
it, but I was in a meeting with Kemp's people until late. All this
trouble, which I guess you're reading about."

Getting down to business pretty quickly, but Elizabeth had
never been one for small talk. She seemed to want to pretend she
had never been away. He tried to accommodate her. "The papers
love a scandal. Are the Blackwell letters really so ominous?"

"Potentially very bad for us, sure. Whoever mailed those
letters—some fucking runner, according to Kemp—is making

it hard to conduct business. Did you see the crowd in front of the Grand last night? The only good news is, they weren't carrying torches."

"So the letters are truthful?"

"I haven't seen them, but it sounds like it. And that's the problem. Do you think we'd be welcome here if the average person knew even the stuff *you* know about us? There's a reason we're careful about what we say. The past is another country, and there's no guarantee of cordial diplomatic relations."

"So Kemp chose to hide the unsettling details. I understand, but maybe it was a mistake. People will think you're ashamed of what you are, now that the truth's out."

"We don't have anything to apologize for. We don't have to apologize for our superior hygiene or our flashy technology, and we sure as hell don't have to apologize because we come from a place where women can vote and black people can hold political office and LGBT people can walk down the street with their heads held high."

Jesse nodded. He had learned about these things when he first came to the City, in a training course aimed at preventing local hires from inadvertently insulting visitors—and, not incidentally, weeding out any employees who were too well-bred or bigoted to endorse a principle of tolerance. "It's nothing to be ashamed of, but it won't win you friends."

"Tell me about it. Maybe we have Walt Whitman or Robert Ingersoll on our side. Otherwise, we're being denounced from every pulpit in the country and in most of these ink-smeared tabloids you guys call newspapers. Which is why Kemp's been so careful about holding this stuff back until the last year, preferably until the *end* of the last year—this is exactly what we hoped to avoid."

A lot of 'we' and 'you' in these statements, Jesse thought. "The letters are premature."

"The letters are deliberate sabotage. Obviously the work of a runner trying to stir up trouble."

"A political radical."

Elizabeth's look became guarded. "Probably."

"Someone who imagines he has a moral obligation to intervene in our history," Jesse said, thinking of Weismann.

"Someone who hates what Kemp is doing. Someone who wants to warn African-Americans and Indians and so forth about what's coming."

"And what exactly is coming?"

"Well, like the compromise Congress enacted to let Hayes take office. The end of Reconstruction. Southern blacks turned into sharecroppers, handed over to chain gangs, worked to death in iron mines or turpentine camps. Legal apartheid that won't be dismantled until the 1950s. Native Americans pushed onto dwindling reservations or killed outright, because 'the only good Indian is a dead Indian'—you know who said that? Philip Sheridan, buddy of U. S. Grant and major general in the old Army of the Potomac, soon to be general of the army." A tourist at a nearby table turned his head, and Elizabeth lowered her voice. "I could go on."

"I guess that's all true," Jesse said, "if you say so, but how are these letters supposed to help?"

"Probably whoever wrote them thinks they'll give some courage to the victims, by saying out loud that this stuff is wrong and that history won't look kindly on it. Failing that, they'll discredit the City and cast doubt on Kemp's official history."

"Seems like a slender victory."

"They're only letters. The world's cheapest weapon. But we don't know what else the writer might have in mind."

Jesse thought again of Weismann, whose idealism required

the murder of an Austro-Hungarian customs clerk. *I'm more radical than some, but I'm not the only one.* "Elizabeth?"

She took a bite from a pineapple wedge. "What?"

"It's good to see you again."

"You too, Jesse."

At least she had used his name. "How are things back where you come from?"

"More or less okay."

"Your daughter Gabriella is doing well?"

"She's fine. I mean, she's healthy and she remembered me. I guess that counts as fine." It sounded a degree short of fine. Jesse remembered a word he had learned from his employers at the City: *suboptimal.* "How about you?"

"I recovered from the blow to the head I received at Onslow's."

"I know. I kept tabs, even from the other side of the Mirror."

"Since then, I've been busy." Riding the fence. Hunting runners.

"Busy is good, right?"

"It helps. Seeing you again is good."

She checked her watch. "Speaking of busy, I'm doing a ride-along with the Manhattan tour in about fifteen minutes—"

"A ride-along?"

The Manhattan tour was part of the so-called Springtime in New York package: dozens of tourists packed into a big horse-drawn omnibus and paraded up Broadway to Longacre Square and around the city's more respectable streets. "Kemp was thinking of canceling it. We have to guarantee the safety of the visitors, but that's hard to do if there are racist mobs following us everywhere."

"Is it as bad as that?"

"Not *yet*, and Kemp's letting the tour go ahead, but he's

laying on extra security. Including me. And I need to check a weapon out of the armory, so . . ."

"Will I see you tonight?"

She hesitated longer than Jesse liked. "You know, what happened between us back at Futurity Station . . . that's not something I can jump back into. I thought about it a lot when I was home. What happened between us can never be anything but temporary. Do you understand?"

"I guess I understand it well enough."

"But we can have dinner tonight if you want. Maybe they haven't told you yet, but Kemp's reassigning you to his personal security detail. Along with me. And we'll be leaving New York before long."

The news rang in his head like a bell, too loud to make sense of, but what he said was, "Partners again?"

"Kind of."

"Back at the City?"

"No. They're sending us to San Francisco."

The summons to Kemp's penthouse lodgings came that afternoon, by way of Jesse's pager. He rode the elevator to the top floor of the Electric Grand, standing next to a tourist couple who were arguing, in the lazy way of the long married, over who was currently president of the United States. "Grant," the man said, "I'm pretty sure it's Grant, his picture was in the brochure," while his wife insisted, "But that was last year. There was an election, I think it's Hayes? Does Hayes ring a bell?"

Should have been Tilden, Jesse thought. Congress had given the contested election to Rutherford Hayes in exchange for letting the so-called Redeemers have their way down South— one of the things the letter-writing runner had complained about. Big victory for the White League and the Red Shirts, big setback for freed slaves, and apparently one reason the City failed to attract many dark-skinned tourists from the future. Grant himself was currently in England, an ocean away from domestic politics.

Jesse got off at the penthouse and passed by three armed guards, each of whom examined his credentials, on his way to August Kemp's suite. It was a pleasant suite, equipped with futuristic amenities including a machine for making coffee and a video screen the size of a door. A window overlooked Broadway, but the curtains were drawn. Kemp stood in front of a mirror, adjusting his tie. He was formally dressed, twenty-first-century style.

"Jesse Cullum," he said to Jesse's reflection. "Good to see you again. Thank you for coming up. You talked to Elizabeth already? She told you I want you for some special duty?"

"She mentioned it in general terms."

"General terms might have to do for now. I don't want to be late for dinner. We're bringing Edison in from New Jersey."

"Edison?"

"Yeah, Edison, Thomas Edison, you've heard of him?"

"The inventor? I read something about him in *Leslie's*."

"Electric light, recorded sound, the movies—we more or less stole his thunder, the poor fuck. Half the stuff we have, he invented, but it's going to be hard for him to get patents for any of it. So I want to make sure he knows how much we owe him, that the *world* knows it. It's only fair. Also, I'm hoping he'll agree to come to the City for an appearance. I'm picturing an interview with, I don't know, Neil deGrasse Tyson, Bill Nye, one of those guys. Wouldn't that be great?"

"I'm sure it would."

"You don't have the faintest idea what I'm talking about, do you?"

This was Kemp in a more brittle mood than Jesse had seen

before. "As far as I can tell, you're talking about using Mr. Edison to make some money."

Kemp's we're-all-friends-here manner had gone the way of the morning dew, but after a chilly pause he smiled. "Okay, yes. On a no-bullshit basis, you're correct. *In part*. But I *also* feel an ethical obligation to Edison. Right?"

"Right," Jesse said.

"For the record."

"I understand."

"So here's the thing. I've put together a group of people doing high-level security, mostly traveling with me, but not just protecting me personally—I need people who can go out into the community when I want them to, people who are loyal to the City but know how to conduct themselves in the world as we find it. I think you might be one of those people. Am I right about that?"

"I guess I know my way around. I've tracked down a few runners, if that's the business you have in mind."

"You'll be briefed about your duties when the time comes. Are you comfortable carrying a gun?"

"I've done it before."

"At Futurity Station you carried a weapon, but you didn't fire it."

"I didn't have an opportunity to fire it. I'm not what you'd call a gunslinger, Mr. Kemp, but I do know how to use a pistol." His father had taught him the basics, and he had learned marksmanship from a Six Companies hatchetman named Sonny Lau.

"We'll make sure you get a little extra training. Also, we're heading west. You hail from San Francisco, right?"

"It's where I grew up."

"Which could be an advantage. You know the city pretty well?"

"I did, at one time."

"You feel comfortable there?"

"I'm not sure I understand the question."

"Any problems with the law?"

"Are you asking whether I'm a criminal?"

"I'm asking whether I'll have to bail you out of jail if a cop recognizes you. Anything like that in your past?"

Much in his past, but no outstanding warrants. As far as he knew. "Nothing like that."

"Okay. Good." Kemp's necktie had apparently achieved a satisfactory state. He turned away from the mirror and put his hand on Jesse's shoulder. "Welcome to the team. Elizabeth can get you set up with a handset and whatever else you need. We'll be leaving Manhattan this week, maybe as soon as Thursday or Friday if I can get Edison to commit to an appearance."

"The runner we'll be looking for," Jesse said. "Is he the author of those letters in the press?"

"When you need to know," Kemp said, "I'll tell you."

Elizabeth returned unscathed from her afternoon protecting twenty-first-century tourists from the indignation of angry locals. There had been no real problem, she told Jesse. A few disapproving stares, but no one was throwing bricks. "Seems like most people don't really care how morally compromised we are."

"Well, this is New York," Jesse said. "They tolerated Boss Tweed for years. People here are hard to shock."

They took supper in the hotel dining room, as opposed to the staff room in the basement. Twenty-first-century cuisine. The waiter handed Jesse a menu as long as his forearm, which contained a great many words not recognizably English. "Does any of this translate into mutton?"

"Live a little," Elizabeth said. "Let me order for you."

"Is that customary?"

"Your manhood won't wilt."

She told the waiter to bring them two California chipotle burgers and various ancillary dishes. And beer of a particular brand, which came chilled, in a bottle with a lime wedge stuck in its neck. "Cheers," she said.

"How were things back home?" he asked for the second time in as many days, because he couldn't think of anything else to say.

"You really want to know?" She shrugged. "It was good to spend time with Gabby. She's a big girl now. Smart. And independent, which is a good thing. My mom does a great job looking after her, and I'm grateful to her . . ."

"But?"

"But mom got religion after my dad died. Not in a good way. Joined a fundie church, and she won't keep quiet about it around Gabby."

"You're not a churchgoer?"

"No. I mean, I don't have strong opinions about how the universe was created or any of that stuff. I'm not a raging atheist. But I don't think Noah's ark was a real thing, and I don't think God hates gays and heathens. If Gabby ever decides to join a church, that's up to her, but I don't want my mom teaching her stuff she'll have to unlearn in biology class. So the arguments start as soon as Gabby's down for the night—my mom's all *you need to get her baptized*, and I'm like, *she's only four, what's religion to her?* Plus Gabby never fails to ask about her father. She knows he did some bad things, that he's in prison for it. But it's like an abscessed tooth, she won't let it alone. 'What did he do that was wrong? Does he want to hurt us? Why can't I see him?' "

"What do you tell her?"

"As much of the truth as I think a four-year-old can under-

stand. But the worst of it? My last day at home, we were taking a walk around the neighborhood, the three of us, me and
my mom and Gabby, and Gabby tripped over the curb and
skinned her knee. The usual kid crisis, but the thing is, she ran
crying to my mom. Not to her mother—to her *grandmother.*"

"It was probably just—"

"Oh, I ran through all the *probably just* excuses. Probably
she isn't used to me being around, is what it boils down to. And
that's exactly the problem. Rock and a hard place. I need this
job to make a real home for Gabby, but I can't make a real home
for Gabby while I have this job."

Their meals arrived. Ground beef on a bun, fried potatoes,
and salad, better than the fast-food equivalents Jesse had grown
accustomed to at the City. The beef tasted like actual beef, for
one thing.

"It's the last year," Jesse said. "You'll be back with her
soon."

"But who's to say another six months isn't six months too
many? How long does it take to lose that mother-daughter
connection? Which is another reason why—"

"What?"

"Nothing. How's your burger?"

"Good," he said. "Hearty. A little complicated, what with
the avocado and onions and all."

"Best of both worlds, in a way—1877 American beef, grain
fed and pharmaceutical free, butchered and stored to twenty-
first-century standards. The hotel's chef has an arrangement
with a local slaughterhouse. Kobe beef's got nothing on it, if
you ask me."

"Why, are your cattle anemic?"

"Two words: *factory farm*. Not that I have much experience
with high-end beef. Half the time, at our house, we do McDonald's like everybody else. My mom's a Doritos-and-Coke kind

of gal when she isn't praying. But I try to make sure Gabby gets enough veggies."

"If she lacks for anything," Jesse said, "it's not a mother's love."

Maybe it was the wrong thing to say. Elizabeth stared at him for an awkward moment. He hoped he hadn't offended her. But she changed the subject: "I guess Kemp told you about San Francisco."

"Not much about it. That we'll be hunting a runner. Maybe or maybe not the infamous letter-writer."

"Are you okay with San Francisco? Because I don't know what happened to you there, but it was obviously bad enough to leave you traumatized."

"Do you want me to tell you about it?"

She frowned. "I'm not asking you to."

"I know."

"I guess the question is, whatever happened, will it affect your work?"

He had lied to Kemp when Kemp asked a less well-informed version of the same question. But this was Elizabeth. "I don't know. It's possible."

"You have enemies there?"

"Yes."

"Okay. I appreciate the honesty. This is strictly between us. But if I need to know something, you'll tell me, right?"

"I give you my word."

An hour had passed, and their plates were as empty as they were going to get. Elizabeth said, "My room is on the third floor."

"The one they gave me is on the fourth."

"And I think we should keep it that way. Like I said, what happened at Futurity Station—"

"When we shared a bed, you mean? Speaking bluntly, which you usually prefer to do."

He had not thought she was capable of blushing, that obligatory act of females in popular fiction. But she came close. "Okay, well, I don't know if we should do it again. Not because I don't want to, necessarily. But because there's no future in it."

Future: How many meanings could such a simple word have?

"The thing is," Elizabeth went on, not meeting his eyes, "I thought about this a whole lot when I was back home. Told myself it was a mistake and unfair to both of us. Unprofessional conduct. Do you know what I'm saying?"

"Yes."

"And we've been apart long enough that being with you now seems kind of overwhelming."

"All right."

"That's it? Just, all right?"

"I don't know what else to say. I know I'm not entitled to expect anything. What happened at the depot is a memory I treasure, but I'm not so vain as to think it means I have a claim on you."

The waiter arrived to clear their table. The rattle of plates and cutlery was the sound of empires falling. They folded their napkins and signed for their meals and walked in silence to the elevators. Jesse got a wave and a wink from Amos Creagh at the reception desk, which he pretended not to see. The elevator door rolled open; they punched their respective destinations into the panel of illuminated numbers.

The elevator rose to the third floor. The doors slid open. The doors slid closed.

"You missed your stop," Jesse said.

"I changed my mind," she said.

10

The Blackwell letters were a problem, but Kemp's declaration to the press that he would publish the true story next December created enough ambiguity for the City to continue conducting its business more or less unmolested. Jesse supposed most folks thought of the visitors from the future as near-mythical beings—like the moon-men the *New York Sun* famously claimed to have discovered back in 1835—and mythical beings were expected to do shocking or unusual things. You'd be disappointed if they didn't. The clergy and the columnists might disapprove, but that counted for little, barring further trouble.

The City train laid over for a week at Futurity Station. Ordinarily it would have dropped off passengers from New York and picked up a new load of tourists bound for San Francisco, all within a span of hours, but Kemp needed more time than that to confer with his managers and make contingency plans. Which left Jesse and Elizabeth with very little to do, not altogether a bad thing. Kemp gave everyone on his personal security team passes to the live shows in both Towers, and on their first night back at the City Jesse had the pleasure of sitting next to Elizabeth for the final performance of a week-long concert series by the Fisk Jubilee Singers, who had been lured home from a European tour with the promise of a substantial donation to the Negro college they represented.

Jesse enjoyed the music well enough, and the audience of mostly white twenty-first-century visitors rewarded the ensemble's performance with a rapturous standing ovation. After that Kemp himself came onstage to present a bank draft for an implausibly large amount of money to one of the group's bass singers, a man named Loudin—enough to sustain Fisk for decades, Jesse imagined. It seemed like a magnanimous gesture, though Elizabeth said sales of recordings of tonight's performance would generate vastly larger sums for Kemp's corporation, far in excess of what he had donated. As they filed out of the auditorium, Elizabeth said, "So you like gospel music?"

"Is that what you call what we just heard? I guess I like it all right."

"I don't know much about your taste in music."

"There isn't much to know. I like to hear a brass band every once in a while. I don't play an instrument, but I guess I can sing as well as the next man. What about you?"

"I download all kinds of things," she said obscurely.

Jesse got a taste of twenty-first-century music at the Cirque du Soleil show in Tower Two the following night. But the show was primarily an acrobatic exhibition, and he was too dazzled by the leaping and the colored lights to pay attention to the score. Much of the music was generated electronically, Elizabeth said, and it sounded to Jesse as if it had been produced by an orchestra of enormous, enthusiastically buzzing insects.

On their third night in the City they attended the much-anticipated Tower One event in which Thomas Edison spoke with a scientific celebrity of the future, whose name Jesse promptly forgot. Edison seemed intimidated by the stage lights and the audience's enthusiasm, while the interviewer's attempts to describe the devices that had evolved from Edison's experiments left him looking bewildered and uncomfortable. But the inventor's mood improved when Kemp came on stage with another bank draft, this one intended "to underwrite Mr. Edison's further research."

No mention was made of any patents that might have been preempted by the publication of *Advice for Engineers from the City of Futurity*. That book and its companion, *Advice for Physicians and Medical Practitioners from the City of Futurity*, had been hurried into print by a Boston publisher just days ago, in the hope that the prospect of safer bridges and more effective anodynes would subdue any incipient moral panic. As a result Kemp convinced his advisors that an immediate evacuation was uncalled for and that the City's tours could safely continue, at least for now. The journey to San Francisco would resume, though any setbacks might make it the last.

On the day the train was due to leave Jesse took a pensive walk around Tower Two, through the ground-floor galleries and high tiled lobbies, the restaurants and theaters on the mezzanine level, the gymnasium and the heated swimming pool, the concrete pad where the Sikorsky airship squatted like a burnished steel damselfly. This was the labyrinth he had inhabited for four years, an illusion he had helped to create and sustain. Once Kemp closed the Mirror, ownership of all remaining City property would revert to the Union Pacific Railroad. The City would still be a tourist attraction. But its new proprietors would not be able to maintain these buildings indefinitely. The machines that made them habitable would wear out, irreplaceable parts would break. One day, Jesse thought, sooner rather than later, this whole vast palace would be a ruin. Barn owls would roost in the rafters of the Gallery of Manned Flight, and mice would nest under the chairs in the Theater of Tomorrow.

These thoughts haunted him as he rode the coach through the main gates toward Futurity Station and the westbound train, looking back at the towers where they stabbed the twilight like alabaster knives. He wanted to fix the image in his memory, to possess it as his own.

"Cheer up," Elizabeth said. "I got you something."

He turned away from the window and stared at her in amazement. She held a small box in her hand. He said, "A gift?"

"I'm a giving it to you, so yeah, you can call it a gift. Here." She thrust the box at him as if it embarrassed her.

"What is it?"

"Nothing, really. It's just an old iPod, plus a solar charger and some decent headphones. I loaded it with tunes from the Apple Store."

"Tunes?"

"Music. Songs."

"Music from the twenty-first century?"

"And the twentieth. I tried to be eclectic."

"You brought this with you from the future?"

"Well, yeah. Once we have some privacy I can show you how it works."

"Elizabeth . . . I don't know how to thank you."

"It's not such a big deal."

"I think it is."

"Okay, I'm glad you like it."

I was on her mind, Jesse thought. *Out there in her unimaginable shadow of a future, I was on her mind.* Just as she had been on his. And that was both a good and a bad thing.

———

The City train was a special train, pulled by one of the special engines Kemp had brought from the future—a coal-burning steam engine constructed with materials and expertise far in advance of anything available at the Schenectady Locomotive Works. The engine's blunt, rounded lines and glossy black finish attracted gawkers wherever it passed, and the passenger cars behind it were almost as astonishing: heated or cooled as the weather required, fully electrified. The sleeping cars were expansive, the dining cars served hot meals at all hours, and all the windows were fashioned of a special glass that would repel bullets in case of an attack. The threat of violence was small but real: The Sioux had ceased hostilities for the most part, and some of the Pawnee had even been hired to stage mock attacks at scheduled hours for the entertainment of tourists, but banditry was always possible, and labor troubles were commonplace. Just days ago a strike against the B&O Railroad in West Virginia had spread to Maryland, shutting down freight and passenger traffic through Cumberland. These same events had happened in Elizabeth's history, but weeks later—an example of what the experts called historical drift.

But at least for now, all these threats seemed a world away. For two days the train sped across the western prairies (*fast as a bullet,* Jesse thought, though Elizabeth seemed to find it quaintly slow), and Kemp summoned them each morning for a brief conference but made no other demands on their time. Jesse and Elizabeth had been assigned separate sleeping compartments but they spent their nights in Elizabeth's room, where there was a sort of folding bed attached to the wall: hardly big enough even for one, but they found ways to make it accommodate two as the train rocked through the western darkness.

They talked, when they weren't otherwise entangled. It seemed to Jesse that their talk became a kind of ethereal lovemaking, a subtler and more complex way of undressing each other. He tried to tell her—on the third night of the trip, rattling through Wyoming under stars as bright as pirate treasure— that the talk meant as much to him as what she casually called "the fucking." But it was hard to explain. He said, "When I was younger—"

"Back in the whorehouse, you mean?"

The light came from an electrical fixture turned to its dimmest setting. Elizabeth sat cross-legged at the far end of the bed, dressed in nothing but the cotton shorts she called "panties" and a white cotton T-shirt. Jesse was down to his City-issue briefs, the kind with a loose flap in front, where his lax manhood was even now threatening to make a reappearance. "Back at Madame Chao's," he said, "I saw more of women's bodies than most boys my age. I got to know cooch the way a farm boy knows chickens."

"Uh-huh."

"The girls at Madame Chao's had a captive boy to scandalize, and they scandalized me until I couldn't be scandalized any longer. The female body held no mysteries for me. The men who came to the door, I knew what they paid for, and I knew how much they paid for it. My father made sure I understood how the business worked, on the grounds that ignorance would be more dangerous to me than knowledge. But there were still mysteries."

Elizabeth nodded, waiting for him to go on. The train ticked and muttered against the tracks. Between the rounds of their lovemaking Jesse had lost all sense of time. It was long past midnight, certainly. A sky like ink behind the bulletproof glass of the window. He said, "Those girls, none of them was born in China. Lots of Chinamen were brought over to work the mines and railroads, hardly any women. Madame Chao was born in Pekin, or so she told us, and she came to California by way of New Zealand, but most of her girls were native to the Tenderloin, born to white whores in the houses that served the Six Companies. Madame Chao dressed them up in cheap silks and gave them music-hall names and taught them the kind of Chinatown patois that impressed the customers, but they mostly spoke English on their own time. Some of them weren't even partly Chinese. We had one girl who was some kind of mestiza from Churubusco, passing herself off under the name Lotus Blossom. Sunday afternoons, or any time the house wasn't open for business, I might walk past an open door and see Lotus and Mei-Ling in nothing but their underclothes, darning socks or playing cards—laughing at some joke, talking the way they never talked during business hours. Times like that, they never invited me in. I think it was because those moments were all they really owned. They didn't own what they had between their legs—they'd show that to a curious twelve-year-old if he asked nicely and didn't take liberties, because it wasn't intimate to them and showing it off wasn't an intimacy—do you understand?"

"I guess so."

"What they wouldn't share were those private moments. And it was the very thing they refused to share that I began to crave—I craved it the way some men crave the fucking. I didn't just want what those women sold, though it would be a lie to say I didn't want it. I wanted the kind of intimacy a woman can't be paid or forced to give."

Elizabeth's face had grown somber. "And did you get it?"

"No. Nor did I expect to. But I think it's why—"

"Why what?"

"Why all this"—the darkened train compartment, the frankness of their bodies—"feels like such a gift."

Elizabeth was silent, and Jesse was afraid he had embarrassed or insulted her. It was the first time he had tried to talk about these things, and he had done it clumsily. But the women he had known best were all whores or widows or working girls. Apart from his aunt Abbie, who lived on Nob Hill, there had been no Boston matrons in his social circle. He was about to apologize when she said, "Those girls—"

"I'm sorry, I shouldn't have talked about them."

"No, it's the *way* you talk about them. Jesse . . . are any of those girls still alive?"

Elizabeth had a disconcerting talent for hearing all the words he was careful not to speak. He said, "A few of them survived."

"We should talk about that."

Maybe so. It was a subject Jesse wasn't eager to discuss— Roscoe Candy and Madame Chao's whores and what had happened to his sister—in part because he could hardly bear the thought of dragging Elizabeth into the sordid history of San Francisco's Tenderloin. But there were things she needed to know, and maybe this was the best place to discuss them, here on a sleek train barreling through a desert night.

But the window had turned more blue than black, a horizon had begun to emerge from the darkness. The high Laramie plains. Purple mountains ahead, fruited plains behind. And before Jesse could frame a word, their pagers, buried under mounds of hastily discarded clothing, began to chime, and the train began to slow, and Elizabeth scrambled to dress herself.

11

"Change of plans," Kemp said. "I'm ordering a full evacuation, beginning right now."

The sun had just risen over the long Wyoming plains, visible through the bulletproof windows of the train as he and Elizabeth hurried forward to Kemp's private car. Blue sky and brown earth, each streaked with red. But he could see none of that now, because Kemp's car was windowless. It was a single undivided chamber, its walls lined with electrical devices and display screens. Jesse knew the train was connected by radio to the City and to the City's outposts in San Francisco and New York, and he guessed Kemp had received some bad news by way of these machines. All of Kemp's traveling security crew had crowded into the car, some twenty people, most in uniform, most with automatic pistols strapped to their hips. Most were male, and tall, and Jesse had to crane his head to see Kemp through a forest of shaved heads and black duckbilled caps.

"We're putting the train on a siding at the nearest depot," Kemp said. "We've got another train returning with a tour group from San Francisco. This afternoon we'll be transferring passengers from our train to the eastbound train, and I need you to help with that. I don't want any kind of panic breaking out. Anybody asks what's up, you can say it's some kind of legal dispute with Union Pacific. We're printing up explanatory handouts—everybody will be getting a full refund, no questions asked. If people grumble I want you to be gracious about it, but we need everybody on the train back to Illinois by sundown. Any questions?"

One large and obvious one, Jesse thought. But no one was bold enough to ask it.

"Okay," Kemp said. "We're also recovering some gear from this depot, so we'll need able bodies to lift and carry. Chavez and Epstein have already been briefed on all this and they'll be forming you into teams. From here you head on over to the common room at the depot for duty assignments. Clear?" The security crew began filing toward the exit. Kemp said, "Jesse and Elizabeth, please stick around."

When the car was empty but for the three of them, Kemp slumped into a chair. He looked exhausted, as if he had been awake all night. So had Jesse, of course, but for less onerous reasons. Elizabeth said, "We can lift and carry with the rest of them."

"That's not what you're here for. Only the tourists are going back to the City. An evacuation takes time and work. We're still bound for San Francisco."

Jesse said, "Do you want to tell us why this is happening?"

"It's not a secret, or at least it won't be much longer. The papers published another fucking Blackwell letter. This one claims we arrived in 1873 with a fortune in counterfeit financial instruments, and it says we used these instruments as collateral to acquire two failing banks, the Union Trust Company and E. W. Clark. It says everything we've done since, building hotels, improving railroads, acquiring property, we did with what was basically fraudulent money."

"Is that true?"

Kemp gave Jesse a long stare. "As a demonstration of the degree to which I trust you, I will tell you the answer is, to a certain extent, yes. The question I would *ask* is, so what? There's nothing we've done I can't defend. But I won't be given the chance. In a few hours, everybody with deposits at Clark or Union Trust will be lining up to cash in their accounts. We'll be lucky if it doesn't trigger another financial crisis. And we won't be forgiven for that. Coming on top of everything else, this is pretty much the definition of a nonrecoverable cluster-fuck. And it gets worse."

"Hard to see how."

"Rail workers in Buffalo went on strike a couple of days ago—they pulled switch lights, greased the tracks, and fought a pitched battle with state militia. A police raid on the home of a ringleader turned up dozens of Glocks and a stash of ammunition. At least one Glock was used in an ambush that killed fifteen soldiers."

"Onslow's guns?"

"Probably purchased through the Chicago connection. But the City is being blamed for it."

"So we're going to San Francisco to speed up the evacuation?"

"Yeah, but I want you two for something more specific. We need to recover a couple of runners."

"Is one of them the author of the Blackwell letters?"

"Don't get ahead of yourself. One of the people I want you to find is the asshole who's writing these letters, but that damage is done—at this point, I don't care about stopping him. He can live or die on this side of the Mirror as far as I'm concerned. But he has someone with him. Someone who's under his influence." Kemp looked like he was about to lapse into another broody silence. "It's my daughter," he said. "I need you to help me find my daughter."

The depot where they stopped had been built to supply water and fuel for City trains exclusively, and the City people had driven their spur line far enough into the hinterlands of Wyoming that few curiosity-seekers were likely to follow. The land here was spectacularly empty and, Jesse thought, beautiful. A high rolling plain, some of it sandstone-red, much of it a calico print of green buffalo grass and yellow wildflowers. Astride the horizon was a tumbled mountain range, hazy as a faded daguerreotype, and the air was cold even in the sharp spring sunlight, as if it had dallied over glaciers on its journey from the west.

The City people had put a building here, but it was nothing like the Illinois towers. It was little more than a wide, low bunker, next to a tin-roofed wooden outbuilding and a high steel tower on which was mounted something Elizabeth called a "microwave relay repeater." There was also a paved road, hundreds of yards long but leading nowhere—it was a landing strip, Elizabeth said, but she didn't know or wouldn't say whether any airship had ever used it. Kemp sent Jesse and Elizabeth to a room in the bunker with dossiers to read: mainly information about Kemp's daughter. But the raucous sound of men dismantling equipment for removal proved impossible to ignore, and at Elizabeth's suggestion they carried their documents away from the building to a quieter place, a grassy mound in the lee of a sandstone outcrop.

Jesse read and reread the pages for most of an hour before he confessed to Elizabeth that there was much in them he simply didn't understand.

"Okay," she said. "Well, it's not really complicated. Mercy Seraphina Kemp, twenty-eight years old. August Kemp's daughter by his third wife—"

"Kemp seems to have divorced his spouses fairly freely."

"Rich guy, multiple marriages, trophy wives, old story. He has five kids, but Mercy was the only one from his most recent marriage. It doesn't say so in the dossier, but according to what I've read in *People* magazine he always doted on her. Private schools, an attempt at a medical degree before she dropped out of Stanford. Bright, athletic, bookish, and since her teen years, political. Spotted at various left-wing demos. She spent a month in Canada lending her name and celebrity status to some aboriginal protest movement."

"Aboriginal?"

"Indians. The point is, she's idealistic and she sides with the folks who don't shop at Hermès or Net-a-Porter. The rebellious aristocrat who embraces the common people. You understand that trajectory?"

"She's a reformer. Maybe for the purpose of annoying her father?"

"Maybe. They obviously had some kind of falling-out. But that doesn't mean she's not sincere."

Jesse nodded.

"For our purposes," Elizabeth said, "the important thing is that her activism put her in contact with a man named Theo Stromberg."

"A Dutchman?"

"Born in Cleveland, so no."

"And this Theo is suspected of being the author of the Blackwell letters?"

"There's an appendix to the dossier—"

"I didn't get that far."

"Theo Stromberg is a guy in his late thirties with a long

history of political activism. He has a poli-sci degree and taught for a while at a community college in California. Wrote a book called *The New Hegemony*, started a grassroots lobbying collective around campaign finance and regulatory issues. Arrested for civil disobedience more than once. Pretty ballsy guy, actually, with a following well outside the academic left. Maybe a bit of a martyr complex, but not a complete flake. Are you processing all this?"

"More or less."

"Theo Stromberg's history intersected with August Kemp's a few years back. Theo agitated against licensing Mirror technology to private businesses even before Kemp started selling tickets. And Theo wasn't content to walk a picket line or write an angry blog post. When Kemp opened his first Mirror resort, Theo tried to smuggle himself through."

"And failed?"

"He got through the Mirror, but they intercepted him while he was still on City property. He was charged with trespassing and reckless endangerment, for which he received a suspended sentence. And when Kemp opened his second resort, *our* City, apparently Theo tried again."

"Wouldn't security have been even more diligent the second time around?"

"They were, but Theo's not stupid, and he has backers with money. He came through the Mirror as a paying customer with credible credentials. Along with Mercy Seraphina Kemp."

"They crossed together?"

"Mercy's been in sporadic contact with Theo Stromberg since she dropped out of college. The relationship is off-and-on but maybe not purely platonic."

"How long has Kemp known about this?"

"The dossier doesn't say. Kemp hasn't had regular contact with Mercy for almost a decade, so not hearing from her

wouldn't have set off any immediate alarms. And nobody identified Theo Stromberg as a runner until fairly recently. I'm
guessing the gun-smuggling investigation turned up evidence
pointing at Theo and Mercy, who may have been peripherally
involved."

Jesse nodded. "So it's a dire revelation for Kemp. His rebellious daughter is a runner, and there's not much time to bring
her home."

"He obviously thinks Mercy is in San Francisco, and he
seems to believe we can find her before it's too late. But yeah,
she's on the wrong side of a closing door."

"Do you think she means to stay here?"

"Based on her history, I doubt it. But Theo might want to
stay. And she might want to stay with Theo."

"You think it's her fondness for Theo Stromberg that's driving her? Or her need to defy her father?"

Elizabeth was slow to reply. Jesse sensed something deeper
in the narrative, some implication not recorded in the papers
Kemp had been willing to show them, something even Elizabeth was reluctant to discuss.

"She might have other motives," Elizabeth allowed. "Not
all idealism is fake."

"Back east," Jesse said, "a runner once told me I ought to
ask Kemp a question. He said I ought to ask him who invented the Mirror." He waited, but Elizabeth didn't speak. "Is the
answer to that question pertinent to Mercy's motives?"

"I don't know. It might be. I'm not really supposed to talk
about it."

"But will you?"

She stood up, brushing dust from her trousers. "Maybe later.
And you can tell me what you're so afraid of in San Francisco."

The eastbound train arrived at the siding as the sun was crossing the meridian. Jesse and Elizabeth helped escort passengers to their assigned cars, Jesse moving through the crowd of nervous twenty-first-century tourists as he had been taught to move among them back at the City: quietly, wordlessly. Kemp had already spoken to them about the need to return to Illinois, had promised refunds and compensation, but it wasn't enough to suppress a current of uneasiness. "Like they just figured out this isn't a giant theme park," Elizabeth said.

"Is that what they come here for?"

"Some, sure. People come here for all kinds of reasons. Curiosity, bragging rights, boredom, who knows. If people want to think of 1877 as unspoiled America, Kemp is happy to let them. But reality tends to get in the way. Little things, like the horseshit in the streets. Or big things, like child labor and people dying of tuberculosis and yellow fever. Speaking of yellow fever, you might want to stay away from New Orleans next year."

"Next year?"

"More than twenty thousand dead in the Mississippi River Valley. At least, that's what happened where I come from. I looked it up on Wikipedia."

In the depot's rail yard, trainmen in orange vests supervised the noisy coupling and decoupling of passenger cars. The eastbound train grew longer; the train that would carry Kemp and his crew to San Francisco grew shorter.

Jesse considered the compound's bunker, now stripped of electronic gear and machinery. "What happens to this place when the Mirror closes?"

"It becomes the property of Union Pacific, like every other spur line and microwave repeater along the line."

"Is Kemp wealthy enough to just throw these things away?"

"It's a concrete box and a steel tower, basically. And he's not really throwing them away. The railroad is supposed to pay him a transfer fee when they take possession."

"In gold, I suppose."

"Gold's negotiable, even in the future."

"Unlike counterfeit specie."

"Well, maybe that's the real business of the City," Elizabeth said. "Turning paper into gold."

The long train full of tourists left the yard at sunset, stirring up whirlwinds of dust. Kemp ordered the westbound voyagers aboard the shorter train as soon as the engine had brought its boiler up to pressure, and Jesse followed Elizabeth aboard as the air grew cool and a legion of stars took possession of the sky.

The next day, as the train rolled through the western wilderness, Jesse resolved to tell Elizabeth about the killer Roscoe Candy.

There was plenty of time for talk. August Kemp had retreated to his private car, ostensibly to work his radio but also, Jesse suspected, to get enough liquor inside him to render the prospect of losing his daughter more bearable. Kemp wasn't an obvious drinker, but he showed signs of being a sly and careful one. As Jesse's father had been.

"Your father was a drunk?" Elizabeth asked.

They sat alone in an empty passenger car, in the plush seats ordinarily reserved for the paying customers. The valley of the Humboldt had given way to alkali desert, which had yielded in turn to the elevations of the Sierra Nevada: rock cuts and tunnels that plunged the train into momentary darkness, lakes that trapped sunlight in lenses of blue water.

All that, Jesse thought, *and the weight of what lay ahead.* "My father was a lot of things. He was a big man, he was a brawler when he needed to be, but he was an educated man. He taught me to read and made sure I practiced the skill. But he drank, yes. He tried not to let it make him weak, but it was wearing him down by the time of his last encounter with Roscoe Candy."

Elizabeth said, "Tell me about Roscoe Candy."

"He's—a criminal."

"Maybe you can expand on that?"

"In a way, there's nothing unusual about Candy. Nobody knows for certain where he came from, but he was working the placer mines before he ever grew a beard. In that kind of life, there are only two ways of getting ahead: luck or intimidation. Roscoe took the second road. He had a talent for it. People were afraid of him from an early age. Afraid of his fearlessness, afraid of his henchmen, afraid of the knives he started to carry. By the time he turned twenty-five he owned a pair of hydraulic mines up around Placerville, deeded to him by the previous owner under suspicious circumstances. But Roscoe wasn't content to lay back and let the money roll in. He was ambitious. He came into San Francisco with a fearsome reputation and a fat bankroll. Such men often gamble or drink their money away. Roscoe didn't have those vices, at least not to excess. His real interest wasn't the money, it was the power he gained from it. He used to say money beat a pistol any day, for the purpose of making a fool dance." Jesse took a sip of water from a bottle he had bought in the dining car. DASANI, it said on the label. "Are there people like that where you come from?"

"Violent narcissistic assholes? Oh yeah."

"What do you do about them?"

"Lock them up, if they get out of hand."

"I don't doubt Roscoe Candy should have been locked up. Maybe in Boston or New York he would have been—unless they elected him mayor instead—but San Francisco's not that kind of town. It was built on a principle of lawlessness."

"Wild frontier gold-rush town, I get it."

"In San Francisco, for all practical purposes, the only law is the difference between what you can get away with and what you can enforce. Roscoe Candy learned pretty soon that he was too coarse in his manners to gain leverage with the opera-house crowd, but he could rule quite neatly in other kingdoms. He used his cash to buy himself into the whore business. Pretty soon half the bawdy houses and cooch dens on Jackson Street were either owned by Roscoe or paying tribute to him. He came up against plenty of rough men in the process, and he used them without mercy. His vanquished enemies usually turned up in the back alleys of the Tenderloin with their throats cut and their tongues pulled out through the slit."

"Sicilian necktie," Elizabeth said, grimacing.

"Roscoe's no Sicilian. They say his father was a Polish forty-niner with a bad leg."

"It's just a name for it."

Jesse looked out the window as the train traversed a mountain pass. Below, narrow valleys of ponderosa pine and brown chaparral. Above, a sky like blue vitreous enamel. "At Madame Chao's we bought protection from a Dupont Street tong. Real protection, not just extortion. They protected us from Roscoe Candy."

"Didn't your father do that?"

"Roscoe wasn't afraid of my father. My father could wrestle a rowdy sailor out the door any night of the week, but he wasn't an army. But Roscoe *was* afraid of the Six Companies. So when Roscoe started making moves on the cooch trade, the tongs sent a man to Madame Chao's to keep an eye on things. I say 'man'—his name was Sonny Lau, and he was a boy not much older than myself, but he was already a seasoned *boo how doy*."

"*Boo how doy?*"

"A highbinder. A hatchetman. Do you understand? He carried a hatchet with its handle sawed short, hidden up his sleeve when he wore Chinese clothes—though Sonny knew how to dress American when he wanted to. Roscoe Candy respected those Dupont Gai knife men, because he was a knife man himself. Sonny's tong was part of the See Yup Company, a faction called the Moon of Peace and Contentment Society, which did business on Dupont and Jackson, small-time gambling and opium dens mainly, though they operated one of the better Chinese theaters. As long as Moon of Peace and Contentment was looking after us, Roscoe kept his distance."

"So what went wrong?"

"Well, Madame Chao wasn't your run-of-the-mill bordello keeper. Among the Chinese in San Francisco, I doubt there's even one female for ten men. A lot of those women came over as slaves, basically. Not Madame Chao. Madame Chao fought her way across half the known world before she got to California, at least according to the stories she liked to tell. She wasn't from the same part of China as all those Canton men. She spoke a fancier brand of Chinese. The girls in her bordello were half-breeds, and she catered almost entirely to the white trade—the tong leaders treated her with a mix of respect and contempt, and she felt exactly the same about them. So whenever Roscoe started to make trouble, Moon of Peace and Contentment would raise the price of protection. And Madame Chao wasn't shy about complaining. But from the tong's point of view, Madame Chao was no bargain even when she paid in full. Much as they hated Roscoe Candy, there was always a risk involved in taking on a white man, especially a white man like Roscoe. And eventually Roscoe realized it would be easier to strike a deal with the See Yups than to fight them."

"You didn't see that coming?"

"It was always a possibility, but the only warning we got was from Sonny Lau, and it came too late."

Speaking about what came next was difficult, even in broad daylight. Watching Elizabeth's face would only make it harder. Jesse turned to the window and fixed his eyes on the sun-shot haze that divided heaven from earth.

"I was down in Chinatown when it happened. It was a Thursday night, hot, with a spit of rain coming down, just enough to wet the streets and slick your collar. Most nights, I worked at Madame Chao's alongside my father. I was as big as him, about as strong, and quicker, though maybe not as intimidating. But the night started slow, and Madame Chao sent me out to deliver a payment to the See Yup man who supplied us with opium."

"So, not just a bordello but also an opium den?"

"The white men who came to Madame Chao's believed a proper Chinese whorehouse ought to serve opium on the side. But no, we weren't a 'den,' strictly speaking. We were a cooch house that let the customers buy a bowl if they insisted on it. Most of the girls liked a smoke now and then themselves—it made their work easier—and Madame Chao wasn't above smoking a pill after the last guests left."

"But not you?"

"I had an idea that sobriety was a weapon. I thought it would give me an advantage over my enemies. I wasn't sober for moral reasons—I was sober for the same reason a man carries a concealed pistol."

"Okay," Elizabeth said.

"So I'm headed back to Madame Chao's when Sonny Lau pops out of an alley and pulls me in after him. His clothes are gaudy with blood. Some of it is his own—his face is cut in a couple of places, the sleeves of his shirt are open on a couple of bad gashes—but most of it's someone else's. He's so worked up he can hardly talk. He's begging me not to go back to Madame Chao's. Sonny speaks English as well as the next man, but he's mixing in Chinese words. Eyes rolling in his head like a mad dog. 'Roscoe's men,' he says, and 'there was too many of them!' There's more, but he can't bring himself to say it, so I have to ask. What about my father, what about Phoebe? 'I stood with your father,' he says. 'We killed some men. But there were too many! He's still inside! Phoebe, too.' "

Jesse felt a pressure on his shoulder, which was Elizabeth's hand, and he appreciated the attempt to comfort him. But if he submitted to her compassion he wouldn't be able to speak.

High above the passing valley, a turkey buzzard circled and circled like a feral thought.

"I leave him and run to the house. There's a mob of Candy's men milling around in front of it. These are white men who followed him from the mining camps for the most part, but they're armed like highbinders, kitchen cleavers in their hands and pistols on their hips. I can see smoke coming from one of the upper windows of the house, one of the girls' rooms, and I can smell it, a cindery stink. There's no chance I can get past Candy's men, but there are other ways inside. Down an alley, up a drainpipe, across the roof of a mercantile shop to an attic window. Inside, the first room I come to is Madame Chao's. She's dead, her throat cut. More blood than I've ever seen in one place, and I'm no stranger to blood. It's a revenge killing pure and simple—revenge on all of us, for the sin of having put an obstacle in Candy's way.

"I have a Bowie knife up my own sleeve, because that's how Sonny taught me to carry it; I'm nobody's *boo how doy*, but I know better than to go out unarmed. I have a short blade, too, a little knife I keep in a leather sheath in my hip pocket, but that's all, and it's not enough to go up against even one of Candy's mob. But it seems like the hatchetmen are all downstairs at the moment, and anyway I'm not in my right mind any longer, so I head for the attic room where Phoebe sleeps, the same room where my father keeps his possessions, such as they are, a few books and mementos, including his Gibbon and his *Pilgrim's Progress*. Some of the rooms I pass on the way to the stairs, the doors are open. Some of them, I can see the girls inside. And they're all dead, in ugly ways. I look because I can't stop myself, but there's nothing I can do for them.

"The door to my father's room is standing open, but I hear movement inside. So I slow down and come up on it quietly, or trying to be quiet, though I'm breathing like there's not enough air in the world to fill my lungs. I put my head around to take look. But all that stealth was futile. Candy's in there, and he has my father in a wrestler's grip, and his flensing knife is at my father's throat, and they're both looking right at me.

"It seems like the world goes silent and motionless. Then I see my father's eyes darting left. I know him well enough to know he's frightened, but he was never a man to panic in a tight place. He's trying to tell me something.

"Candy says, 'You might as well step in, boy. You got nowhere else to go.'

"So I step into the room. Candy's wearing the kind of ridiculous clothing he favors, a vest as green as a beetle's wing, a schoolboy cap, a clawhammer jacket half a size too small for him. All drenched in blood, and blood on his face like scarlet freckles. He knows me as my father's son. He smiles.

"I realize my father is gesturing with his eyes at the wardrobe in the corner of the room. I know better than to stare at it. The wardrobe, hardly bigger than a steamer trunk standing on end, is where Phoebe hides out whenever there's trouble in the house. She must be in there now. In the dark, trying not to cry out.

" 'Best put down that knife,' Candy says to me.

"The Bowie knife is in my right hand. I was foolishly about to take it in my left. I'm left-handed, but Candy doesn't know that. There's nothing useful I can do with the knife now that Candy's seen it. So I put it on the floor. With my right hand.

" 'Now step away from it,' Candy says.

"I take two sidelong steps away from the knife toward the only other real furniture in the room: a writing desk. The desk has a drawer. I know my father keeps a loaded pistol in the drawer. It might still be there.

"The fire at the other end of the house is spreading, and a haze of smoke rolls along the ceiling. I hear myself telling Candy to let my father go. Candy says, 'Well, why would I do that? I'm here to kill him! *Watch*.' So he slides his flensing knife through my father's throat. My father is still looking at me as it happens, as the knowledge of his own death comes into his eyes. While the blood's still gushing Candy makes another long slice, belly to rib cage, right through my father's shirt. Three bone buttons drop to the floor and rattle like dice. My father's insides also fall to the floor—as much of them as he can't catch in his hands. Then he follows them down.

"What I do next I do without thinking. I take my small knife from my pocket. With my right hand. And I hold it in front of me, point toward Roscoe Candy. Who's delighted to see it. He can't take his eyes off it. Like it's the jolliest thing he's ever seen. He wipes his bloody flensing blade on the tail of his blood-soaked vest and grins. 'Come on, boy!' he says. 'Come on, then! Take me! Take me, while your old man's lights are still warm—*take me!*' "

Jesse realized he was shouting. But the passenger car was empty except for him and Elizabeth, and Elizabeth had only flinched.

The train cornered a bend. Sunlight tracked along the rows of seats like a moving finger.

"I wave that little knife as if I'm looking for the best way to cut him—and maybe I am—but my better hand is behind my back, and my better hand has ideas of its own. By the time Candy gets tired of waiting and rushes me, my left hand has opened the desk drawer and found the pistol there.

"I don't know for certain it's loaded. But there's no point just showing it to him. As I level it, he's almost on me. I pull the trigger and the pistol jumps in my hand."

Elizabeth said, "You shot him."

"I shot him."

The *emptiness* of that declaration: It had felt the same way when it happened. A vulgar anticlimax. Roscoe grabbing his pendulous belly and screaming, falling to the floor next to Jesse's father and writhing there, the flensing knife forgotten even as Jesse kicks it away from his flailing hands.

"And Phoebe was in the wardrobe?"

"Yes."

"Was she all right?"

"No." After a time he added, "She'd run away from Roscoe's highbinders when they came into the house, but not before one of them cut her. Maybe Roscoe himself. Her face was—well. She lost an eye."

"But she was alive?"

"She was alive."

"And Candy?"

"The hatchetmen heard the gunshot and came boiling up the stairs, but I took Phoebe out a back window. The flames were spreading fast. I left Candy in a burning house with a bullet in his gut. I imagined there was no way he could survive."

"But he did."

"So I've been told."

"You think it's true?"

"I don't see how. But I suppose stranger things have happened."

"And . . . Phoebe?"

"I hope to see her soon." He had no more words to offer, on this or any other subject, but he realized Elizabeth was staring at him. "What is it?"

"Your hands."

His hands were in his lap, clenched so tightly the nails had drawn blood.

Jesse cleaned himself up in the passenger car's absurdly luxurious bathroom. By the time he rejoined Elizabeth he was calm again.

They moved to the club car for a meal. There were only a half dozen other diners present, all from Kemp's security staff. The waiter, a local hire who must have been accustomed to serving crowds of well-heeled twenty-first-century tourists, greeted Jesse and Elizabeth with the nervous volubility of a man who knows he's about to lose his job. Outside, the sun had retreated behind the mountain peaks. Jesse wasn't especially hungry but he ordered what Elizabeth ordered, steak and a salad and a beer. She said, "This thing about you not drinking—"

"You know I'm not a teetotaler. I never claimed to be. I just don't drink to the point of stupidity."

"That's reassuring."

"That I drink beer?"

"It makes you seem a little more human."

"As opposed to?"

"Never mind. You realize this is our last night on the train? We'll be in San Francisco tomorrow morning."

"Yes."

"In the middle of an emergency evac procedure. And once we get this thing with Kemp's daughter sorted out—"

"You'll go home. I know. But we don't have to dwell on it."

"I guess we don't."

"May I ask you something?"

"Sure."

"Back where you come from, someone like me must have lived and died. Exactly as I would have if the City had never appeared. Is that true?"

She hesitated. "Actually, I Googled you a couple of times."

"I probably shouldn't ask what that means."

"Historical records and all that. But your name never came up."

"There was no record of me?"

"No. I'm sorry, Jesse. I guess that must feel weird."

"I'm flattered you thought to look. But no, I'm not sorry there was nothing to find. Better men than me have lived and died unnoticed. It's not a bad company to be in." Though it was a melancholy thing to contemplate, as the light faded from the sky.

The waiter delivered their salads. "Another question," he said.

"Ask."

"I asked it once already. It's the one about the Mirror and who invented it."

"Ah," Elizabeth said. "Okay. Kemp doesn't like us talking about it, but I guess we're past that now. But it's complicated, Jesse. There's the official story. There's the real story. And there's the conspiracy theory."

"Tell me the real story."

"I would, but I don't know what it is."

"Well, then what's the official story? And who declared it official?"

"The official story is that the Mirror technology came out of a research project at DARPA. DARPA's an agency that does cutting-edge scientific research for the military. DARPA supposedly stumbled on a way of creating what the wonks call 'material translations in ontological Hilbert space' while working on ultra-high-energy lasers. No, I don't know what that means any better than you do. The idea is that they discovered some weird new physics that, unfortunately from their point of view, turned out not to be weaponizable in any practical way. So the core concepts were farmed out for civilian research and potential commercial applications. So far, the only enterprise that's managed to turn a profit with the technology is August Kemp's. Kemp's people patented a technique for scaling up the Hilbert translation, making it possible to send large objects from our own universe to one that resembles our past."

"The Mirror, that is to say."

"The Mirror."

"But not everyone accepts this story?"

"Well, the Mirror looks pretty strange even by twenty-first-century standards. It's not like rockets. People understand rockets—a moon rocket is just a Fourth of July rocket, scaled up. But the Mirror? Traveling into a past that isn't actually *our* past? Basically unprecedented. So a bunch of alternative theories started to circulate, usually involving aliens or the Antichrist. But one story in particular got a lot of traction. It goes like this. Shortly after 9/11—you know about 9/11?"

"An attack on New York City by Mussulman fanatics." Jesse had overheard enough talk among the tourists to make that obvious deduction.

"After 9/11, national and local security agencies start

looking hard at anyone with suspicious ID or travel histories. Supposedly, two dudes with no fixed address get red-flagged by some such agency, and when they're brought in for questioning they turn out to be not entirely human. They're only a little over five foot tall, their IDs don't check out, a medical examination reveals all kinds of weird physical anomalies, and when they're questioned they clam up—even under torture, according to some accounts. But their movements are traced back to a house where investigators find something even stranger concealed in the basement: a version of the Mirror. In this story, DARPA is assigned the work of reverse-engineering the technology, basically taking it apart and figuring out what it does and how it works. Amazingly, they succeed at that. You see where this is going?"

Jesse said, "You were visited from some version of your own future. The visitors were arrested and their Mirror was impounded."

"Uh-huh."

"Do you think there's any truth to it?"

"Probably not, but how would I know? In some versions of the story the visitors died in captivity. In others, they're being held in a secret government facility—Area 51 or like that. Like most of these fringe theories, there's not much evidence you can pin down. The most plausible corroboration comes from a highly classified Defense Department memo, part of a batch of documents leaked by a whistleblower a few years ago. But the language is ambiguous. It might be talking about ordinary terrorist detainees, not post-human gnomes from the far reaches of Hilbert space."

"The story was never confirmed or disproved?"

"Not as far as I know."

"Why, in that case, would a runner tell me to ask August Kemp who invented the Mirror?"

"I guess to fuck with you. Or to fuck with Kemp. This runner you talked to, was he politically motivated?"

"He was planning to prevent the conception of a man named Hitler, not yet born."

"Oh, for God's sake. So *yes*, politically motivated. Like the anti-Mirror movement back home, most of these political runners take the conspiracy theory seriously. They think Kemp knows the truth and is hiding it so he can exploit the technology to his own advantage."

"The runner in San Francisco, Theo Stromberg—he shares these beliefs?"

"He wants to be taken seriously, so he distances himself from the wacky stuff, but he doesn't deny it altogether."

"And Mercy Kemp?"

"She's on record as a believer."

After the meal Jesse followed Elizabeth to her stateroom. It was their last night on the train, and he thought he should say something more about the dangers that might be waiting in San Francisco. But she put her finger to her lips as she closed the door behind her. "No more talk. I want music. You have that iPod I gave you?"

He took it from his kit bag. She used a cable to connect the device to a port on the wall of the room. Jesse said, "Are there loudspeakers?"

"Built into the ceiling."

"Are all trains so luxurious where you come from?"

"Hardly. We're living like the one percent tonight."

A drumbeat began. Elizabeth turned up the volume. Jesse said, "Music from your time."

"From before my time. I have an uncle in New Hampshire who teaches a course on the theory and history of popular music. Very cool guy. When I was younger he used to send me CDs and downloads, so I got to hear all kinds of things."

"What we're hearing, is it something you like?"

She unbuttoned her shirt. "It's a classic album. Hendrix, *Axis Bold as Love.*"

"It's very loud."

"It's supposed to be."

"Axes? Bold as love?"

"*Axis.*"

"Is love bold?"

"I don't know. Maybe. Shut up and take off your clothes, let's find out."

PART THREE

The Siege of Futurity

—1877—

12

Jesse woke to a pounding on the stateroom door.

He had slept as soundly as he had slept in months, and it took him a moment to place himself. The train was motionless. *End of the line,* he thought, which would be the terminal at the Oakland Long Wharf. There was nothing to see beyond the window but a tangle of telegraph wires, a billboard advertising vinegar bitters, and a flat gray sky. But he knew by some animal instinct that the train had brought him home, or close to home: to the shores of San Francisco Bay, a ferry ride away from Market Street.

It wasn't a good feeling.

Beside him, Elizabeth sat up and said, "What the hell?"

The pounding continued. Jesse had just succeeded in pulling on his briefs when the door flew open. The impatient party in the corridor was August Kemp. In his hand Kemp held a newspaper, which he threw at Jesse's feet. "We're fucked!"

It was outrageous behavior. Kemp had burst in on a woman while she was in a state of undress. Jesse suppressed an impulse to throw him out of the room—Elizabeth put a restraining hand on his shoulder—and picked up the paper, a spindled copy of yesterday's *Examiner* "What's this about?"

"Read it and weep. Both of you. Conference in the terminal cafeteria at eight. And Jesse? I want a word with you after that."

Four years ago this wing of the terminal building had been refurbished by City architects, who had turned it into a glittering arcade with plate-glass skylights and a forest of electrified signage. Ordinarily, the arrival of a City train would have filled it with twenty-first-century tourists. Today it was a ghost town, nobody present but a skeleton crew of nervous-looking City employees and the few dozen passengers and security people Kemp had brought along with him. Jesse settled at one of the empty tables in the cafeteria and unfurled the newspaper Kemp had thrown at him. The story that had alarmed Kemp was on the front page. GUNS OF FUTURITY DISCOVERED, the headline said. Jesse read the article carefully, then offered the paper to Elizabeth.

She gave the close-set columns of type an unhappy glance. "Is it about the Glocks they recovered in Buffalo?"

"In part. But other guns have turned up."

"Turned up where?"

"Well, the post office found a futuristic pistol in a seized package bound for Chief Joseph of the Nez Percé. The Nez Percé are restive—they're due to be removed to a reservation in Idaho, but they don't want to give up their tribal lands. How did that play out, back where you come from?"

"I don't know. I'm not really a history buff. I'm guessing it ended badly."

"It was only one Glock, with a single clip, but apparently it came with a letter warning of an attack on a Nez Percé camp on the Clearwater River."

"Like the Blackwell letters."

"Written in the same hand, some say. One pistol doesn't amount to much, but the warnings in the letter could have given the Nez Percé a real advantage in a fight. Does that sound like something that might interest Theo Stromberg?"

"Forcing an entire native population to move from its ancestral land is considered a human rights offense where I come from, so yeah. Is that all?"

"Not by half. A similar weapon was found in the hands of a group of Negro Republicans in Caddo County, Louisiana. The pistol was confiscated before it could be loaded or fired, but Congress is making a scandal of it. No one knows whether the gun also came with a letter, because the Negros were lynched before they could be questioned."

"Jesus," Elizabeth said.

"Added to that, the labor troubles. There's been discontent among rail workers ever since the Baltimore and Ohio cut wages. The Cumberland line's been shut down for days. The Governor of Maryland called in the National Guard, and the troops were fired on in Baltimore. Another Futurity gun was involved, according to some accounts. The facts are still muddy, but politicos are rushing to blame the City for all of this. There's talk of issuing a warrant for the arrest of August Kemp, though it's not clear who has the jurisdiction to do that."

Kemp came into the cafeteria as if summoned by the mention of his name. Jesse and Elizabeth shouldered into the crowd that formed as Kemp stepped up onto a cafeteria bench to address them. He started with a summary of the current situation, not much different from what Jesse had distilled from the pages of the *Examiner.* "We're in no immediate danger," he said, "but this is a problem that's only going to get worse, and the situation could deteriorate quickly. Our New York site got the evacuation order two days ago—everybody east of the Mississippi is either back at the City or on their way—but we still have vulnerable personnel in San Francisco, and securing their safe return is our highest priority right now."

The most direct route from San Francisco to Oakland was by water, either via the regularly scheduled ferries or the City's own steam ferry, *Futurity*. Ordinarily, tourists were ferried into San Francisco and accommodated at a City hotel on the Point Lobos toll road. All such tourists had been evacuated as of yesterday, but there were City employees still stationed at the Folsom Street docks, and they needed to be at the Oakland terminal by Wednesday morning—because, Kemp said, "that's when the last train's leaving."

Two days from now. An absurdly short span of time in which to locate and recover Kemp's daughter. Jesse looked at Elizabeth, who shook her head in disbelief.

Kemp went on to parcel out duties to various factions of his security crew and declare the meeting over. He approached Jesse as the crowd dispersed. "I've set up a temporary office in one of the function rooms off the east corridor. Follow me there."

Elizabeth said, "Sir, I—"

"No. Not you. Just Jesse. You can wait here for us. This won't take long."

Jesse followed Kemp to a room furnished with a desk and a single chair. Both the desk and the chair were twenty-first-century items, unadorned and bluntly functional. Both men remained standing. Kemp said, "You've been drawing a paycheck for what, four years now?"

"About," Jesse said.

"And you understand your term of employment is about to come to an end?"

"Yes, sir. Obviously."

"We've been generous to you in terms of salary, correct?"

"Yes."

"And you saved some of that? You won't be left penniless when we shut down the Mirror?"

"I expect I'll do all right."

"Your contract specifies severance pay if you're employed to the end of the City's tenure. Are you worried about getting that payment?"

In truth, Jesse hadn't given it much thought. Given the questions surrounding the City's banking practices, maybe he should have. "You've always been as good as your word."

"I'm sending you and Elizabeth into San Francisco to find my daughter. Right now that's your one and only job. I know Elizabeth won't have a problem with it. She's a loyal employee and she wants to go home with a commendation and money in her pocket. I trust her because I know where her interests lie. But you're in a different position. *This* is your home. And right now it could be dangerous for you to be identified with the City of Futurity. So you might be thinking how easy it would be to just walk away, especially with the trouble at the sandlots."

The sandlots were a patch of unimproved ground outside City Hall, favored territory for rabble-rousers. "Has there been trouble?"

"Last night there was a big rally. Assholes with torches and pick handles, basically, but they stopped short of marching on Chinatown. There might be worse tonight or tomorrow."

"A few Kearneyites don't scare me."

"I believe you, and that's why I chose you for this assignment. But human nature is human nature. So I want to show you something." Kemp went to the desk and opened a drawer and extracted a leather drawstring bag. He hefted it to demonstrate its weight and loosened the string to expose a glitter of coins. Eagles and double eagles, mainly. "Gold," Kemp said. "Not specie. Not bank drafts. This is your severance pay, Jesse. This is what you get when you bring Mercy back. Do you understand?"

Jesse looked at Kemp and the bag and tried to decide whether he was being bribed or insulted or both. Most likely both. "I understand perfectly."

"Good. Because the rules for runners don't apply right now. I need you to be absolutely clear on that. Find Mercy, bring her back. Willing or unwilling. I don't care what laws you break and I don't care who you hurt. I want her unharmed and on board the last train to the City when it leaves. Do you accept that commission?"

"What about Theo Stromberg? Under the rules, I'm obliged to offer him the chance to go home."

"I don't give a shit. Was I unclear about that? Fuck the rules! The rules were made to protect the paying customers, not Theo fucking Stromberg."

Jesse heard a faint ticking in the ensuing silence. He guessed the sound came from Kemp's wristwatch. Like the double eagles in the leather bag, the watch appeared to be made of gold. "I understand," Jesse said.

"Okay. We're on the same page? Good. Then let's get you outfitted. There's no time to waste."

An hour later Jesse was aboard the ferry *Futurity* with Elizabeth beside him, standing at the rail as the vessel drew away from the Oakland docks.

He had been given a calico travel bag containing two Glocks with ammunition, a pair of Tasers, a portable radio, and a selection of stun grenades—Kemp seemed to feel Theo might put up a fight. Jesse felt conspicuous in his City-issued trousers and cotton shirt, which seemed too crisp and unsullied to be entirely plausible, and Elizabeth plucked at her Velcro-fitted day dress as if she found it binding. She turned to him and said, "Does this bustle make my ass look fat?"

"No."

She laughed. "It's a joke. Sorry."

"Is it? I've seen those magazines tourists leave behind. Women as bony as tubercular mules."

"Fashion models."

"You're not like that."

"Okay, yeah."

"You're much more wholesome and . . . rounded."

"Right, thank you. Sorry I mentioned it."

The sun was bright and a spring breeze kicked up chop in the water. *Futurity* sounded its whistle and began to move through the traffic of other vessels, a motley assortment of crowded ferries and cargo boats laden with produce, but the only passengers aboard *Futurity* were Jesse and Elizabeth and a few local hires headed for San Francisco to recover what remained to be recovered from various City-held sites. Elizabeth grew moody, clutching her hat as the vessel passed through scrims of coal smoke toward the scalloped hills. At one point she turned to him and said, "Do you think we can do this? Find Mercy, I mean?"

"Probably we can find her. Whether we can find her before the last train leaves is another question entirely."

"Do you know where to start? Because I don't."

"I have an idea or two," he said.

Elizabeth lapsed into silence, though she was briefly excited when a humpback whale surfaced off the starboard side of the ferry. Maybe whales were as scarce as bison or passenger pigeons where she came from. Jesse rummaged in his bag and found the iPod she had given him. He put the earpieces in his ears and tried to remember how to instruct the machine to play music. He wanted *Axis Bold as Love* but ended up with an entirely different suite of songs by the same composer, *Electric Ladyland.* A song called "Crosstown Traffic" was grinding away like a cakewalk for steam engines and steel barrels by the time the *Futurity* docked at its Folsom Street mooring. The strange and raucous music seemed perfectly suited to the crowded wharf, but Jesse was careful to remove the earbuds and conceal the device before any locals spotted him with it.

Ashore, they were met by a harried-looking City employee who escorted them through the busy terminal to the street, where a horse and a two-person buggy had been procured for them. Jesse took the reins, and before long they were fighting for a place in a merciless roil of carriages and carts. Elizabeth said, "Where are we headed?"

"California Street Hill."

"What's there?"

"The house where my sister lives."

"We're going to see your sister?"

"Yes."

"You know we're working a deadline, right?"

"I know."

"So is your sister going to help us find Theo and Mercy?"

"She might," Jesse said. "One way or another."

13

Elizabeth knew Jesse well enough to expect an explanation from him. She also knew he wouldn't give it to her until he was ready. So she relaxed, as much as it was possible to relax while clinging to the seat of a loosely sprung buggy as it was dragged up steep grades by an enthusiastically farting dray horse, and tried to enjoy the ride. There was architecture to look at. Weird old San Francisco architecture, especially as they worked their way from the tobacco-spit districts to the fancier environs of Nob Hill: big houses with stone turrets and what looked like minarets, window's walks, gabled roofs. Things architectural students would know about. The question she wanted to ask was: How had Jesse's sister, raised in a whorehouse, come to live in a wealthy neighborhood like this?

Jesse brought the rig to a stop near one of these grandiose stone piles, humming what sounded like a version of Hendrix's "Crosstown Traffic." Jesse had taken to Hendrix in a big way, surprisingly. Elizabeth would have put him down for country and western, maybe classic Dylan, but his tastes seemed more adventurous than that. Fortunately, the playlist she'd downloaded for him was eclectic: For all she knew he might develop a fondness for Kanye West or Taylor Swift. There was no predicting. Nor would she ever find out, given that tomorrow or the next day would be the last of their time together.

She didn't like to think about that, not least because it reminded her how precarious her own position was. She was going to be one of the last people to leave Kemp's 1877, no matter how well or badly this expedition turned out, which increasingly felt like being the last person out of a burning building. The road home was long, and it ran through an obstacle course of mountains, deserts, and hostile locals. Home, where Gabriella was waiting for her. Or forgetting about her.

She recalled something her drill instructor used to say: *One foot at a time.* Which meant, *Don't think too far ahead. Work the problem that's in front of you. Let other people worry about strategy.* So fine: The problem in front of her was Mercy Kemp. Or maybe the problem in front of her was Jesse, who had decided to pay a visit to his San Francisco relations instead of getting on with the search.

He said, "This house is where Phoebe lives. She lives with a woman named Hauser. Abigail Hauser. Have I mentioned her?"

"Obviously not."

"Abbie is my father's sister. My aunt."

"You have a wealthy aunt?"

"Aunt Abbie's a widow. Mr. Hauser was a partner in Hauser, Schmidt and Odette, a Washoe Valley mining firm. Very wealthy man. He was inspecting a dig near Virginia City when a steam pipe burst and scalded him to death. That was 1866. Aunt Abbie inherited his fortune, but most of it evaporated in the crash of '73. She still has the house, and she keeps up appearances, but don't be deceived. She's only a few pennies better off than the Tenderloin crowd. After my father was killed, this is where I brought Phoebe."

"I don't mean to pry or anything, but if your father was

related to a wealthy family, how come he was working as a bouncer in a whorehouse?"

"My father and Aunt Abbie weren't on speaking terms back then. But my father sent us up here for visits, sometimes for as much as a month at a time. It was his way of showing us that life that wasn't always hard and unforgiving. Aunt Abbie tried to give us an education, which I didn't always appreciate. But she has a big library, and I took advantage of it."

"Which I guess explains why your grammar is better than most of the local hires. You always did seem a little too polished for somebody who was raised on skid row."

"My father didn't neglect our education. We were raised decently enough."

"I'm not trying to insult anyone."

"Abigail Hauser is a Christian woman. A little stiff, but forward thinking and kind at heart. She has principles. I've told her a little about you—try not to shock her."

Jesse drove the buggy up to the front of the house and set the brake, and Elizabeth managed to climb down without snagging her ridiculous clothing on anything. She watched as he walked to the door and raised his fist to knock. It was hard to read his mood. Catch him at the right moment and he was one big human emoji, all joy or rage. But right now his face was blank. He knocked five times. A minute or more went by. Elizabeth adjusted her hat and tried to appreciate the breeze, which was blissfully free of the reek of the city below.

An Asian woman with a duster in her hand, presumably not Mrs. Hauser, opened the door. She gave Jesse a wide-eyed look.

"Hello, Soo Yee," Jesse said.

Soo Yee's pleasure at recognizing him evolved into what appeared to be equal parts fear and awe. "Jesse, Jesse, come in," she said, giving Elizabeth a sidelong glance: *You too, whoever you are.*

The entrance hall was cool and quiet, rich with sunlight filtered through panes of opalescent glass. A crystal vase holding cut flowers stood on a side table. Soo Yee was a small woman, and the sound of her footsteps on the oaken floor made Elizabeth think of water dripping from a palm leaf. "I'll tell Mrs. Hauser you're here," she said, disappearing down a shadowed hallway. Moments later Jesse's aunt emerged from a deeper part of the house.

"Aunt Abbie," Jesse said. Some complicated mix of emotions put a burr in his voice, though he was trying not to let it show. "I apologize for not telling you I was coming. There wasn't time to write."

Abigail Hauser was tall and lean. She wore a black bombazine dress and appeared to be in her forties, not young by the standards of 1877, but there was a liveliness and wariness in her eyes that Elizabeth immediately liked. "Jesse," she said, embracing him. "It's a surprise to see you, but a most welcome one. And you brought a friend!"

"This is Elizabeth DePaul. Elizabeth, my aunt, Abigail Hauser."

"Right," Elizabeth managed. "It's, uh, nice to meet you." No doubt failing some important test of etiquette, though Aunt Abbie gave her a genuine-seeming smile.

"This is the woman you wrote about in your letters?"

"Yes."

"Then I'm very pleased indeed to meet you, Miss DePaul. A woman from the twenty-first century! I'm not sure I know what to say . . . I feel quite out of place."

"I'm the one who's out of place. You can call me Elizabeth."

"Thank you, Elizabeth. I'm Abbie. Come into the parlor and sit down."

Abbie led them to a smaller room crowded with chairs and ornate sideboards. "Jesse, I know you'll want to see Phoebe. She's in her room, practicing her violin exercises. Soo Yee can fetch her."

"No," Jesse said, "I'll see Phoebe soon enough. I'm sorry if that sounds unsociable, but it can't be helped. As for Soo Yee, I want you to send her down to the city."

"What for?"

"To fetch Sonny Lau."

There was a silence. Abbie said, "Are things as bad as that?"

"Well, I don't know. They might be. You didn't tell me in your letters that Roscoe Candy is alive."

"No," Abbie said, "I didn't. We knew, of course. But I was reluctant to trouble you about it."

"Has he been a problem?"

"It was only last year that he emerged from the shadows. I have friends who watch the property market, and they noticed him making purchases in the less respectable parts of the city, just as he was accustomed to do before you shot him. Then Sonny Lau sent word that Candy was back in the Tenderloin, living in a low house with his band of thugs. He seldom appears in public, and no new murders have been attributed to him. If he knows anything about Phoebe, we've had no sign of it. Had there been even a hint of trouble, of course I would have contacted you at once."

"How did he survive, Aunt Abbie? He was gut-shot—pardon me for saying so."

"You needn't apologize for speaking plainly, least of all on this subject. I don't know how he survived. Lesser wounds have killed better men. A cruel joke on the part of nature, I suppose." Abbie took a bell from a side table and rang it. Soo Yee appeared a moment later. "Soo Yee, will you ask Randal to drive you into town, please? We need to speak to your brother."

"You want me to find Sonny?"

"Yes, please."

"And bring him back?"

"Yes. And I gather it's urgent. So go on now. Quickly, please."

Soo Yee hurried away. Jesse looked at his aunt and cleared his throat and said, "Perhaps I'll see Phoebe now."

"Go on. You know how to find her room, I imagine, even after all these years. Jesse?"

Jesse turned back.

"Are we in danger?"

"I wouldn't bring danger down on you. You know that, Aunt Abbie. I've always kept this house apart from the other aspects of my life."

And from me, Elizabeth thought.

Abbie said, "Are *you* in danger?"

"Not yet," he said.

Elizabeth listened to Jesse's footsteps as he mounted the stairs. There was a briefly audible bar or two of violin music, which must have been Jesse opening the door to his sister's room. Then silence.

Which left Elizabeth and Abbie in the parlor trying not to stare at each other. Elizabeth thought she ought to say something polite, but the best she could come up with was, "Thank you for welcoming me into your home."

Abbie smiled. "I could hardly have left you on the doorstep. Jesse has written me a little about you, Elizabeth. And I've followed stories about the City of Futurity as long as Jesse has been associated with it. But I never dreamt I might meet a woman from the twenty-first century. Is it true you're a soldier?"

"I served in the army, yeah. I mean yes."

"And you saw combat?"

"I was in signals intelligence. Not really front-line stuff. I was at a base in Iraq that took mortar fire a few times, but nothing serious. And that was a few years ago. I'm a civilian now."

"And you've voted in elections?"

"Sure, yeah."

"And is it true that a black man was elected to the presidency?"

"For two terms," Elizabeth said cautiously.

"Please don't think I disapprove. Before I married Mr. Hauser, I advocated for abolition. I've read Mr. Douglass's writings. And I pay attention to the controversy over women's rights—I'm a great admirer of Mrs. Stanton, though I disapprove of her statements against the Fourteenth Amendment." Abbie paused. "Do you understand me at all, Elizabeth?"

"I think so."

"I don't fear the future."

"Okay, good."

"Even if it includes something as alarming as marriage between persons of the same sex. Which Jesse has told me in his letters that it does. It's strange, of course, and I would be helpless to defend it to a clergyman, but I think I understand the logic of it. In fact I have a cousin who—but that's beside the point. What I mean to say, Elizabeth, is that I approve of you."

"Thanks."

"I'm not sure you approve of me, however. No, let me speak frankly. I'm not sure you *ought* to approve of me, especially if Jesse has told you anything about me."

"He hasn't said a whole lot, Mrs. Hauser—Abbie."

"My life illustrates the principle that it's easier to care for strangers than for members of one's own family. My brother Earl—Jesse's father—fell out of favor with our parents when I was just three years old. Earl was fifteen years my senior, and the reasons for his disgrace were never discussed with me, but it became obvious that he had married a woman not respectable enough to bring home. That would have been Jesse's mother. Earl sacrificed the prospect of a career in the family business for the sake of a woman he loved. Maybe that was foolish, maybe it was brave, but I was raised to see it as unacceptable, and I never questioned the verdict. If Earl ever tried to contact my parents, they didn't speak of it to me."

"That's harsh."

"It *was* harsh, but I didn't see it in that light. For me it was as if Earl had died in some mysterious, unspeakable way. I didn't hear from him—or, to be honest, think much about him—until I married Mr. Hauser. When our engagement was announced in the *Boston Daily Advertiser* I received a letter forwarded to me from the newspaper. The letter was from Earl. He offered his best wishes and he told me his wife had died. He said he was living in San Francisco, and that I had a nephew and a niece, Jesse and Phoebe. He supplied an address at which I could write to him."

"Did you?"

"I'm ashamed to say I did not. I was too vain—too naïve—and too much distracted by my new position as a wealthy man's wife. A few years passed. Mr. Hauser kept a home in Boston, but his business took him west more often than I liked. It suited us both to move to California, though it was a terribly long trip. The next time I gave any serious thought to Earl was when we took up residence in this house. I was all too aware that the address he had given me was within riding distance, in a part of town where nothing good ever happens. The knowledge began to weigh on my conscience. Eventually I relented and wrote him a note. A *brusque* note, but it told him I was in the city and that I hoped my niece and nephew were well."

"And he wrote back?"

"Almost at once, and he begged a favor from me. He said Jesse and Phoebe were healthy but in need of education and decent circumstances, neither of which he could provide. He wondered if they might be allowed to come live with me."

"That's a big ask."

"I've never heard it put that way—but yes, it certainly seemed like a 'big ask.' I resented it, and Mr. Hauser wouldn't hear of it. But Mr. Hauser passed away only a month later. We had no other family in the city. So, belatedly, I did what my conscience had been urging me to do. I couldn't take the children and raise them as my own, but I offered to take them periodically, especially if Earl thought they were at risk. He brought them to me a few days later. Their first visit lasted for six weeks, over the hottest part of the summer."

"It must have been strange, seeing your brother again after so many years."

"It surpassed strange. It was daunting. Chastening. Earl had lived a hard life. His clothes were ragged and his breath smelled of liquor. We spoke very briefly, and although we corresponded sporadically after that, we never became close. But I tried to think of my brother as a good-natured man who was walking a difficult path. His love of his children could not have been more obvious. He nearly wept when he left them with me."

"You got along with them okay?"

"They were wary at first, and so was I. Ultimately, yes, we got along. What they lacked in discipline they made up for in natural curiosity. But, Elizabeth—" Abbie bowed her head and clutched her hands in her lap. "I could have done so much more."

Women like Abbie had a vocabulary of hand and head gestures, explicitly feminine ways of expressing guilt or anger. Elizabeth couldn't fake that stuff and found it difficult to read. But Abbie's regret seemed authentic, as far as she could tell. "Phoebe lives here now, Jesse said."

"Phoebe has lived here since the day her father was murdered."

"When Jesse took her away from the burning, uh, house."

"Jesse and Sonny Lau brought her to me. I summoned the doctor who treated her."

"Sonny Lau is the Tong hatchetman?"

"Jesse's friend. And Soo Yee's brother. Yes. That was a terrible day. Phoebe's injuries were terrifying. The doctor is a war veteran, and he knows all the ways a human body can come to harm. But even he was shocked. He sewed her up as well as he could, but he couldn't save her left eye. Jesse left town after that, because he knew Candy's men might try to hunt him down and kill him, and he didn't want to lead them here. It was sheer luck he was hired by the City. Luck for Phoebe and for me, I mean. Every investment I inherited from Mr. Hauser more or less vanished in the financial crisis, and we would be in a difficult position if not for the money Jesse sends every month."

"But you can afford to keep Soo Yee as a servant."

"It was an agreement Jesse made with Sonny Lau. A job and, in effect, a Western education for Soo Yee, in exchange for which Sonny uses his familiarity with the criminal element to keep watch for any threat that might arise. If Candy's henchmen had started hunting for Phoebe or Jesse, Sonny would have warned us. And if we need to get in touch with Sonny, we can do so through Soo Yee."

"Like now," Elizabeth said. "So why do think Jesse wants to talk to Sonny?"

"I'm very much afraid to ask. Don't you know?"

The conversation was interrupted by the sound of footsteps: Jesse and Phoebe, coming downstairs.

Elizabeth had pictured Jesse's younger sister as shy and damaged. But it was obvious as soon as she entered the room that Phoebe wasn't shy. She went straight to Elizabeth and offered her hand, which Elizabeth shook. "You're the woman from the future!"

"Call me Elizabeth."

"Thank you! I'm Phoebe," said Phoebe.

Phoebe wore a blue silk scarf tied into a kind of skewed hijab that concealed the left side of her face. The only injury that showed was some scarring above her lip. But Phoebe's good eye was lively and alert, and her smile was obviously genuine. "Pleased to meet you," Elizabeth said.

"You're from the future."

"Yes."

"Have you ridden a flying machine?"

"Phoebe," Abbie said, "you mustn't put our guest through an inquisition."

"Oh, I'm sorry—"

"It's okay," Elizabeth said. "Yeah, I've ridden a few flying machines."

"How amazing!"

"You get used to it. At least, most people do. Not everybody likes flying. For me, there's almost always a moment when I look out the window and think, wow, I'm thirty thousand feet over Idaho or whatever."

"I'm sure I would feel the same way," Phoebe said. "And is it true your people are shipping pistols to the Indians?"

Abbie was visibly scandalized. But it didn't seem like an

unreasonable question, Elizabeth thought, given what had been in the newspapers. "Not 'our people' exactly. Those guns were smuggled through the City against regulations."

"Don't you support the cause of the Nez Percé? From what Jesse wrote about you, I thought you might."

"I don't know much about it. Where I come from, it's more or less agreed that the Indians got a bad deal. Worse than a bad deal. But I don't see how shipping them pistols is supposed to help."

"Apparently someone disagrees."

Apparently so, Elizabeth thought.

"Perhaps," Abbie said, "we can discuss something less contentious? Phoebe, why don't you tell Elizabeth about your study of the violin."

Which Phoebe proceeded to do, at length. It became a monologue about the difficulty of arranging lessons and her problem learning to hold the instrument correctly, with tacit reference to her facial disfigurement. Despite the relentless talk, or maybe because of it, a less confident Phoebe began to show through. Her shoulders tensed and her voice took on an anxious edge. Finally Abbie said, "*Thank* you, Phoebe."

Phoebe fell silent, looking abashed.

"I'd like to hear you play sometime," Elizabeth said.

Phoebe brightened. "Do you play an instrument?"

"No. I enjoy music, but I'm just a listener."

"What is it like, the music of the future?"

"Well, we have all kinds. Ask Jesse. He was listening to some of it today."

Phoebe turned her good eye on her brother. "How is that possible?"

Elizabeth said, "I gave him a thing that plays recorded music. It's in his pocket."

"May I see it?"

Jesse looked alarmed. "I don't think—I mean, the kind of songs it plays—"

"We don't have to play Hendrix for her," Elizabeth said. "I loaded all kinds of stuff on that iPod. Here, give it to me."

Jesse passed her the device, frowning. Elizabeth scrolled through the playlist. She had put together the contents with Jesse's taste in mind—or what she had imagined Jesse's taste might be—but she had also tried to include representative music, not just personal favorites. Songs that were big even if she didn't especially like them. So what was suitable for a teenage girl circa 1877? The sound track to Elizabeth's adolescence had included a lot of LL Cool J and Cypress Hill, maybe not the best choices. Pressed for time, she cued up Lady Gaga's "Born This Way." It was a song Elizabeth remembered only dimly, but it was up-tempo and optimistic and she guessed Phoebe would find the lyrics too obscure to be truly shocking. "You'll need to put these in your ears," Elizabeth said, holding up the earbuds. "I can help you."

Silence ensued. No one moved. Elizabeth was briefly bewildered. Then she realized Phoebe couldn't put the buds in her ears without taking off her scarf.

Finally Jesse said, "It's all right. Elizabeth knows what happened. Elizabeth was a soldier, Phoebe. She's seen all kinds of things."

Phoebe said, "Is that true?"

"Yes. But you don't have to do this if you don't want to."

"No. Please! I want to hear the music." Phoebe unwrapped her head in a single decisive motion, balling up the scarf in her lap. "There," she said defiantly. "Well? *Have* you seen worse?"

Elizabeth had once visited a friend at Landstuhl Regional, the big US military hospital in Germany. A guy named Felipe, a division MP. Shrapnel from a mortar had carved off his right arm and a chunk of his face. The surgeons had saved Felipe's life, but he was looking at the prospect of multiple rounds of prosthetic and reconstructive surgery. "Yep," Elizabeth said flatly. "I've seen worse. Okay, so these little plastic thingies? They go in your ears."

Phoebe's disfigurement was evidence of a vicious attack. From the number and pattern of the scars, it looked as if she had nearly been scalped. Her vacant eye socket had healed badly, with knots of scar tissue filling the violated space. "How strange," she said, taking the iPod in her hand. "How does it know when you touch it?"

"Beats me. You'd have to ask a geek. I mean, an expert."

"You don't know how it works?"

"I know how to work it, and I have a *vague* idea how it works, but I'm not an electronics engineer. It's like—you understand a steam engine, basically, right? But if I asked you what a particular piston or valve does . . ."

"Yes, I see. But how marvelous it is!"

"I'm going to keep the volume, the loudness, pretty low. You can adjust it if you want."

"What will I hear?"

"Just a song. Nothing fancy. A song that was popular once, back where I come from."

Elizabeth hit play.

What seemed to strike Phoebe first was the simple novelty of reproduced sound. She sat upright, openmouthed, unmoving. Then, a minute or so into the song, her fingers started to move—counting beats, Elizabeth guessed—and her O-mouth compressed into a fascinated smile. No one spoke as the song ran out its four minutes and change. By the time it finished, Phoebe was grinning. "It's wonderful! But it stopped."

"You can play it again if you like."

"May I?"

Elizabeth showed her how. The second time through, Phoebe

closed her eyes and tapped her buttonhook shoe against the floor. Abbie leaned toward Elizabeth and said, "She seems to enjoy it very much. Is it possible I could—?" She mimed putting earbuds into her ears.

"Of course," Elizabeth said. Assuming the iPod's battery was up for it.

She turned to Jesse then, thinking about the other tech devices in his bag—in particular, the radio that was their only real connection to Kemp's base at the Long Wharf in Oakland. Because another hour had passed, and they were no closer to finding Mercy Kemp. She would have to check in soon—what was she supposed to say? But the expression on Jesse's face stopped her.

Not that he was showing much obvious emotion. His stone-face emoji was fully engaged. But Elizabeth knew him well enough to read the clenched jaw, the rapid blinks. There was a lot going on inside him. Happiness at seeing his sister, she guessed. Pleasure at the way Phoebe responded to the music. But darker things, too. Echoes of his own trauma. Maybe guilt. Phoebe would spend a lifetime learning to deal with what had happened to her at the hands of Roscoe Candy, but Jesse would spend a lifetime dealing with the knowledge that he had failed to protect her from it.

So no need to mention August Kemp or the fucking radio. At least not right now.

Not until Sonny Lau showed up, which happened a couple of hours later.

14

Phoebe had changed in ways Jesse found both pleasing and dismaying.

Her disfigurement was no surprise. Her missing eye was a tragedy, and her other wounds had healed badly, but those marks and scars weren't what troubled him. Something nervous and wary had taken up residence inside her. She talked too eagerly, or not at all. She laughed as if laughter hurt her throat. Jesse supposed it was a symptom of the disease Elizabeth called PTSD. Jesse himself had caught it from his last encounter with Roscoe Candy, and it was natural that Phoebe, who was more sensitive, had come down with a more serious case. There was no easy cure, according to Elizabeth.

Jesse felt his own old rage churning inside him, faded memories suddenly burnished to a high shine. He nearly jumped out of his chair when Soo Yee came through the front door with Sonny Lau behind her. It was as if his years at City had never happened, as if he was still the whorehouse boy who ran with the *boo how doy*. Aunt Abbie stood up and said, "Come with me, Phoebe, we'll make ourselves useful in the kitchen. Elizabeth, would you like to join us?"

"No," Jesse said before Elizabeth could answer. "She stays."

His aunt and sister left the parlor by one door as Sonny entered by another. Jesse gave his old friend an evaluating look and got one in return. Sonny had become a man, thicker and more muscular than Jesse would have anticipated. And while he had always been a careful dresser, Sonny's taste in clothes appeared to have sharpened: He wore a knee-length frock coat, a poppy-red vest, and a silk four-in-hand tie. His braided queue dangled as far as his waist. If he was carrying knives or pistols, they were well concealed. Sonny put out his hand, and Jesse shook it.

Sonny spared a glance for Elizabeth. "Who's the woman?"

"She works for the City of Futurity," Jesse said, "just like me."

"I heard as much." Sonny's English was deliberately, almost aggressively formal. "Is she from the future?"

"She is."

"I would have thought she'd be wearing trousers or smoking a cigar."

"Pass on the cigar," Elizabeth said. "But yeah, I wish I'd packed a pair of jeans."

"Can we speak in her presence?"

"Yes."

"Freely?"

"Yes."

"Without being interrupted?"

"Well, I hope so," Jesse said.

"Good. I expect you called me here to talk about Roscoe Candy?"

"That," Jesse said. "But not *just* that."

"What else?"

By way of an answer Jesse reached into his calico travel bag and took out a Glock 19 and set it down on one of Aunt Abbie's gleaming sideboards. "Have you ever seen a pistol like this one?"

Sonny Lau stared at it. "What an interesting question."

Sonny didn't know how Roscoe Candy had survived his gunshot wound. It must have been a near thing, he said, because after the burning of Madame Chao's whorehouse Candy had disappeared for almost three years. And when he did eventually turn up, consolidating his old San Francisco properties and occasionally strutting down Market Street with a cohort of Sacramento thugs in striped jerseys, he was gaunter and grayer than he had been before. Tong men who had dealt with him said Candy still suffered chronic pain from his wound and was obliged to wear a truss he had ordered all the way from Chicago. None of this had improved his temperament, though it had changed him subtly. Candy had once seemed to delight in his own wickedness, but the new Roscoe Candy was differently vicious: He hurt people more methodically and with less emotion. He still cut his victims, Sonny said, but now he cut them as professionally and as indifferently as a butcher cuts a beeve.

None of which meant Candy had forgotten about Jesse Cullum. As soon as Candy was back in San Francisco he had offered a generous reward to anyone who spotted Jesse or could provide news of his whereabouts. "He expected you to come back sooner or later," Sonny said, "as a dog returns to its vomit. Have you been seen?"

"I only just arrived."

"Candy has eyes all over town. That's something you'll have to reckon with, if you stay. Especially if you stay *here*."

"I won't be staying here."

Sonny cocked his head. "You didn't come back just because of Roscoe Candy, did you?"

"No."

"He's only a complication."

"I hope that's all he is."

"Soo Yee could have told you most of what I just told you. I thought you called me here because you wanted help going up against Candy. But that's not it. So what *do* you want from me?"

Jesse didn't answer, only glanced at the pistol on the sideboard as if it were an explanation. Sonny said, "Ah, that. May I hold it?"

"Go ahead."

Sonny picked up the Glock, keeping his fingers away from the trigger guard. He weighed it in his hands, puzzled over the clip, admired the metalwork. "It's a well-made thing. As pretty as it is dangerous. A City thing."

"Seen one before?"

"Not with my own eyes."

"Heard of one?"

Sonny nodded slowly. "I'm not supposed to say. But yes. Little Tom has one. The heads of the other Six Companies also claim to have one."

Jesse exchanged a look with Elizabeth, whose expression was a gratifying combination of genuine surprise and oh-I-get-it-now. "They acquired these pistols recently?"

"I don't know, but I first heard of them a month ago."

"How did they come to possess them?"

"About that, no one speaks. Why? Do you want me to find out?"

"I'm looking for the man who brought these guns into the city."

"Again, why? What's your business with him?"

"He doesn't belong here, Sonny. He needs to go back where he came from."

"Are you a bounty hunter now?"

"Bounty hunter for the City, you could say."

"The City of Futurity is drying up faster than spit in a desert. You must be in a hurry to find this man."

"We are. And I don't like to impose on our friendship by asking for more than you're willing to give, but—"

Sonny Lau said, "You're not my friend."

Jesse was startled. "Say that again?"

"Honestly, what's Jesse Cullum to me? I have lots of friends. Most of them know better than to ask difficult favors of me. But you're not my friend. You may be older now, but you're still just a shirttail whorehouse bouncer with shoulders like a buffalo's and cast-iron balls. A worthless piece of Tenderloin shit with more pride than sense. You want me to risk my reputation and my career by poking my nose into the business of people who could have me killed just for looking at them the wrong way? I wouldn't do that for a friend. No true friend would ask. Only an impertinent bastard like Jesse Cullum would ask." He grinned. "And Jesse Cullum's one of the few people I would do it for."

Now that the conversation had passed on to mutually congratulatory masculine bullshit and reminiscences, Elizabeth gave herself permission to leave the room. She took the bag of tech gear with her, after putting the Glock back inside.

Abbie Hauser's mansion was big but Elizabeth got the feeling that a lot of the rooms had been closed off and abandoned. There were, as far as she could tell, two live-in servants, Soo Yee and a middle-aged black man, Randal, who had put in a brief appearance after driving Soo Yee to town and back. A staff of two was probably picayune stuff by Nob Hill standards. Abbie and Phoebe were in the kitchen helping Soo Yee fix the evening meal, something that probably didn't happen in the tonier households.

Elizabeth retreated to the entrance hall, where she took the clunky two-way radio from the bag and pushed the button to connect her to August Kemp. He must have been waiting for the call, because there was no hesitation, just a flat electronic beep followed almost instantly by his voice: "Elizabeth? Where are you?"

"Somewhere up Nob Hill, actually."

"You have something to tell me?"

"Just that we're making progress."

"What's that mean?"

"We have a lead."

"You found Mercy?"

"Not yet, but we have a line on somebody who's been distributing Glocks, presumably Theo Stromberg."

"Do you know whether Mercy's with him?"

"We're working on that assumption, but we don't know for sure."

"How soon can you find out?"

"It depends on our informant. I doubt we'll find out much more until tomorrow." Which might be absurdly optimistic, but she wasn't sure Kemp could bear the weight of the truth right now.

What followed was a pause so lengthy she began to suspect the radio was defective. "The thing is," Kemp finally said, "there have been some developments. Major upheaval. Rail strikes everywhere, malcontents greasing the tracks and fucking with signal lights. The Chicago yard workers are coming out in sympathy. Worse, Hayes has mobilized federal troops to arrest me and occupy the City."

"Can they do that?"

"Not before we evacuate. We can hold them off. But it's making everything a lot more difficult. Pretty much every editorial writer in the Union blames us for instigating a labor revolt and a race war, thanks in large part to Theo fucking Stromberg. I had to send the last City train back to Chicago this afternoon."

"You—what?"

"Don't worry. I have other means of extracting us when the time comes."

Suddenly all Elizabeth could think about was Gabriella. A thousand miles of physical distance and a century and a half of Hilbert space stood between Elizabeth and her daughter, a divide deeper than any of those misty Sierra Nevada canyons they had crossed on the way here. Now Kemp was telling her he had torched the only bridge. "*Other means?*"

"Look, obviously I have no intention of being stranded. I'll get you home, Elizabeth. You and Mercy both. I promise. But first, you have to find Mercy."

Elizabeth mulled over the news while Jesse said good-bye to Sonny Lau. The tong man left with barely a glance at her, probably confused about the role a badly dressed white woman might have to play in this game of guns and threats. She was a little confused about it herself.

She wanted to tell Jesse what Kemp had said, but they were called to dinner before she could speak to him privately. It was a lengthy meal—Soo Yee served each course with great ceremony, and Jesse made a point of praising everything—but to Elizabeth it just seemed like Something Soup followed by rounds of Boiled Something. *Other means*, she kept thinking. Soo Yee turned up the gaslights as daylight faded (here was something else that made Elizabeth feel uneasy, all these little fires burning in their sconces like promissory notes of disaster), and Abbie began to talk about the future. Or, as she pronounced it, *The Future*, the words spoken reverently, as if she were talking about a sacred grotto in some Greek myth. "I think some people resent the City of Futurity because they feel chastised by it, especially since those rogue letters have been published. But I wonder if that's fair. If there is such a thing as moral progress, the future will inevitably seem to admonish us for our sins."

The remark was meant to be flattering, or at least to communicate Abbie's open-mindedness, but it sounded too much like the kind of high-minded bullshit August Kemp's copywriters produced for the press back home. "I'm not admonishing anybody," Elizabeth said.

"No, Elizabeth, of course not. All I mean to say is that, for instance, concerning the rights of women—"

"Okay, *stop*. I mean, there's some truth in what you're saying. I can vote, which is great, and we don't get yellow fever and we don't hang people for stealing horses, but the idea that what I have waiting for me back home is some kind of Utopia? *No*. Sorry." This wasn't how polite conversation was supposed to go, but Elizabeth felt as if she had lost the ability to steer the words, much less stop them. She flashed on all the times when her friend Chanelle had come over to the house, Friday nights when Gabriella was still in her crib, how they would share a couple of glasses of wine or even a joint (furtively, in the bathroom, with the ventilator fan turned up to carry away the smoke) and complain about Elizabeth's jailed husband or Chanelle's troubles as a Walmart sub-manager, letting the indignation boil over until it turned into laughter or tears. "It's true I was a soldier, but you have no idea what it means being a woman in the armed forces, the kind of crap you put up with on a daily basis, and sometimes worse than crap, sometimes very much worse, and good fucking luck if you try to complain about it. I'm a veteran and a single mom, and the reason I'm here isn't because I enjoy outdoor plumbing and coal smoke. It's because this is the only job that'll pay the rent on my falling-apart house and buy groceries for me and Gabriella and maybe leave enough after taxes that I can think about moving as far as possible from my crazy ex before he gets out of prison. Which is something else we have a lot of—prisons—though you won't hear Kemp boasting about it. We also have wars, not big scary wars but little wars that go on for years and years and never seem to accomplish anything. Wars without victory, whatever victory would amount to. And good luck if you come home needing help, because the VA hospitals—they, uh—"

Jesse and his aunt Abbie were staring. So was Phoebe. Even Soo Yee had gone stock-still in the servants' doorway. Elizabeth's urge to talk evaporated as suddenly as it had come.

"I'm sorry," she finished. "I mean, if I used offensive language."

Silence followed, one of those weighty silences that accompany a weapons-grade breach of etiquette, until Phoebe spoke up: "Jesse said in his letters that even the best people of the future are freer with their language than we're accustomed to. He made it sound quite comical, the way he described it."

"Yeah, well, maybe not so comical at the dinner table. I apologize. It's been a long day."

"He often wrote about the unusual words he heard at the City of Futurity. Didn't you, Jesse?"

"The printable ones," Jesse said stiffly.

"And I committed them to memory," Phoebe said. Elizabeth was chastened by how hard the girl was working to make her feel better. "*Smartphone. Video game. Cool* and *uncool.* Elizabeth?"

"Yes?"

Phoebe's smile curved under her scarf, up into the papery white scar tissue there. "I think you're cool," she said. "I think you're *awesome.*"

15

In the morning Jesse prepared to venture into the lower part of the city. He left the buggy he had arrived in with the servant Randal and arranged to borrow Aunt Abbie's more spacious carriage and two horses from the stables.

He had slept apart from Elizabeth even though it might have been their last night together. It couldn't be helped—Aunt Abbie's views on courtship were modern but not infinitely elastic—and he wasn't sure Elizabeth would have wanted his company in any case. The news that Kemp had sent the last train east had unnerved her. She was worried about getting caught on the wrong side of the Mirror. It was a reasonable fear, but it had made her sullen and temperamental. When he asked whether she had slept well, she said, "Not really. Nice bed and all, but this mansion? The wallpaper, those creepy little bronze statues everywhere? It looks like every haunted house in every horror movie that ever came out of Hollywood."

Jesse couldn't imagine a home as spacious and well-appointed as Aunt Abbie's ever seeming haunted, a word he associated with séances and European castles, though Elizabeth might have a point about the statuary—he remembered his own uneasy fascination with the miniature bronze of the Capitoline Wolf on the table at the top of the stairs.

He hoped Elizabeth's judgment hadn't been affected by recent events. In truth, he wasn't sure how helpful her presence would be. She was a deft hand with a pistol, he had learned that from experience, but they might need to go places where a woman would be unwelcome or outrageously conspicuous. But nor could he proceed without her. Kemp had sent her on this mission for many reasons, not the least of which was to make sure Jesse persisted in it.

Jesse told his aunt and his sister he'd be back to see them soon. Probably he would. But first he had to find Miss Mercy Kemp and deliver her to her wealthy father. And after that— unless he wanted to live the rest of his life in abject fear—he would have to come to terms with Mr. Roscoe Candy.

Only then could he consider the future. Not the City future, not the flying-machine future. His own future.

Should he have one.

He had arranged to meet Sonny Lau at noon in a trinket shop off Dupont Street.

Jesse adjusted his slouch hat to shade his face, but he felt vulnerable and exposed holding the reins as the carriage rattled down California Street. After four years at the City of Futurity, the streets of San Francisco seemed both utterly strange and intimately familiar. As they approached Chinatown he half expected to see his younger self darting through the crowds, all the red-painted doorways once again known to him, the cellar cigar-rollers, the eating houses with smoked ducks and pigs' heads hanging in their windows, the houses where you could buy a bit's worth of twice-laid opium, the noisy Chinese theaters, the gambling houses with their spring-lock doors: a foreign land that was simultaneously his native land. San Francisco defied geography the way the City of Futurity defied time.

Editorial writers liked to play up its squalor, but by daylight the Chinese quarter was safe enough to walk through and attracted plenty of white tourists. Jesse braked the rig at a curb not far from the trinket shop where he was supposed to meet Sonny. He wished now that they had arranged to meet at a place where Jesse was less likely to be recognized—Cliff House, say, or Woodward's Gardens. But the trinket shop was busy and there were enough tourists in it to make the presence of another white man and woman unremarkable. The proprietor, an old man with a queue that dangled below his waist, nodded at Jesse, exchanged a few words with his equally ancient wife in what Jesse recognized as Dupont Gai dialect, then disappeared behind a beaded curtain. Moments later the curtain parted again, just long enough for Sonny Lau to beckon Jesse and Elizabeth inside.

Beyond the curtain was a small room furnished with a simple table and a few scuffed chairs. Sonny was courteous enough to pull out one of those chairs for Elizabeth, though he gave her the same puzzled look he had given her yesterday. "I talked to Little Tom," he said.

His See Yup boss. "About the pistols?"

"Yes. He owns one. And he knows where it came from. Each of the heads of the Six Companies received one, along with a letter saying the Companies need to unite because we're going to be attacked by Kearneyite mobs and the police."

This was the connection Jesse had come to the city hoping to discover. His hope had rested on three established facts. The first fact was that Theo Stromberg was physically present in San Francisco. The second fact was that Theo liked to send Glocks to parties he considered oppressed and endangered.

The third fact was that San Francisco's Chinese population fell into that category. Kearneyites and others had been stirring up mob warfare against the Chinese for years. So, Jesse had reasoned, there was at least a chance Theo had sent weapons to the Six Companies.

But none of that would matter if Theo had been careful enough to cover his tracks. "Is that all?"

"You think Little Tom would waste his time talking to me if there wasn't more to it? I told him there's a man from the City who wants to find out who mailed the guns."

"You mentioned me?"

"Not by name, but I had to tell him something. Little Tom is curious by nature, and the pistol aroused his curiosity as soon as it came into his hands. Like you, he wanted to know where it came from."

"And did he find out?"

"Yes."

"He knows how to find Theo Stromberg?"

"Yes. And it didn't take him long to make a connection between Theo Stromberg and those letters the newspapers have been publishing. But that was as far as he took it. Little Tom doesn't see anything to be gained by involving himself in the business of the City of Futurity."

"I don't care about Little Tom. It's Theo we want. Can you give us a street address?"

"Make an offer."

"What do you mean?"

"If you want this man, offer us something in return."

"What's the going price for that kind of information?"

"Make an offer, I'll take it to Little Tom, and if it's acceptable he'll tell you what you want to know."

"I can't dicker at one remove. I don't know anything about

Company bosses or what they want. The only Chinamen I know are highbinders and sing-song girls—no offense."

Elizabeth spoke up: "This Little Tom, does he *like* his Glock?"

Sonny gave her a condescending stare. "I believe he does."

"Would he like another one? Suppose we offered him another pistol from the future, a different kind. You think he might take that in trade?"

"You have such a thing?"

"Yes."

Sonny Lau looked at Jesse. Jesse thought about the contents of the calico travel bag and guessed she was talking about a Taser. Jesse had taken Taser training when he was hired as City security. It was an unimpressive weapon, in his opinion. "Tell Little Tom we'll give him an X3 handheld electroshock weapon in exchange for the whereabouts of Mr. Theo Stromberg. Tell him it's the only X3 in the state of California."

Sonny looked skeptical. "Is there really such a pistol?"

"Yes."

"When can you bring it?"

"Whenever he's willing to make the exchange. The sooner the better, from our point of view."

"Better for us, too. All this talk about mobs, it's not just talk. Last night there was a big crowd at the sandlots, screaming about burning down Chinatown. Tonight it might be more than talk. Meet me back here, two hours."

Jesse's pocket watch had been given to him by August Kemp especially for this job. The watch looked like any other cheap pocket watch, but its inner workings were digital, meaning the watch didn't tell time so much as calculate it. It was more reliable than a conventional watch, but it ticked just as loudly, for the sake of verisimilitude. Jesse took note of the time as he left the trinket shop. Two hours. He wondered if Sonny owned a reliable watch.

Elizabeth climbed aboard the carriage, still struggling against the bulk of her counterfeit dress, and Jesse drove them from Dupont Street to a place near Market, a nameless alley next to a draper's warehouse. The alley wasn't much wider than the carriage itself, but it was usefully private. Brick walls blocked the sunlight and kept the air cool, as if the morning's fog had lingered in the shadows. It was a place where no one would see them, a place where they could speak freely. He said, "It's like that double exposure you told me about."

"What?"

"You once told me about a double exposure—two photographs developed on one paper."

"I know what a double exposure is. What about it?"

"All this neighborhood seems like a double exposure to me. Familiar but strange. Do you take my meaning? But maybe it isn't the neighborhood. Maybe it's me. Maybe I'm the double exposure. That boy who lived in a Tenderloin parlor house, and whatever the City of Futurity made of me."

"We're both double exposures, in that case."

"Are we?"

"That's what the City does to you. Last time I was home, back in North Carolina, it felt like I was the one out of place. I mean, God knows I don't belong *here*—no offense—but it was like I didn't belong *there*, either."

"What you said at the table last night, about the future—is it really so bad?"

"I was just tired of Abbie looking at me like I'm the ambassador from Utopia. I should have kept my mouth shut."

"But is it as bad as you said?"

"I don't know. It depends. Not necessarily. But it's definitely not paradise."

"I figured that out quite a while ago. If the world you come from was paradise, you wouldn't be such a cool hand with a pistol." He tried to think of a way to speak his thoughts that wouldn't seem sentimental or maudlin or offensive. "So you're not the ambassador from Utopia, and Dupont Street sure as hell isn't paradise lost. But I'm glad you could see a little of the place where I grew up. We're what the world makes us, Elizabeth. Two cities made me, Futurity and San Francisco. And it pleases me that you exist in both of them."

Her expression made Jesse suspect he had not entirely avoided sentimentality. "You know," she said, speaking softly but startling him nonetheless, "it's going to burn."

"What?"

"San Francisco. All these buildings, Jesse. All of them. First an earthquake, then the fire."

"Truly?"

"Truly."

"When?"

"In 1906. April, I think, but I'm not absolutely sure. I should have Googled it when I was back home. But if you're still here, twenty-nine years from now? Take a spring vacation."

He looked away. There was a Kearneyite handbill plastered to the brick wall beside him, one of many such he had seen this afternoon. It advertised tonight's mass meeting at the sandlots. Beside it was another handbill, written in Chinese letters. He couldn't read it, but he recognized it as a *chung hong*—an announcement of impending war. "We might not have to wait thirty years," he said, "to see it burn."

Back at the trinket shop, the owner waved Jesse and Elizabeth through the beaded curtain to the room where Sonny Lau was already waiting. Sonny's expression was somber, and Jesse wondered whether he ought to expect bad news.

Sonny said, "Do you have the pistol?"

Elizabeth took the Taser from the calico bag. The Taser was an awkward weapon and not a lethal one—both drawbacks, in Jesse's opinion. It would incapacitate a man briefly but make an enemy of him for life. But he didn't share these reservations with Sonny, whose eyes widened at the sight of the thing. It had a suitably intimidating appearance: black and yellow, fang-toothed, ready to spit venom.

Sonny weighed the Taser in his hands as Jesse explained how to operate it. It required no ammunition, he said, but what he did not say was that it would need recharging, which would be impractical for another half century or so. Sonny said, "I'm instructed by my employer to make the exchange if the weapon seems authentic."

"It's authentic, all right. They don't come any more authentic than this one."

"All right," Sonny said. "If you say so."

"So you can tell me where to find Theo Stromberg?"

"Little Tom traced the package containing the pistol to its source, if that's what you're asking."

Elizabeth spoke up: "How do you trace a package in this day and age?"

"Bribery," Sonny said, giving her his by now familiar look of bewildered condescension, "and the threat of violence. How else?"

"Where is he, then?" Jesse asked.

"Little Tom was surprised to discover that the package had been sent by a man living in a hotel on Montgomery Street south of Market. Not the worst hotel in the city by a long stretch, but nothing like the best. The man has been living there for more than a year, along with a woman he calls his wife."

"Did Tom or any of his men approach him?"

"My employer kept this knowledge to himself. At first he assigned men to watch the hotel, hoping to learn something more revealing. But the man and his wife spend most of their time in each other's company. They leave the hotel for meals, or to take long aimless walks, or to attend the theater. The man often mails letters, though he never seems to receive any. He pays his rent promptly. Little Tom saw no advantage and much risk in attempting to contact him. Does that sound like the man you're looking for?"

"Close enough. All we need is an address."

Sonny Lau passed over a folded slip of paper, and Jesse put it in his pocket.

The business was done. Sonny tucked the Taser into a leather carry-all. "I'd lay low for a while after this, if I were you. Little Tom asked a lot of questions."

"What did you tell him?"

"Only as much as I had to. I told him someone I knew had been hired by the City of Futurity to hunt for a fugitive. That you had approached me and asked me to negotiate this exchange. I invented a name for you. But curiosity has been aroused. I may have been followed here. You ought to know that."

"It doesn't matter." Or so Jesse hoped. "I thank you for taking the risk."

"There's always risk. Risk is unimportant, as long as the house won't be endangered." The house on California Street, Sonny meant: Phoebe and Aunt Abbie and Randal and Soo Yee.

"Good," Jesse said, standing.

"You're happy with what I brought you?"

The address on the paper might be fraudulent, though Jesse doubted Little Tom would stoop to hustling a City agent. Or it could be a trap. Roscoe Candy had business connections with the See Yups, though they didn't love him. But if anyone could be trusted, it was Sonny Lau. "I'm in your debt."

They shook hands then, more as old friends than to seal the bargain, but Sonny still looked troubled. Jesse said, "Are *you* in danger?"

"No more than any of us. Today the highbinders are tying up their queues and sharpening their hatchets. Try to be somewhere else after dark."

The handshake ended. Sonny turned to Elizabeth and made a curt bow. "Pleased to have made your acquaintance."

"Likewise," Elizabeth said.

Jesse left the carriage at a livery stable on Market and walked with Elizabeth to the address they had been given. It was a three-story hotel on Montgomery near Market, just as Sonny Lau had said: not the plush Grand Hotel, which had impressed a younger Jesse as probably the finest hotel in all creation, or the even plusher Palace, which had been constructed in his absence. The Royal, as it was called, was older, less elegant, not exactly shabby but as close as it could get to that description while justifying the price of its rooms. The lobby smelled of oiled wood and boiled cabbage, halfway between a church and a cookhouse. The clerk behind the desk was a bald man with a vast gray beard and pitiless eyes. He looked at Jesse and Elizabeth, and at the calico travel bag in Jesse's hand, and seemed to find their presence in his domain plausible if not entirely convincing. "A room for you and your lady, sir?"

The price he quoted seemed high, but renting a room was

the easiest way to gain access to the upper floors, and in any case it was Kemp's money they were spending, not their own. Jesse didn't want to put his true name on the register, so he signed as "John Comstock and Wife." He was aware of the tension in Elizabeth's body as she waited, the way she scanned the empty lobby as if it might at any moment fill up with hostile forces, wary as a lioness closing in on her prey.

"So do we knock on the door?" she asked as they climbed the stairs, having waved off a disappointed elderly bellboy. According to Sonny's information, the room in which Theo and Mercy were staying was on the third floor. Number 316. "Or do we knock the door down?"

"Might as well knock first," Jesse said. "See where it goes from there. Assuming anybody's home."

At the third-floor landing he took a pistol from the travel bag and made sure it was loaded and ready to fire. Elizabeth did the same, keeping the weapon in her hand but concealing it against the billow of her day dress. Outside the door marked 316, Jesse put the bag on the floor within easy reach. He glanced at Elizabeth, who nodded her readiness. *Now we come to the cusp of the thing*, Jesse thought. He kept the pistol in his left hand and knocked on the door with the knuckles of his right. Four sharp raps.

Long seconds passed. Then the latch rattled and the door opened inward, revealing a young woman. Mercy Kemp. She fit the description and matched all the pictures in the dossier. She was tall, like so many of these twenty-first-century women. She wore a pale yellow dress of no particular distinction. Her blond hair was shorter than most women wore it. Her face was flawlessly symmetrical and her skin was almost supernaturally unblemished. "Yes?"

Jesse said, "Miss Mercy Kemp?"

"You must be from the City." She turned away and called out, "Theo! They're here."

It seemed prudent, as they came inside and closed the door behind them, to keep their weapons visible. But Theo Stromberg offered no resistance. "What were you expecting," he asked, nodding at Jesse's pistol, "a fire fight? You won't need that."

"I hope not. But I'll hang on to it for the time being."

Mercy and Theo stood together by the room's long window as if framed in a photograph. Theo Stromberg, for all the deviltry he had committed, looked about as menacing as a hummingbird. He was a wiry man, and he gave the impression that there wasn't quite enough of him to fill his clothes. He was clean-shaven and dark-haired and nervous. Like Mercy, Theo would not have seemed remarkable if you passed him on the street. But put these two together and they looked unmistakably like visitors from the future—unformed, too perfectly made, lacking all the scars and marks that distinguish real people from store-window mannequins.

On top of a bureau was a leather travel bag, open but almost fully packed. Most of what it contained was women's clothing, presumably Mercy's wardrobe. "Getting ready to go somewhere?"

"Yeah," Theo said amicably. "Home."

It wasn't clear what he meant by that. Elizabeth said, "We're here to take you into custody."

"Fine, good," Theo said.

Mercy added, "We expected my father to send someone. I'm surprised it took so long. We're finished here. We're ready to go with you."

"Another day and you'd have missed us," Theo said. "We

figured we should head east before the strikes shut down rail service west of the Mississippi."

Elizabeth said, "You're telling us you're willing to go back?"

"We don't want to be stranded here. That was never part of the plan. So when we heard the news—"

"What news?"

Theo looked at Mercy, Mercy looked at Theo. Theo pointed at a copy of the *Chronicle* lying on a chair, pages askew. Jesse took his eyes off his nominal captives long enough to spot the pertinent headline at the top of a long column of dense type:

FEDERAL TROOPS BESIEGE CITY OF FUTURITY

Elizabeth didn't trust the apparent docility of the captives—if Theo had offered even a hint of resistance she would have been happy to put him in wrist restraints—but she left them under Jesse's surveillance and took the radio into an adjoining room.

She pictured her signal bouncing from Montgomery Street to Oakland, flying across the bay like a weightless bird, outstripping the ferries and freight boats. Radio before Marconi. She guessed Marconi was just an Italian kid in short pants circa 1877, if he had even been born yet. Something else she could Google at her leisure, if she ever got home.

A voice she didn't recognize answered her call and told her to stay on the air. Then there was an interval of noise, cosmic rays crackling down from distant stars, until Kemp's voice drowned it out. "Elizabeth? What's your status?"

"We have her."

A pause. Then, "Thank God. Oh, Christ. It was a close thing, Elizabeth, I won't shit you about that."

"We have Theo, too. They both say they're willing to come back. No argument."

"Theo's a liar. Don't take him at his word. Especially not as long as my daughter is under his influence."

"Understood. But I'm assuming you want us to bring them both in."

"Obviously, but it's Mercy who matters. Keep that in mind."

"We will."

"Okay. Things are a little chaotic here—"

"It was in the papers," Elizabeth said, "about the siege."

"We're dealing with it. It's not as bad as it sounds. Fucking reporters, half the time they're just making shit up. It's true Hayes has an infantry brigade at the gate. Some laid-off local employee told the Chicago papers about the attempt on Grant's life—Congress and the press are making a big deal of it, on top of everything else. But we still have a few friends in high places. We'll make it back safely, I promise, but time is tight."

"So what happens next?"

"We're dealing with local hostility here on the Oakland side. The City's docks and property are more or less under police control right now, so we're working out of private facilities the authorities don't know about. Getting you out of San Francisco is going to be a little tricky. We should be able to have an unmarked boat for you at the Market Street wharf by nine tonight, but we're still working out the details. Can you stay where you are for another few hours?"

Elizabeth wasn't sure how to answer that. Jesse might have stirred up a hornets' nest by bartering with the tongs. But it was hard to imagine hired killers storming the Royal Hotel. "I guess we can sit tight."

"Stay by the radio and be ready to move when you get the word. How far are you from the docks?"

"Jesse would know better than I do, all this horse traffic, but maybe half an hour, three-quarters of an hour?"

"Okay, noted. As for Jesse, tell him he'll be paid when you deliver Mercy to the boat. He doesn't need to come across the bay with her. Once I have my daughter back, his work is done. And that's the last you'll see of him. Understood?"

"Understood," she said, hating him for making her say it.

Jesse didn't like the idea of waiting in the hotel for orders from Kemp. This was a place known to his enemies, and every instinct he had learned as a bouncer's boy told him to keep moving and stick to the shadows.

But orders were orders. He was only hired help, and he would be hired help for a few hours more, until Kemp, or someone from the City, paid him off with a bag of double eagles and a handshake. Then he would be his own man again. And Elizabeth would go home to her daughter. And the rest of his life, which seemed to Jesse like an ominous void waiting to be filled, could begin.

In the meantime there was nothing to do but sit at the window of the hotel room and watch the sun creep down behind a billboard advertising Kopp's Pills for Cough and Grippe. It was the time of day when San Francisco's respectable citizens began heading for their comfortable homes and lockable doors, while everyone else—that is to say, the city's majority—prepared to conduct the kind of business that thrives after dark. Elizabeth, seated across the room from Theo and Mercy and cradling her pistol in her lap, seemed not to want to talk. But Jesse was bored and saw no reason to suppress his curiosity about the two runners. He'd talked to many runners in the course of his work, and he didn't despise them as a class. So when Theo ventured to ask a question—"How exactly did you find us?"—Jesse said, "The City tracked you to San Francisco. There must have been postmarks on some of those letters you sent."

"That's not surprising. And we weren't exactly hiding. But how'd you track us to the Royal?"

"Talked to one of the Six Companies. They like to know the whereabouts of the people they do business with."

"Okay, I get that, but how did you connect us to the Six Companies?"

"The weapons you've been giving away tend to end up in the hands of people with grievances. Hereabouts, that's one of two groups—Chinamen and wage workers. I happen to know some people in Chinatown, so that's where we started. If that didn't pan out I would have talked to the Kearneyites."

"What if I hadn't given pistols to either group?"

"Then we wouldn't have found you so quick, and you wouldn't be going home."

"Well," Theo said in his piping voice, "you're wrong on two counts. One, I would never put a weapon in the hands of the Kearneyites. Denis Kearney talks a lot about the working man, but he's a fucking racist. The way it worked out where I come from, Kearneyite mobs attacked the Chinese and a lot of innocent people got killed. It seems likely to happen here just the same. Second, I have no desire to stay behind after the Mirror closes. If that's what August Kemp thinks, he has no idea what I'm all about."

"He thinks you'll face legal trouble if you go home."

"He can bring charges, sure, but on fairly trivial grounds— transporting dangerous goods, trespassing on City property. The weapons I arranged to smuggle through the Mirror were legally purchased, and there's no law about what I can do with them on this side. I mean, Kemp imported weapons, too, in the hands of his security people. They say a local was killed by City agents at Futurity Station last year. Is Kemp going to answer for that? No—not back home, not in a court of law. Given that, does he really want to initiate a lawsuit that'll put *my* testimony into the public record? I *hope* he does, but I doubt he's that stupid."

Jesse didn't react when Theo mentioned the man killed at Futurity Station. Nor did Elizabeth. But it raised a question. He said, "Some of those Glocks ended up in the wrong hands, didn't they?"

The glow of moral certainty vanished from Theo's face. "Not everyone in my supply chain was reliable. I had to work with locals and low-level City employees. The guns were never supposed to be more than symbolic. One pistol, one clip, a dramatic way of proving to the people I wrote to that the warnings I sent them really came from the future. But more weapons came across than I ever intended."

"A piece or two got sold that shouldn't have, in other words."

"Apparently."

"Private buyers."

"I suppose so."

"Including the man who tried to shoot Ulysses S. Grant. Which is another reason you might be eager to get out of 1877."

Theo didn't have an answer for that.

Out on the street, the shadows had grown and merged. The air was still, the sky the color of blue ink. A horse car rattled up Montgomery. From time to time, passing men glanced up at the hotel. Jesse said to Elizabeth, "Too many people know this room number. We already rented a room upstairs—we should go there."

He was afraid she might accuse him of paranoia, a twenty-first-century word for unreasonable fear (and apparently a common malady in that world). But she nodded curtly. "Good thought."

Mercy Kemp looked at her bag. "I can finish packing—"

Jesse said, "You won't need all that, and we'll travel lighter without it."

She gave it a moment's thought and shrugged. *Sensible attitude,* Jesse thought. Moments later they were in a nearly identical room one floor up. According to his pocket watch, another hour had passed without further word from August Kemp.

It seemed to Jesse that Mercy had a little of her father about her. It was nothing obvious, just her quick brown eyes, a sort of economy of motion, a hint of the elder Kemp's natural authority. Jesse knew she was a woman who had once been made to feel special and permitted to expect obedience from others, but there was something chastened in her, too—a humility she must have learned, not inherited. He asked how she had come to join Theo in the adventures that had landed her in a hotel south of Market.

She shrugged. "I believe in the cause."

It sounded like a well-rehearsed answer to a foolish question. "The cause of bankrupting your father?"

"The cause of letting people know what he's doing here and stopping him from doing it again."

"By 'here,' you mean San Francisco?"

"I mean your whole world."

"And what's he doing to it, in your opinion?"

"Exploiting it, corrupting it, deceiving it, and abandoning it as soon as he's extracted enough gold to turn a profit."

"He might say he's given as much as he's taken."

"I'm sure he would. But that would be a lie."

"Do you hate your father, Ms. Kemp? Did he raise you badly?"

"That's a *People* magazine kind of question." She gave him an impatient look, then sighed and said, "I don't hate my father.

I mean, he wasn't around a lot, so maybe I have some issues. But that's not why I joined the movement, and it's not why I'm here."

She seemed reluctant to say more. "Well, I won't press—"

"She's a truther," Elizabeth said.

Mercy sat upright. "That's an insulting word."

Elizabeth said, "Truthers are conspiracy theorists. Mercy's a time-travel truther. She thinks the government's covering up the real source of the Mirror technology."

"It was invented by gnomes from the far reaches of Hilbert space," Jesse said. "Isn't that what you told me?"

Mercy's indignation turned her face a brickish shade of red. "They weren't 'gnomes.' They were normal for where they came from. They were kept in captivity for a couple of years before they died."

"No one's ever proved that," Elizabeth said.

"Because the evidence has been suppressed. But the facts are coming out piece by piece, and it makes the elites nervous."

Jesse said, "What facts are those?"

"The fact that our entire political and economic system is driving us into a lethal dead end." Mercy turned to Elizabeth. "The people you call 'gnomes' came from almost a thousand years in our future. They're small because, where they come from, *everybody's* small. Their bodies are unusual in a lot of ways, according to the autopsies, which were never officially released. They process food more efficiently than we do. They're built for survival in a hot, depleted environment. That's an uncomfortable truth for anyone who wants to go on doing business as usual, given that business-as-usual is cooking the planet. But it gets worse, for people like my father. The visitors' economic system is different, too—egalitarian in a way that makes wealthy and powerful people uncomfortable. "

Jesse turned to Theo. "Do you believe this as well, about the utopian gnomes?"

Theo looked uncomfortable. "I haven't seen the kind of evidence Mercy's seen. But I agree that there needs to be a whole lot more transparency. And, you know, the irony is pretty inescapable."

"What irony is that?"

"That we suppress information about the future on the grounds that making it public might create chaos. But somehow it's okay for us to come here and stir up the exact same shit. It's a double standard."

"My father's doing things here that are inexcusable," Mercy said. "You should be angry at him."

I may yet work myself up to it, Jesse thought.

By the time it was fully dark, two fire wagons had gone rattling and clanging down Montgomery Street. There was nothing else the window view could tell him, but it was a safe bet that there was trouble in Chinatown, just as Theo had predicted. Jesse was relieved, then, when the radio emitted a chirp that indicated an incoming message. Elizabeth put the device to her ear and said "yes" or "okay" at various intervals; then she tucked the radio into the calico travel bag and said, "We're supposed to be at the Market Street wharf by ten o'clock. An unmarked boat will take us across the bay to Oakland."

Jesse checked his pocket watch. Ample time to make the deadline. "All right," he said. To Mercy and Theo: "We have a carriage big enough to carry us all. If anyone's watching they'll see us leave the hotel, but I can't do anything about that—we only have to get to the stable around the corner on Market. Once we're in the carriage we should be safe enough, though we might need to take the long way around if there's trouble between here and the wharfs. Understood?"

Nods all around.

"Downstairs, out the door, up Montgomery to Market. I'll reclaim the carriage, then we head for the docks. All right?"

No objections. The ladies put on their hats.

Jesse opened the door of the room and surveyed the hallway beyond. The Royal Hotel wasn't a complicated building. He could see the entire corridor from the north end to the stairway on the south, and there was no motion but the flicker of the gaslights. "Come ahead," he said.

They made it to the third-floor landing before they encountered anyone else. In this case it was a man in a top hat, escorting a woman who looked too furtive to be his wife. The man was clutching a room key in his right hand.

The couple walked past the door marked 316, Mercy and Theo's old room. Jesse wouldn't have given it a second thought, save that the woman tugged her companion's sleeve and said, "What kind of hotel is this? This door's had its lock broken."

Elizabeth guided Mercy and Theo a little ways down the stair, out of sight. Jesse waited for the top-hatted man to convince his female friend to continue on to their own room. Once they were out of the corridor he made a cautious approach to 316.

The door was ajar. And yes, the lock had been forced—with a crowbar, it looked like. The wood of the jamb was splintered and broken.

Jesse pushed the door open and stepped inside.

The room was empty. Nothing had been disturbed except Mercy's suitcase, the contents of which had been dumped on the floor. All else was as they had left it earlier in the day. The thieves had not found what they had come for.

Because what they came for, Jesse thought, *was us.*

The break-in wasn't entirely surprising. The question was, who was behind it? Little Tom or some other tong boss, looking for more City weapons? Or Roscoe Candy, looking for revenge?

They passed through the lobby of the Royal into the street, where the evening air smelled of refuse and wood smoke. The pedestrians on Montgomery were mostly male and mostly respectable, none obviously threatening. Haphazard light and deep shadow provided cover but made it harder to spot potentially hostile strangers. Jesse walked a little ahead of Mercy and Theo; Elizabeth walked a pace behind them, as if she were afraid they might dart away into the crowd.

The traffic on Market Street was denser and even more lively, but the livery stable where he had left the carriage bore a crude sign that said CLOSED. There was no visible light from inside. Jesse pounded his fist on the barn-sized door, but no one came. Which was worrying. There were animals inside— he could hear the nervous whinnying that followed his knock— and at this hour there should have been a hostler there to tend them. He looked at Elizabeth, who shrugged.

The big door wasn't chained, so he pushed it open. The reek of horses and fouled straw wafted out of the darkness, along with the sound of the animals shuffling in place. There was no lantern at hand. Jesse had been carrying his pistol on his belt under his shirt; now he took it in his hand and kept it at his side. "Stay by the door," he told Elizabeth. "Keep Mercy and Theo where you can see them." She nodded and drew her own pistol from a pocket sewn into her day dress.

Jesse hugged the shadows as he began to move deeper into the building. On his right was a row of stalls; on his left an assortment of carts, wagons, and carriages. A tall window at the rear of the shed admitted enough reflected light to allow him to navigate without bumping into anything. As he passed a small alcove he spotted an oil lamp resting on an anvil, as if it had been left there in haste, and he paused long enough to lift the mantle and light the wick with a paper lucifer of the futuristic kind. The lamp gave off an acrid glare that penetrated into the dark places of the shed and made it instantly obvious why no one had answered his knock.

The stable hand who had accepted Jesse's horse and carriage only a few hours ago lay motionless, sprawled behind a quenching barrel in the blacksmith's alcove. The blacksmith in his apron lay facedown on a drift of urine-soaked straw, arms akimbo. The throats of both men had been cut. Their blood had collected in rusty pools. It had been there long enough to begin congealing.

Jesse felt himself grow cold—a literal coldness, a winter wind that seemed to travel from his heart to his extremities.

Some years ago, a knife-wielding Placer County miner had assaulted one of Madame Chao's girls because she couldn't make his pecker stand up. Jesse had helped his father evict the man. It hadn't been easy, and he had taken a few cuts in the process, but the miner got the worst of it. Later, Jesse had tried to describe to his father the feeling that had come over him during the fight, a radiant chill that didn't make him weaker but made him strong. *I know all about that*, his father had said: It was a Cullum trait, a blessing and a curse. Helpful in a fight because it numbed the nerves and left the mind cool and clear; dangerous because it made you less likely to turn and flee— almost always the wisest course of action.

Tonight Jesse didn't turn or flee, just took the lantern in the icy fingers of his right hand and gripped his pistol with the icy fingers of his left. The coppery stink of shed blood was obvious to him now. It was what had made the horses skittish: They snorted and shuffled at every move he made, which convinced him that there was no one else here—no one living—except himself.

And he still needed a vehicle and an animal or two to draw it. So he pressed on until he found Aunt Abbie's carriage, parked at the back. He was about to call in Elizabeth so she could help him put a horse in its traces when a faint odor caused him to pause and open the carriage door.

A body tumbled out and folded at his feet.

The smell of blood became overwhelming. The horses in their stalls rolled their eyes and began to rear and kick.

Jesse brought the light of the lantern to bear on the corpse's face.

The dead man was Sonny Lau, though he wasn't easy to recognize. His throat had been cut and his tongue pulled out through the bloody gap.

16

Elizabeth stood with Mercy and Theo at the stable doors like a good soldier, keeping an eye on passing strangers. Jesse was taking too long, though she could hear him moving down the straw-littered length of what was essentially a large barn, accompanied by the various unintelligible noises made by horses in their stalls. She glanced inward when a flicker of light caught her eyes. He must have found a lamp. Then a span of silence, more motion, ultimately a muffled thump.

Then Jesse was back at the entrance, beckoning her and the two runners inside.

He closed the doors behind them. She could see by the glow of the lamp that his face was clenched into an expression of shock and rage so intense she had to suppress an urge to back away. "What happened?"

He took her aside and answered her question in a monotone. He had found three corpses, he said: two men dead of knife wounds and Sonny Lau mutilated in the cab of their carriage. Sonny had been killed in the signature style of Roscoe Candy: "It's his calling card," Jesse said.

Anger boiled off of him like the reek of an overdriven motor. Although, Elizabeth thought, the metallic tang in the air probably had some other source. Reluctantly, she acknowledged the stink of spilled blood. "So what do we do?"

"We can't use the carriage, it's a charnel house, but we can steal another of these rigs. Help me harness the horses, and then—"

He trailed off. "What?"

"I don't suppose you can drive one of these? Or maybe Theo—if he knows the way to the docks—"

"What are you saying?"

"Think about what happened. We left Sonny at the trinket shop. Sonny might have followed us, but why would he? My guess is that Candy's men caught him not long after he talked to us. Maybe they were watching him the whole time."

"Why would they be watching Sonny Lau?"

"Candy might have known that Sonny had a connection to Madame Chao's. And if Candy's men were watching Sonny, they would have raised a red flag if he met with an out-of-towner matching my description."

"We saw Sonny twice today, and nobody stopped us."

"By the time Roscoe got wind of it we were probably already headed for the Royal."

Elizabeth pictured Sonny Lau as she had last seen him, an arrogant young Asian guy dressed like a riverboat gambler, and tried not to imagine how he must look now, butchered gangland-style by Roscoe Candy. "What do you think he told them?"

"As little as possible. Sonny would have put up a fight. But he's only human, Elizabeth. In the end, he probably told them whatever they wanted to know."

"Including the room number at the Royal."

"But when they came looking for us, the room was empty. So they would have asked Sonny a few more questions."

"Why here?"

"This is the closest livery stable to the hotel. Candy might have been lying in wait for us. But he's not a patient man by nature."

"You think he killed the stable hands, then Sonny?"

"Probably the other way around—killed Sonny on an impulse, then killed the witnesses. Leaving Sonny in the carriage was a message, aimed right at me. Candy wants revenge. He doesn't care about Mercy Kemp or the City of Futurity."

Elizabeth stared at him as the implications began to sink in. "They asked Sonny why you were in town. They asked how you contacted him. They would have asked—"

"About Phoebe."

"He wouldn't have given her up, would he? His sister lives in the house, too."

"We don't know what Sonny might have said. He might have given up Phoebe to *protect* his sister. And they left his body for me to find, because Candy knows the first thing I'll do is go to Phoebe. They set a trap, Elizabeth. And I don't have any choice but to walk into it."

"But we have to deliver the runners to Kemp's boat."

Jesse said nothing.

"Tonight," she said.

"I'll take a horse of my own. You can take the runners to the dock. They're not resisting. Hire a cab."

"But you won't get paid."

Jesse gave her a scornful look.

"Anyway," she pressed, "if Candy's at your aunt's house he'll have his troops with him. You can't take him on alone."

"Can't I?"

"You don't have to. I'm a veteran. I've been trained. I can handle weapons."

She had his full attention now. He put his hands on her shoulders. Big hands, but cold. "There's no time for this. I thank you, Elizabeth. But you have a daughter to go home to."

"Even if I miss the boat, Kemp won't leave me behind."

"Won't he?"

"Not if we have his daughter."

Jesse was slow to answer. "You can't—"

"*Yes* I fucking *can*," she said, realizing she meant it.

"Why would you take such a risk?"

"Because Kemp was wrong, he's always been wrong, this isn't a fucking diorama—it's real, you're real, Phoebe is real, this is a real place, and I'm in it, I'm right here, I'm real, too, and I can help." *And you can't stop me,* she added silently.

Jesse just stared. His hands tightened on her shoulders, as if he was about to push her away.

But he didn't. "In that case," he said, "we're wasting time. Get Mercy and Theo into a carriage. Any carriage but the one we came in. And don't forget the weapons. I expect we'll need them."

Two panting horses pulled the stolen rig up the slope of Nob Hill.

The people who lived here called it California Street Hill. But it was Nob Hill to the people who lived south of Market, Jesse had said, and Nob Hill was the name that would stick. The angle of the grade and the finite strength of the horses made their progress agonizingly slow, which meant Elizabeth had time to glance over her shoulder from time to time. California Street offered a comprehensive view of the business district, the rattletrap neighborhoods south of it, and all of the Chinese quarter. Which was burning.

Elizabeth counted at least five individual fires. "It looks like the mobs went after the Chinese theaters," Jesse said. "Some of those shows go on for days, in installments. A lot of people inside."

Fire bells rang out a continuous clangor. In places the flames had turned whole streets incandescent, like hostile zones on a digital grid. "Will it spread?"

"It might."

"Will it come up here?"

"Most likely not. At least not tonight. I guess none of this was in your history books?"

Not exactly, no. This version of 1877 had come undocked from history and was drifting into uncharted space. Elizabeth's guess about what came next was no better than Jesse's.

She sat with Jesse on the driver's bench of the carriage. Mercy and Theo were enclosed in the cab, if "cab" was the correct name for the passenger box of the vehicle. When Aunt Abbie's house came within sight Jesse tugged the reins, looking for a place he could stop without either blocking traffic from the burning city or revealing himself to any hostile forces watching out for his approach.

Abbie Hauser's late husband, for all his wealth, had not built the finest house on California Street. That prize would have gone to a building farther up the hill, the mansion of someone named Leland Stanford, an Addams Family spook house inflated to the size of an aircraft carrier. Abbie's house was more human in scale but just as baroque, a quarry's worth of stone folded into tesseracts of Italianate complexity. "Okay," Elizabeth said, "what now?"

Jesse gazed at the house a few moments more. "You see the lights in the second-floor windows, south side?"

"So?"

"Most of those rooms haven't been used since Abbie was widowed. Phoebe and I used to play hide-and-seek in them. They were never lit up at night."

"Abbie or Phoebe might have gone up there to see the fires."

"They would have more likely gone to the widow's walk," Jesse said, meaning the balcony surrounding a stone turret at the highest part of the house.

"So what conclusion are you drawing?"

"I'm betting Candy and his men are already inside."

He said this in a flat voice, but Elizabeth knew him well enough to hear the envelope of rage around the words. "So it's basically a hostage situation. We have to find a way to get Abbie and Phoebe out without getting them killed."

Jesse nodded, but he counted off on his fingers: "Phoebe. Abbie. Soo Yee. And the hired man, Randal, if he was present when Candy's hatchetmen moved in."

"We don't know how many men Candy has."

"No."

"I've been trained in counterterrorism and hostage-rescue operations," Elizabeth said, which was sort of true. She had received basic infantry training, though her SIGINT work meant she'd spent most of her tour of duty behind a monitor. And when she joined the nominally civilian company that provided security to the City of Futurity she had gone through a truncated version of the FBI's Quantico training, including simulated responses to simulated attacks in a grid of fake doors and walls representing a generic urban environment. "We need a plan," she said, already conducting a mental inventory of the contents of their traveling bag: four flash-bang grenades, four automatic pistols with spare clips, one unsold Taser, a sheath of plastic pull-tie wrist restraints—plus a radio, their essential link to August Kemp. Thin pickings, but better than nothing.

"I'll go in and kill Candy and his men," Jesse said.

"That's—not a real plan."

"I disagree."

"So what am I supposed to do, wait in the carriage?"

"Yes."

"Waste of resources, Jesse. If you go in by yourself, that means I have to go in on my own after you get killed. If we do this together—"

"You're a soldier, I understand that, and I'm thankful for your help. But I know the house better than you do. I can get close without revealing myself."

"So, without revealing yourself, can you find out roughly how many men Candy has and where they're situated with respect to the hostages?"

"I suppose so."

"Then do that. Scout the house, come back here, and we'll make a plan that uses what we have to maximal effect."

"One thing we don't have is time."

"So keep an eye on your watch. If you're not back here in thirty minutes I'll assume you're dead or captured."

"And what if I am?"

"I'll act accordingly."

"What does that mean?"

She wasn't sure what it meant, to be honest. "Let's try to avoid finding out, okay?"

He stared at her. Then he nodded and took out his pocket watch. "Thirty minutes?"

"Starting now."

Jesse understood that the urgency of his task and his fear of failing at it might interfere with clear thinking. So for the purposes of this scouting expedition he tried to pretend he was still the fifteen-year-old who had taught himself the secrets of the house well enough to come and go at will, undetected.

The house had seemed huge to him back then, the very definition of a rich man's palace. Today he knew better. Mr. Hauser had never been quite as rich as he appeared to be, and the house on California Street was a modest one compared to the grandiose stone piles other millionaires had erected before or since. Nevertheless, the construction reflected the Comstock Lode money that had fueled it: It was big, boastful, smug in its complexity. It was not unusual for California Street nobs to surround their properties with walls, often for no other purpose than to spite a neighbor by blocking his view—Hauser's silver-mining wealth had probably been great enough to allow for such extravagances, but his Bostonian sense of propriety had kept him from indulging it to its fullest extent. As a result Aunt Abbie's mansion possessed only a handful of spare bedrooms and no more than a half dozen common rooms serving as library, parlor, study, dining room, etcetera. There was a small section set aside for servants' quarters, not much used now that the employed staff was reduced to Randal and Soo Yee. It was also down to Hauser's comparative modesty that the stone wall surrounding the house on three sides was only a little taller than Jesse's head. It had never presented much of an obstacle to him, even when he was an inch or two shorter. And he knew all the least conspicuous angles by which to approach and scale it.

He came up and over on the north side of the property, landing in a patch of overgrown moonshadow that had once been Aunt Abbie's azalea bed, with the family's small greenhouse situated between him and the mansion. He crouched there for a while, in case he had been seen. The half moon hanging over the house cast a light that was both useful and dangerous.

No one came to chase him, so he moved slowly and more or less silently along the base of the wall until he could see the front of the house. Two carriages stood in the drive. They were flashy and expensive-looking, just the kind of conveyances

Roscoe Candy favored. How many men could he have brought
with him in these two vehicles? Not more than ten, Jesse
thought, probably fewer, but he made ten his provisional as-
sessment. Say ten criminals including Candy himself, which—
if Abbie, Phoebe, Soo Yee, and Randal were all present—made
fourteen people in the house. Ten villains and four hostages.
(*Assuming Candy kept the hostages alive*, a traitorous fraction
of his thoughts reminded him.)

Where exactly were the hostages? To answer that question
he would have to get inside the house. He checked his pocket
watch, but in the pale moonlight it was all but unreadable. He
guessed at least five of his allotted thirty minutes had passed,
and he wished he'd held out for forty.

Years ago, when he had first taught himself to sneak in and
out of this house, Aunt Abbie had been a sterner presence in
his life. It had been no secret that she thought of her niece and
nephew as half savages, raised amid corruption by a drunkard.
Jesse's habit of roaming the streets at will had been anathema
to her, as her Bostonian sense of propriety had been to him.
Prevented from leaving by the customary exists, he had been
obliged to resort to other means.

He had been younger then, and less well fed. The years he
had spent as an employee of the City of Futurity had put weight
and muscle on him, not that he had been small to begin with.
He doubted he could shinny up a drainpipe without tearing
it free of its moorings. But there were many ways inside, some
of which involved the kind of climbing that turned his strength
into an asset. The easiest of these was the one that looked most
difficult: by way of the high turret of the house.

Mr. Hauser had hired a prominent San Francisco architect
to design his home, which was to say he had hired someone
who combined the skills and sensibilities of a stonemason and
a lunatic. Aunt Abbie once told him the building's "elements"

had been copied from European architectural history, including the turret, a miniature tower that projected from the second story and poked its cap above the highest roof. The turret housed two circular rooms, one above the other, and the uppermost of the rooms opened onto a narrow balcony, the widow's walk, that formed a half circle where the turret projected from the flat stone walls.

The turret looked as unassailable as the medieval towers it was meant to emulate. But looks were deceptive. The turret route had been Jesse's most reliable way in and out when he wanted to go undetected, precisely because everyone assumed it was unclimbable. In fact the route was perfectly simple: from the top of the greenhouse to the crenellated stone wall, where gaps in the masonry made for natural foot- and handholds, to the gently sloping roof of the stables, to the angle where that roof met the innermost point of the widow's walk, then up and over the railing and through the door. No harder now than it had ever been, but there was a complication: It seemed that Roscoe Candy had posted a guard on the widow's walk.

Jesse spent a couple of minutes watching as the guard did a lazy tour of the walk and stopped to light a cigar. A stupid move, but the behavior of Candy's men had always reflected their leader's cockiness. The flare of the man's match showed a bearded face, a slouched hat. As soon as the guard turned to walk the other way, Jesse crossed the exposed patch of lawn to the corner where the greenhouse met the wall of the mansion, deep enough under the contours of the turret to conceal him from sight. The greenhouse was a low structure, barely tall enough to stand up in, once used to winter perennials but now empty. It was an arrangement of iron struts supporting sheets of leaded glass; the trick, he had learned, was to put your weight where the struts were. Jesse stood on his toes and reached until he got a grip on the outer edge of the greenhouse roof; then he used the adjoining wall to help lever himself up.

The next part of the climb was safely hidden from the widow's walk but exposed to anyone who might step out onto the lawn, so he moved up the wall as quickly and quietly as he could. The quarried stone had been crudely cut, and his shoes dislodged cascades of pebbles, an unavoidable noise, though the street sounds helped to conceal it. Jesse was obliged to freeze in place when one such pebble rang against a pane of greenhouse glass below him. The guard paused, peered into the shadowed garden, and eventually went back to his rounds— no harm done, but it cost time.

Jesse's arms and thighs were burning with fatigue by the time he gained the lower end of the sloped roof, but from there he made fast progress: across the shingles to the place where the widow's walk met the wall, a quick vault over the ironwork railing, then he was behind Candy's guard, who sensed his presence and began to turn at the same time Jesse put an arm around his throat and tightened it into a choke hold he had learned in his City training.

Jesse's father had taught him never to kill an enemy, unless his enemy was the kind of snake that could be rendered harmless no other way. Jesse figured all of Candy's hatchetmen qualified as snakes. He wrestled to the man to the floor and planted a knee on his back and wrenched the man's head sideways until something broke. When he was sure the man was dead, he took the guard's revolver and added it to his own arsenal, consisting of a Glock tucked under his belt, spare clips in one pocket of his pants, and a flash-bang grenade in another—everything he could carry without weighing himself down or leaving Elizabeth defenseless.

Time was passing. Jesse saw through the windows that the

upper turret room was empty. He stepped inside and shut out the night behind him.

Elizabeth checked her watch.

Fifteen minutes had passed since Jesse had left. Half the time allotted for his scouting expedition. Long enough to plan her next move. She climbed down from the driver's seat of the carriage and opened the door to the enclosed cab where Mercy and Theo were sitting.

All she had told them was that the trip to the docks had been delayed and that Jesse needed to "clean up a problem" before they could leave San Francisco. Probably they assumed it was something connected with the riots in Chinatown. She guessed they'd be willing to sit tight while Jesse and Elizabeth tried to secure the hostages, but she couldn't be absolutely sure of that. Theo was a professional troublemaker, after all. So she climbed into the carriage and locked eyes with him. "Take off your pants," she said.

"Excuse me?"

"I need something to wear that won't get in my way, unlike this fucking dress. And I need you and Mercy to stay put and not leave the carriage. So, two birds with one stone. Give me your pants, Theo."

Theo blinked and said, "I'm not sure they'll fit you."

Theo was built like a prep-school tennis player, so the remark might have had some warrant. But he bought his clothes locally and they didn't look especially close-fitting or well tailored. Plus, he was pissing her off. "I'll risk it."

"Look, I promise I won't—"

"I'm not negotiating here. This is not a request."

For a moment she thought he was going to resist, which might have required physical persuasion, perhaps at Taser-point, but Theo seemed to run that scenario through his mind and realize how well it was likely to go. So Elizabeth ended up with the trousers and Theo ended up in a pair of cotton shorts, huddled in a corner of the carriage and glaring indignantly.

Elizabeth's fake dress opened down the side along a single Velcroed seam, so it was relatively easy to wiggle out of it and shuck herself into the pants. Which were, yes, uncomfortably tight across the thighs and a little difficult to button. She put the dress back on over them, as camouflage; she could step out of it easily enough when the time came. "Now give me your hands," she said.

Theo looked ready to work himself into a fresh round of outrage. "Why?"

"Do you have to ask?"

She flex-tied Mercy to Theo at the wrist. She was wagering they wouldn't leave the coach, given that a woman hand-cuffed to a man without pants would draw instantaneous attention. Then she checked her watch again. Jesse was due back in less than ten minutes. Still no sign of him.

Jesse moved more confidently now that he was inside the house.

He managed to navigate the spiral staircase from the upper room of the turret without causing the risers to groan or squeal. The room below was a circular space furnished only with a few small oval windows. The door to the second-floor corridor had been left slightly ajar, admitting a faint wedge of light. He peered through the gap.

The corridor was vacant. Gaslights blazed in their sconces, their glow reflected in yellow highlights on the brass-and-copper fittings of five bedroom doors and the walnut side table that decorated the landing above the grand staircase. The two doors nearest the landing were Phoebe's and Aunt Abbie's bedrooms. All these doors were closed, and everything looked normal enough, except that a vase on the side table had been overturned, spilling water and wilted violets at the base of the brass miniature of the Capitoline Wolf. And he heard the sound of voices from somewhere below. Men's voices, with the burl of smoke and meanness in them.

He had to face a stark possibility: that Abbie and Phoebe and Soo Yee and Randal might already be dead. Roscoe Candy had known the murder of Sonny Lau would draw Jesse to the house. He had come here with his men, bullied his way inside, and cowed the occupants. He might then have abused and violated the women or simply killed the hostages outright. It would have been characteristic behavior. On the other hand, Candy might have wanted to keep the captives alive as leverage in case something went wrong. Or—perhaps most likely—Candy might have decided to postpone the brutalization and murder until he could force Jesse to watch.

Jesse didn't bother consulting his watch. He guessed his allotted time must be nearly up, but he had hardly learned anything useful yet. And retreating the way he had come would only waste more vital minutes. He needed to do something practical.

As he was deliberating he heard footsteps ascending the staircase. A man came up to the landing, one of Candy's henchmen, some ex–placer-miner past his prime, it looked like, with a bandolier of bullets across his chest as if he were playing a Mexican rebel in a music-hall review. The man's movements were slow and approximate: He might have been drinking. Maybe all these men had been drinking. Jesse hoped so. But if that was the case, they must have brought their own liquor. Aunt Abbie ran a dry household.

The bandit knocked twice at the door of Phoebe's room. It opened, and another man peered out.

"You can go on down and get something to eat," the bandit said, "but you'd best hurry. The old woman's larder is none too generous. Any of them giving you trouble?"

A question that quickened Jesse's pulse.

The other man responded with a mumble that sounded like a no. What was happening here, Jesse realized, was a changing of the guard. The hostages, maybe all of them, maybe just some, were alive and were being held in Phoebe's room.

Suddenly the bandit gestured down the hall at the turret rooms—at Jesse himself, as it seemed. "Wheeler seen anything from his perch?"

He was talking about the lookout on the widow's walk. Wheeler must be the name of the man Jesse had killed. "If he did, he didn't tell me about it."

"Somebody ought to take him a chicken leg."

"Wheeler can go hungry for all of me."

The guard who had been relieved headed down the stairs for his meal as the bandit stepped into Phoebe's room and pulled the door shut behind him. Jesse waited until the only sound he could hear was a steady murmur from below. Then he left the turret room and moved down the corridor, just as if it were 1870 and he was sneaking back from some nighttime mischief. When he came to the landing he peered out as far as he dared but saw no one in the entrance hall below. It sounded as if Candy and his men had occupied the front parlor and made it their headquarters.

He turned back to the side table where Aunt Abbie's flower vase lay on its side next to the bronze miniature, the one Elizabeth had called "creepy," the Capitoline Wolf, from a story about Romulus and Remus, the mythical twin founders of Rome, who were supposedly protected and suckled by a she-wolf. It was the suckling the sculpture depicted. Two cherubic infants with their faces upturned to the wolf's wine-sack-like dugs. *Either a very big wolf,* Jesse thought, *or very small infants.* The bronze was heavy. Jesse picked it up by the wolf's blunt muzzle and raised it over his head. With his right hand he knocked at Phoebe's door, not quite loudly enough to be heard downstairs.

The bandit opened the door and put his head out. He began a word that might have been "What," but the final consonant had not yet emerged before Jesse brought down the Capitoline Wolf on the man's head. This was followed by gasps from inside the room, but the reaction was fortunately muted. Jesse caught the bandit's body as it fell and lowered it to the floor, pushing it inside so he could close the door behind him. The Capitoline Wolf was still in his hand, the wolf's dugs flecked with blood. He was ready to use it a second time if necessary, but the bandit's head was clearly broken. After a sort of guttural hiccup, the man stopped breathing.

That was the second of Candy's men Jesse had put away. He looked up from the body to the hostages. There was no need to count them. Phoebe, Abbie, Soo Yee, and the hired man, Randal. Of these, all were alive except Randal.

Randal had been shot very neatly through the heart, and at close range, judging by the blood and spent-powder stains on his vest. The three women appeared unhurt, apart from a purpling bruise on Abbie's cheek. Soo Yee was in a bad way, trembling and clutching at the hem of the comforter where she sat on Phoebe's bed, but she seemed not to have been physically abused. Phoebe was also obviously frightened, and her scarf had been taken from her, so that her scars stood out against her pale skin like the crenellations of a desert landscape, but her good eye was furiously alert. "Thank you," she whispered.

None of them rushed to embrace him, perhaps because of the bloody Capitoline Wolf in his hand, and that was good, because as much as he wanted to stay here, he could not. Not without making a hostage of himself. Nor was it practical to take these women out of the bedroom. There was no plausible way out except down the stairs and through the gauntlet of Candy's soldiers, which was, as the City people liked to say, "not doable."

But he might be able to pick off a few more thugs before initiating a full-blown shootout. So he put the Capitoline Wolf on the floor and nudged it into a corner, pulled the corpse of the bandit to a less conspicuous position behind the bed, put a finger to his lips to emphasize the need for quiet, and asked a single question: "How many?"

"I think ten men altogether," Abbie whispered. Phoebe closed her eyes as if counting the assailants in her mind, then nodded in agreement.

"All right," Jesse said. "Wait for me."

Then he slipped back into the hallway and headed for his hiding place in the turret room. He was halfway there when gunfire broke out downstairs.

The deadline came.

The deadline passed.

Five more minutes followed it into oblivion.

No sign of Jesse.

Elizabeth was alone. Profoundly alone, existentially alone, as alone as she had ever been in her life: She had no backup, the Mirror was half a continent away, and not even August Kemp could find her unless she radioed him her location. Which she was not prepared to do, at least until this problem was resolved. By her calculation, the City boat that was supposed to carry her and the runners back to Oakland had probably just docked. Within minutes Kemp would get a *they're-not-here* call from the foot of Market Street. And several varieties of hell would then break loose.

Not her problem, not right now. She was about to walk into a firefight. The last time Elizabeth had fired a weapon in earnest was when she had taken out the gunman at Futurity Station. Before that, all her targets had been cardboard silhouettes. The men she was about to go up against had learned their skills differently. They had practiced their marksmanship on warm flesh.

On the other hand (or so she told herself), they were ignorant criminals armed with knives and antique revolvers. She had the advantage of superior knowledge, superior armaments, and surprise. She might be able to kill at least a few of them before they had time to put up a unified resistance.

Unfortunately, "killing a few of them" was the only plan she had. If Jesse was still operational, it would help. If not—

She promised herself she'd retreat if the battle became too one-sided. A memory of Gabriella hung in her mind's eye, Gabriella when she was still a baby, barely old enough to grab the edge of a chair and haul herself upright, tumbling down on her diaper-padded bottom as often as not—*Gabriella*, she told the memory, *I'll be home soon.* Even if it meant leaving Jesse for dead.

But until that choice was forced upon her?

She had work to do.

She remembered the layout of the house from the night she had spent there. A drill sergeant had once told her she had "excellent tactical memory." Basically, she was facing a house occupied by an unknown number of lethally dangerous men who were expecting to be attacked. Her sole advantage was that they were not expecting to be attacked by a woman. It made a frontal approach possible.

She walked up the drive in plain sight, her Velcro dress covering the borrowed trousers, her ludicrous hat on her head, the calico travel bag clutched in both hands like a purse.

What surprised her was how close she managed to get before anything happened. Had the bad guys failed to post a lookout—were they that confident? Or had Jesse already reduced their numbers? No matter—she was nearly to the front steps when the door opened. Three men stepped onto the veranda, forming a thou-shalt-not-pass scrimmage line in front of her. They were dressed like gamblers, and their body language gave off a smug don't-fuck-with-me vibe. All were conspicuously armed, though they kept their pistols holstered. The man in the middle said, "What do you want here?"

Elizabeth widened her eyes in mock surprise. "Is Mrs. Hauser at home? Abigail Hauser?"

"She's indisposed just now. What's your business with Abigail Hauser?"

"Well, I don't like to say. But I borrowed money from her last year, a *great deal* of money—she was very generous—and I've come to pay it back."

Two of the men seemed to find this declaration fantastically funny, judging by their efforts to keep a straight face, but the one in the middle managed to sustain a somber expression. "Well, Mrs. Hauser can't be disturbed, but I'll give her the money if you like. Is it in that bag there?"

Behind this banter lurked Elizabeth's memory of what had happened to Sonny Lau and her knowledge that these men had participated in it. The pretense was bound to fail before long. "Yes," she said, "it's here," reaching into the bag. "And there's a message that goes with it."

"All right, then, what's the message?"

What the bag contained was a Glock with a full clip. "The message is, Sonny Lau says hello."

She had shot the first two men before the third recovered enough presence of mind to reach for his Colt, and his hand failed to make it as far as the grip before he joined his friends. Then Elizabeth was running around the side of the house with the familiar shooting-range ache in her wrist and her heart doing gymnastics in her chest. She had just killed or critically injured three strangers. Two with wounds to the upper torso, not survivable without immediate medical intervention, and one with a head shot, so obviously deadly that nothing short of divine intervention could repair it. But she couldn't allow herself to dwell on that.

She had half hoped more of Candy's henchmen would come boiling out at the sound of gunfire—more easy targets—but that didn't happen. They were presumably smart enough not make that mistake a second time. And that gave her a fleeting moment to think about what *would* happen next.

The house was set far enough from the street that the gunfire failed to draw attention, the sound probably muted by hedges and walls or lost on passersby distracted by the Chinatown inferno. So she was still on her own. The calico bag was empty (she had dropped it as soon as she took out the gun), but its other contents were concealed on her body under the fake dress. Which she ought to think about losing, for mobility's sake, now that it had served its purpose as a distraction. Then maybe a flash-bang through the window she was crouching under, which would create enough chaos for her to circle around to the back. And from there—

She never completed the thought.

She felt the pressure first, a pricking just under her rib cage. She flinched away reflexively and felt a second pressure, an arm encircling her throat, now tightening like a noose, and where had this come from, how could she not have heard or seen the man approaching? A question that ceased to matter as soon as it occurred to her. "Drop your gun," a voice said, intimately close to her ear, a male voice, unhurried and unafraid. "Right now."

A voice accustomed to being obeyed. Her fingers opened. The Glock thudded into moist earth.

The pressure under her ribs was the point of a knife. Her head was immobilized but she could see the hand, the hilt, a wedge of steel brighter than the darkness around it. The hand moved slightly; the blade advanced a fraction of an inch. It had already pierced her skin. The pain wasn't bad. Yet. But she felt a drop of blood trickle down under her layers of clothing. She gasped for breath against the arm that clamped her throat, and the arm tightened.

The voice (and she was almost certain it belonged to Roscoe Candy) whispered, "You're the one that was with him, aren't you? You're Jesse Cullum's woman."

She couldn't get air enough to give him an answer. He seemed not to expect one. The tip of the knife was in her, and now it went a little deeper. Her eyes clouded, some combination of hypoxia and tears, and she thought again of Gabriella, so impossibly far away.

Then the tongue of the knife touched bone, her bottommost rib, sending an electric arc of pain through her body, and her spine arched, driving the knife deeper.

Then, suddenly, the pain relented.

"Come inside," Roscoe Candy said, "where we can talk."

Jesse stayed in the lower turret room with his eye to the door after the shooting stopped. *Elizabeth*, he thought, but there was no way of knowing what she was up to, and although he could charge down the big staircase with guns blazing—he gave it some thought—such a move would likely leave him dead and the hostages in danger. So he bit his lip and watched the corridor for several long, futile minutes, trying to make sense of the agitated voices drifting up from down below.

After a few interminable minutes more, he heard the sound of multiple footsteps on the stairs.

A crowd came up to the second-floor landing. Jesse counted seven people all together. Five of them were Candy's henchmen, all cut from the same cloth: men with the upper-body strength of miners, all dressed in flashy clothing and all conspicuously armed. They varied in the details—younger, older, bearded, clean-shaven—but they were uniformly unhappy, snarling and gritting their teeth at whatever had just happened.

After them came Roscoe Candy himself. It had been years since Jesse had set eyes on him, and Candy had diminished in the interval. Part of that was surely an illusion: The memory was larger than the man. Some of it was a genuine physical diminishment. Candy had not died of the wound Jesse had inflicted on him, but the wings of death had brushed him. He wasn't the bean-shaped, muscular force of nature he once had been. His belly had shrunk and looked lopsided. His face was scrawnier. But his wide, deceptively gentle eyes—like the glass eyes they put in porcelain dolls, Jesse thought—had not changed. Nor had his taste in clothing: He wore a red-and-white-striped jersey, like a sailor's jersey, and a striped schoolboy cap. Nor had he lost his love of honed blades. He carried a long-bladed knife, like a flensing knife, in his hand. He was holding it at Elizabeth's throat.

Elizabeth was the seventh person on the landing, and she was Roscoe Candy's captive. Her dress was soiled and stained with blood. The blood came from her left flank, just under the ribs. The wound was messy but apparently not disabling—and a deep cut in that place would have taken her down quickly. She was pale and seemed frightened but not panicked. Her eyes repeatedly strayed to the knife in Candy's hand, as if she were wondering how best to take it from him. Which, for all Jesse knew, she had been trained to do. But she didn't know Roscoe Candy. How famously fast he was with a blade. How difficult to deceive or surprise.

Candy's men were arguing fiercely. Jesse caught the name Wheeler, the name of the lookout on the widow's walk. Wheeler had been remiss in his duties was the gist of it; Wheeler had failed to warn them of something, presumably Elizabeth's approach. Candy nodded at one of the five men and said, "Wake up that dog and send him down—tell him I want a word with him. And you stay up there and keep your damned eyes open. If this one's come for us,"—meaning Elizabeth—"the other won't be far behind."

The designated man headed down the hallway, straight toward Jesse's hiding place in the turret room. The others approached Phoebe's room, inside of which they would find one of their men dead—testimony to the fact that Jesse was already in the house and prepared to fight. But he could do nothing about that right now.

He hurried up the iron staircase to the upper room and out onto the widow's walk, stepping over the body of Mr. Wheeler, whose open eyes had gone cloudy. The moon shone down through a red, smoky haze. Jesse put his back to the wall and waited.

Candy's henchman came up the staircase as subtly as a buffalo, every footfall a bell-like clank. He came through the door onto the widow's walk and looked at the corpse of Wheeler at his feet and blinked as if he thought Wheeler might only be asleep, at which point Jesse shot him through the head. Unpleasant residue flew between the struts of the iron railing to the shadowy garden below.

By now Candy must have discovered the body in Phoebe's

room. Had he also heard Jesse's gunshot? Maybe, maybe not. Jesse didn't want to be cornered, so some misdirection was called for.

He took from his pocket one of the two flash-bang grenades he had brought with him. The flash-bang, also called a stun grenade, was a simple device: a black canister about the size of a can of beans, with a bright metal ring hanging out of it. Like the Taser he had sold to Little Tom, it was one of a class of weapons the City people called "nonlethal." The concept of a nonlethal weapon had sounded idiotic to Jesse when he had first been introduced to it—what was a nonlethal weapon supposed to do, *annoy* your enemies?

No. In the case of the flash-bang, it was supposed to render your enemy temporarily blind, deaf, and disoriented—for thirty seconds or so, maybe longer if you factored in surprise and lingering confusion. But this particular flash-bang didn't need to do any of that. It just needed to be loud.

Jesse depressed the safety lever, pulled the ring, and dropped the grenade over the railing of the widow's walk.

He didn't wait for the concussion but hustled into the turret and began to take the stairs two rungs at a time, no longer worried about the noise he was making. *Plenty more noise to come,* he thought. The grenade was on a two-second delay. It detonated as he was halfway between the upper and lower turret rooms. The stone walls of the house were impervious to anything short of artillery fire, but the concussion was audible even here. With any luck, it might have broken a window or two.

He reached the door to the hallway in time to watch from hiding as Candy's men reacted. Three men boiled out of Phoebe's bedroom with Roscoe Candy's curses following them: "Find that son of a bitch before the whole of California Street comes crowding in to see what blew up," which was a real possibility, Jesse hoped, though the city's fire brigades and police were almost certainly busy in the Chinese quarter.

The three men headed downstairs, guns drawn. Which left Candy and one other man in the room with the hostages. Which sounded to Jesse like tolerable odds. Unfortunately, his only option was a frontal assault. Phoebe's room had but a single door, and Candy was more than shrewd enough to have anticipated a hostile approach.

But the time for subtlety was past. Jesse took a Glock in each hand and ran down the hallway. At Phoebe's door he slowed and swerved and hit the door, which wheeled inward, revealing one of Candy's gunmen braced against the opposite wall with a revolver aimed and ready. The gunman fired first, and Jesse felt the bullet as a sharp blow to his right arm, but it only turned him a little and he was able to get off a shot that passed through his opponent's throat. The gunman gawked blankly and slumped down the wall, leaving a smeary trail of blood. Jesse ducked to make himself a smaller target and swiveled to survey the room, and here was Roscoe Candy himself, a gleam in his eye and a smile on his face and his flensing knife still pressed to Elizabeth's throat. "Put your pistols down," he said.

Jesse hesitated. But he had no real choice but to obey. And he didn't have to ask what Candy's next move would be. Candy would cut Elizabeth's throat and force Jesse to watch her die.

"*Now*," Candy said.

Jesse held the pistols by their grips and bent at the knee, keeping his eyes locked on Candy's. Peripheral vision told him a few interesting things. Including the fact that Phoebe, Abbie, and Soo Yee seemed not to be present.

"They're in the closet," Candy said. "Your sister, the old lady, the slant-eyed girl. But are they alive or are they dead? That's the question!"

It was not a question Jesse wanted to consider. He placed the City pistols on the carpet and straightened up.

"Now empty your pockets."

Jesse's pockets were full to bursting. He had Wheeler's pistol, spare clips for the Glocks, another flash-bang, and his iPod. He removed these items, taking as much time as he guessed Candy would tolerate, and spared a glance at Phoebe's closet.

It was a big space, he knew. Unless her habits had changed over the last five years, Phoebe didn't keep much in it. Three people could stand in there and feel only moderately crowded. Or it could hold three corpses, stacked like cordwood. Jesse sensed no motion from inside. Heard no sound of movement.

"You can't help them," Candy said.

Jesse was careful about where he put his weapons as he arrayed them at his feet. Wheeler's pistol behind the two City pistols. The stun grenade behind that, almost at his heels. He touched the power button of the iPod as he set it down at the front of this collection. The screen lit up as he straightened, icons arranging themselves in a grid of Easter-egg-colored squares. Candy frowned and took a sidelong step, pulling Elizabeth along with him, as if the device might fire a bullet at him. "What is that?"

"It's harmless," Jesse said.

"Step away from it."

"It can't hurt you."

"Step back, you dog! I know better than to trust you."

Blood had begun to flow down Jesse's arm from the place where Candy's henchman had shot him. His right hand was slick with it. The pain, radiating from a place between his elbow and the ball of his shoulder, wasn't unbearable. But three of his fingers had gone numb, a bad sign.

Misdirection, he thought. Something his father had once said, teaching him larcenous card shuffles. *Misdirection, the invisible weapon.* He took a step back, just as Candy had ordered him to. The heel of his left foot came to rest on the pin of the flash-bang. Candy was troubled and distracted by the eerie glow of the iPod and failed to notice.

But Elizabeth noticed. Even with Candy's knife at her throat, she managed to cant her jaw in a shadow of a nod.

Footfalls sounded on the stairway beyond the door, Candy's men coming back to report on the situation downstairs. Maybe Candy wanted them here to see what happened next, beginning with the death of Elizabeth. Jesse's margin of time had run out. He held his empty hands before him in an imploring gesture. "Please," he said.

Candy's madly joyous expression grew even more gleeful. "If you mean to *beg*, Jesse Cullum, go right ahead! I won't stop you!"

"*Please*," Jesse repeated. The heel of his right foot trapped the pin of the stun grenade and he stepped on the barrel of it with his left, compressing the safety lever as he kicked it away from the pin. The flash-bang rolled behind him, toward Phoebe's bed and perhaps under it—he dared not look to see where it had gone.

"Please *what?*" Candy demanded.

One second. Two seconds.

"Please go to hell," Jesse said.

Elizabeth jammed her hands between her throat and Candy's wrist. She squeezed her eyes shut, and Jesse did the same.

Shutting his eyes gave him a little protection from the flash, a fiery red starburst, but not from the bang. The bang did what it was designed to do—it boxed his ears, disabled his sense of hearing, induced dizziness and confusion, and interfered with rational thought.

When Jesse opened his eyes, the room was reeling around him. Smoke gusted up from the floor in a sickening chemical reek. He was deaf, but it wasn't a silent deafness, it was a deafness made out of the ringing of a hundred church bells and the roaring of a thousand dynamos. He saw, in a rolling succession of lightning-flash images:

Elizabeth, who had stumbled out of Candy's embrace, tugging frantically at the Velcro seam of her trick dress (an angry red line on her throat where Candy's knife had touched her, but only a drop or so of blood)—

Roscoe Candy, his schoolboy cap askew and both hands empty, his flensing knife on the floor where he had dropped it, weaving in place—

And the door of the room, the knob of which began to rotate as one of Candy's remaining henchmen turned it from the hallway.

Jesse lurched toward Candy, leaving an open line of sight toward the door for Elizabeth. Elizabeth was peeling off the dress, revealing a cotton undershirt, a pair of ill-fitting men's trousers, and a small arsenal strapped to her body.

Jesse recovered fully functional vision and a degree of muscular control at about the same time Roscoe Candy did. The murderer locked eyes with him, and Jesse sensed the furious calculation going on behind that reptile stare. *He'll go for the knife or one of the guns,* Jesse thought. But which?

Candy was a knife man. Always had been. The knife, Jesse thought. He dived for it himself, hoping to turn it on its owner.

But he had miscalculated. Candy went for the nearest pistol, dropping to the floor with his right arm outstretched and fingers scrabbling at the grip.

Elizabeth had managed to raise her own pistol just as the door flew open. She squeezed off multiple shots, sounds fainter than a parson's farts to Jesse's tortured ears, but he felt the concussions in the air like a series of blows.

Jesse took the flensing knife in his hand. The handle was still warm where Candy had been holding it. Candy had got his hand on the grip of the pistol and his finger inside the trigger guard, but before he could raise it Jesse rolled on top of him, kneeling on Candy's gun arm and pinning him in place with the weight of his body. He brought his other knee hard up against the place Jesse had hurt him once before, that old but still vulnerable wound, and Candy howled loudly enough for Jesse to hear him above the sound of phantom bells.

Elizabeth fired two more shots, perhaps needlessly. The door wheeled fully open, revealing two men dead and another clearly dying—and no one else in sight.

Jesse put the knife to Candy where the point could pass between the slats of his ribs to his heart. No mistake this time. No hesitation. He punched the blade past bone and gristle and the glutinous resistance of dense flesh. He leaned into it, using his weight to keep Candy's right arm immobilized. Candy flailed fiercely, his heels kicked the carpet, his body bucked like a bull at a Wild West show, but Jesse pushed and kept pushing, surprisingly hard work, like butchering some leathery old hog, until the knife was buried right up to the guard.

It had found a vital point. Roscoe Candy died screaming, but not before he managed to squeeze off a few shots from the pistol, in the only direction he could point it: at the door of Phoebe's closet.

17

Mercy Kemp wasn't frightened until she heard the detonations from the California Street mansion.

Well, that wasn't strictly true. She had spent much of the last two years in a generalized state of anxiety, bordering on fear. Living as a runner, with a man who might as well have had a target painted on his back, had conditioned her to it. But the idea that she could actually be left behind, that she might be permanently stranded in this instantiation of 1877, had only recently begun to feel real. And it felt particularly terrifying now that she was cuffed to Theo Stromberg, in a closed coach on a street above a burning city.

Theo hadn't taken any of this gracefully, but that wasn't surprising. Mercy's infatuation with him had long ago shriveled into an abstract admiration for the work he was doing. From the beginning of their journey into this tranche of Hilbert space, Theo had proved himself to be dogmatic, narcissistic, and arrogant, a textbook pain in the ass. And she was resigned to that. Fact: Important work was often done by unpleasant people. "Can you see anything?" he asked for the third time.

Mercy peered around the edge of the isinglass shade, but

nothing had changed. She could see the spectacularly ugly Italianate mansion into which Jesse Cullum and Elizabeth DePaul had apparently vanished, she could see the glow of the distant fires, and she could see the gathering crowd. "No."

The flex-tie handcuff chafed her wrist. Theo kept tugging at it, pointlessly—even gnawing at it with his teeth at one point—though this only made the irritation worse. Mercy had stopped sleeping with Theo (that is to say, fucking him; they still shared a bed when it was necessary) three months into their sojourn here. Despite that, the collegial aspects of their relationship had remained more or less intact. She had composed more than one of his famous letters for him, and she knew why they had to be written. Though she had always been uneasy about the guns.

"The guns are tokens," he used to say. "To prove we're who we say we are. The progressive papers might be satisfied with a few fulfilled prophecies, but what does that mean to Chief Joseph or a black family in Grant Parish?" He had never included more than a single clip of ammunition with any of the Glocks he shipped to endangered communities. "It's a way of saying, expect violence. Of saying, we have seen the future, and it fucks you over, and some of us aren't okay with that."

The part about expecting violence was undeniably true. That violence was erupting all around them, in the repeal of Reconstruction, the murders in the South, war between workers and the railroads—in the mob attack on Chinatown, maybe even in this Nob Hill mansion. She had heard two detonations in the last few minutes, the first and louder of them accompanied by a burst of light. She remembered, two summers ago in Paris, a seminar for activists that had taught her the basics of noise cannons, kettling, tear gas, and concussion grenades. Bright light, big noise, no flame—was it actually possible that Jesse or Elizabeth had detonated a flash-bang?

She wasn't sure what to make of Elizabeth DePaul, who worked for Mercy's father but who seemed a little more thoughtful than the job description would suggest. Jesse Cullum was even more enigmatic, a local hire whose term of employment was obviously coming to an end and whose loyalty to August Kemp had probably reached its best-before date. Which was maybe why they had come here to do whatever they were doing, rather than taking Mercy and Theo to the docks as had been arranged. Some urgent and violent errand of Jesse's, Mercy guessed, which must have gone bad in a big way, if grenades were being deployed.

But on a purely intuitive level, for no defensible logical reason, she wanted to trust Jesse Cullum. Elizabeth, on the other hand . . . had Elizabeth really learned that this slice of Hilbert space was not Frontierland? Or was she still clinging to the illusion the City fostered, of the past as a kind of disposable virtual reality, a dream that vanished as soon as you took the goggles off?

"We might have to get out of here," Theo said; this, too, not for the first time. "If things get completely crazy."

"But not yet."

"But if we *do* have to get out, even without this fucking wrist cuff—"

"You can tie my jacket around your waist, so you won't get arrested for public indecency, if that's what you're wondering about."

But what then? Where would they go? Theo's accomplices in this world, mostly runners, had set up bank accounts he could draw on in an emergency. But the evacuation of City people from both coasts had thrown that network into disarray. All but the most fanatical runners had already decamped for the plains of Illinois.

We're a long way out on a thin limb, Mercy thought; and it was making Theo crazy.

She looked outside again. Events at the house had attracted the attention of the crowd that had gathered to watch the fires consuming the Chinese quarter. But the house was surrounded by walls, and although the gates were open, the onlookers stayed outside them, out of some instinctive deference to the property and prerogatives of the rich. Nothing new, she was about to tell Theo, but then a figure lurched out of the darkness, heading straight for the coach.

A meaty hand landed on the door handle and yanked it open. Jesse Cullum leaned inside.

Mercy almost failed to recognize him. His expression was a mask of grief or outrage, and worse, his face was speckled with blood: There was a dime-sized spot of it above his right eye and smaller dots clustered around his cheek, as if he had been flecked with a blood-brush. He looked at Mercy but didn't seem especially interested in her. "Sit tight," he said in a flat voice. "I'll drive the rig up to the house. Once we're inside, you can talk to your father by radio."

His right hand was bloody, too. The blood, oily black by moonlight, seemed to be leaking from the cuff of his shirt, also sodden with blood. "Are you hurt?"

"A little. There are people inside who are hurt worse."

"I can help," she said.

He looked at her dubiously.

"Seriously," she said. "I volunteered at a hospital when I was doing pre-med. I'm not squeamish, and I can do basic first aid."

"All right," Jesse said. He closed the door, climbed onto the driver's bench, and set the carriage in motion.

———

Elizabeth improvised a compression bandage for Phoebe's wound while Jesse was out retrieving the carriage.

He came back into the house with Mercy and Theo trailing behind him, rubbing their wrists where Jesse had cut away the flex cuffs. Mercy rushed to the sofa where Phoebe was lying, muttering something about her med-school training. Elizabeth was skeptical—she had pegged Kemp's daughter as the kind of dilettante who wears Prada to a sit-in—but she stood back while Mercy examined the unconscious girl. "Good job stanching the wound," Mercy said, "but you must know she needs more than a bandage."

"Her name is Phoebe. And yeah, I do know that."

"She's bleeding internally, her pulse is weak—she needs serious medical attention as soon as possible."

"Obviously. I was about to radio your father."

"Call him now," Mercy said, which was fairly presumptuous for someone who had recently been cuffed to a guy without pants. But there was nothing wrong with the advice.

Elizabeth nodded. "I will. In the meantime you should look after Jesse's arm."

"If he'll let me. Are there any other injuries?"

"Nothing serious. There's a stack of bodies upstairs, but the survivors are all down here."

"What about you?" Mercy was eyeing Elizabeth's shirt where she had bled into it.

"When you have time," Elizabeth said.

Elizabeth took the radio to an adjoining room. The radio reminded her of an antique mobile phone: It had a collapsible antenna, which she extended to its fullest length, and she stood by the window to use it, as if it might work better if it had a clear view toward Oakland.

This wasn't the easiest call Elizabeth had ever made, but it was probably the most urgent. The voice that came crackling back at her was August Kemp's, and he was pissed. "*Where the fuck are you?* You missed the rendezvous—what's your status?"

"We're halfway up Nob Hill, and we have injured requiring evac."

"Is Mercy—"

"Mercy's all right. She's here, she's okay, but there's no way we can get her to the docks tonight."

"Okay . . . so who's injured? You?"

"Jesse and I sustained minor injuries, but we're basically okay. But we have a young woman who took a bullet and needs attention ASAP."

"A local?"

"She was hurt while we were on City business." Not strictly true, but it was a useful lie.

Kemp said, "We're not in the business of patching up locals."

Mercy Kemp came into the room. Elizabeth turned to face the window. A reef of cloud had rolled in from the sea, reflecting the glare of the Chinatown fires, as if the clouds themselves were about to burst into flame. "She'll die without help."

"I'm truly sorry to hear that, but there's nothing I can do."

"We have a moral obligation—"

"You picked the wrong time to lecture me about morality. Give me your location and I'll arrange to evacuate you and my daughter. And here's a clue: The next words out of your mouth should be 'yes sir' and 'thank you.'"

Elizabeth stared at the radio. This was going south even faster than she had feared.

Mercy put a hand on Elizabeth's shoulder. "Let me talk to him."

"What?"

"Just let me talk."

Elizabeth was annoyed, but anything that might change Kemp's mind was worth a try. She showed Mercy the send/receive button and handed over the device. After that, all she could hear was Mercy's end of the conversation:

"It's me."

Pause.

"Yes!"

Pause.

"No, I *want* to go back. But—"

Pause.

"I understand that, but we have a medical emergency."

Pause.

"No!"

Pause.

"Bottom line, I'm not leaving this house unless she does."

Pause.

"Of course I know what it means! This isn't negotiable."

Pause.

"I'm standing by a door, and there's nothing stopping me from walking out of it."

Pause.

"All right. Yes, all right."

Mercy handed the radio back to Elizabeth.

August Kemp said, "You heard that?"

"This end of it."

"My daughter is acting irrationally. I need you and Jesse to take her into custody. I trust you can do that without hurting her. Handcuff her if you have to."

"Sir—"

"What?"

"I'm not in a position to do that."

"Say again?"

"It's not currently possible to comply with that order."

"Bullshit!"

"It's the situation on the ground."

Elizabeth closed her eyes. After everything she had been through today, the prospect of losing her job seemed trivial. But she had probably just guaranteed that outcome. She heard Kemp talking to someone else, barking out unintelligible orders with his thumb still on the transmit button. Then he said, "Get your runners ready for transport. We'll discuss this face to face."

Jesse stood by his sister, watching her. Her bleeding had been stanched and her wound bandaged, but she was still unconscious and grievously hurt.

One of Candy's bullets had passed through the door of the closet and pierced Phoebe's gut. He had found her slumped and gushing blood, and he had carried her to the parlor sofa, cradled in his arms as if it were not too late to protect her, as if the idea of protecting her had not become a foolish joke. He stood over her now, calculating all the ways he could have prevented this. He replayed the memory of his struggle with Candy as if it were one of the songs in the iPod Elizabeth had given him, until he felt a gentle touch at his shoulder.

"Come away," Aunt Abbie said. "Elizabeth and Miss Kemp need to prepare her so she can be moved."

It was a common belief that women were useless in an emergency, but Jesse had known it for a lie long before he went to work for the City of Futurity. Abbie was just one more item of evidence. Women were soft, it was said; they tended to faint or succumb to hysteria; but Jesse had often seen in the women he knew something precisely the opposite: a polished, refractory hardness. He forced himself to turn away and allowed Aunt Abbie to steer him to the room she used as a library.

He had much to apologize for. In a single night he had made a charnel house of her mansion and changed the course of her life irrevocably. But she refused his mumbled contrition. "The people responsible for the carnage are dead, Jesse, and if not for you I might be dead in their place. Don't take on the weight of Mr. Candy's sins." She said this confidently, though her hands, Jesse saw, were shaking. He wondered if she was coming down with PTSD. It would be a miracle if she were not.

"Aunt Abbie . . . what will you do now?"

"When you call me Aunt Abbie you make me think of the boy you were when your father first delivered you here. Do you remember that day? How wide your eyes were when you walked into this room! You said you'd never seen so many books in your life. And in the end, it was easier to let you read them at whim than to give you a proper education. Don't worry about me, Jesse. My home was invaded by armed criminals, who will trouble us no longer. No one will mourn for them and the police will be grateful, on balance, to find them dead. Anything more difficult to explain, such as the use of unusual weapons, I intend to blame on you and your connection to the City of Futurity—assuming you're safely far away. Is that all right?"

"Blame me for bank failures and bad weather, too, if it serves you. I don't mind. But what about the house? It's damaged, and it'll become notorious if the newspapers take up the story."

"I'm not bound to this house. Notorious or not, it can be sold. I wouldn't be sorry to go back to Boston, if it comes to that. This was a good place for Phoebe, on the whole, but now—" Her words stopped as if they had hit a wall. "Do you think she can be saved?"

"The City people know how to save her." It was not as positive an answer as he would have liked to give.

"Is that where you'll take her, the City of Futurity?"

"That's where they have the tools and machines to save her life."

"According to the newspapers, the City is under siege."

"Don't believe everything you read. I expect August Kemp knows how to find his way inside."

"I hope so. But, Jesse—" She became stern. "I don't hold you responsible for what happened to your sister, or to Randal, or for anything else that went on here. But I'm entrusting you with Phoebe, and I *do* hold you responsible for what happens next. You must do your very best to help her, and if in the end you *can't* help her, you must comfort her. Save her or soothe her dying. Will you do that?"

They were terrible words to pronounce, terrible to hear. "I won't abandon her."

It was a binding promise. Aunt Abbie nodded. Jesse said, "How is Soo Yee?"

"She's in the kitchen, keeping to herself. Randal was killed in front of her, and she hasn't spoken since she learned of Sonny's murder. Soo Yee has a place with me as long as she wants it, of course . . ." Before Jesse could speak again she looked over his shoulder at the window, startled. "My goodness, what's that *light*?"

Jesse left his aunt in the library and hurried up to the widow's walk. Elizabeth was already there. The radio was in her hand, and she was talking to it.

Two of Candy's men had died here, but Jesse had dragged the bodies into the turret room and out of the way. Sooner or later, an undertaker would be called to remove the numerous dead. The blood that had been tracked underfoot would be difficult to get rid of, but he guessed it could be done. Memories were harder to eradicate. He could hardly blame Aunt Abbie for wanting to close the house and sell it. It would be many years before the sum of its tenants exceeded the sum of its ghosts.

The light that had startled Abbie was moving up California Street from the south, a circle of artificial daylight swinging like a bucket at the end of a rope. Its source was airborne. Jesse said, "A helicopter."

Elizabeth kept the radio to her ear, but no message was coming through at the moment. "Yep."

"Did it come all the way from the City?"

"Hardly. The helicopter at the City isn't the only one Kemp imported. It's not even the only aircraft. There are at least two fixed-wing planes stashed at isolated hangars within range of both coasts. Multiple redundancy."

"First I've heard of it," Jesse said. There had been rumors, of course, but there were always rumors, some more plausible than others.

"All the aircraft and associated gear came through the Mirror before construction on the towers was finished—probably before you were hired. Kemp was never going to let himself get caught in Manhattan or San Francisco without a guaranteed escape route. And a Plan B, and a Plan C, in case of emergencies."

"Like this."

"I doubt he imagined an emergency quite like this. But yeah."

The radio crackled again as Mercy came up the stairs from below.

Jesse looked out at the crowd in the street. The Chinatown fires were burning brighter than ever, but the crowd had turned its attention to the airship's fulgent glare and clattering roar. The helicopter's searchlight flitted over the homes of the wealthy like the attention of a jealous god. A few people began to run haphazardly or to crouch behind walls, and Jesse hoped no one would be bold or stupid enough to pull a gun and fire at what frightened them.

"There's no protected place to land," Elizabeth said, raising her voice above the noise, "so they want to do a rooftop evac, like they do with flood victims."

Mercy stepped up next to Jesse. "Do they have a litter?"

"A Stokes basket, yeah," Elizabeth said.

"Tell them to send it down first. I don't want my father dropping a security team on us."

Elizabeth relayed the request and listened to the answer. "They say they'll lower the basket for casualties as soon as you're safely on board."

"Not acceptable. There's no way I'm going aboard before Phoebe. If I see anything *but* a basket coming out of that helicopter, I'll be out the front door and running."

Jesse's respect for the woman went up another notch. Mercy looked as skinny and insubstantial as the women whose pictures appeared in glossy twenty-first-century magazines, but she possessed considerable grit.

The airship was almost directly overhead now. Its metallic underside glittered balefully, and it broadcast a false daylight that turned the lawn a phosphorescent green. "No, he's right here," Elizabeth said, and handed the radio to Jesse.

Jesse accepted it reluctantly. The next voice he heard was August Kemp's. "Elizabeth says you're injured. Is that true?"

"My right arm, but I can still use it."

"And my daughter is there with you?"

"Yes."

"Listen carefully. Don't speak, just listen. I don't want you to hurt her, but I want you to take her into custody. Right now. Handcuff her if necessary."

Jesse pretended to think about it. Neither Mercy nor Elizabeth had been able to hear the exchange, but both eyed him warily. He let a few more seconds slip by. Then he said, "I won't do it."

He waited another long minute, but Kemp said nothing further. He gave the radio to Elizabeth. She pressed its buttons, without result. Then a man wearing a helmet and orange-colored overalls appeared in the side door of the airship, swinging out a metal-frame bed—Elizabeth had called it a Stokes basket—on a system of ropes and pulleys. Jesse hurried into the house, calling out to Theo and Aunt Abbie to help him carry Phoebe up the stairs.

18

Aboard the airship there was a City physician, a solemn black man, who examined Phoebe without speaking. She had been sweating and moaning when Jesse carried her up the stairs, but the doctor administered a drug and plugged a bag of fluid into her arm, and soon enough her eyes closed and her face became peaceful.

Jesse would have thanked the man, but the roar of the helicopter was as oppressive on the inside as it had seemed from the outside. Meaningful communication was almost impossible for anyone not wearing a headset, and Jesse had not been given one, so he sat wordlessly on a bench in the cramped interior as the doors were sealed and the airship hurtled higher into the air. Through the small window at his shoulder he was able to see the whole of San Francisco below him, brightest where it was burning, and all the moonlit land and the sea that enclosed it, until vertigo made him turn away and close his eyes.

When he felt well enough to look again, there was nothing but a plain of cloud, as wide as the world and flowing like an ethereal river. Mercy had bandaged his wounded arm for him, and he cradled it against his body to minimize the pain. After a time the clouds opened to reveal misty hilltops, moon-shadowed valleys, moon-blue rivers, a perspective that belonged by right to God himself; and it made him feel lonesome and fragile to be suspended over this abyss of air by nothing more than burning vapors and whirling steel.

It wasn't a prolonged journey. A helicopter couldn't fly all the way from San Francisco to Illinois without refueling, apparently. The airship gradually lost altitude until it was hovering over a patch of pavement somewhere in the western desert: a landing strip marked with yellow lights, a horizon of dry hills under a firmament of fierce, bright stars.

Mercy Kemp's clothes were bloody from the first-aid work she'd done—the entire cabin of the helicopter reeked of blood and hot metal and spent gunpowder—and she had exchanged fewer than ten words with her father since the rescue. Instead she had elected to sit with Theo and let herself drift in and out of sleep.

She was still shaking off her fatigue when she stepped onto the landing pad and was surrounded by a phalanx of security people in City uniforms who separated her from Theo and the others. Theo began to object, loudly, and Jesse Cullum looked ready to attempt a rescue if she needed it, but her father stepped out in front of the procession and said, "I want to have a word with my daughter in private. There's a fixed-wing aircraft being fueled, and in a few minutes we'll all be on it, *all* of us, so *calm the fuck down.* Nobody's being left behind."

So he said. But Mercy was inclined to believe him. Abandoning employees and runners wasn't his style, especially when he knew she'd carry the story back home. "It's all right," she called back to Theo.

She followed her father to a windowless room in a concrete-box building, where she sat in an office chair while he received a verbal report from the station's radio operator. The news was all bad. Pitched battles between railroad workers and federal troops had turned Baltimore into an inferno. There was rioting in Charleston, for reasons as yet unclear. In the South, dozens of black towns and neighborhoods had been burned by hooded vigilantes. The coal miners of Schuylkill County were on strike; Pinkerton men hired as strikebreakers had killed fourteen men and three women in the town of Shenandoah. Documents seized at certain banks had substantiated charges of counterfeiting and financial fraud against the City. John D. Rockefeller and Jay Gould—prominent men who had been dining with her father and bragging about it only a few months ago—had publically called for the arrest and trial of August Kemp.

Which obviously wasn't going to happen, at least not in this slice of Hilbert space. As soon as they were alone in the room, Mercy said, "This is worse than last time, isn't it?"

Her father stared at her. His eyes looked sunken, as if he hadn't slept for days. "I'm not prepared to discuss that with you."

Not that he had ever been a heavy sleeper. As a child Mercy had often heard him moving around their Long Island house after midnight, a comforting sound once she learned to recognize it. Five bells, all's well, Daddy's making his rounds. She was a light sleeper herself. As a teenager she had occasionally played the game of being awake when he was awake and moving from room to room without revealing her presence—watching TV in the basement while he plodded around the kitchen; fixing a snack in the kitchen when he was at work in his study. On rare occasions, important people visited; when that happened, and especially when conversation continued into the small hours, Mercy had amused herself by pretending to be a spy, eavesdropping from the top of the stairs or the nook behind the basement door.

Mercy's mother had been wholly uninterested in August Kemp's business affairs, but Mercy had been ardently curious about them, if only because business was never discussed in her presence. She knew her father was a wealthy man and that he owned many hotels and resorts and other properties around the world; she knew he had been married more than once, and she had met, if not especially liked, most of her step-siblings. And she knew he had friends in high places, including the high places of national politics. (A Democratic Speaker of the House had once spent the night in the guest bedroom. He turned out to be an obese and hilariously flatulent but otherwise perfectly ordinary man: The most interesting thing about him had been his job description.) It was during a late-night conversation between her father and two solemn-looking men in business suits that Mercy had first heard him mention the visitors from Hilbert space.

Much of what he said was incomprehensible to her, and not only because she heard it through the grate in the bedroom above her father's study. But in those days she had been keeping a diary (saved to a thumb drive she hid on her bookcase behind a copy of *Harry Potter and the Chamber of Secrets*), and she recorded in it what she believed she had heard. So, years later, when the truth began to leak out, either through rumors or by way of certain documents published by Wikileaks, it had only confirmed what Mercy had already guessed.

She was a first-year student at Stanford when the Department of Defense documents were published on the Internet. By that time it had become obvious to everyone in the family that Mercy was not the purse-dog-bearing Upper East Side fashion clone some of her half-sisters had become. She often talked to her father about current affairs, and he had seemed vaguely proud of her precocity, but any attempt to engage him about the Mirror—his first paratemporal resort had just opened—was met with a wall of platitudes and generalizations.

So she had formed her own ideas about the so-called visitors, presumed to have died in custody in 2003 or 2004. Wikileaks and her diary agreed: Where the visitors came from, humanity had survived a massive global die-back in which population numbers had plummeted to eighteenth-century levels. The survivors had responded by modifying not only the terrestrial environment but the human genome. Arguably, although they were descended from *Homo sapiens*, they had made themselves a distinct species. And they regarded twenty-first-century humanity with a combination of sympathy and contempt.

As they should, Mercy thought. But her father and his powerful friends didn't see it that way. What her father saw was the catastrophic ascendance of an effete, genetically engineered socialism. Hijacking the visitors' technology to build the City of Futurity had been his cry of defiance and denial.

She had said all that to him, back when he closed down the first of his Gilded Age resorts and before he opened the current City. He had told her she was foolish, that she had fallen under the influence of radicals, that she could believe such nonsense only because his money had sheltered her from what he called "the real world." (She wondered: *Which one?*)

The argument had turned into an angry mutual repudiation. They hadn't spoken since then. But he had worked hard to track her down and bring her to safety, now that the City of Futurity was sinking like an ocean liner gored by an iceberg, and she appreciated that, even if his motives were more calculated than sentimental. On some level, August Kemp still cared about her. Duly noted.

"I'll have a Beechcraft ready to take off inside of ten minutes," he said.

"The sooner the better, for Phoebe's sake."

"That's the name of the injured girl?"

"Yes."

"What is she to you?"

"Does it matter?"

"I was hoping she could be treated here—"

"And what, abandoned? What's she supposed to do, pick up her saline drip and hike across the Sierra Nevada?"

"We're not far from a rail spur. I could make arrangements. I'm not heartless. But neither am I in the business of rescuing random locals."

"We're not talking about random locals. We're talking about one particular person."

"I know that. Drop the condescending tone, Mercy. You're not on any moral high ground here. Your boyfriend is the one who smuggled in weapons. Like dropping matches into a barrel of gunpowder."

She refused to be drawn into an argument. "Phoebe needs to go to the City."

"If that's the case, I won't object."

"And I'll stay with her until she's stabilized."

"We're closing the Mirror. There are time limits."

"This isn't a negotiation. If you want to take me home in cuffs, you might as well call the guards now."

He stared at her. "Be careful what you ask for."

Jesse, Elizabeth, and Theo followed Phoebe as the City doctor wheeled her to the more distant of two concrete blockhouses, this one set up as a makeshift hospital. The doctor wore a plastic name tag announcing him as A. TALBOT, and he took

Phoebe into an adjoining room Jesse and the others were not allowed to enter.

Minutes passed. A guard—a local hire with an automatic rifle lax in his hands—blocked the exterior door, but there was only one of him, and he looked more sleepy than dangerous. Jesse exchanged a few desultory words with Theo Stromberg, who kept hitching up a pair of trousers he had been allowed to borrow from Randal's quarters back at the Nob Hill mansion, until Talbot came out of the back room and said, "She's stabilized for travel—which one of you is her family?"

Jesse stood up. "I'm her brother."

"Can you tell me her name?"

"Phoebe Cullum."

"And you are?"

"Jesse Cullum."

"Okay. Well, here's how it stands. We've stabilized Phoebe, but she needs surgery, so we'll transport her to the City. If the infirmary is intact, she can be treated there. But getting the bullet out of her and patching the internal damage isn't the end of it. Far from it. She's going to need post-surgical care. And that's going to be a problem, given that the City is about to be evacuated and abandoned. Am I correct in assuming she's a local?"

"Yes."

"Then she'll have to stay on this side of the Mirror, and you'll have to care for her."

"As long as there's life in me," Jesse said.

"I can set you up with antibiotics, sterile bandages, and some basic instructions, including how to handle a surgical drain. But after that, you'll be on your own. If there are complications—"

"Is that likely?"

"It's a real possibility. Infection, renal failure—you won't have the resources to deal with that."

"You mean she might die."

"I want to give you the tools and knowledge to prevent that. But she's going to have a long recovery even under the best circumstances, and you should be prepared for all possible outcomes."

"That's a gentle way of putting it."

"I'm sorry I can't be more positive. We'll do everything we can for her, Jesse. Right now we need to get her on the plane for the next leg of the trip."

Theo spoke up: "You said something about the infirmary maybe not being intact?"

"It was fine when I left there two days ago. But there were already federal troops with artillery caissons outside the wall." Talbot hesitated. "You're Theo Stromberg, aren't you?"

"Why, did Kemp put up a wanted poster?"

"No. I saw you speak at a rally. Chicago, summer of 2016."

"You attended a rally and then went to work for August Kemp?"

"I'm an old army medic, Mr. Stromberg. I like field work, and saving lives isn't political. Given how Mr. Kemp's first resort turned out, I took the job when it was offered it to me. I thought this one might need my services."

"Looks like you weren't wrong," Theo said.

Talbot wheeled Phoebe out of the blockhouse toward the new airship, and Jesse followed behind Elizabeth and Theo.

The guard at the door gave a little contemptuous sniff as they passed. Jesse turned back. "You have something to say?"

"No sir. Not to you."

"Last day on the job?"

"It looks that way. I was hired out of Carson City six months ago. Just to sit around this patch of nowhere in case I'm needed. Which I never was. I told them I'll make my own way to the railhead after they turn the lights out. As for the City of Futurity, those goddamned towers can fall down for all of me. Better if they do. You're one of us, you must know what these people are."

"And what are they?"

The guard spat a plug of tobacco into the darkness. "Whores, fancy boys, Chinamen, niggers . . ."

"They pay your salary, friend."

"Not much longer they don't." The guard shouldered his rifle. "Nor yours, either."

He walked away without looking back. Abandoning his post, Jesse thought, but that didn't seem to matter anymore. All sorts of things were being abandoned. It seemed like everyone was going home, or leaving it.

19

The next leg of the flight was faster but more terrifying, more terrifying because faster: The fixed-wing airship flew more like a bullet than a bird. It was probably the largest single thing to have been imported through the Mirror, and Jesse was not surprised Kemp had kept it hidden from local tourists and the press. One did not, in this vehicle, float. One hurtled.

He closed his eyes and gave himself over to his fatigue. The pain in his wounded right arm had become a hot rhythmic pulse, Morse code stuttering a single letter, but he managed a few rounds of dream-haunted sleep despite it. He dreamed of the days of his life divided into leaves and bound into a book that could be read only backward. He dreamed of those gnomes Mercy believed in, visitors from a century even more distant than the twenty-first, and in his dream they marched out of the frame of a vanity mirror, pale and serene as clouds, and one of them (it might have been male or female or both or neither) stood before Jesse and told him that all things change and in the end nothing endures but change itself.

After an incalculable time the airship landed at another remote strip, somewhere in Illinois but west of the City, where he helped transfer Phoebe to another helicopter for the last leg of the flight. Jesse was tempted to sleep again, and he dozed a little, until a band of daylight struck his eyes as the helicopter made a banking turn: Morning had come. He tried to make himself alert as he glanced around the cabin. Mercy Kemp and Theo Stromberg were safety-belted next to Elizabeth and the dark-skinned physician, Talbot. Phoebe was strapped to a gurney—alive, though she looked as pale as death—and August Kemp rode near the front of the airship, wearing a headset that allowed him to communicate with the pilot.

Reluctantly, Jesse steeled his nerve and looked out the window.

The view by daylight was as disorienting as it had been by night. The sun had just cleared a reef of cloud on the eastern horizon. Empty prairie scrolled beneath the airship, green with wild grass and stitched with the silver thread of rivers and creeks; a flock of passenger pigeons wheeled over a blue-green bog in the shadow of a low hill. Ahead, two distant needles caught the rake of the sunlight: the twin towers of the City of Futurity. Talbot had taken a digital device from his pocket and was holding it to the window—recording video, Jesse assumed, just as the twenty-first-century tourists habitually did.

Elizabeth left her seat and moved next to Jesse. She had been talking to Mercy and Theo—more like shouting at them, given the unrelenting noise of the engines—and sparing occasional sour glances for August Kemp. Jesse's understanding of the argument between Kemp and his daughter had deepened over the past day. His first impression—of Mercy Kemp as a pampered daughter who needed rescuing from the consequences of her fashionable radicalism—had been too hasty. Mercy wasn't stupid or obviously foolish, and her presence here was more than an act of petulant rebellion. It was a disagreement about money and power and purpose, imported (like so many other bewildering things) from the age of the Mirror. Mercy believed her father was extracting profits shamelessly while dodging responsibility for the crisis he left in his wake. And as far as Jesse could tell, that was true.

But it had ceased to matter to him. His business now was with Phoebe, saving her life by any means possible. After that, Phoebe, if she lived, would go back to Aunt Abbie, and Jesse would revert to what he had been before he ever stumbled into the City of Futurity: a drifter, without employment or prospects, but generally sober and good with his fists. Maybe he would go back to San Francisco, now that Roscoe Candy was truly dead; maybe he would live and die where God had put him, in the gap between Pike Street and Dupont.

Elizabeth leaned into his shoulder. "Something's going on!" she shouted. "Kemp's talking to someone at the City, and he doesn't look happy!"

Jesse glanced forward. She was right. There was no way to know what Kemp was saying, but he looked like a Thomas Nast caricature of an infuriated Irishman.

"Probably about *that*," Elizabeth said, nodding at the window. Jesse turned to take a second look just as Talbot crossed the aisle, aiming his phone in a new direction.

They were close enough to the City now to see that the newspaper stories had not been exaggerated. A small army was arrayed before the wall, with what looked like caissons and supply wagons enough to fight another Bull Run. Smoke rose from cooking fires as men in blue uniforms milled about, treading the prairie grass to bare earth. The airship made a sweeping turn, revealing powder scars on the City's gaudily painted wall where it had been struck by cannon fire. Struck, but not breached—the wall was massive, and the City had its own small army of uniformed men arrayed along the top of it.

From this altitude it all looked peaceful enough, until a federal cannon gouted flame and a canister exploded just short of the gate.

The City's soldiers fired a volley in response, and the troops at the vanguard hastily pulled back, but their artillery emplacements were beyond range of the wall-top gunners, and now they began to fire in earnest. Smoke and dust rose from the battleground as if a giant had pounded the earth with his fist.

Kemp shouted into his mouthpiece again, and the airship veered toward its landing pad outside Tower Two.

They touched ground with a bounce that suggested the pilot's haste. Outside, a committee of grim-faced security personnel waited for the rotors to slow. All other open space within the boundary of the City walls was empty. Jesse had seen the City grounds deserted during snowstorms, or in the hours before dawn, but never on a sunny morning like this, and the reason was as obvious as it was shocking: at least a couple of artillery rounds had overshot the walls and struck the north face of Tower Two, shattering windows and scarring the concrete façade.

He waited until Phoebe's wheeled bed had been hoisted out of the airship, then followed Elizabeth and the others to the lobby doors. The medical facilities were in Tower One, where visitors from the future customarily stayed, so Kemp's security team hustled everyone down an inclined ramp to the underground tunnel connecting the buildings. A pair of junior medics took charge of Phoebe, one at each end of the gurney, with Talbot following close behind, as Elizabeth came up beside Jesse and said in a low voice, "This is worse than I expected."

The siege, she meant. He said, "The wall is bound to come

down sooner or later. There'll be federal troops in both towers before long."

"It'll be bad for Kemp. Back home, I mean. He'll try to blame all this on Theo, of course. But if it gets out that City employees fired on American soldiers, even in self-defense, Kemp will be out of business for good."

She had told him on the train—days ago, though it seemed more like months—that Kemp's first City of Futurity had ended badly: Three people had been killed when a former Confederate soldier entered the City's pavilion at the Centennial Exhibition in Philadelphia and opened fire on the crowd. It wasn't much compared to what was happening here, but it had emboldened activists like Theo Stromberg and raised questions about the ethics of time travel. "If *any* of this gets into the press back home—I mean the bank fraud, the riots, the attempt on Grant's life, this siege—it'll be all over."

"Will Kemp be put on trial?"

"Maybe not a criminal trial, more likely a Congressional investigation, but yeah—that's what Theo Stromberg's hoping for."

"And will you be called to testify?"

She seemed startled by the idea. "I guess it's not impossible."

"Would you testify against Kemp, even if it cost you your job?"

"I wouldn't lie to save him. And he's already pissed at me, so losing the job is probably a done deal. Sure, I guess I'd testify. Theo's a fanatic, but he's right—Kemp's reckless, he hurts people, and he ought to be stopped."

The tunnel was busy with City operatives rushing back and forth, some riding on electrical carts, some laden with boxes or luggage. Large-scale goods too valuable to be abandoned would have been taken to the Mirror by way of the enormous freight elevators at ground level, while City personnel and any remaining civilians lined up for the less gargantuan staff elevators here. It looked as if the City's twenty-first-century employees had all been moved to Tower One to wait their turn to leave, while local hires were segregated in Tower Two to wait for something else—the inevitable entry of federal forces, to whom they could surrender, presumably, and plead innocence.

Kemp's people arrived at a doorway that marked the border between Tower One and Tower Two, where a pair of security men had been stationed to scrutinize everyone who passed through. The men doing the scrutinizing, Jesse realized with dismay, were his old enemies from Tower One, Dekker and Castro, two men who done as much as anyone to convince him that the future had not abolished vindictiveness or petty jealousy.

August Kemp stood next to Dekker as his party began to pass through. Phoebe on her gurney, pushed by the medics, then Elizabeth, Mercy Kemp, Theo Stromberg, then Dr. Talbot—but Kemp stepped forward and put a hand on Talbot's chest and said, "Your phone, please, Doctor."

"My phone?"

"For security reasons. You'll get it back once we're home."

He would get it back with all the dangerous images purged from it, Jesse thought. Talbot looked like he might object, then sighed. "If you insist," he said, handing the phone to Kemp, who passed it into the meaty hand of Dekker, who pocketed it, grinning. Talbot was allowed to pass. Then it was Jesse's turn.

Except that it was not. "Hold on, chief," Dekker said.

Kemp took Jesse's arm and steered him aside. "I'm afraid we can't allow locals beyond this point."

"My sister's a local," Jesse said, "and she's already beyond this point."

"Phoebe's your sister? Mercy didn't mention that. It looks like Phoebe got caught in the crossfire when you were doing whatever it was you were doing in that Nob Hill house. That was personal business, wasn't it? No connection to the job you were hired to do."

Jesse didn't venture an answer. Beyond the doorway, Elizabeth turned to look back but was hustled away by the press of people.

"I promised Mercy we'd take care of the girl, and we will. And as soon as she's patched up, we'll deliver her to you at Tower One. I'm a man of my word. And I promised you something else, didn't I? This." Kemp reached into his jacket and extracted a bag of jingling coins. Gold eagles, Jesse assumed, maybe the same bag Kemp had shown him back in Oakland. "Severance pay. I'm not sure you've earned it. You put my daughter in danger, and I'd be justified in cutting you off without a penny more than you've already been paid. But I'm not vindictive and I don't hold a grudge. Take it. Go on. Take it, Jesse."

Elizabeth and Dr. Talbot had already disappeared. So had Phoebe. Jesse considered his options. He continued to meet Kemp's cynical stare.

But he took the money.

"Some advice," Kemp said. "That arm looks pretty ugly. Have someone take care of it before it gets infected. And if you're afraid of how the army might treat you, as a City employee? Don't be. You're the man who saved the life of U. S. Grant. A fucking hero! Tell them that. Tell everyone! Talk to the press, play it up. A book, a lecture series—you could make yourself a rich man."

Kemp pushed through the doorway and was gone. Jesse hung back, watching the passage. Dekker and Castro stood on each side of the door, eyeing him in return.

Jesse waited.

After a few minutes the crowd began to thin. These were the last of the City people, Jesse thought, abandoning Tower Two to the local employees. Soon the crowd was scant enough that the mechanical doors slid shut from time to time, so that stragglers had to use a pass card to open them. Jesse chose one of these empty moments to approach the door again.

Dekker's grin expanded. He clearly relished the prospect of a fight . . . perhaps particularly because of the wound to Jesse's right arm, blood from which had stained the sleeve of his shirt and was leaking through the bandage even now. "Need some help, chief? You're headed in the wrong direction."

"I ought to be with my sister."

"Well, but that's not possible."

Castro kept quiet and looked uneasy. Jesse narrowed his attention to Dekker and only Dekker. "I mean to pass through, so you might as well get out of my way."

"Not happening, bro. As an alternative, I suggest you go fuck yourself."

Jesse charged him. These twenty-first-century security men were unnaturally tall and densely muscled, but Jesse was a big man for his time and his skills were brutally practical. It gave him a grim pleasure to step inside the radius of Dekker's beefy arms and deliver a blow that rocked Dekker's head back and sent a spurt of blood from his nose.

But Dekker wasn't on his heels for long. He recovered quickly enough to close Jesse in a grip that trapped his injured right arm. And as Jesse struggled, flailing with his free left hand, Dekker began to squeeze. The man's strength was astonishing. The pressure ignited a furious pain, as if the flesh itself were screaming. Jesse endured it until a new freshet of blood flowed down his forearm to the wrist and began to spatter the tiled floor. Dekker put his mouth to Jesse's ear and said, "Had enough, chief?"

Jesse refused to speak.

"I can do this forever, asshole. Had enough?"

Jesse managed to nod his head, once.

"Say it. Seriously. Say it."

"Enough," Jesse gasped.

Dekker relaxed his grip, but followed with an open-palm blow that rocked Jesse's head and sent him reeling. "Just head on back to Tower Two," Dekker said. "They'll send you your sister when they're done with her. Chief."

Jesse gave himself credit for staying upright. The damage to his arm was significant. An ominous numbness, almost worse than the pain, propagated through his right hand. Some of the fingers were reluctant to obey him. He turned and walked away. The sound of Dekker's laughter followed him as he stumbled down the tunnel.

Dekker was savoring his victory. He would probably continue to savor it, Jesse thought, right up until the moment he realized that in the course of the struggle Jesse had taken from him both his pass card and Talbot's phone.

Local employees of the City of Futurity had been herded into the commissary in the basement level of Tower Two, where they could surrender *en masse* to federal forces once the evacuation was complete and the Mirror shut down. None of these people was responsible for August Kemp's crimes, and in principle none of them had anything to fear from the troops. But guns had been fired in earnest, and City employees were understandably nervous about the consequences of that. The crowd consisted of a hundred people or so, and some of them must have recognized Jesse, but apart from a few startled exclamations they left him alone. Limping slightly, bleeding from his arm, his clothes ragged and bloodstained, he guessed he looked as if he might be followed by an undertaker or a flock of carrion crows.

He spotted Dorothy, the war widow who used to sell him muffins from the Starbucks booth, seated on an upturned trash bin. Her eyes widened at the sight of him, but she was brave enough not to flinch. "Jesse Cullum, is that you?"

"Yes, ma'am. I was away, but I got back this morning."

"How is that possible—did you fly over the wall?"

She meant it facetiously, but he nodded. "In fact I did."

"I'm tempted to believe you. You're hurt!"

"Not fatally. Tell me, have you seen Doris Vanderkamp today?"

"Do you see how few of us are still here? Most of the local hires left as soon as the evacuation was announced. The rest of us took cash bonuses to stay behind and help, for better or worse. If Doris had been prudent she'd be long gone. But when was Doris ever *prudent*? I saw her heading for the dormitory section a few minutes ago, probably packing up what's left of her possessions. Jesse, do you know what's going on? We haven't heard from management for hours. Has the wall been breached?"

"Kemp's people mean to hold off the soldiers until the Mirror is shut down. But I'm guessing you'll see soldiers inside by nightfall."

She smiled wanly. "I liked it here, Jesse. Oh, I know it was all pretend. The amity, the smiles. Past and future clasping hands in friendship. But it was a *pretty* dream, wasn't it?"

Jesse felt a surge of affection for this solemn woman who had served him coffee on countless winter mornings. "For some of us it was. Best of luck to you, Dorothy."

"And to you, Jesse Cullum, wherever you're hurrying off to. Have someone see to that arm!"

He found Doris Vanderkamp in her cubicle in the dormitory wing, just as Dorothy had said. The door to her room was half ajar, but he knocked so as not to alarm her. It didn't work. She saw his face and emitted a small shriek. "Jesse!"

"Yes," he said, "it's me."

She came to him and took his arm—his uninjured left arm, luckily—and steered him inside. He sat on her bed and let a wave of dizziness wash over him. "Lord," she said, "you're bleeding like a butchered hog!"

A coin-sized drop of blood stained the bedsheet. He gazed at it dully. "I'm sorry . . ."

"You need a bandage."

"I already have one."

"Then you need a fresh one, or a tourniquet."

"It's a kind thought. But what I really need, Doris, is a uniform."

"What? I thought you said 'uniform.'"

"I did. A City security uniform."

"Are you drunk? That's the *last* thing you need. All of us here already traded our uniforms for civilian clothes. The army will be inside sooner or later, and you don't want to get caught wearing City colors. It would only make a target of you. Lie down and let me look at that wound."

"Did you take medical training in my absence?"

"No, but I can tie a cloth."

He was tempted to take her advice, at least the part about lying down. But if he closed his eyes he might not open them again for hours. "My case is different. I'm serious—I need a uniform that fits me."

Her eyes narrowed. "What business are you caught up in now?"

"It's a long story, Doris, I'm sorry. A City uniform—can you get me one?"

"The lockers are full of them." She sighed. "If you're willing to wait here, I'll bring you one. I guess anything would serve you better than that bloody rag of a shirt."

"One more thing. Do you have paper and a pen?"

She waved at her desk, the kind with which every dormitory cubicle was equipped. "Top drawer."

"I thank you," he said. But she had already left the room. Time was slipping away from him. He located a pad of paper embossed with the City logo and a City pen with a rolling point. Paper in his lap, pen in his left hand, he gathered his unruly thoughts and began to write.

He had filled two pages by the time Doris returned with a uniform that looked as if it might fit him. He set aside the pages and let her help him trade his civilian pants for City trousers. That was easy enough. The shirt was more difficult. He took Dekker's pass card and Talbot's phone from his pocket and put them on Doris's desk.

"That's an iPhone," she said.

"How do you know about such things?"

"I was courted by a Tower One man last winter, when you were off chasing runners or whatever you were doing. He had a pass card like that. He used it to sneak me into his quarters. And he had an iPhone, too. He liked to take pictures with it. Moving pictures," she said, waggling her eyebrows suggestively.

Jesse understood that Doris liked to think she possessed the power to make him jealous. "What kind of moving pictures?"

"The *intimate* kind."

"The cad," he said, to please her.

Doris grinned triumphantly. "I didn't mind! He said there are women who do it for a living, where he comes from, and they're perfectly respectable, and I'm as good at it as any of them."

"Seems like you were born too soon."

"Are you making fun of me?"

"Far from it." He clenched his teeth and pulled off his shirt. The shirt and the bandage beneath it and the flesh of his arm had been glued together with blood. Peeling it all apart caused black spots to cloud his vision. Doris sucked in her breath when she saw the exposed wound. "Jesse . . . *I think I can see bone.*"

He wished she hadn't spoken. "Bind it," he said. "Any old cloth. Tear a strip from my shirttail if you have to. Bind it for me, Doris—I can't do it myself."

She looked queasy but followed his instructions. The bleeding wasn't stanched, but it slowed. He used his old shirt to wipe some of the spilled blood from his arm, and he covered up the rest with the fresh City shirt and the blue City blazer with the City of Futurity insignia on it.

"And I got these for you," Doris said.

A pair of Oakley sunglasses. The kind he had once considered supremely desirable. Tinted plastic and a thimble's-worth of aluminum. He put them on and regarded himself in Doris's mirror.

"You look as City as they come," she said.

He pocketed the pass card and was pocketing Talbot's iPhone when an idea occurred to him. "Doris, have you really used one of these devices?"

"I said so, didn't I?"

"To make moving pictures?"

"Yes."

"I'm going up to the observation deck to find out what's happening. Will you come with me?"

"Those elevators don't open to us anymore."

"They'll open for me. It'll only take a few minutes. Will you come?"

She seemed flattered and curious in equal parts. "Yeah, all right," she said.

The observation deck of Tower Two, like the rest of Tower Two, had been designed to impress guests who had never seen a building taller than three stories. Jesse had been up here occasionally during his tenure at the City, and for him, as for most guests, the effect was an amalgam of fascination and dread. The floor was not divided by interior walls, and the outer walls were made of thick transparent glass. It was like standing on an open platform suspended from a cloud.

Not everyone enjoyed the experience. Every week a few visitors, by no means exclusively women, fainted at the sight. Others begged to be taken back to solid ground. And even Doris's pleasure was not unalloyed, it seemed to Jesse. Or maybe it was the risk of a stray artillery round that made her uneasy.

He went to the north side of the deck, where he could see the wall and the army arrayed beyond it. From this angle it was clear what the City's strategy had been. The army was separated from the wall by a broad swath of empty prairie, a sort of no-man's-land, marking out the effective range of a twenty-first-century rifle. The City's soldiers were posted atop the wall itself, which was more than broad enough to accommodate them, and they were all armed with automatic weapons. Any infantryman who ventured into the no-go zone would be rewarded with a bullet. And City rifles were accurate at distances that made even the finest Winchester seem like a farmer's musket.

The gate itself was a smaller steel barrier set into the wall, and the soldiers had trained their artillery on that target, perhaps hoping to eventually blow it open and enable a massed charge. Or maybe they were simply restraining themselves in hope of a negotiated surrender: They could have shelled the towers at any time, as a few stray shots had demonstrated.

The steel gate was sturdy, but it wasn't as massive as the wall itself, and there was enough accumulated rubble at the base of it to suggest a breach was possible. As Jesse watched, another artillery round burst against it. The City's defenders responded with rounds of automatic-rifle fire.

"Kemp wants to buy time to finish the evacuation," Jesse said. "The Mirror is a bottleneck. It's hard to say how long this will last. You can record moving pictures with this phone?"

"For the last time, yes! But I don't mean to stand close enough to the window to do so. I'll go back down, if you don't mind. I feel like a flea on a flagpole."

"All right, but will you show me how to do it?"

She spent a few grudging minutes adjusting Talbot's device until it needed only the touch of a finger to begin capturing images. Jesse thanked her. She said, "You're bleeding again."

He was, but it wasn't a problem he could address just now.

"And you're pale as a ghost."

"I can take care of myself from here on out. Thank you for your help. You're a good girl at heart, Doris."

He thought the words would please her, but she frowned. "Do you mean that?"

"Of course I do."

"Then say it like I was one of *them*."

"What?"

"You know what I mean."

"Woman," he corrected himself. "You're a good woman."

She smiled. "And you're a gentleman."

"I left you something," he said, "back in your cubicle."

He used Dekker's pass card to open the elevator for her. She stepped inside and gave him a longing look. Those big eyes of hers were what had drawn him to her in the first place, against his own better judgment. She said, "We were a good pair, weren't we? While we lasted?"

No, not especially. "Sure, we were."

She smiled and kissed his cheek. "Keep safe."

Keeping safe was not an option. But he nodded as the doors closed.

In truth, he would have liked to get off his feet. There was something lulling about this bright, vacant aerie. It provoked an urge to sleep, despite the thunder of guns. The tiled floor began to look like a bed to him. But he dared not give in to that temptation. It was the siren song of his faltering body. He pictured Phoebe in his mind's eye. Phoebe and Elizabeth. He would sleep when they were safe.

Now the federal cannons began to fire *en masse*, a concentrated volley that probably represented some frustrated commander's failing patience, all focused on the main gate. Swaying at the edge of the observation deck, Jesse took off the Oakleys Doris had given him and dropped them at his feet. He raised the iPhone to eye level, peered at its screen and at the diminishing row of bars that predicted its useful life, touched the icon that caused it to record moving pictures. The device captured images of rising smoke and City soldiers firing fierce volleys, the steel gate trembling under the artillery barrage. At least two shells arced over the wall and struck Tower Two as the battle went on, impacts that shook the floor under Jesse's feet.

He was still recording all this when a vast shape hove up at the periphery of his vision, close enough to rattle the window. It was the City helicopter—the one that used to give rides to tourists—but there were no tourists in it now. As it canted toward the besieging army Jesse saw an open door and figures with rifles at the ready.

It was as if a monstrous but formerly pacific creature had been provoked to deadly violence. The airship crossed the City's boundary and bore down directly on the federal lines. What happened next seemed dreamlike, framed in the luminous display of the iPhone: federal marksmen firing futile volleys at the airship—the airship tilting to give its own gunners a field of fire—then rounds pouring down from above in a sudden, furious rain. Here was Thermopylae, Jesse thought madly. Here was Bull Run.

Blue uniforms blossomed with blood.

He went on recording until the phone's screen dimmed to darkness. In a matter of minutes the besieging army was reduced from ordered ranks to terrified chaos, its flags trampled in a panicked retreat. And now the victorious City men began to abandon their positions atop the wall, hurrying down interior stairways and across the open courtyard toward Tower Two as the attacking airship circled back to its landing pad.

Which could only mean that the evacuation was nearly complete.

Which meant Jesse had to hurry.

He used Dekker's card to call an elevator, hoping the artillery impacts hadn't damaged the machinery. Hours seemed to pass before the door slid open. He stumbled inside, leaving boot prints in the blood that had puddled at his feet.

———

Down in the sublevels, in the tunnel that connected the towers, he joined the crowd of men who had just left the wall. He recognized none of them, and none of them recognized him. They were all from the future, new arrivals recruited to act as a rear guard for the evacuation. A few of them saw the blood he was trying to conceal and urged him to hurry to the Mirror or to go to the clinic in Tower One while there were still medics available. It was this last advice he chose to accept. His body had grown mysteriously heavy, but he refused all offers of help. Better not to involve strangers. He found the designated elevator and used Dekker's card to summon it.

The door opened on a hectic crowd of men and women in white gowns, uniformed security men, distressed civilians. Jesse stepped out of the elevator and tried to orient himself. The Tower One medical clinic had originally been a small part of this arcade floor, but the broad central corridor was lined with cots and gurney beds now; shop stalls had been curtained off to create makeshift surgical rooms where physicians patched up security men who had been injured in skirmishes and civilians who had been hurt by stray artillery rounds. No sooner had Jesse stumbled out of the elevator than a medic pushed a loaded gurney past him: It looked as if casualties were being hurried to the Mirror as soon as they were stabilized.

He caught the attention of a woman in a green surgical gown. "I need to find Dr. Talbot."

"Are you in from the wall?" She looked him over, and her eyes widened. "You need to be triaged."

"Talbot," Jesse insisted.

"I'm sorry, but you need attention right now."

"Not as much as I need to find Talbot."

"I don't have time to argue. Triage is by the fountain. I think

Dr. Talbot is working over there,"—she waved vaguely—"in what used to be the spa. Take your pick."

It was only a scant few yards to the sign that said MASSAGE/ HYDROTHERAPY/FACIAL AND BODY SCRUBS, but the journey seemed immensely long. Jesse kept his eye out for Talbot, but in the end it was Elizabeth he found. She came barreling out of the crowd so eagerly that he had to turn away to protect his damaged arm. "Jesse!"

He hugged her, or leaned on her, a little of both.

"I wanted to kick Kemp's ass when I realized he shut you out, but by then we were deep into Tower One and I figured I ought to stick with Phoebe. They handcuffed Theo and Mercy and took them to the Mirror, but—are you all right?"

Not entirely. He ignored the question and asked where Phoebe was.

"Talbot's with her" was all Elizabeth would say.

His thoughts had grown unreliable, but he remembered the iPhone. He took it from his pocket and presented it to her. "It's the one Kemp's people confiscated," he said. "I took some extra pictures with it. The kind August Kemp doesn't want anyone to see."

Phoebe lay on a table in a back room of the former spa with bags of fluid attached to her body. Her face was alabaster-white, her eyes were closed. Dr. Talbot took Jesse by his good arm and steered him to a chair. "You need attention," he said.

I need to stay awake a little longer, Jesse thought. *That's what I need.* "How is she?"

Talbot took a vial of liquid from the heap of medical supplies on an adjacent table and drew some of the fluid into a syringe. "Under the circumstances," he said, "I can't help her."

Jesse focused on the words until they made sense. Even then, he refused to believe it. He had come too far to be dismissed so cavalierly. "With all your futuristic medicine—"

"Jesse, listen to me. I can't help her *here*. We X-rayed her, and the internal damage is too extensive for a quick repair. There's a good chance she'll survive, but only if she gets careful surgery and post-surgical support. And I can't give her that— *here*."

Five years, Jesse thought. For five years all he had done, from working at the City to killing Roscoe Candy, had been for Phoebe's sake. To protect her and to redeem her from the ugliness of the world she had been born into. And he had failed. He closed his eyes.

Elizabeth came close to him. "Jesse," she said. "There are dozens of injured people being taken back through the Mirror. No one's checking their ID. Do you understand? Jesse? If Talbot puts a tag on Phoebe's gurney, he can take her through the Mirror. No questions asked. Hell to pay when they find out, but by the time that happens she'll be getting real treatment. It'll save her life. *But she can't come back*. Once the Mirror's closed, there's no opening it again. Do you understand? *Jesse?*"

He struggled to find the meaning of her words in the increasingly cavernous space his thoughts now occupied. If he understood correctly, she was offering him a ghost of hope. It meant he would never see Phoebe again. But Phoebe might live.

"Yes," he said. "Yes. All right. Take her."

"And you?"

"What about me?"

Talbot hovered into view, still holding a syringe. "She means you're a plausible invalid. If I hook you up to a saline drip and give you something to make you sleep, odds are I can get you to the other side along with your sister. If that's what you want."

The medication to make him sleep might not be needed. His

vision narrowed until all it contained was Elizabeth. Her face, her eyes.

The floor shuddered under him. The lights flickered, there were shouts of alarm. *At least one of the federal artillery emplacements must have survived the helicopter assault,* Jesse thought. Tower One was being shelled.

A Klaxon sounded, everything was in motion now, an oceanic roar of voices, the smell of blood . . . "It's up to you." Elizabeth's voice, taut as a piano wire. "It won't be easy either way, but you have to choose."

He understood that he was being offered an invitation, but to what? To Futurity, he thought; to the diorama world, spaceships and luminous cities; but no, Futurity was a myth. That was a fact the City had taught him. Futurity was nothing but a place. A faraway place. Another country.

Her voice again: "Help me get him on a gurney."

Hands lifting him.

"Jesse, can you hear me? We don't have much time. Last call. Where do you want to go?"

The question required an answer. He summoned what remained of his strength. "With you," he said, or meant to say, but darkness took him before he could be sure.

EPILOGUE

Magnificent Ruins

—1889—

Long ago, in his first letter from Illinois, Jesse had described the towers of the City as "an architecture fit for angels." And in his last letter he had written, "They will make magnificent ruins."

And he was right, Abbie Hauser thought. The prophecy had been fulfilled with remarkable speed.

Ten years and more had passed since Jesse's final communication. During that time she had often resolved to make this visit, and for years she had put it off, distracted by her situation and the daily business of coping with it. And while she dithered, both she and the City had grown old. Her bones ached on winter mornings, her digestion was irregular, intimations of mortality intruded on her thoughts. And the City of Futurity had been given up to wind and rust and nesting birds.

"Is that it?" Soo Yee asked. "There on the horizon?"

Their carriage crested one of the rolling mounds that passed for hills in this part of Illinois, on a road that had once been smoothly paved but had been crazed and broken by seasons of sun and ice. There it was on the horizon, the City of Futurity, dark against the pale opacity of an October morning. Two man-made buttes, as if the Illinois bedrock had lifted its arms to the heavens. Abbie tugged her shawl and sighed. "Yes."

"Like gravestones," Soo Yee said.

"Memorials, perhaps. Not gravestones. Phoebe and Jesse aren't dead, Soo Yee. At least, I don't believe so. They're just— not *here*."

They were not dead, but this was the place where they had left the sensible world, and that was why Abbie had wanted to come. She carried with her Jesse's last letter, written under the letterhead of the City, on crisp white paper made soft as cloth by years of handling. She didn't need to look at it. She had committed it to memory long ago.

Dear Aunt Abbie,

Please forgive my brevity. I have not much time to write. If you receive this letter it will be by the graces of a woman named Doris Vanderkamp. I have also given her a large number of gold eagles in the hope that she will deliver at least some fraction of them to you. Doris is kindhearted but of questionable reliability, so I cannot depend on her to do more than put this letter in the mail, care of your family in Boston in case you have sold the house on California Street. I hope my words, if nothing else, reach you safely.

Several carriages and an omnibus arrived in the courtyard inside the pitted wall of the City.

Abbie had arranged to join a guided group tour, organized by the Women's Auxiliary of the Illinois Grange and consisting mainly of females. It was an end-of-autumn tour, at a discounted price. The weather was chilly, and low cloud obscured the heights of the two immense towers; but the summer crowds were absent, which Abbie considered a benefit. She left the carriage and joined the crowd of thirty or so women assembling around the hired guide, a young man who worked at the City on behalf of the Union Pacific Railroad, the nominal owner of the property.

Doris Vanderkamp had arrived on the doorstep of Abbie's Boston family late in the summer of 1877, bearing the letter and three gold coins. Doris had impressed Abbie as less virtuous than Jesse wanted to believe, and those coins had once, quite obviously, had many companions, now absent. But a certain Christian charity of spirit prevented Abbie from resenting the theft, if it could be called that. Doris, an unmarried woman in a perilous world, had surely needed the money more than Abbie ever would. And Doris had faithfully delivered the letter itself, which was more precious than any coin.

"The towers are tall," the guide said, "but you ladies needn't worry that they might fall down. They are built around steel skeletons and are immensely sturdy. Buildings constructed in the same manner are rising in our big cities even now. Soon enough, structures tall as these may be commonplace in Chicago and New York! Join me as we enter the lobby of the nearest tower."

The tower's doors and windows were dark in the long October light. The buildings had been damaged by artillery fire in the long-ago siege, and a wind like the breath of Boreas blew through their many gaps and hollows.

Phoebe's wound is being treated as I write. I am at the City of Futurity now. Its two great towers are under siege, and will soon be abandoned—I think they will make magnificent ruins, with time. But I must speak bluntly. If this letter is all that reaches you—if months or years have passed and neither Phoebe nor I have contacted you—you should think of us as lost. Just what that means I cannot at present say.

Abbie and Soo Yee hung back from the crowd as the guide began his work in earnest. First they passed into the grand lobby of what had once been Tower Two, a room as big as a cathedral but cold as the autumn prairie. In its heyday these spaces would have been heated and illuminated by electricity and filled with astonishing displays. The original contract, which Mr. August Kemp had signed with the railroad, had provided for fuel and spare parts to be left behind after the Mirror was closed, to allow the City to operate as a tourist attraction for a few years more. But that genial agreement had come to grief in the City's final confrontation with the forces sent to arrest Mr. Kemp. Whatever had not already been stripped from the buildings by Kemp's men had been looted or vandalized by the victorious troops, or shipped off to the Smithsonian Institution in Washington.

Of course, the building was an astonishment even in its present condition. Its current owners had attempted to replicate some of its former glory, with recreated models of airships, crude wood and plaster dioramas, and murals, less than expertly painted, of the so-called world of futurity. "Not *our* futurity," the guide was careful to point out, "as even our visitors were willing to admit."

"Where *were* they from," Soo Yee asked in a whisper, "if not the future?"

Supposedly, from another leaf in some great (perhaps infinite) Book of Worlds, a book in which each page was an instantiated moment. Which meant—Abbie had given the subject much thought—no moment every truly ceased to exist. Every "now" was inscribed in a vaster Now. "The mind of God?" Soo Yee asked.

Soo Yee had lately joined a church, at Abbie's urging, and her question was in earnest. "Perhaps so," Abbie said.

"And the people who built this City, all those adulterers and Sodomites, they knew how to travel through God's mind?"

"Some say they learned the trick from others, wiser than themselves."

I apologize again for the events that injured Phoebe and defiled the house you so generously shared with us. It is a consolation to me and I hope to you that you will never again be troubled by Mr. R. Candy.

I expect many hard things will be said about the people of the future and their presence among us. Much of this disapproval they have earned and richly deserve. But not all. Do not judge them by Mr. August Kemp's behavior, no matter what the newspapers say. Remember that Elizabeth DePaul is one of them, and Elizabeth has adopted the cause of Phoebe's welfare as her own, and has been invaluable in getting her the care she needs.

The tour did not include the high parts of the Towers. There had been attempts, the guide said, to restore or replace the original mechanical elevators, but not even Mr. Thomas Edison's people (on loan from Menlo Park) had been able to find a safe way of doing so. The stairs were intact, and special tours were sometimes arranged for the physically fit, but such a climb would of course be too strenuous for the ladies. However, the guide said, photographs taken from the famous Observation Deck could be purchased at the conclusion of the tour.

Abbie supposed at least some of the fairer sex might have been willing to attempt the climb; but she was, admittedly, not one of them, not with the persistent dull pain that had lodged in her hip this last year. The views were said to be incomparable, but she would leave the Observation Deck to the athletes, the crows, and the four indifferent winds. It was the ruin of the Mirror she especially wanted to see.

Soo Yee wondered aloud, as they descended a lantern-lit stairway to an underground tunnel connecting the towers, how such a corrupt people could have built such astounding things.

"Engineering is not an art reserved exclusively to Christians," Abbie said.

"What do you mean—were they Freemasons?"

"No, of course not. What are you learning at that church you attend? No, I mean they may have been great builders, as the ancient Egyptians were, even without the enlightenment of Scripture. And at least some of the visitors *were* Christians, or claimed to be."

"Their Christianity isn't like ours."

"Shall we judge them on that basis? I don't want to sound like a pagan philosopher,"—thinking of Heraclitus, about whom she had read in an article in *Godey's*—"but all things change with time—perhaps even Christianity."

"A truth is a truth forever," Soo Yee declared, hurrying after the tour group, which threatened to disappear around a bend in the tunnel.

"I'm sure you're right."

A gentle lie. Abbie was sure of no such thing.

I lived among the City people for most of five years, and I must admit some of them were smug and self-satisfied in their attitude toward us. Others revered us, and saw us as the beau ideal of rugged self-reliance, but this too I have come to think of as a kind of condescension—as if we should be admired for our deadly diseases, the mortal vulnerability of our children, or our makeshift laws and customs.

In any case, their foolish admiration rankles less than their disdain. We don't like to be found abhorrent on the grounds that we will not share a meal with a Negro or allow a woman to enter into marriage with another woman. And we've retaliated by denouncing the City people as race-mixers, or feminists, or Sodomites—I have heard all these hateful words applied, and worse.

"We must not denounce what we do not understand," Abbie said, "simply because we do not understand it."

Here at the entrance to the Hall of the Mirror, one successful restoration had been achieved. The shafts that had once contained the City elevators had been excavated and the machinery replaced with the sort of commonplace lift that carried coal miners to their work. Soo Yee was reluctant to enter the wooden cage at the top of the shaft; she said it made her think of the entrance to Hell. "You take too literally the things your pastor tells you," Abbie said irritably. "We're only going a few yards under the earth. I'm sure Hell lies much deeper."

Abbie had postponed this pilgrimage for too long, out of a vain and unspoken hope that Jesse and Phoebe might yet appear on her doorstep. Much had happened since 1877. James Garfield had served two terms as president, despite a prophecy (in one of Mr. Theo Stromberg's letters to Lucy Stone, which the press insisted on calling the Blackwell letters) that he would be assassinated—or perhaps the prophecy had prevented its own fulfillment. Prophecies had been fulfilled or overthrown on many fronts as the influence of the City continued to ripple through the world. August Kemp's gift of practical knowledge had effected huge advances. Scientific hygiene, vaccination against disease, electric lighting, even gasoline-driven motor cars, all were becoming commonplace . . . though one also had to take into account Theo Stromberg's warning about the profligate use of what he called "fossil fuels."

But labor had not thrived under Garfield, the Negro of the South had been reduced to a peonage almost indistinguishable from slavery, the vote for women was no nearer than it had ever been. Kemp had told a pretty lie, Abbie thought, that in the future we would be ruled by the better angels of our nature; and Theo Stromberg had told a harder truth, that such angels do not arrive on clouds of glory but are born of travail and, too often, blood. (*And did we not already learn that lesson at Fort Sumter, Appomattox, Richmond? Have we forgotten it so completely and so soon?*)

The Hall of the Mirror, deep underground, could have enclosed two cathedrals and a shipyard. In its original state (the tour guide said as they stepped out of the lift, his voice disappearing into the cavernous space like a penny dropped into well), the chamber had been brightly illuminated. The current owners had installed a dynamo to produce alternating current, but it could bring the bank of ceiling lights to little more than a tepid glow, and lanterns were necessary to supplement it. "Allow your eyes to accommodate to the darkness," the guide advised.

Abbie waited patiently as shapes and properties slowly became distinct. The labyrinth of side rooms, the elaborate scaffolding, the loading bays, the detritus of strange machinery did not especially interest her. As soon as she could see well enough to do so, she walked to the foot of the Mirror itself. It was a steel semicircle, like a giant's wrist bracelet standing on end, as tall as the room was tall and as wide as it was wide, barnacled with fragments of copper and wire. In its prime it had enclosed a reflective but immaterial surface, a shimmering boundary between two worlds. Huge motors, railroad cars, even airships had passed through that boundary, along with hundreds of visitors. Now the Mirror opened onto nothing more than compressed earth and old Illinois stone.

The tour group moved from one novelty to another, but Abbie remained in place. She recalled what Doris Vanderkamp had told her: *When the soldiers came, all of us who worked at the City got rounded up and sorted out to find if any visitors were among us. I looked for Jesse, I waited for him, but he wasn't to be found. Nor his sister that he talked about. Maybe they found a way to escape the troops, but I doubt that, since Jesse was in a bad way with his wound and his sister was also hurt, or so he told me. My own guess is that they went through the Mirror. It's against the rules but the rules were being broken right and left. That's what I think, anyhow. They're safe there in the future, I think, probably flying through the air or visiting the moon.*

That was the belief Miss Vanderkamp had chosen to adopt, and Abbie had adopted it as well.

"It's like a tomb in here," Soo Yee said, shivering.

"No more a tomb than a gravestone."

Soo Yee said, "I'm sorry. They were like your children, I know."

Jesse and Phoebe Cullum. "Their father was a well-meaning drunkard, and I was a poor substitute for a real mother. But yes, I loved them, in my way. Not a tomb, Soo Yee, because I think they are not dead."

It was her benediction. The words were swallowed by darkness and the mineral smell of old earth, deep rust, autumn rain. And what was changed by her coming here? Nothing she could name. And yet.

Take care of your sister, Jesse.

"Are you praying?"

"Yes."

"But the tour is leaving. I don't want to be left behind."

"Then let us join them." Abbie turned away from the empty Mirror. "I'm ready for daylight now." Daylight, and whatever came next.

Were they our betters? No. They are people like us, Aunt Abbie, no better than some and no worse than others. From what I have learned of their world I can say with confidence that they have not brought forth a paradise on Earth.

But if there is such a thing as progress, perhaps Futurity is entitled to some part of the disdain with which they regard us.

Until the world is perfect we pay the price of progress by acknowledging the sins of the past. It is the business of the future to chastise us, and we ought to accept that chastisement. One of the secrets of these people is that they, too, were chastened by visitors from a distant future. Mr. Kemp is among those who refused the chastening. That is what makes a lie of all his rosy visions, and that is why his plans for us have gone so wrong.

Time is short and I do not know whether I will see you again. If not, I thank you for your countless kindnesses and I apologize for all the hardships I exposed you to. Don't fear for me, Aunt Abbie. No matter where I

might find myself at the end of all this trouble, I will try
to conduct myself in a way that would make you proud.

I make no other predictions—as always, the future is
unclear.

Yours truly,
Jesse Cullum